FORGOTTEN REALMS®
Ed Greenwood
Swords of Dragonfire
The Knights of Myth Drannor Book II
D0595654
Wizards of the Coast®

YA

The Knights of Myth Drannor, Book II

SWORDS OF DRAGONFIRE

Published by Wizards of the Coast, Inc. FORGOTTEN REALMS, WIZARDS OF THE COAST, and their respective logos are trademarks of Wizards of the Coast, Inc., in the U.S.A. and other countries.

Printed in the U.S.A.

Cover art by Matt Stewart (www.duirwaighgallery.com)
Map by Todd Gamble
Original Hardcover First Printing: August 2007
First Paperback Printing: April 2008

9 8 7 6 5 4 3 2 1

ISBN: 978-0-7869-4862-8
620-21732740-001-EN

U.S., CANADA,
ASIA, PACIFIC, & LATIN AMERICA
Wizards of the Coast, Inc.
P.O. Box 707
Renton, WA 98057-0707
+1-800-324-6496

EUROPEAN HEADQUARTERS
Hasbro UK Ltd
Caswell Way
Newport, Gwent NP9 0YH
GREAT BRITAIN
Save this address for your records.

Visit our web site at www.wizards.com

Ed Greenwood

Shandril's Saga
Spellfire
Crown of Fire
Hand of Fire

The Shadow of the Avatar Trilogy
Shadows of Doom
Cloak of Shadows
All Shadows Fled

The Elminster Series
Elminster: The Making of a Mage
Elminster in Myth Drannor
The Temptation of Elminster
Elminster in Hell
Elminster's Daughter

The Cormyr Saga
Cormyr: A Novel (with Jeff Grubb)
Death of the Dragon (with Troy Denning)

The Knights of Myth Drannor
Swords of Eveningstar
Swords of Dragonfire
The Sword Never Sleeps
August 2008

Stormlight
Silverfall: Stories of the Seven Sisters
The City of Splendors: A Waterdeep Novel
(with Elaine Cunningham)

The Best of the Realms, Book II
The Stories of Ed Greenwood
Edited by Susan J. Morris

praesto et persto

This one's for six great ladies, for six different reasons.

So, to you: Abby, Calye, Cathy, Laura, Sarah, and Tish.

May all your lives be brighter, with each passing day.

Then did I ask him: What, if it pains you not too much to tell it, happened next?

And Azoun of Cormyr smiled, and shook his head, and spake thus: "They make not heroes like those, any more, in these latter days. Peerless idiots, yes, but heroes, no. I've shouted at the gods about that a time or two, but am still awaiting an answer."

Well, so am I, Ruling Lord of Cormyr. So am I.

Tilzarra Rahlaera of Athkatla
Bright Remembrances and Dark Moments:
Thirty-Six Summers As A Lady Escort
published in the Year of the Tankard

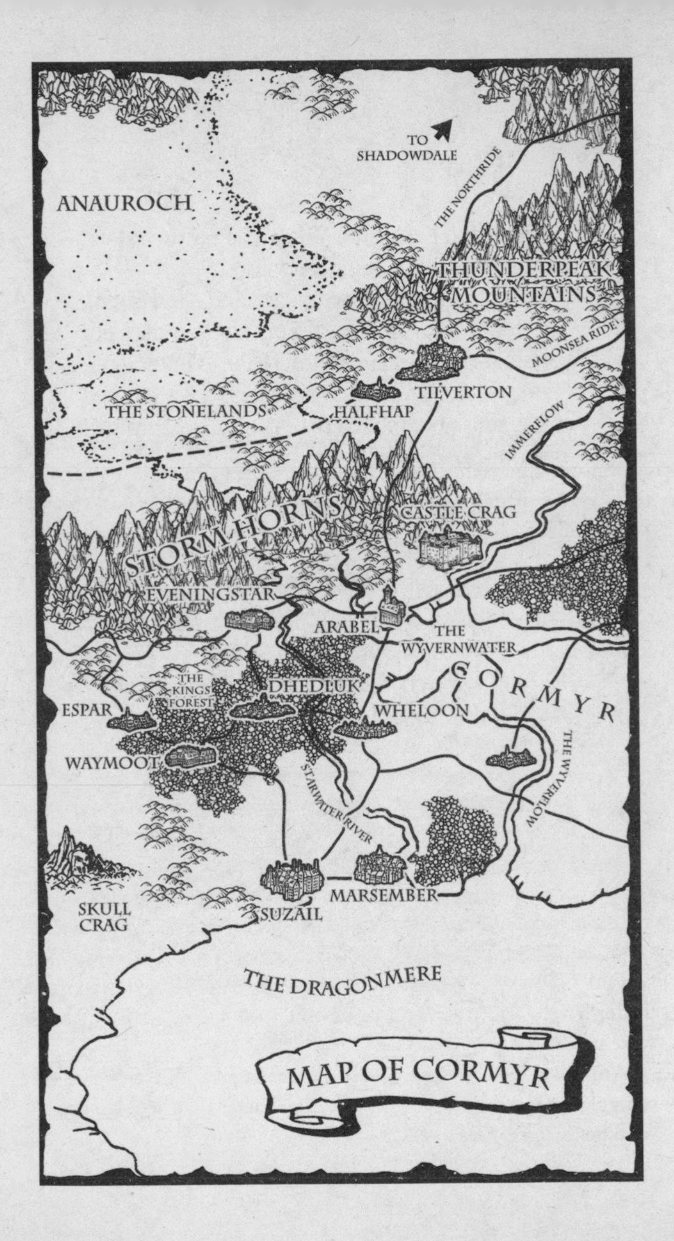

TO SHADOWDALE
ANAUROCH
THE NORTHRIDE
THUNDERPEAK MOUNTAINS
MOONSEA RIDE
TILVERTON
HALFHAP
THE STONELANDS
IMMERFLOW
STORM HORNS
CASTLE CRAG
EVENINGSTAR
ARABEL
THE WYVERNWATER
THE KINGS FOREST
DHEDLUK
CORMYR
ESPAR
WHELOON
THE WYVERFLOW
WAYMOOT
STARWATER RIVER
SKULL CRAG
SUZAIL
MARSEMBER
THE DRAGONMERE
MAP OF CORMYR

Prologue

Many flickering enchantments flared up in pale warning at Old Ghost's approach, as he drifted along the grim stone corridors of the Citadel of the Raven. Wherefore, he moved cautiously among their menaces, hurrying only as much as he could. New wards and locks and illusions that hid doors and locks and sliding wall-panels were everywhere among the older barriers—and no wonder.

The Zhentarim were prospering in this Year of the Spur. The Citadel seemed overrun with bright-eyed and cruel young magelings, all seeking to impress the senior mages so as to rise to places among them. Preening fools.

Fools who had to be kept out of moots where a handful of them could pounce on and overwhelm a hurrying slave or servant—or one of their own fellows they'd taken a dislike to. Not that any of them were very likable.

Some of them were at least energetic, and it was that verve and vitality, that superior life-force of an entity gifted with arcane ability, drive, and ambition, that Old Ghost wanted. Hungered for. All right, the Watching Gods be his witness: needed.

Old Ghost was recollecting as much, ruefully, as he seeped under a very old door and came out into a room where chains were rattling.

Amid a trio of three grinning magelings, a helpless prisoner struggled vainly against massive iron manacles that held her upright with her arms spread wide.

Teeth clenched, she snarled and sobbed her way to exhaustion, and then sagged down in her chains—only to stiffen and stare in horror at a sudden roiling glow occurring just above her own belt. "What—?" she gasped.

The three wizards grinned.

"Delzyn of the Zhentarim am I," one of them said grandly, stepping forward and drawing a long, curved dagger, "and mine is the spell you're now feeling."

He slashed through her rope belt with a flourish, and the upperworks of the breeches beneath, not quite cutting skin.

The garment fell. The prisoner screamed, or tried to, but Delzyn was still slicing away most of the front of her jerkin to bare her from breasts to clout—and display a long, wriggling worm of her own flesh that had drawn away from the red, wetly glistening organs beneath. As four gazes watched, it arched, undulated, and grew a blind, snakelike, fanged head.

The magelings chuckled and murmured in approval as the snake-thing reared back from the terrified prisoner—and then struck at her, its needlelike fangs biting viciously into the very body it had been fashioned from.

"Notice," Delzyn commented, ignoring the raw screams of agony now erupting from right beside him, "how swiftly it devours the—"

The screams stopped abruptly as Old Ghost plunged through the unfortunate woman from behind, leaving her empty-eyed and silently staring.

"Say, now," one of the watching Zhentarim commented, "*that's* not supposed to happen, is it? Delzyn, your spell must need—"

Delzyn's eyes bulged. He made an odd, urgent choking sound, lifting a hand to claw vainly at the air as if it were pressing in upon him. He swayed, his eyes going from frantic fear to emptiness, and then toppled.

The two other Zhentarim sprang hastily back to keep clear, and let Delzyn's bones shatter on the flagstones. They wanted nothing to do with whatever had gone wrong with the spell. It was obviously—

Plunging through them, too—faster than they could do anything about it. They trembled for an instant each, something almost visible flickering between them, and then fell on their faces to join Delzyn in death, on the floor.

Old Ghost rushed right on out of the chamber, seeking the swiftest way up to the sentinel who must also be slain. Usually he liked to linger when he fed, basking in the slow, warming drift of life-energy into him, but just now he was in some haste.

He dared not be late for this particular secret meeting.

In a high chamber far across the Citadel from the room where a dead woman sagged in chains with three lifeless Zhentarim at her feet, Ilbrar Thaelwand, duty-sentinel of the Brotherhood, stared hard into the glowing scrying-sphere in front of him, shaking his head in disbelief.

No matter how often he murmured over it, touched it, and even slapped it, the scene in the sphere didn't change. Something had happened at last, after months of bored staring at nothing unremarkable. Bane forfend, he'd just seen some sort of wraith fly *through* Delzyn and the others, and drain them as it did so. Drain them dead.

Hissing in apprehension, Ilbrar turned to strike the alarm gong—and recoiled from what came right at his eyes: a disembodied man's left hand, reaching at him out of thin air and gliding closer . . . closer . . .

Ilbrar gabbled in fear and swatted at it, seeking to strike the hand aside, but it ducked deftly under his frantic arms and swooped up to touch him.

Whereupon Ilbrar's panted curses became a sizzling sound, and he slumped over with smoke curling in gentle wisps from his eyes, nose, and mouth.

Hissing at the haste that denied him this chance to bask and gloat, Old Ghost raced away again.

Behind him the gong remained silent, flanked by a sentinel forevermore mindless, his brain cooked inside his head.

In another room of the Citadel that was far older, darker, and better hidden than the previous two, a wizard whose left arm ended at the wrist stood calmly watching that stump as his hand slowly faded back into view.

When it seemed whole and solid once more, he waggled his fingers experimentally, seemed satisfied with the result, and turned to face the lone door of the room.

It was closed and locked, but that seemed to pose no trouble at all for the sinister shadow that was now seeping through it, and gliding upright into a ghostly shape that was vaguely manlike—and sharply menacing.

Old Ghost was good at seeming menacing.

"Hesperdan," the wraith-thing asked, by way of greeting, "why did you summon me? I mislike showing myself so boldly."

"Your behavior regarding Horaundoon was so intemperate," the wizard replied, "that I felt it necessary to re-examine your aims and beliefs. And eliminate you, if necessary."

"I, too, feel *necessities,*" Old Ghost replied, and thrust open doors in his mind that he'd held firmly closed for some time, to glare at the words of fire blazing behind them.

In answer to those breaches the air shimmered in four places in the room, opening like windows into four chambers distant indeed in Faerûn, in each of which stood a blank-faced mage with a wand in his hand. Murmuring mindlessly, the four unleashed the magics of their wands.

Ravening spells howled forth and struck Hesperdan from all sides, wrestling and raging in the air—but somehow failed to touch the calmly watching wizard. Instead, something unseen turned aside the spells into writhing, crackling chaos.

Through the roiling tumult Old Ghost arrowed forward, plunging into Hesperdan with a snarl of glee.

Only to emerge beyond the unmoving wizard, much diminished and smoldering. He gasped in a voice trembling with pain, "How did you—?"

The wizard shrugged. "Continue wondering. *I* mislike imparting information so boldly. Suffice it to say that you may continue to exist—for now."

"Please accept my thanks for that benevolence," Old Ghost said. "Is there a price?"

"Of course. Answering me fully and honestly: Do you still consider yourself a loyal member of the Zhentarim?"

"Yes." The wraith-thing's tone was as firm as it was sullen.

"Loyal to whom, exactly?"

"The High Imperceptor. You. Lord Chess."

"Until you can slay us, of course. Yet you act against the Zhentarim, repeatedly, in matters both large and small. Why?"

"For the reasons I have always done: to thwart and ultimately eliminate Manshoon, who has so perverted our Brotherhood into a fellowship at war with itself, and his personal tool of influence and domination."

Hesperdan crooked an eyebrow. "And to confound him, you destroy *other* members and plans of the Zhentarim?"

"I do. Those who obey him more than our founding causes are part of his stain and shadow upon us. His self-serving schemes are not ours, and the more he achieves them the more his power grows. The Zhentarim are torn aside from what they should be."

"To specifics: Why did you act as you did in the matter of the Red Wizard Hilmryn?"

"The Thayan dared to use his spells to influence the minds of a few of our magelings—a weakness no one must be allowed to conclude exists. So I rode him into turning on his fellow Red Wizards with reckless slaying spells, and exacted a toll high enough, before they blasted him to wet dust, that all Red Wizards will think twice about daring to meddle with any Zhentarim again."

Hesperdan nodded. "How will you deal with Horaundoon, now that you've . . . become as you are?"

"He is my rival and a blundering fool, still wildly seeking to escape his new nature even as he learns it, but when he calms—if he strays not into tactics too dangerous—I will aid him in working against the Brotherhood, to weaken Manshoon's rule."

"And your intentions for the Knights of Myth Drannor?"

"Are my own."

Hesperdan raised a hand, and there was suddenly a shining web-work of force all around Old Ghost, thrusting sharp lance-points of crackling energy at him. "Fully and honestly," the wizard reminded.

"They are capable steeds that both Horaundoon and I know now how to ride comfortably and exactingly. And they are headed closer to where we want them."

"Away from the Hidden House, that neither of you dare approach," Hesperdan replied silkily, "and closer to the decaying mythal of Myth Drannor, whose energies you can call upon."

Old Ghost paused. "So," he hissed, after a time of tense silence. "You know."

"Of course," Hesperdan replied. "I helped raise that mythal; I can feel your attempts to draw on it."

"You. . . ?"

"Awed disbelief becomes you not, Arlonder Darmeth. Let us see if you wear obedience better. Do as you please to Manshoon and the Zhentarim—but neither drain nor harm any Knight of Myth Drannor. They are *my* unwitting tools. So ride or hamper them not. In the slightest. 'Or else,' as they say."

The wizard smiled then. It was a cold smile, like that of a prowling wolf—and for the first time in longer than he could remember, Old Ghost found himself shivering.

He hadn't known, until then, that he *could* still shiver.

This shuffling old Zhent had been part of creating the mythal of Myth *Drannor?*

And just how, by all the Watching Gods, was it that he knew Old Ghost's name?

Who *was* he?

As if he'd shouted those thoughts aloud, Hesperdan said quietly, "By all means entertain yourself seeking to find out. Yet go. Now. We both have more important things to do than tarry here trading menacing words."

Old Ghost went, trying not to hurry.

But failing.

Chapter 1

Doom comes reaching

Doom comes reaching for a Knight or two
And the taverns fall suddenly empty,
Fires crackling in silence where boasting
And swaggering held sway but moments ago.
Leaving a little quiet for true heroes
To hear themselves think, for once.

Mirt the Moneylender
Proof I Cannot Write Poetry:
A Fat Man's Chapbook
published in the Year of the Saddle

Deep in the undercellars of the massive stone building known as the Royal Court of Cormyr were chambers that no one but certain senior Crown-sworn wizards of the realm ever willingly entered. The doors were as thick as stylish horse-carriages stretched wide, and barred with great beams that required several sweating men to shift. The brightest lights those large, nigh-empty chambers ever saw were spell-glows.

The chambers were one of the places that the war wizards of Cormyr cast dangerous and unpleasant spells that—hopefully—weren't too explosive. Spells that were necessary, but better kept hidden.

The silently raging, vivid blue fires of mighty spells flared and flickered busily in one of those rooms, making eerie masks of the grim faces of the two war wizards who stood watching a third at work.

Laspeera Naerinth and Beldos Margaster made not a sound. The dragontail rings on their fingers spat tiny lightnings in response to each of Vangerdahast's powerful spells, but otherwise they were still.

Those magics raged and swirled, and finally each died down in turn, and faded away. After a long, silent time, the Royal Magician of Cormyr turned wearily away from the unconscious man on the cot.

"I've done all I can," Vangerdahast growled. "Margaster?"

The elderly man who'd once been the trusted confidant and messenger of King Azoun's father, the second ruling Rhigaerd, shook his head grimly. "As well cast as I've ever seen," he said grimly. "If they work not, then the gods meant this one's life not to stretch longer. If we confine him, the worms will eat his head hollow from within."

Laspeera nodded—and then three wizard's heads turned as one, as they all watched something black and slimy gush from Florin Falconhand's nose, lift from the cot like a wet and unwilling bat, and sail through the air to land with a *splat* in the brazier in front of Laspeera. She lifted both of her hands in command. The brazier's flames roared up obediently, and the black thing sizzled.

Suddenly it popped, sending Laspeera reeling back—but Margaster was ready. Something streaked from his pointing finger, consuming the black fragments in a tiny, raging sphere of flames that drew the fire of the brazier up into it, extinguishing the blaze, but reducing the blackness to nothing at all.

"That's the last of his mindworms," Vangerdahast said. "We're almost done."

All three of them turned rather reluctantly to look across the room at another cot. It held all that was left of Narantha Crownsilver, a bloody heap surrounded by more spell-glows. From the waist up, she was nothing but wet, amorphous gore.

"So ends *that* fair flower of the Crownsilvers," Vangey muttered. "She's riddled with them, and must be burned, I'm afraid. Lasp?"

Laspeera nodded grimly, and cast a careful spell that enshrouded the cot with magic that ignited—and, spiraling slowly, drank—all within it. Narantha's funeral pyre rose into softly reaching flames and smoke that became part of the rising shroud, twisted into it, and then dwindled.

The three wizards watched until nothing was left but ashes on the stone floor. Vangerdahast cast a spell of his own on them, sighed, and announced, "This threat to the realm is ended."

He strode briskly to the door. "Now for the next one!"

✦ ✦ ✦ ✦ ✦

Master Understeward-of-Chambers Halighon Amranthur strode grandly to the double doors and flung them wide, seven liveried doorjacks at his heels. "Now we must make haste," he commanded, "because the Knights will be here in less than a bell, and all must be—"

He stopped, blinked at the four people sprawled quietly in the most comfortable lounges at the northeastern corner of the room, and snapped, "And who are you? How did you get in here?"

The woman who looked like a burly, almost mannish farm lass looked up at him and said calmly, "Islif Lurelake. At your service, courtier."

"Courtier? *Courtier?*" Halighon almost spat the word, voice rising into full and scandalized incredulity, his shoulders prickling with the (quite correct) realization that the doorjacks were undoubtedly exchanging delighted grins behind his back. "Wench, I am no mere courtier, let me assure you! I am—*hold!*" His voice sank down into the deep, hissing whisper of real shock. "Are those *weapons* upon your persons? Here, in the Royal Wing?"

A smaller, darker woman in form-fitting leathers put her feet up on the best cushions and drawled, "Yes, sirrah, your eyesight fails you not. And *such* swift, keen wits you have, too! These are indeed weapons upon our persons. Here, in the Royal Wing."

As the understeward stared at her in shock, mouth gaping and face pale, she inspected her nails idly and told them, "Oh, yes; Halighon, be aware that I am best known as Pennae. And whereas Islif politely places herself at your service, *I* expect *you* to service *me.*"

In the silence that followed that serene observation, a doorjack snickered—and Understeward Halighon lost his last desperate hold on his temper, stormed to a bellpull beside the door, and tugged it so savagely that the cord tore and was left hanging by a few threads. "This—this is *scandalous!*" he snarled.

"When the Purple Dragons storm in here," Pennae murmured imperturbably, "be sure to introduce us properly. This personage of dainty carriage is Jhessail Silvertree, and this handsome but quiet priest of Tymora is Doust Sulwood. Two of our companions are absent, but should join us shortly: Semoor Wolftooth, a holy man of Lathander, and Florin Falconhand, who's—"

A paneled section of wall burst open and a dozen bright-armored men streamed through the revealed opening into the room, swords drawn. They peered alertly in all directions, eyes stern and faces grim.

"Who sounded the danger-gong?" the foremost snapped, from behind a formidable mustache. "Where's the peril?"

Pennae pointed languidly. "Behold the sounder of the gong *and* the only peril we face in this chamber, all in one man: Understeward—ah! Pray forgive me—*Master* Understeward-of-Chambers Halighon Amranthur."

"I—ah—that is to say . . ." Halighon faltered, as the Purple Dragons strode nearer, giving him hard looks.

Then he gathered himself visibly, reddening in the process, and glared at Pennae. "How is it you know my name? And who *are* you—all of you, your two absent friends included? Just how did you get in here?"

Pennae smiled. "Answer the first: Fee—ah, pray pardon, *Queen Filfaeril* to you—told me. Answer the second: we are the Knights of Myth Drannor, royally chartered adventurers. Answer the third: Vangey—ah, forgive me again, I am unused to court protocol—*Royal Magician* Vangerdahast brought us here through that same secret door the loyal Purple Dragons have just employed, and bade us remain here until he brought Florin to us. Florin is meeting privately with Vangey, Laspeera, and Margaster elsewhere in this quaint pile. War wizard business, I'm given to understand."

Master Understeward-of-Chambers Halighon Amranthur had slowly gone a dirty yellow hue, as of old bone, and was now trying to manage a hue as white as fresh linen.

The Purple Dragons gave him contemptuous glances, sheathed their swords pointedly, and exchanged rolled eyes with some of the doorjacks. At a curt nod from the Purple Dragon commander, the doorjacks departed the room.

That commander dispensed another pointed look that sent his own men filing back through the no-longer-so-secret door, and ere following them, turned to favor Halighon with a cold glare.

After the door closed softly behind them all, leaving the understeward alone with the Knights, Halighon regarded the four folk on the lounges with open loathing.

"Adventurers," he hissed. "I *hate* adventurers."

"I quite agree," said an all-too-familiar voice from right behind him, sending the courtier up into the air with a little shriek of startlement. "However, it's not politic to say so, out loud, when we can perhaps still get them to do something useful for us. *Lesser* Understeward Amranthur."

Halighon Amranthur tried to sink right through the rich furs underfoot, but as they lay upon a solid stone floor and yielded not a fingerbreadth, he settled for toppling into a senseless heap.

Court Wizard of the Realm and Royal Magician of Cormyr Vangerdahast sighed, stepped over the unconscious courtier, and regarded the grinning Knights with what some might have described as a "jaundiced eye."

"Can't you lot keep out of trouble for *less* than a bell? Do you know how much it costs to train good servants?"

"Ah," Pennae replied serenely, pointing at the huddled heap on the floor. "That must be why you haven't gotten around to training *him.*"

Behind Vangerdahast, one of the two grandly sinister war wizards who'd accompanied him into the room snorted with mirth.

Vangerdahast sighed again. Patiently.

"Your Florin will live," he growled, "and his wits are his own. More than that, he seems to have as many as most folk need in life. Which is better than I can say for some of you." He turned his head slowly, to give all four Knights a warning glare.

"You may enjoy royal favor, and a proper charter, but let me remind you that you do *not* command any license to thieve freely through every grand house and noble mansion in Suzail or Arabel or anywhere *else* in the realm. Nor is making foes of loyal servants of the Crown a wise road on through life, no matter how tiresome they may seem to you. Cormyr presents the appearance of a tolerant land, but believe you me, Cormyr has a way of *dealing with* irritants."

"The war wizards and their master with his oh-so-subtle-threats?" Pennae asked archly. "Or were you speaking of some other way?"

The Royal Magician of Cormyr regarded her expressionlessly for a long moment, and then said flatly, "I managed to save Florin Falconhand. I could not save the Lady Narantha. Her father will not forgive that. And before you feel moved to shrug that away with more insolence, I bid you—all of you—remember three names: Martess Ilmra, Agannor Wildsilver, and Bey Freemantle. Three who are too dead to be Knights of Myth Drannor any longer."

He turned away.

"Lord Vangerdahast?" Islif asked quietly, from behind him, rising from the lounges. "May we thank you for our Florin's life?"

"You may."

"Thank you," Jhessail said fervently, standing up in turn.

"Aye, thanks," Pennae added quickly, still lounging with her boots up. "Do all his bits still work?"

Making sure they could not see his smile, Vangerdahast sighed again. Loudly.

* * * * *

The boom of distant double doors being violently flung open brought the two casually lounging Highknights into stiff, impassive alertness. An instant was all they needed to assume formal stances, halberds crossed in front of the door into the royal study.

In the distance, a fast-striding figure turned a corner and began the long walk toward them, cloak swirling. It did not slow as it approached, but merely snarled, "Get out of the way!"

Lord Maniol Crownsilver was already in a towering rage. As the halberds moved not a fingerwidth, his eyes widened, his face reddened, and his lips drew back in a snarl ere he burst out, "Underlings, *move!* I demand audience with the king! As is the right of every noble-born Cormyrean!"

The Highknights might have been two statues, if statues could regard sputtering nobles with coldly withering contempt.

"Obey, gods curse you!" Crownsilver roared. "How low has this fair land come, when insolence rules its very Palace drudges?"

Silence was the only reply they gave him, even when his howlings rose into curses commenting personally and quite specifically upon their ancestry, social habits, and thankfully armor-hidden physical attributes. They stood like statues when Crownsilver clawed at the hilt of his ornate court sword and then drew it on them.

"Must I hew you like tree trunks?" the lord ranted, swinging hard—and striking the metal-clad haft of a halberd with a ringing clang that numbed his arm right up to the shoulder, but moved the halberd not a whit, that he could see. "A little *obedience* is all I expect!"

He swung again as he spat, "And is that too *much* to expect, in the Cormyr of here and now?"

Another ringing clang and another, the halberds moving smoothly to catch and deflect his strongest blows.

Panting, the noble used his favorite trick: thrusting at one expressionless face and then swooping his blade down viciously at the flaring top edge of that guard's codpiece—only to have the other guard do something blurringly fast with his own sword, that sent Crownsilver's halberd back over his head to clang off the passage ceiling and clatter somewhere behind him.

Lord Crownsilver stared at the two guards in speechless disbelief. He'd been disarmed with casual ease, and lo, they were back in their statuelike poses again as if he weren't there at all!

He whirled away, seething, and spat out the worst insults he could think of, one after another, as he clawed at the floor with numbed fingers for his blade.

Recovering it, he spun around in case one of the guards was considering his backside a suitable target for a kick, snarling, "And your stone-faced insolence betrays a lawlessness that bodes the realm ill, in its brazen disregard for rightful rank! You may think yourselves clever, you lowborn pizzle-heads, but no statue of a sentinel is revered by pigeons, and I've half a mind to down my breeches and serve the both of you the same—"

Which was when he noticed that the study door behind the two impassive guards had quietly opened, and the King of All Cormyr was standing in the doorway not quite succeeding in keeping a smile off his face, as he silently beckoned his visitor in.

And Maniol Crownsilver suddenly ran out of words to say.

* * * * *

"Fool! You bear the wasting curse that now afflicts all of you Knights of Myth Drannor! You shall all soon be as I am, if you tarry west of the Thunder Peaks! Doom reaches for you, Semoor Wolftooth! Doom!" intoned the mage, ending his spell with a flourish that made the unicorn-headed ring on his fingers flash in the lamplight.

In his mind, he watched the skeletal wench melt to nothing in the distant—and astonished—Semoor Wolftooth's arms. The Knight's fearful flight, an instant later, made him chuckle.

"Alluring flesh to bones to terrifying nothing! A night or two more of this," the War Wizard Ghoruld Applethorn told himself gleefully, "and they'll bolt for the swiftest road out of the realm no matter *what* Vangey threatens them with! Hah!"

He strode to the door, and began making the complicated passes and murmurings that would part ward after ward—the same wards that kept Vangerdahast himself from spying on what Applethorn or anyone else did in this secret chamber.

Only Vangerdahast was supposed to know of this room—but the Royal Magician was *so* busy, and had so many secret chambers all over the realm, and so many distractions to keep him from noticing from when someone who knew how slipped into one and used it for a breath or two.

"Yes," Applethorn gloated. "Let them off to the Dales to dance at the Blackstaff's bidding among the hayheads and hairy lasses, out of my way but handy if I need them to wear blame." He chuckled. "Hah! Talking to myself again! Ah, well, as long as I don't fall to arguing with myself. Or worse yet, *losing* those arguments!"

He snorted mirthfully at that thought, parted the last ward, opened the now-unlocked door, and hurried off. Vangey *so* hated to be kept waiting.

✦ ✦ ✦ ✦ ✦

Mortification had left Maniol dumbstruck, but his still-flaming rage and the king's kindly manner gave him a boldness that would have surprised him if he hadn't been so angry.

"Azoun—Majesty—don't make me plead!" he snarled. "I must have the throats of these villainous Knights of Myth Drannor! Here, in these hands, I must have them!"

He shook his hands, like two upturned claws, under the nose of the seated king. "My wife they've taken from me, and now my daughter!" Then he whirled away, pacing down the room to cry, "I demand justice! Give them to me, for me to butcher fittingly while all the realm watches. All will see what it means to dare to slay a Crownsilver!"

"No, Maniol," the king said, and his voice was stern. "They did *not* take your wife from you. Nor your daughter. Foul magic did that; foul magic your wife nurtured and was part of! She forged the doom that slew her, and it infected your daughter. More than that, it infected the some of Knights, and those who have not followed your Narantha into the arms of the gods may well soon!"

Crownsilver stared at him, mouth working, a dreadful hope openly warring with grief and disappointment on his face.

"Demand not justice too loudly," Azoun told him, trying not to let any trace of the disgust he felt at Crownsilver's reaction show in his face or voice. "For when you loose it, who knows whom it'll strike down?"

The noble took a few unsteady steps nearer, whimpering.

"Fear not," Azoun said. "The Wizards of War are at work on the Knights right now. Any who may yet live when our mages are done with them will no longer be welcome in Cormyr."

Lord Crownsilver stared at his king with widening eyes—and then burst into sudden tears, staggering forward almost blindly. Azoun rose from the chair swiftly enough to embrace and comfort him, crouching to enfold the shorter man to his chest.

Maniol Crownsilver buried his nose in a royal armpit and cried like a baby.

Chapter 2

A HASTY DEPARTURE

I daresay there's not an adventurer alive
West of the Plains of Purple Dust
And north of the hot southern seas
Who hasn't had to make a hasty departure or two.
Those who tell you differently are lying
Or undead, and talking from beyond the grave
Because they left off leaving until it was too late.
When's that? Well, when her father thrusts her
Bedchamber door open, and bare and hasty as you are,
You discover you can't fit through the window.

Tamper Tencoin
A Life's Cargo of Mistakes
published circa the Year of the Bloodbird

Knights," the old steward Orthund said gravely, "pray enter, and fall on your knees before Her Most Gracious Highness, Filfaeril Obarskyr, Queen of Cormyr!"

He stood aside from the door he'd just opened, revealing a familiar regal figure standing in flowing robes in the center of the room beyond.

Florin felt as weak and pale as he looked. He lurched through the doorway a little unsteadily. Islif moved like lightning to take his arm and lower him gracefully to his knees, descending with him.

Behind them, Jhessail and Pennae entered and knelt too, leaving Doust and Semoor to bring up the rear and going down on one knee only, as all priests did.

"Rise," Queen Filfaeril said, "and take your ease. Orthund, leave us and pull the doors to. We are not to be disturbed by any less a personage than the king himself."

Obediently, the Knights rose. The steward deftly drew the doors together behind them. The room, somewhere deep in the royal apartments, was richly paneled and carpeted, but sparsely furnished: it held only a chair and two polished, magnificently carved doors, both closed. The Dragon Queen occupied the chair, flanked by two robed men the Knights had come to know rather well over the last few days: the Royal Sage Alaphondar, and the eldest-looking war wizard they'd yet seen, a quiet, fatherly man called Margaster.

"All talk in Cormyr echoes most loudly here in Suzail, and tongues wag nowhere more energetically than in the passages and antechambers of the Royal Court," Queen Filfaeril said gently. "Wherefore, my Knights, you cannot be unaware of the rising mood in the realm."

Florin and Islif both nodded slowly, but said nothing. Nor did the other Knights behind them.

"Our Court is teaching you tact already," Filfaeril added, her smile as wry as it was sudden. "That will never do. One more reason that it's best that you immediately and covertly depart Suzail and hasten to Shadowdale, as Khelben urged you to do."

"Your Highness, may we know the other reasons?" Doust asked quietly.

"Of course. That which I alluded to: the rising anger of many noble families, across the realm, who out of ignorance or for their own purposes choose to blame you for the deaths of Lady Greenmantle and both Lady Crownsilvers. To say nothing of another and more just cause of noble fury: thefts from many nobles, here in Arabel."

The queen turned her head to look meaningfully at Pennae, who looked demurely magnificent in a plain storm gray gown, but blushed guiltily under the direct and knowing royal gaze.

As that reddening raced down her throat and across her bodice, the obtainer among the Knights shrugged and became suddenly and intensely interested in the state and hue of her fingernails.

Semoor rolled his eyes at that, and asked his own diffident question. "So we'll cause the Throne trouble by staying?"

Filfaeril nodded. "And goad some noble or other into trying to show the realm who holds *true* power in Cormyr by hiring someone to slay all of you—despite Our royal protection."

"Your Majesty, we are honored to obey," Florin said. "Command us."

The queen smiled and rose. "Have my thanks. Such unhesitating obedience is gratifying. It is an art too few here at Court seem to have mastered." She went to one of the beautifully carved wooden doors in the back wall of the chamber, drew it open by means of one of the many entwined dragons standing forth from its edges in bold relief, and waved at the Knights to pass through this inner doorway.

They did so, finding themselves in a stone room where a row of six chairs faced a group of gravely murmuring war wizards, who all fell silent and turned to regard the arriving Knights.

In turn, the adventurers beheld Vangerdahast, Laspeera, and five unfamiliar war wizards, one of them female and all of them looking very solemn.

"Be welcome, Knights of Myth Drannor," Laspeera said with a smile, stepping forward. "May I present Melandar Raentree, Yassandra Durstable, Orzil Nelgarth, Sarmeir Landorl, and Gorndar Lacklar."

All five wizards nodded unsmilingly as they were introduced. Pennae, who customarily looked first at the eyes and then at the hands of everyone she met, noticed that Melandar, Yassandra, and Orzil were all wearing unicorn-headed rings, Sarmeir and Gorndar wore no rings, and the rings on Vangerdahast's and Laspeera's fingers had been fashioned to look like the sinuous, scaled tails of dragons. Just what did those rings—or their lack—betoken?

Vangerdahast gave her no time to ponder. Like an impatient battlemaster, he waved the Knights to sit in the waiting chairs, his gesture an imperious command, and then took up a stance in front of them, frowning as if he were the coming storm of doom and their punishment were at hand.

Laspeera was already leading the five war wizards she'd just introduced past the Knights, heading for the door.

"Oh, Tymora," Doust murmured under his breath, "*this* doesn't look good."

"Vangey *never* looks good," Semoor whispered back, taking the seat beside Doust. "I think he battles nigh-constant indigestion. Either that or he's just sick of all of us."

By then Laspeera and the five mages had reached the door—where they turned, behind the Knights, and pointed to enact the same silent spell in unison.

And the six seated Knights slumped over, instantly deep in magical slumber.

The war wizards looked to Vangerdahast for approval.

"Well, what're you waiting for?" the Royal Magician asked them curtly. "I want this mess off my hands as fast as you can work your spells!"

* * * * *

Princess Alusair Nacacia Obarskyr had now seen thirteen summers, and they had proven more than enough to make her headstrong and rebellious, honing her hauteur and a quick temper, but failed utterly to quell her ever-welling curiosity. Wherefore, servants and courtiers alike had learned to avoid—and certainly never to rebuke or even to try to proffer suggestions—the young princess who so moodily prowled the Palace, forbidden to break blades with Purple Dragons or down tankards in any tavern or do much of anything on her own.

Alusair was a familiar sight in the Palace passages, all gangly arms and legs, a "lad in lasses' clothing" who climbed where she shouldn't, got dirty every chance she could, and seemed to wear a permanent scowl as she pointedly turned away from everyone who looked at her. Especially her everpresent war wizard and Purple Dragon minders and bodyguards, whose silent scrutiny she bitterly resented, almost as much as she hated their all-too-frequent interventions to stop her "having any fun at all." They watched *everything* she did, from bathing to filling chamberpots to picking her nose—hrast them. There was nothing she liked better than an adventure in the dungeons, deep well chambers, vaults, and other dark, unfamiliar, and off-limits parts of the Palace—and it seemed there was nothing they liked better than preventing such forays.

Wherefore, when she paused in a dim, little-used chamber she was strolling through to get from the Chamber of Three Dragons to Runsor's Robing Room, to look into a cloudy old crown-to-ankles looking glass and sneer critically at her oak brown eyes and swirling, honey-hued hair—and her ever-curious fingers traced the carved berries of its frame, finding and pressing the one that sank inwards, in the heart of the cluster—her heart leaped in quickening delight when the mirror shuddered and swung open.

Princess Alusair cast a swift glance back the way she'd come. Old Alsarra hadn't yet turned the corner, and was probably flirting with the drooping-mustached doorjack she seemed to fancy so.

She swung the mirror open, to reveal narrow shelves of dusty old tomes.

The racing of her heart slowed a little, but then she smiled and shrugged. After all, a secret stair *was* unlikely, with a main hallway just the other side of this wall. What might these books hold? Forbidden spells? Descriptions of Palace trysts? The court gossip of yesteryear? Being ever-curious was *good*.

Alusair thrust fingers up both her nostrils to keep from sneezing, and with her other hand plucked forth the most intriguing-looking volume: a slender black book with no lettering down its spine. A musty smell, rag-paper pages that seemed to be wanting to return to being rags, and some of the most crabbed and dry poetry she'd *ever* tried to read. Ugly words in uglier phrases—" 'Ywis my bonden heart now doth for thee bounding-hart-leap high/All across fair Cormyr in answer the realm's maidens all tremulous sigh"—ughh! She slid it back into place, and with both hands wrestled out the thick maroon volume next to it, a squared-corners, metal-bound book as fat as her own arm.

It proved to be latched, the metal black with tarnish that dearly wanted to be on her hands, and to be an account of naval sailings of six long-ago reigns, with informed debate as to the best riggings to use in particular winds and specific waters. Alusair rolled her eyes, flipped its pages in hopes of finding a battle at sea or a map or *something*, and heard something metallic clink and then slither down the *inside* of the book's spine.

With mounting excitement, she cupped her hand over the bottom of the spine to keep whatever it was—a key?—from falling out, turned so as to block Alsarra's view of what she was doing—should her overshoulder spy finally wrest herself away from Lord

Hairylust—and shook the heavy book as hard as she could. Its weight almost defeated her slender wrists; she had to go into a hasty crouch to keep from dropping it end-over-end.

Which is when, of course, she heard the expected cry, "Princess? *Princess!* Alusair, what're you doing on the *floor,* child? Are you well?"

Alusair sat down with a thud, scooped the book into her lap, and worked its covers back and forth frantically with both hands—whereupon the slithering something fell out. A ring!

An *old* ring, silvern and smooth-flowing in shape, like elven work. Not a stone on it, but it was on the first finger she could slip it onto in a trice, and—she gasped and shuddered as it shifted gently to resize itself, and a window seemed to open in her mind, showing her . . . showing her . . .

"Child, what have you gotten yourself into *now?*"

The trouble with Alsarra was that she acted like a disapproving old aunt, and that both Alusair's father and mother confirmed her in full authority to do so, almost once or twice a tenday, very firmly and enthusiastically. Alusair wanted to tell the old watch-hound—watch-*bitch,* yes?—to run and plunge face-first into the mud of a castle moat, preferably a castle somewhere north of shining Silverymoon, half Faerûn away, and never stop eating that mud, but . . .

Bony hands were plucking the book from her hands, wrinkled lips were clucking as if she were some sort of disobedient barnfowl, and Alusair sighed, folded her hands together (the one without the ring over the one now wearing it), and announced, "I found some old books, and wanted to look at them. The only ones I looked at were very boring, but this one was so heavy I almost dropped it, and one"—she dropped her voice into viciously accurate mimicry of Alsarra's own tones—"should *never* damage a book, so I—"

"Sat down to try to forestall the fall? Quite so, child, quite so—and may I say an *admirable* sentiment and deed for a younger princess, whose deportment and manner will be such an asset to House Obarskyr in time soon to come!"

So I can be married off like a prize cow, Alusair thought sourly.

"I say again, as I've said so oft before, that you should watch your sister Princess Tanalasta, and strive to act as she does!"

Alusair nodded out of unthinking habit, and Alsarra smiled and went gushing on, words flowing in a sharp and exclamatory flood. She restored the book to its place and hauled the wayward princess to her feet so the mirror could be closed, Alusair's dust-soiled breeches could be exclaimed over, and Alusair could be chided once more for refusing to wear a *gown* that any fair woman-to-be would find fitting and suitable, to say nothing of a royal princess of Cormyr. Alusair nodded absently and heard not a word of it all.

Instead, she raced excitedly back and forth through the new thoughts and images in her head that the ring had put there, telling her that it was old and mighty, and had three powers: teleportation, to four set places that were unknown to her; something called a "non-detection shield," that would make her, whenever she willed, invisible to all magics that sought to detect or locate her, or read or influence her mind . . . and something else, too, that she didn't understand. Warm delight grew in her like a comforting fireside flame. With this, she had the chance to slip away from her everpresent war wizard and Purple Dragon watchers. She was *free*.

"Alsarra," she said firmly, "I must find a garderobe. My near-fall, you understand . . ."

"Oh, but of course! Are you sure an examination would not come amiss? We really should—"

"If there's blood, I'll *hasten* to let you know, Alsarra," the princess said very firmly. "Now, stand out of the way, or this royal bladder will—"

"Of course! Of course! Oh, gods and guardian spirits forfend! Here I am, a foolish old woman, a-twittering while—"

Well, at least you *know* what you are, Alusair thought sourly, slipping past her watcher. Wouldn't you just be *delighted* if there were blood? Then I'd be fertile, and you could lock me up straight and proper, never again to set foot out of my bedchambers except to appear at feasts and be put on display for suitors—until one of them bit, and my life of *true* slavery could begin.

She sped down a narrow passage to the filigreed gates of the nearest ladies' garderobe, and instead of turning left into its comforts, turned right, ducking through the hanging to the unlit, steeply descending servants' stair. Standing in the darkness at the head of its steps, she told the ring: *hide me*.

And the adventure began.

First, to find herself a sword, a dagger, and some proper traveling boots! Then a little food, a belt flask of something to drink, and—

Alusair faltered, halfway down the stair, as she discovered she could *feel* the alarm of the war wizards who'd been their usual bored selves, magically spying on her. Their minds rushed past her like frantic wraiths who couldn't see her. They were far from bored now. Her knife-abrupt disappearance from their scrying spells had them shouting at each other and ringing gongs!

She snickered—and then spat out a curse. Those ringing gongs were even now summoning thunder-booted Purple Dragons and irritated senior war wizards to start a search for her.

"Ilmater's pain, but I hate this place," she murmured, as lamplight spilled out into the hallway at the bottom of the stair. She hurled herself down the last few steps, her heavy pendant smacking her across the face, and just had time enough to duck around a corner, thankful for her soft slippers, before servants rushed out into the hall and up the stair she'd just left.

"Has anyone seen the Princess Alusair?" a maid asked sharply, in the room where the lamp was. "We're to find her and bring her to the nearest war wizard. Drop all and get up into the staterooms, all of you!"

"Drag Little Lady Pouting-Trouble half the length of the Palace to find a spellhurler? And get beheaded for our troubles? *After* she kicks all our organs clear up and out of our bodies and pulls every last hair out of our heads?"

"Well, she won't have much hair to pull on your shining pate, Jorlguld!"

"I've got nose-hairs, ye know," Jorlguld said darkly.

"Well, there won't be all that much dragging; every chamber of the Palace is filling up with war wizards, just as fast as they can—"

Alusair whispered something very rude, and went in search of a sword and dagger. Her purse would have to buy her the rest, once she was out of here.

This passage ran along to an end stair with a Purple Dragon ready-room. Normally it was a place she'd want to stay well away from, if she was trying to hide, but with the alarm raised, surely they'd all have rushed upstairs to poke and pry and waste much time before they got around to thinking a high-and-mighty princess might go below, down into the dark, dank servants' halls. And not only did Purple Dragons never close doors unless someone ordered them to, they always had extra weapons in their armories. Lots of extra weapons.

Yes! The ready-room stood empty of men, the wooden racks on its walls a-gleam with swords and daggers in plenty.

But nary a scabbard for any of them, or even a cloak. Alusair peered around in dismay, and then shrugged, took down a sword she liked the look of, and then a dagger, likewise, and—

"I saw *someone* along here, I tell thee, and it could have been a lass!" The man's voice echoed, still far down the passage.

Alusair spun around to face the door, hefted her sword and dagger—the sword was a trifle too heavy for comfort, but it would have to do—and thought about the ring. Hard.

And being elsewhere, to that first destination. Wherever it was.

Obligingly, the Palace whirled away, and she was suddenly falling, falling endlessly through chill blue mists. . . .

Chapter 3

More Leavings

My life has been full of leavings—some tearful, some contented, and many of the sort that kings tend to term "not a moment too soon."

Tamper Tencoin
A Life's Cargo of Mistakes
published circa the Year of the Bloodbird

"The Royal Magician—?"

"Has other pressing matters to attend to," Laspeera said. "However, *I* trust myself and you five to translocate six sleeping Knights from here to Arabel. *Now.*"

It was rare for the warm, kindly manner of the woman most Wizards of War fondly called "Mother" to slip, even for a moment, and the mages around her blinked, carefully made not the slightest reply, and devoted themselves to swift, accurate spellcasting.

Wizards, chairs, and the sleepers slumped in them were suddenly no longer in an inner chamber of the Palace, but in a smaller, dingier room with boarded-over windows, that by the sounds of clottering hooves and creaking wagon wheels, stood hard by a street or drovers' alley, somewhere slightly colder than Suzail.

"Mother," Wizard of War Sarmeir Landorl asked cautiously, "do I risk my neck at this time, if I dare to ask you some questions about this matter at hand?"

Laspeera's sudden smile was as bright as a flaring flame. "Of *course* not, Sarm. You need not fear my 'brisk moments' in the slightest, so long as you obey me with alacrity during them."

"Huh," muttered another mage. "Vangey says the same thing."

"Indeed, Orzil, wherefore it should come as no surprise to you to learn you'd do well to believe us both," Laspeera said, "and conduct yourself accordingly. Your questions, Sarm?"

"This is the hideaway-house in Arabel, yes?"

"Yes," Laspeera confirmed pleasantly.

Sarm waited for her to add more. In vain. As the silence started to stretch and Laspeera's gentle smile wavered not at all, some of the other wizards started to grin.

"So," Sarmeir said carefully, "that being the case, why didn't we just march the Knights through the usual portal?"

"Sarmeir," Laspeera replied, "we may need half the Dales *not* to know about that particular portal for a little while longer. Moreover, none of our snorers here are keyed to the portal, and I don't want them to know about *that,* either."

"Why would they need to be keyed?"

"Doing so cuts down on vanishings, and they're carrying a pendant we do *not* want them to lose."

"Vanishings?"

"Have you never wondered why—given that all sufficiently gifted folk can craft portals—merchants still struggle overland, through mud and stinging flies, brigands and blizzards, to carry, say, candles from the hamlet of Hither to waiting townsfolk at the market of Yon?"

"Well, *no,*" Sarmeir replied. "We seem to receive far more encouragement to do as we're told, and leave 'wonderings' to the likes of Vangerdahast, and Margaster—and you."

"Shrewdly struck, Sarm. I reel, but recover." Laspeera's dimples told the now tensely watching war wizards no eruption was about to occur. "Harken, then, to the new, emerging danger of portal travel: vanishings."

"You mean people going missing?"

"No, that's hardly a *new* danger. I speak rather of the matter of the portals themselves betimes melting away things taken through them—trade goods, the sword in a wayfarer's hand or on her belt. Suchlike."

"Ah," Orzil put in, "the old matter of 'on dread deeds bent, I charge through the waiting way full-armored and sword in hand—and arrive at the other end grinning at my foes, naked and weaponless.'"

"Indeed."

Yassandra, the darkly beautiful lady war wizard, frowned at that. "I thought sages of matters arcane always blamed such vanishings on snatchings done by creatures watching over or guarding the portals. The same creatures who sometimes do or intend far greater ill to portal-users."

"They do. *I* thought alarphons were better schooled than to believe them."

Yassandra flushed and said sharply, "None of us, so far as I know, have been told anything of portal vanishings. If I understand you correctly, they are why portals will never replace caravans for overland trade, yes?"

Laspeera nodded. "And why we still use mass teleport spells, yes."

Sarmeir frowned. "But we've been told that a teleportation done purely by a spell can't be traced later, whereas a portal jump—particularly by a keyed individual—*can*. So was that a lie, and these vanishings the real reason?"

"No. War wizards use portals whenever possible because they are both more reliable and for tracing reasons. If you run into trouble, the rest of us can more easily trace you, and if you are pursued and hide a document or item to keep foes from seizing it when they take you, colleagues investigating later can follow your portal uses and know where to search. Yet everyone not already sworn to the Crown of Cormyr and standing high in both service and trust who learns the location and nature of a portal opens a gap in the shared armor of the realm. Wherefore we avoid portals and cleave to spells instead when time and circumstances allow, when shuttling common citizens and outlanders around Cormyr. Keying can't be done on the sly; even if a person we do it to is unaware of what we're doing, he soon discovers what we did, and what powers he's now gained. That's why we don't tend to key just-risen adventurers, whose loyalties may stray far from us—" She waved her hand at the row of sprawled and sleeping Knights of Myth Drannor, just as Doust started to slide off his chair. Laspeera launched herself across the room in time to catch him and thrust him back onto the seat, turning back to the younger wizards with a shushing finger to her lips, and concluded, "—but do key Crown messengers and envoys."

* * * * *

"And why," the Wizard of War Ghoruld Applethorn purred, smiling at the unwitting face of Laspeera in his glowing scrying crystal, "I can trace everyone who uses any portal in the Palace."

He beamed at her unseeing beauty and told her unhearing ears, "Vangey has trusted me too much, for too long. And trust, as better men than our dear Royal Magician discovered to their costs long ago, is a blade with two sharp edges."

* * * * *

Florin came awake very suddenly, and found himself looking into a pair of alert dark brown eyes. They belonged to a slender, dark-haired, handsome man in robes, now bending over him, that he'd seen somewhere before, recently, but . . . oh, yes: this was a war wizard, one of the five Laspeera had introduced to them, in—

Quick glances told him his fellow Knights were still sitting on chairs beside him, Islif as awake as he was, the others seemingly asleep. But they were in no room Florin knew or had ever been in before. And of Vangerdahast, Laspeera, and the other war wizards, there was no sign.

"Where are we?" he asked. "And why?"

"This is Arabel, and you are here in obedience to the queen."

"Departing the realm forthwith," Islif said. "And you are . . . Melandar ah, Raentree."

The handsome war wizard nodded, his smile tight, his face revealing nothing. "At your service. You were magically transported here while you slept. I have been assigned to oversee your departure."

"Well," Semoor grunted, "I suppose it *is* too much to expect the queen to trust us—we being her sworn Knights, and all."

"We being *adventurers,*" Jhessail told him, her smile rueful. It seemed everyone was awakening.

"Well met again, fellow weaver of the Art, and Holy of Lathander," Melandar greeted them both. "Not much time has passed since you spoke with Her Majesty, but by means of magic you are now in Arabel. This is a—well, a nondescript backstreet house owned by the Crown, that stands hard by a busy stable. Wherein await mounts for all of you, saddled and ready. Purple Dragon mounts when this day began, but yours to keep now."

"Oh?" Semoor's eyes narrowed. "How many Purple Dragons know this? And how many are going to be riding hard after us, eager to chain and dungeon us as horse-thieves?"

Florin frowned. "This is . . . very swift. The Lady Narantha Crownsilver lies not even in her family crypt yet, and *no one* has paid the price for her death. Something I mean to attend to, before *I* depart Cormyr!"

The war wizard nodded gravely. "I understand your feelings, believe me—but betimes our oaths of loyalty must govern us sternly, and we must set aside revenge until a better time."

The look Florin gave him then was stony. "And did Narantha's murderer choose a 'better time' to bring doom down upon her?"

Jhessail turned and laid a gentle hand on her friend's shoulder. "Florin," she murmured, "nothing we do—or don't do—will bring her back. Please find some calm inside you, and listen. Vangerdahast promised me that her death would be fully investigated, and the *queen* said so too. I trust her to see that he does what he promised—and he can do far more, with his spells and working among nobles he knows and has some authority over, than we could ever hope to do. We can't *threaten* nobles into confessing or aiding us; we have nothing to threaten them with."

"Not now we've been ordered out of the realm," Florin said bitterly, "but do any of them know that yet?" He glared at Melandar. "How long will it be before they all know?"

"Sir Falconhand," the war wizard replied carefully, "please listen to the wise words of Lady Knight Silvertree, and depart the kingdom—for now—without delay or dispute. If you knew exactly who was guilty and how to reach them, and they happened to be here in Arabel, I myself would aid you with my spells to get into their presence, and keep what you did as secret as possible. Yet such is not the case, and it could take you years of blundering around asking questions and waving your sword before you learned anything useful about whom you *should* be seeking. If, that is, this or that noble didn't have you killed out of sheer irritation, first."

Florin turned his head to look down the line of chairs. "Well?" he growled. "What do the rest of you think?"

Doust held up a hand to quell what others might have been going to say, and replied quietly, "I hate to leave Cormyr. This is not what I intended, when I dreamed of adventure. Yet I like even less the thought of disobeying a royal command as almost our first act as Knights."

"Pennae?"

The thief shrugged. "When a queen lets on that she knows all you've been up to, and in the same breath tells you to get out of town . . . let's just say that as I'm not a disguised dragon or arch-lich able to overthrow thrones whenever I please, minstrels' fantasies notwithstanding, disobeying Queen Fee is *not* my first instinct. Nor yet my sixth or seventh."

Melandar winced visibly at that "Queen Fee," but said nothing. His look in Islif's direction, however, was as clear as if he'd snapped an order.

Islif gave him a thin smile and then turned to Florin and said, "I, too, am reluctant to leave our beloved Cormyr—but I am *not* interested in being hunted by nobles or rushing around looking for culprits, just now. It will end in our having to fight some of our countrymen, and *that* will end with us imprisoned, exiled for good, or dead. Florin, if you stay now to avenge Narantha, I'm afraid you'll do so alone. And this is a war wizard standing in front of us; you won't be free to flit around Cormyr by night and put your sword through suspected culprits—unless you do so as Vangey's puppet. Not quite the adventurers' glory *I'd* be seeking."

Florin stared at her grimly, then looked at Jhessail, and in the end glared at Melandar again. The war wizard said nothing.

From somewhere nearby, there came a muffled crash, some shouts of men disagreeing enthusiastically over something, and a series of thuds, as if heavy things were being stacked up and shifted around.

Pennae looked questioningly at Melandar, who murmured, "This house stands hard by a warehouse too—just the far side of the stable. There's always bustle, night and day."

The war wizard's gaze never left Florin's face, and a silence fell—broken only by the creaking and clottering of a cart passing, outside—that ended only when the ranger looked up and said through clenched teeth, "Very well. We go. For now."

"Good," Melandar said. "This is an ideal time to depart Arabel. Night has fallen, and it's raining lightly. Few folk will be out on the streets to get a good look at your faces as you ride by."

Doust frowned. "But if 'tis after nightfall, the gates—"

"Strangely enough," Melandar said with a wry smile, "we've taken care of that."

✦ ✦ ✦ ✦ ✦

The rain dripped from Norandur's cloak in loud and swift abundance. "S'come on to rain," he said, unnecessarily.

"Um-hmm, so it has," Ornrion Dauntless growled, looking up from his desk. "So, who are these war wizard highnoses, who need all our best horses so suddenly?"

Norandur snorted. "The adventurers we chased all over that warehouse," he rasped, as a raindrop descended from his nose, "that the queen knighted. Seems she has some private little mission in mind for them."

Dauntless stared at the Purple Dragon with his mouth open, his face slowly going white with anger.

Norandur stared back, impassively. This ought to be entertaining.

The dripping First Sword wasn't disappointed. Dauntless slammed the quill in his hand down on the table so hard that it seemed he was trying to drive it *through* the thick, scarred wood. It snapped, and the blow caused his inkpot to skip off the table and shatter noisily on the flagstone floor. "Tyr and Torm blast me if they deserve any such thing! Private little mission *where?*"

The soldier shrugged. "I know not. There's just one war wizard left with them now, and he gave me the cold eye when I tried to talk to them."

"Well, we'll just let our eyes serve where our tongues can't!" Dauntless snarled. "They won't ride a horselength without us seeing it, from now until—"

"Until I order you to do otherwise, Ornrion Dahauntul," the wizard Laspeera said coldly, materializing out of empty air at his elbow. "As I'm doing right now. Clean up that ink and see to your work here, and the Knights of Myth Drannor will just ride out of all our lives. If Tymora smiles on us."

The blue mists were suddenly gone, and Princess Alusair found herself in a city, standing outside in the night, in gently falling rain. She was on a slick but almost level slate rooftop. She blinked at a huge and impressive wall of stone spires soaring up beside her—nay, towering over her. A temple rooftop.

Alusair peered around through the wet night, until she was sure. Yes, familiar towers and gables, a streetmoot she knew; she was in Arabel, though she couldn't remember just which god this holy place belonged to.

No matter; she was here, and she was alone at last. Adventure!

The roof under her feet was nothing but a rain-cover, to give shelter to a coach or wagon loading area, where a temple door opened out into a cartway running back to a stable. At its outward end (she walked cautiously away from the towering temple), it ended at a stone wall enclosing the temple grounds, a wall crowned with a rusty row of iron spikes. A man's boot wouldn't fit between those spikes, but her slippered feet could.

Beyond, she could just see a narrow alleyway in the night-gloom, running along the shabby, shuttered-windowed backs of shops and homes that were nothing compared to the temple behind her.

The temple that must be full of priests and their magic, and possibly guardian beasts and enchanted stone sentinels too!

Alusair shivered in sheer thrill, getting wet but not caring, and went to the row of spikes in an excited crouch, planting the sword in her hand like a staff to balance with. Adventure at last!

She'd been to Arabel twice or thrice that she could remember; the Rebel City, some courtiers called it. "Almost outside the kingdom," as some in Suzail never missed a chance to describe it, or even "the fortress that keeps the Stonelands at bay."

Not that she believed half the wild tales of dragons and worse that the Stonelands were supposed to be a-crawl with. Why—

Enough. She was getting wet through. She needed her adventure to feature a warm fireside or at least a cloak soon.

Alusair drew in a deep breath of wet Arabellan air, smiled at the uncaring night, and set one foot carefully between two spikes. She shifted her weight back to make sure she could lift that foot easily back out of its wedged position, found that she could—and stood up tall, swinging sword and dagger wide with a flourish, to step boldly forward, into a feet-first jump down into the dark alley below.

Her landing jarred, and she crushed something wet and squishy that she was glad she couldn't see—her slippers slid in something that felt like hair or fur—underfoot. Springing away to her right, Alusair trotted down the alleyway, finding it evil-smelling and strewn with rotten fragments of wood and what looked like slimy remnants of leaves that were beyond rotten.

Her heart leaped as something moved in the gloom ahead. A man! A lurching, bleary-eyed man in worn leathers and a tunic that looked more like a rag than clothing, who peered at her and mumbled, "S'truth! The l'il *lasses*'re a-waving swords and daggers, now? Are the orcs come again, then?"

He reached out for her with shaking fingers, but she swiveled her hips, quickened her pace, and was past, giving him a smile but no reply—and trailing her sword behind her to discourage him following. She looked back, a few breaths later, to see no sign of him in the night shadows.

The alley stank, of dung and rotting food and worse, everchanging smells overlaid by woodsmoke and the occasional lovely aroma of a cooked meal, but Alusair breathed it all in deeply and happily, running along in the rain with a smile on her face. She was having an adventure!

And not a war wizard in sight! Nay, she was—

The hand thrusting out of the darkness this time was swift and strong, taking her by the shoulder and spinning her around before she could do more than utter a startled *eeep*.

Adventure. . . .

Chapter 4

Swords in the Rain

Of that night, I remember mercifully little
Beyond too many friends falling dead
And striking aside swords in the rain.

Onstable Halvurr
Twenty Summers A Purple Dragon:
One Soldier's Life
published in the Year of the Crown

Ho, now! Hold hard there, my lad! Where d'ye be going, so hasty-like, on a night like—"

This voice was deeper than the first drunkard's had been, and came with a reek of stale drink that was almost stupefying. Alusair reared back, bringing her sword and dagger up between her and that half-seen face. The hand abruptly let go.

It returned, coming in a little lower, thrusting past her bared steel to press hard into her chest and send her staggering back. "*Away* with that war-steel!"

Then the drunkard made a surprised sound at what his fingers had found, and growled, "A lass? A *lass,* out in the night like this? Running from a murder, are ye?"

"Nay," Alusair said, trying to make her voice snap in command as she'd heard her father do many a time, "but there *will be* a murder in this alley if you lay hands on me again!"

"Whoa, now! Easy!" The reply seemed a step or two farther away, as if the man had retreated. "A lass, light-dressed, out in the rain and the night with no lantern, carrying war-steel unsheathed . . . a slip of a lass, too, with a sword too heavy for her by half . . . ye're an acolyte of Tempus, ye are!"

He sounded almost proud, as if he'd won some sort of prize. "The Lord of Battles keep ye and honor ye, Swordmaiden! Fair even to ye, and pray accept the apologies of ol' Dag Runsarr—not the least of the King's Dragons, in my day! Saw the king himself I did, once!"

Alusair resisted the urge to tell old Dag that she'd seen the King of Cormyr a thousand thousand times, and sometimes felt she saw far too much of him, yet at the same time not enough. "Fair even, Dag Runsarr," she said, instead. "Tempus defend thee and watch over thee."

That grand speech was rather spoiled by a sudden loud grumble from her stomach. Old Dag chuckled and shuffled off down the alley, in the direction she'd come. Leaving the youngest princess of Cormyr suddenly aware of just how hungry she was. She'd last eaten at morningfeast, and last sipped some spiced clarry just after high-sun . . . and the night was well begun, now.

A tavern. A tavern would still be serving food. So would a feasting hall, but she had no idea if Arabel even *had* any fine feasting halls. So a tavern it would be.

Alusair hurried along the alley and came out into a narrow cobbled street lit by two lonely, distant hanging lamps. She could see nothing but houses in either direction—and the alley continuing on, across the road. She crossed, returning to the darkness almost thankfully. A distant dog barked, but she knew she had little to fear: dogs in Arabel were working beasts, and only fools let their workers stand out in rainstorms to get chilled and fall sick. It would be a rare alley that would have wild dogs waiting for her. Rats, now . . .

That cheerful thought carried her right into a smell that made her stomach complain again. Stew!

Just ahead, where the alley met with another street, and started to reek like men spewing up too much ale, was a small, dingy tavern, its signboard dangling from one hook and too dark to read anyway. Light was spilling out into the night all around its warped, ill-fitting door. Much chatter came from within, and pipesmoke too. Reversing sword and dagger downward, and transferring them both into one hand, Princess Alusair thrust open the door and stepped inside.

The taproom was small, low-ceilinged, thick with drifting smoke, and crowded. She paused for a moment, expecting the room to fall silent in reverence, but no one seemed to so much as notice her—one more wet, bedraggled visitor from the night outside. When she peered around, she saw a few eyebrows, here and there, lifting in surprise at the blades in her hand and then at her gender, but everyone looked away, and no one remarked. Wise Arabellans tended not to comment on such things.

Alusair found an empty table and sank thankfully down into its lone chair, setting her blades carefully on the table and running her fingers back through her sodden hair to get it out of her eyes. Two none-too-clean men facing each other over tankards at the next table leered at her and then turned back to their converse. Their noses were long and sharp, their eyes sharper. Alusair ducked her head a little so the curtain of her wet hair hid her eyes from them, and tried not to seem like she was listening.

"Darthil, see the one in green? That's him," one of the sharp-nosed men said.

The other turned a ring on his tankard hand a little with his thumb. The ring caught the candlelight with a flash, and Alusair saw it had been polished mirror-bright—to serve, in fact, as a mirror.

"Aha. My, he's the prance-dandy, isn't he? We'll deal with him later," the other muttered. "But Mhaulo, tell me: Who's the old mountain of meat beside him? His bodyguard we'll have to fight?"

"No, far from it. Another he owes coin to, more likely. Gulkar *has* no bodyguards, not after—" Mhaulo cast a glance across the taproom at the white-haired, heavily muscled man sitting beside Gulkar, turned back in almost the same movement, and said with a smirk, "That, Darth, is Durnhelm Draggar Lenth B. Stormgate."

Darthil lifted an eyebrow. "He's called all that? No wonder he has shoulders that broad, if he has to carry all those names around. What's the 'B' for?"

Mhaulo's smirk widened. "Blade. But I'm not done; 'tis better than that. Old Durn asked his mother why he was called Durnhelm

Draggar Lenth. She said those were her best three guesses as to who'd sired him."

Darthil sighed. "Her last three lovers?"

"Her brothers."

Darthil gave Mhaulo a decidedly disbelieving look, lifted his tankard, and said cautiously, " 'Tis a good thing she only had three brothers."

"Oh, I don't think that matters all that much. Blade was the name of her horse."

Princess Alusair suspected her face was reddening, and turned away swiftly to lean her chin in her hand and so block any view Mhaulo or Darthil might have of her. She found herself facing a weary-looking woman in an apron, who'd just stopped by her table and asked, "What'll it be, good-lass?"

"That stew I'm smelling, and—" Alusair caught sight of some sweet buns on another table, and pointed. "Oh, and what wines d'you have?"

The serving maid's voice sharpened. "None, lass, 'til the new vintage comes in. High-coin cellars are for grander houses. Here in the Hound, we serve good honest ale." She started to turn away, and then said, "And being as you're not wearing a face I know and you've blades bare on the table before you, I'd best ask for coin up front."

Alusair stared at her. "Why—" She started to make the airy gesture that would refer the maid to the chamberlain at her shoulder, and then remembered there *wasn't* any chamberlain at her shoulder.

And princesses a-prowling around the Palace didn't carry purses full of coins at their belts. She had nothing.

Panic stabbed at her—until something caught the candlelight, on the table in front of her, and she remembered she was wearing several rings besides the magic one that had brought her here.

The plainest was a band of plain gold surmounted by a single small, dainty pearl. She twisted it, hoping her wet fingers would let it come off easily, and the gods smiled on her. Alusair held it up triumphantly. "With this."

The serving-woman's eyes widened, and she pointed at the sword and dagger. "Lass," she said helplessly, as heads turned at tables all around them. "Lass, you didn't slice up a husband with those and go running out into the storm, did you? Tell truth, now."

Alusair blinked at the woman angrily, and then drew herself up in her chair, throwing her shoulders back as she'd seen courtiers do all her life, and snapped, "I *always* tell the truth. The realm depends upon it."

Alsarra and many other maids and guardians and courtiers had instructed her to say—and do—as much, from before she could walk.

"Ooooh," said someone at a table nearby, in mocking mimicry of a haughty, oh-so-pompous noble—the very sort of parody Alusair loved to indulge in herself. She cast a glance around, and saw astonishment on many hard-bitten faces.

"Lass," a fat man asked, from a table not far off, "who *are* you?"

Alusair stood up slowly, planted her fingertips on the tabletop, stared at the serving maid, then slowly turned her head to survey everyone around her, as far to the left and right as her stance permitted.

"Folk of Cormyr," she said proudly, "I am your princess. The Princess Alusair Nacacia Obarskyr, daughter of the Purple Dragon himself."

Her last few words reminded her that in troubled Arabel, every last man of the local Watch was a Crown-sworn Purple Dragon, and as her eyes fell on Mhaulo and Darthil, gaping at her in staring astonishment, she added sternly, "It is my royal command that none of you, here or after departing this place, tell any man of the Watch or war wizard of my presence."

In the awed silence that followed, she held out the ring again to the serving maid, who shrank back from it as if it were red-hot and flaming from a forge.

"By all the Watching Gods, are we to *believe* this wild-tongue work?" a tall merchant scoffed, from far across the taproom. "If this drab is Princess Alusair, I suppose then I'm Vangerdahast, wearing the crowns of all the dead kings of Cormyr as I play my grand games, lifting up the king and queen and setting them as his unwitting playing-pieces, and—"

"Be still!" Another man was on his feet, a gray-haired trader in once-fine robes, his voice shaking with anger. "You dishonor us all, man! I have been to Suzail, and been slipped into a grand revel to watch from a balcony as the royal family swept in—and this *is* the princess."

And in the sudden, utter silence, he went down on his knees to Alusair.

✦ ✦ ✦ ✦ ✦

In the warehouse next door, men growled instructions, grunted with effort, and hastened to and fro as new stacks of crates and coffers were shifted by lanternlight. The stable, however, was dark and silent except for the sounds of horses tossing their heads and pawing at the straw.

The most restive horses seemed to be the ones made ready for the Knights, their reins tied to pillars. Things did not improve as the Knights mounted up.

"Fare you well, Knights of Myth Drannor," Melandar said, walking along the row of horses with a hand that glowed faintly. He calmed each horse at a touch. "Your horses now all know the way to the Eastgate, and will desire to go only there. The gate will open at your approach. Know that the good wishes of Cormyr go with you, and that agents of the Crown will bring word when you are welcome back."

"Thank you," Semoor murmured. "Is that word expected in our lifetimes?"

The war wizard gave him a wry smile, said gently, "Of course it is, Sir Priest. This is no exile nor punishment. Consider it a personal service to the queen. I will not be surprised to see all of you back at Court far sooner than you expect to be there. Yet now I must leave you to attend to my next task."

His wave was the last of him that the Knights saw. His body

vanished, swallowed by some silent magic or other, his moving hand winking out last.

Florin sighed, shook himself as if coming out of a deep slumber, and said, "Well, we'd best get out of Arabel without delay, as such is obviously expected of us, and—"

Something moved in the darkness, swift and near. Islif ducked to let a knife flash past, then lifted an arm to strike aside a dagger whirling at her. Jhessail's horse reared and screamed. Pennae launched herself from her saddle at a man who dodged out from behind a pillar and a heap of hay, running at them with a drawn sword and dagger in his hands.

Another man sprang up beside Florin's horse, knife flashing. The ranger kicked out as hard as he could, taking the man under the chin.

Florin could feel the man's neck and jaw shatter as his boot heaved the writhing, spasming man up into the air. A few teeth flashed back lanternlight momentarily as their owner spun away. Florin's mount bucked and screamed in fear, and he wrestled with the reins to stay in the saddle.

Doust cried, "Tymora be with us!"

At the same time Semoor chanted, "Lathander's light sunder this night!" and light flared in the air around them—only to be extinguished an instant later, by a spell that made the air all around the Knights crackle and crawl.

The horses screamed in terrified unison, a horrible sound that was cut off as abruptly as if by a slicing knife, leaving only silence. A silence that swallowed everything except a man's cold, cruel laughter.

"Die, Knights of Myth Drannor," the unseen man said, "at the hands of the Zhentarim. Faerûn will be much improved by the removal of a queen's toys before they have any chance to become annoying. You are as nothing—so *be* nothing!"

* * * * *

"There are six Knights of Myth Drannor now. Behold, and mark them well. All but one from the flourishing, upcountry spired-city of Espar."

The guards chuckled, but went on peering at the glowing spell images. Even the house wizards of minor nobles were apt to be testy with underlings who treated their orders with anything less than eager attention.

"This tall, handsome ladies-swoon hero is Florin Falconhand. Honest, true, swift with a sword, and a lot more naive than his manner will make you think—or than he thinks he is. This ruddy-faced farm lass who looks capable of wrestling him to the ground is Islif Lurelake. Strong, doesn't say much; you know the sort. The dainty little thing with the big elflike eyes is Jhessail Silvertree, who knows a spell or two. Looks like a little girl just ready to flirt, eh? Beware her—aside from *this* one, skulking here at the end, she's the most dangerous if the Knights ever step over our threshold."

"And will they?"

The house wizard shrugged. "Who knows? They're saying these Knights now serve the queen—and you know what *that* means."

"I know what it usually means, but notorious adventurers with blades hanging off them are hardly effective spies."

"Aye, but they can be effective *distractions*. And threats too." The wizard's voice sharpened. "Which we can speak of later. For now, learn these last three. The dangerous one is the outlander: Pennae, she calls herself, though she's used a score of other names across Sembia in the last ten winters. A sneak-thief, and a good one. Learn her face if you remember none of the others."

"And the holy men? Aren't they mere novices?"

"They are. This handsome one is Doust Sulwood, dedicated to Tymora. Shy, unassuming, but misses little. The other's Semoor Wolf-tooth, of Lathander. He's ruled by his smart tongue and inability not to use it *all* the time. What comes out of his mouth will give us all the excuses we need to attack, imprison, or run off these Knights, if they show up here. Any questions?"

"Have they any weaknesses?"

The house wizard sighed. "They're *adventurers,* Dlarvan. Therefore they're reckless fools, by definition. *Inexperienced* reckless fools. Surely you can deal with a handful of such dolts?"

"I'm sure we can," Dlarvan said—at the same time as a guard somewhere in the shadows well behind him muttered, "Well, we deal with a *wizard* every day."

The look the house wizard gave them all then was his best withering glare, but they looked back at him with identical expressions of moon-faced innocence. Motherless bastards.

• ✦ ✦ ✦ •

Black-clad men were everywhere in the darkness, swords flashing in the gloom of the stables. Pennae threw a dagger into one man's face, then leaped in another direction to stab a half-seen warrior.

Doust threw himself awkwardly out of his saddle, bare moments before a sword stabbed at where he'd been. Its wielder ducked around the hind end of Doust's horse—and was flung hard against a pillar as the horse kicked angrily.

Jhessail reached out for a rafter, to try to haul herself off her bucking, kicking horse, but arched back and away with a little shriek as a man swung down out of the loft to thrust a sword along the beam she'd been reaching for.

In the eerie spell-silence, with her fellow Knights fighting for their lives all around her, Islif spat out an oath that no one heard.

• ✦ ✦ ✦ •

People were crowding around the preening princess, as she sipped thankfully from the cooling-spout of the most ornate soup bowl in the tavern, and sighed her appreciation. Everyone was trying to get a good look at royalty, and many faces wore a hesitancy that betokened an inward war between wanting to touch the princess for good luck, and not daring such a boldness lest it offend—and cause spell-hidden war wizards and Purple Dragons melt out of the air to slay anyone so profaning an Obarskyr.

Old retired Purple Dragons shuffled forward in reverent silence, and outlanders peered and even stood on chairs to feed their curiosity. Among all the others seeking to gaze upon the Princess Alusair, no one noticed a lone diner—a quiet little man in a dark weathercloak, tunic, and breeches—eyeing the princess *very* thoughtfully from his nearby table. He nodded, as if in respect, rose, edged out of the press of awed Cormyreans, ducked through a curtain into a back room, and failed to emerge again.

Chapter 5
Rescuing a Princess

It's not all the bowing and fawning
over princesses as turns my stomach
whilst giving me bloody wounds and white hairs.
No. It's rescuing the princesses—again!—
when they blunder witlessly into doom
after doom. Hard life lesson after hard life lesson
that our heroics let them ignore.
No wonder they learn so little.

Horvarr Hardcastle
Never A Highknight:
The Life of a Dragon Guard
published in the Year of the Bow

The eerie silence faded. Florin's lunging, rearing horse almost brained him on a low crossbeam for the third time. He gave up on staying in the saddle and flung himself sideways into a heap of hay.

Pennae rolled over and over on the floor, viciously stabbing the man she grappled with, her dagger wet and glistening to her very knuckles. As the man's groans ended, she rolled to her feet, giving Florin a cheerful grin, and sprinted across the stables to pounce on a man who was trying to haul Jhessail out of her saddle.

As her dagger found the man's ribs from behind, the lashing hooves of Jhessail's terrified mount crashed into him from the front. The man crumpled, Pennae coolly slitting his throat as they went into the straw together. Florin saw a trail of three sprawled corpses behind the one he'd seen her slay.

Three brightnesses flared from someone's fingertips at the far end of the stables—and streaked through the air, curving around pillars to follow the hastening, battling Knights—and Florin saw Pennae gasp and reel as one of the spell-bolts struck her. An instant later, Islif grunted and stiffened in midparry, her attacker seizing the chance to drive her blade aside and send her staggering back. As Florin launched himself at the man, the last missile struck Doust and slammed him head-first into a pillar. He fell without a sound.

Florin's charge carried him into the swordsman with a solid crash. The man went down. Florin trampled him and ran on, heading for the spot where some Zhentarim wizard had cast that spell. Islif could handle her foes without his aid, but if that mage took it into his head to, say, blast a few of the pillars with a fire spell that brought the stables down on top of them all and set it afire. . . .

The Zhents all seemed to wear motley leathers and everyday traders' vests and boots, and to be wielding similarly mismatched swords and daggers. They also seemed to be dying very swiftly—behind him, a man screamed suddenly and started choking wetly, and he heard Pennae laugh and call, "I've run out of foes again! Over here, all craven assailants!"—which would *not* be viewed favorably by the Watch of Arabel.

Was this whole affair a trap? These men had appeared the moment the war wizard took himself away. Who was left to attest that the Knights had been given these mounts and weren't just horse-thieves in the night?

Those thoughts took Florin up a dimly seen hayloft ladder, a fleeing black robe flapping not far ahead of him, and out through an open hatch in a frantic, stumbling run so he could get through before the wizard readied any sort of spell, onto a rooftop of old shakes slippery in the slackening rain.

The wizard was backing away from him with an uncertain sneer, as more Zhent warriors waving swords and daggers came hurrying from the warehouse roof to surround him in a protective ring—and then advance on Florin. Ten . . . a dozen . . . Florin planted himself, and wondered how long it would take a newly knighted young ranger from Espar to die.

In the back room of the Old Warhound tavern, Andaero Hardtower of the Zhentarim hissed fiercely into the face of the short man in the dark weathercloak, "Ravelo, I don't care if *all* the kings of every last *Border Kingdom* are out in the taproom—and all their jeweled strumpets too! I'm late reporting in and the scrying crystal's starting to glow and I *must be alone!* Get gone!"

Scowling, Ravelo whirled around and ducked out—just as the palm-sized crystal ball in front of Hardtower flickered into sudden glowing life, and a cold voice asked, without bothering with any greeting, "Well? What idiocy are you up to *now?*"

"N-none, Lord Sarhthor!" Andaero gasped excitedly. "All but a handful of my forces are busy carrying out Lathalance's orders right now!"

There was a sigh. "And just what orders did Lathalance give?"

"He bade us see this night to the elimination of the Knights of Myth Drannor. They have a pendant we are to seize. Lathalance says slaying them and getting that bauble will shatter and once and for all *end* the schemes of the Royal Magician and the Blackstaff of Waterdeep and their confounded Harpers, and hand Shadowdale to *us*."

The glowing crystal was showing no image in its depths—and that suddenly seemed like a good thing to Andaero, as it erupted in a stream of snarled curses that ended in an exasperated, "Stop them, fool!"

"T-too late," Hardtower stammered. "They're fighting the Knights right now!"

"Do you command a drunken rabble," Sarhthor inquired icily, "or Zhentilar warriors?"

"A-a drunken rabble, Lord. All the men you trained have been killed fighting the Knights *and* all the roused Dragons in Arabel, with Baron Thomdor leading them! These we have now are our spies and lazynecks, plus all I could induce with coin to fight for us—or coerce by threat of exposing them to the Dragons—in a day. Neldrar leads them."

"Then let them die, and Neldrar with them, and get yourself well away from it all," Sarhthor ordered coldly. "*Now.*"

As the crystal started to dim, Hardtower heard the fading beginnings of an incantation, and shivered as he recognized it.

✦ ✦ ✦ ✦ ✦

The tall, slender double doors of flame-hued, glossy copper parted, and a cloaked half-elf who was also tall and slender stepped through them and drew them firmly closed behind him. Even before they closed in velvet silence, the dwarf who'd been leaning against a curved wall, waiting, stepped forward to block the half-elf's path, and squinted up to ask gruffly, "And what was all that about, aye?"

"Well met, Raurig," the half-elf said with a smile that hinted otherwise, but added smoothly, "The High Lady desires closer ties of trade and friendship with the Forest Kingdom, Cormyr."

"And so?"

"And so will shortly announce the investiture of a new envoy to the Royal Court of King Azoun, in Suzail."

"Who will be—? Gods above, Laroncel, getting specifics out of ye is like prodding a sullen orc prisoner!"

"Oh? Well, that seems fitting, Raurig. Entertaining your questions always seems much akin to answering an angry orc trying to browbeat replies out of a captive! I have good reason to believe Lady Alustriel still possesses a mouth—"

"Heh! I'll *bet* ye do!"

"I see no need at all for low coarseness, Raurig, nor for allusions to matters not now under discussion. As I was saying, the Lady Alustriel still having a mouth permits her to make her own announcement as to the identity of her envoy, as is customary, and I see no reason at all for me to—"

"Ah, I quite see. Just as *I* see no reason not to inform her Lady Lovehips as to yer little meeting with Jesper of Luskan, a night back, regarding—"

"*Ahem*, Raurig, if we could *just* refrain from mentioning matters so personal, I was about to say that I saw no reason not to inform someone so *discreet* as yourself as to the identity of the envoy. Yes? Good, I'm glad we so plainly understand each other."

"I, too, am overwhelmed with gladness. Out with it, Brightears!"

"Raurig, *please!* Leave me some small shards of dignity! Very well, though I dislike speaking of such delicate matters out here in this very public passage, let it be known to you—and *only* to you—that Silverymoon's new envoy to Cormyr will be the Lady Aerilee Hastorna Summerwood."

"Huh! *That* loose-skirts! Serve Azoun the Lusty well, won't she?"

"I believe that opinion was just privately imparted, yes, though *not* by myself."

"That fails utterly to surprise me, Laroncel. Same bloodlines as ye, every bit as tall—ye'll miss her, won't ye?"

Laroncel Duirwood smiled as if remembering something very pleasant, and murmured, "Yes, but my aim has improved steadily."

As he strode off down the passage, he decided that the dwarven chuckles from behind him could best be described as "dirty."

* * * * *

Florin ducked and thrust and sidestepped, fighting furiously just to stay alive. Rather than trying to wound, he used his reach and strength to tumble foe after foe off the roof, and was succeeding—which was a very good thing, because ever-more men were rushing at him from all sides.

One of the largest swordsmen, who'd come stumping cautiously across the slimy roof rather than rushing Florin, reached the ranger at last. He wore a belt bristling with sheathed daggers, but wielded only a huge sword, using both hands to raise his fearsome weapon back and to the side. In a moment, he'd come at Florin and swing it around in a great body-slicing slash, with all of his weight behind it.

Florin feigned a slip, "falling" forward onto the fingertips of his free hand—and as the man chuckled and started his great hacking swing, Florin sprang froglike to his right and rolled over, leading with his blade, scything the man's ankles out from under him and sending the swordsman toppling with a shriek of startled pain.

Right behind him, another swordsman charged at Florin with his blade drawn back. Florin rolled frantically and came up with his sword lifted. One swift dodge and the man impaled himself on Florin's blade, solid and heavy and almost hilt-deep.

Then light blossomed in the night, and the swordsmen running across the roofs at Florin faltered, stopped, and turned to stare.

The wizard Florin had pursued up onto the stable roof swayed, startlement clear on his face—a face that all could see clearly in the rainy night because the Zhentarim's body was starting to glow, hitherto-invisible runes all over his robes burning into scarlet life. The wizard stared down at the runes; a cold voice arose from them, speaking what sounded like an incantation. Except for the one now collapsing over Florin's blade, the swordsmen were all watching and listening now, like so many dark statues in the night.

The wizard stared past them all at Florin, horror in his eyes, and screamed, "No! *Nooooo!*" as the incantation rose to a triumphant end. The runes exploded, the wizard vanishing in a shattering burst of flames that hurled blazing swordsmen in all directions. Florin flung himself toward the edge of the roof.

* * * * *

"Follow me not," the princess had grandly commanded everyone in the Black Hound, sweeping out into the night with the cloak some fool of a merchant had given her swirling around her. Not wanting to be noticed doing just that by a tavern-full of awed Arabellans, Ravelo Tarltarth had slipped boldly into the servery and out the back door, to become one more alley shadow in the wet night.

It had not been difficult to spot the princess, still waving her sword and dagger around as she turned along a street and headed for grander lanes, where beyond a few stables and warehouses, balconied mansions rose many-windowed into the rain.

Ravelo didn't have to skulk. He could stroll openly, this royal lass was so careless—and so predictable. Not that he was known to the local Watch, yet. Short, silent, and balding, he looked more like a weary shopkeeper than a Zhent spy. One of the better "eyes" for the Zhentarim in the Forest Kingdom, he judged himself; one who remained unnoticed by the Crown, despite war wizards poking their noses into everything—including everyone's minds—in Cormyr every second breath or so.

Ravelo took a side-alley, trotting swiftly in the wet darkness, and then turned along a cross-alley, back to the street where the Princess Alusair was walking, once he was sure he'd gotten ahead of her. He crouched in the mouth of the alley, weathercloak drawn close around him. Yes, here she was now, looking like some sort of bad actor in a fancy-play, sneaking along having an adventure.

Ravelo's lip barely had time to curl before he and the princess both became aware that something of interest was happening on the roof of a stables not far ahead of Alusair. Men were rushing around in the rain there, fighting with swords, and many of them, one after another, fell or were hurled off the roof, to crash down out of sight behind a warehouse that still had lanterns lit and men sorting and shifting coffers and crates around. Those, that is, that hadn't stopped to gape up at the fighting.

There were occasional yells, and even a shriek or two. The princess slowed, but her sword and dagger came up as if to deal death, and her eyes shone with excitement. Ravelo's sneer slipped into a grin.

A sudden glow came into being up on the roof, coming from the front of someone—a wizard—in robes, and illuminating a dozen or more men with sword and daggers, who seemed to have been converging on a lone man, but who were now turning to look at the glowing wizard. Ravelo's eyes narrowed. Was that Neldrar of the Brotherhood? Yes, he was almost certain it was Neldrar, whose cold commands Ravelo had heard and obeyed a time or two, and—

A blinding-bright burst of flame suddenly split the night, an ear-smiting blast that seemed to come from Neldrar.

It echoed off taller nearby buildings and hurled men with swords in all directions. Writhing men plunged through the air and smaller, unseen things came pattering down all around.

Ravelo watched the princess shrink back as what was left of a torn and boneless human arm bounced in the street in front of her boots and rolled bloodily past her. Half a dozen dead or senseless Zhent warriors crashed heavily into the street, swords and daggers clanging and skittering away across the cobbles. A pale-faced Alusair turned as if to go back the way she'd come.

Mouthing a silent curse, Ravelo stepped out of the alley to glide after her—but ducked back in as he saw her stop, and heard and saw why: a Watch patrol was pelting down the street, swords drawn, their boots raising a rising thunder of their own. A dozen Purple

Dragons in full chain mail, with the Dragon of Cormyr on their surcoats—and one glimpse of that badge had the princess turning and running right for the mouth of Ravelo's alley.

Grinning like a fox, Ravelo waited for her, his knife ready. If the Princess Alusair were found murdered here in so-often-rebel Arabel, Cormyr would rouse to arms.

And in the wake of a royal killing, the kingdom should be so beset by confusion that the Brotherhood could covertly enact all manner of killings and thefts. If they spread the right rumors, to manipulate the citizenry effectively, they could quite possibly start a civil war.

His Zhentarim superiors would take the credit and claim all the rewards, of course, but one Ravelo Tarltarth, opportunistic low-ranking Zhent spy, should be able to steal loot in plenty for himself in all the tumult.

And all because he undertook the moment's work of slitting the throat of one pampered fool of a girl.

Princess Alusair Nacacia darted into the alley, right past the crouching Ravelo. As he turned, rising and shaking off his weathercloak, he thumbed forth the magic token that had ridden for so long clipped to the inner face of his belt buckle, and slapped it to the cobbles. It winked, and utter silence fell.

The princess was already turning, having seen *something* moving in the darkness nigh her elbow. Her eyes widened in alarm, her mouth opened—and Ravelo, hefting his knife, grinned broadly. Silent screams summoned no aid.

His murderous intent was unmistakable. The young royal parried wildly, her sword long enough to drive aside his first thrust.

Ravelo chuckled. It was splendid steel, but too large and heavy for her slender arm, and she'd just entangled her cloak on it, dragging it down. Ah, but this killing would be *easy.*

Easy enough to enjoy a bit. . . .

He slashed at Alusair's face, expecting her to shrink back, but she clenched her teeth and brought her sword arm up sharply, swirling cloak and all—so Ravelo showed her what a slaying-sharp knife could do, slicing through thick wool and sasheen lining as if they were but mist, slicing a neat, shallow cut in the royal sword arm.

Alusair shrieked soundlessly, her face going pale. She staggered back, hand falling open. Her cloak came off her shoulders and dragged her sword from her fingers—and she spun around and fled, cloak and sword falling together in her wake, dagger flashing in her other hand.

Ravelo sprang after her. It would be the work of a moment to pounce on the princess, a knee in her back to bear her down hard onto the cobbles, and slit her throat while she was still bouncing and wallowing to try to get her breath.

Yet she was, yes, running to a tall, ornate iron gate in the alley wall, a gate Ravelo knew. He slowed, his grin widening.

It was the back way into the mansion of the Delzuld noble family. Better and better. If her murder were blamed on the Delzulds—and how could it not be, if she were found sprawled in her blood in the Delzuld grounds?—given their nigh-certain reaction, and those of their allies, it *would* mean civil war.

Panting soundlessly in the spell-silence, Alusair shook the gate. It was locked, and she clawed her way up it in a frenzy, slipping twice or thrice on the wet iron.

At the top she slipped again, risking impalement on the row of spikes that crowned the gate.

Ravelo strolled to just below her kicking feet and waited. If she did die on the gate, he'd climb up and leave his knife hilt-deep in her, but 'twould be better if—

Alusair sobbed in fear, staring blindly into the dark wet night, and when a hand reached down out of nowhere to take firm hold of hers, it seemed to her as if the Watching Gods themselves had reached down to deliver her from doom.

Chapter 6

Waywards Return

In the end, all waywards return.
The trick is doing so alive.

Horvarr Hardcastle
Never A Highknight:
The Life of a Dragon Guard
published in the Year of the Bow

The blast plucked up Florin Falconhand in mid-dive and hurled him over the stableyard and the grand wall beyond. He tumbled helplessly through an endless instant of whistling wind—to a bouncing, bruisingly hard landing on the roof of the Delzuld gatehouse.

Skidding to a halt, he rolled over, fighting for breath. It was not a place he recognized, but seemed much safer than the stable roof and its plentiful supply of murderous swordsmen. He came weaving to his feet, still a little dazed and winded—only to stare down into the terrified, wide-eyed face of a young girl clawing her way up the gate with an alley skulker just below her.

She took his proffered hand, and Florin hauled her bodily up onto the roof, out of the way, and drew his dagger. His sword was deep in a Zhent's gut, back on the stable roof—if there *was* a roof anymore.

As Florin brought his dagger up, her would-be slayer was already up the gate and—smashing the ranger off his feet, driving Florin down hard on his backside. As they skidded back along the roof, a needle-sharp dagger stabbed like an icicle into Florin's shoulder.

He grunted in startled pain. The slayer clawed his way over Florin reaching his dagger for the girl's throat, but she struck his blade aside with a knife of her own. Florin's stabbed arm was useless, but he twisted under the man and slammed his other hand into the man's throat. The slayer stiffened. Florin closed his fingers around that throat and squeezed, as hard as he could.

The deadly dagger came at him again, and Florin rolled desperately away, taking them both across the roof as the slayer's knife waved wildly, the strangling man fighting for balance.

The knife swept down, and Florin shoved hard, flinging the man into a last roll over and then half-under him. The slayer ran out of rooftop, ending up scrabbling right on the edge, still clutching Florin.

Florin pulled his feet up to his chest and kicked out, thrusting the slayer upright, arms windmilling, and away.

The man's foot came down awkwardly on the roof-edge, and he fell over backward, toppling right onto the gate-spikes, where he slumped, hanging helpless and dying, spikes thrusting up through his chest like red fangs.

Florin could see the man's fate, illuminated in the light of lanterns bobbing nearer, below. Wincing, he rolled over, breathing hard, and made for the back of the roof, as far as he could get from the Purple Dragon patrol now stalking along the alley. His shoulder felt like his arm was dangling by shreds, about to fall off.

The lass shrank back a little as he crawled up to her, and no wonder; he must look fearsome, drenched in blood and dragging one arm, his face twisted in pain.

"Are you all right?" the ranger gasped, shifting so the shadow of his body shielded her face from the lanternlight. Behind and below, the gate rattled and Purple Dragons snapped terse words back and forth.

"I am, goodsir," she murmured, frowning, "but you're hurt."

"Sorely, as they say," Florin hissed, managing a crooked grin, "but I mustn't be found here. I must get away somehow."

The lass plucked a long pendant from around her neck, put it into his good hand, and whispered, "Break it with your fingers! Now!"

Florin looked at her wonderingly, and did so. A pale, tingling radiance washed over his fingers and ran up his arm, and he found himself gasping and shuddering in a rapture that washed all his pain away. He could *feel* his wound closing, the sliced muscles knitting together again . . .

When he could see again, Florin blinked, swallowed, and said, "Lady, you have my deepest thanks." He was completely unhurt, healed as if he'd never been wounded. "Who are you?"

The lass gave him a rather superior smile—gods, she could not be more than thirteen or so!—drew herself up, and announced, "I am Alusair Nacacia Obarskyr, Princess of Cormyr."

From behind them both came curses of amazement, and then a more startled oath as the Purple Dragon at the top of the gate lost his footing in his astonishment and fell back among, or onto, his fellows.

"Princess—Highness—I am honored," Florin stammered, "but I *must* go."

He knelt to her, on the roof, and Alusair put her hand on his, so light and swift a caress that it seemed almost as if a breeze had touched him, and said quickly, "Of course. Pray begone, and may the gods guard you."

He gave her a smile, nodded, and thankfully raced away along the broad top of the ornate mansion wall.

Behind him, he heard a Purple Dragon gasp, "It *is* her, hrast all the gods! Princess, how came you to be *here?*"

Florin caught hold of the top of some sort of carved stone ornament adorning the wall and turned to swing himself around and down—but paused for a moment to watch what befell the princess.

"I am unaccustomed to giving any account of myself to passing Purple Dragons," she snapped, her voice rising in anger as she saw the soldiers hastening to encircle her.

Various Purple Dragons converged on her on the gatehouse roof, holding up their lanterns. Florin was in time to see the Princess Alusair smile triumphantly and vanish, winking out of their clutches.

The Purple Dragons swore in hearty and collective earnest.

* * * * *

Ghoruld Applethorn, Master of Alarphons of the Wizards of War, chuckled in glee at what was unfolding in his scrying crystal. This particular wet night in Arabel offered superb entertainment.

The crystal winked as lightning split the sky somewhere between Arabel and Suzail, and the unicorn ring on his finger winked back at it. The surging energies made the hargaunt restless; it slithered across the floor, a mottled rippling curtain with a tail and ever-shifting tentacle-arms, and started to climb Applethorn's leg.

The battle in the stables was over, Purple Dragons converging on the place and rushing around with shouts and brandished swords. Idiots.

"Better and better," Applethorn purred. "These Knights are going to prove *so* useful. How many war wizards and overambitious nobles can I manage to get them to kill before they're out of the realm?"

He ran a toying finger over the warm, yielding skin of the hargaunt, now slithering up his thigh, and murmured, "Out of the realm for now, that is. Until I need them to deal death again."

* * * * *

Stepping through the blue mists that took Laspeera at a single stride from Arabel to the Palace seemed a mere moment ago; a moment that had been spent hastening to a robing room to exchange her wet, clinging garments for dry robes, and then hurrying on, by secret ways, to the queen's apartments, where the hurrying would end. The regular duty of guarding the queen overnight thankfully involved very little haste and tumult.

Yet no sooner had the Wizard of War Laspeera settled into this night's attendance on Queen Filfaeril than a seldom-heard chime sounded.

Laspeera looked up, frowning sharply. The triggering of that warning-spell meant that someone had just traversed a nearby portal. Specifically "the Back Way," a wardrobe that stood in one of the few rooms of this wing of the Palace that wasn't heavily warded against translocation magics, and had probably been created in the days of the Royal Magician Amedahast. Kept for emergencies, it was known only to Azoun and his queen, a handful of Highknights, and a few senior war wizards. Or so she'd thought.

"Something's wrong," Filfaeril murmured. Laspeera pulled a wand from her belt, and a secret panel slid open with the faintest of whisperings to admit Margaster, who stepped into the room with a heavy black rod in his hand that crackled with blue glows and arcings of awakened power. Filfaeril took up a dagger and a magic orb from a sidetable. "If my Az—"

Tapestries billowed aside as Dove of the Harpers shouldered through them and strode into the room, carrying an unconscious Princess Alusair in her arms.

The queen went white, but Dove gave her a smile and said firmly, "She's alive and unharmed. Her slumber's due to a spell of mine."

The slack mouth and lolling head of the princess made her look a lot worse than asleep, and Filfaeril looked less than reassured as the tall, burly woman in worn leathers stalked across the room to arrange her royal burden gently upon a cushion-strewn lounge. "Where—?" Filfaeril began.

"A hilltop near Jester's Green," Dove said over her shoulder, "where I happened to be meeting privately with a fellow Harper. Your daughter appeared rather abruptly between us—thanks to magic, obviously—soaked through as you see her, and seemed profanely disinclined to follow my suggestion to accompany me back here."

Laspeera started to smile. "So you . . ."

"So I cast a little spell on her, which sent her off to visit her dreams for a bit, while she was still threatening both of us with her little dagger. Fee, your little one is growing teeth, and starting to use them."

The Dragon Queen almost smiled. "Did she say where she'd been, and what she had been doing?"

"No," Dove said calmly, "so I then used a little more magic on our sleeper here to learn what she'd been up to. I could scarce resist. How often these days do minstrels have a chance to cast spells on sleeping princesses?"

Laspeera's smile vanished. "You dared use magic on an Obarskyr? Do we not have an agreement, between Harpers and Crown?"

"We do," Dove said firmly, drawing herself up to give Laspeera a steady look. "Yet we *Chosen* agreed with Baerauble and Amedahast and Thanderahast and Jorunhast and now Vangerdahast, as to exactly what we can and can't do regarding the Dragon Throne. An understanding quite separate from what the Harpers have agreed to. Moreover, Lasp, I'm unlikely to accept any rebuke on using magic on anyone from a *war wizard*. You do the same, and more, daily. Yet worry not. Before Mystra I swear that all my magic did was compel Alusair to sleep, and then peer at her most recent memories—and *only* her newest memories."

She turned to the queen and added, "Learning something of her . . . activities, I relieved her of this ring"—Dove turned back to Laspeera, and handed her a ring that certainly hadn't been in her fingers a moment earlier—"that this night took her to Arabel before she dropped in on us, and then I brought her home to you."

She spun around again to face Filfaeril, and murmured, "Fee, you must promise me you won't cage your younger daughter—or let your war wizards do so. They'll only make matters worse if they try. Instead they're going to have to shadow her—*unseen* by her—as she spreads her wings into womanhood. Ready to rush in and rescue her if needful, of course, *but* taking care not to rush in too soon, and in doing so rob her of making her own mistakes and darings."

The Dragon Queen lifted her chin. "You certainly have my promise on that, Dove. Yet you speak as if you suspect otherwise. What dark things did you learn from my Alusair's mind?"

"That she feels caged right now. She bitterly hates being shut into the Palace and hounded by ever-watchful servants and courtiers and war wizards. She hungers for adventure—so strongly that just going into a tavern alone, to eat stew and some buns, delights her as adventure."

Laspeera sighed. "I know you're right, Dove. I've been watching her. Yet eating in a tavern isn't all she did, is it?"

"No," Dove said, putting a comforting arm around the Dragon Queen before she added, "She went for a walk along an alley or two, and met some drunks and a Zhentarim."

Filfaeril started to shake, silently, and Dove spun her gently around into a full embrace, folding her arms around the queen. For all her iron will and sharp tongue, Fee had never gotten over the murder of her infant son Foril, and what this particular Chosen of Mystra was going to have to say to her next certainly wasn't going to help her do so.

"A Zhentarim," Dove repeated softly. "Not a wizard, but a spy with a knife. The Princess Alusair came very close to being slain, as unpleasantly as possible—and knows it, thank the gods. Her life was saved by a young man known to you, the chartered adventurer Florin Falconhand."

She felt Filfaeril stiffen, and saw Laspeera stiffen too.

"He took the knife-thrust meant for her," she added, "on a rooftop, in the rain, though he knew not who she was until after. Or so, at least, she believes and remembers it."

Queen Filfaeril tugged free of Dove's embrace, and turned to look at her almost helplessly, and then at Laspeera. Tears streamed down her face as she murmured, "And I sent him away—I sent them all away. To the Nine Hells with Khelben's schemes, and Vangerdahast's too! Can't we call them back?"

✦ ✦ ✦

Far indeed from the castle in Cormyr where a queen known to the citizenry of Suzail for her icy manner sobbed helplessly, a man who was no longer a man pondered life as it now was.

Horaundoon might have lacked a body of his own, but he had all the bodies of living folk of Faerûn to choose from. King or commoner, mighty-thewed bodyguard or curvaceous veiled dancer, human or snake-man or tentacled, slithering thing—he could "ride" them all.

No longer a cringing, middling mage of the Zhentarim, he could now wield the Brotherhood like a weapon, manipulating it or possessing those who gave orders within its ranks . . . or he could destroy it, butchering his way through those same ranks until none remained to menace the Realms.

Yet increasingly he found such struggles and schemes beneath him, or no longer mattering all that much. Being a wraithlike spirit was changing him, and the changes excited him, scared him, and thrust him ever onward into . . . an unknown life.

He still often plunged murderously into people, burning them out from within in the space of a few breaths as he drank their life-energies. Sometimes he did so just to lash out, dealing death as much out of furious frustration as out of his need for life-force to empower him.

Yet Horaundoon was learning to enjoy the rides, and to cherish his steeds as well as destroying them.

Just now, he was riding a hapless wealthy merchant of Amn, one Unstraburl Hordree.

Cloak swirling out behind him, Hordree was striding home through the glittering streets of Athkatla, rubbing his hands in satisfaction. His trotting bodyguards formed a grim ring all around him as he hastened along, teeth bared in a wider sharklike smile than was usual.

Horaundoon was broadening that smile with his own pleasure, having just ridden voyeur on Hordree's lovemaking, at his secret loveden of enslaved-with-drugs mistresses.

Hordree was the third man Horaundoon had ridden for days on end without harming him all that much. He was learning.

Mastering his rage at what had been stolen from him, and learning to control humans rather than just drain them. Growing comfortable with being a wraithlike spirit, and starting to see the possibilities of his new existence.

Mindworms and stolen elven spells were behind him.

Nobles, adventurers, and royalty in Cormyr were just playthings, and he was past all that now.

No fearful, skulking retirement in hiding awaited him. No hargaunt and no fear of being hunted at Manshoon's orders.

Why, if he went about things deftly and patiently, he could well slay all of his former rivals in the Zhentarim, by drinking their very lives. Lathalance and Sarhthor, Eirhaun Sooundaeril . . . and Manshoon himself.

Yes.

After all these years, if he kept well hidden—and who would be looking for "dead by his own hand" Horaundoon?—he could finally dare to strike at Manshoon.

Destroying Manshoon . . . now that would be *true* power.

* * * * *

"Well met, Dragon," Dove said, as King Azoun strode back into the room. "You've been told all?"

Azoun nodded. "I have, and I thank you. We still have two daughters this night because of you."

"Because of Florin Falconhand," Dove corrected him. She looked at Queen Filfaeril. "I must leave you now, I'm afraid. Other business"—one of her fingers brushed her harp-shaped belt buckle for an instant, a momentary gesture unseen by Laspeera or Margaster through the intervening royal bodies —"presses me sorely. So you must guard your own princesses."

Azoun gave her another grim nod. As he stepped forward to clasp her hand, he asked, "Margaster?"

The old war wizard bowed. "My king?"

Azoun waved at the sleeping Alusair. "The Dragondown Chambers?"

The war wizard nodded.

"Both Tana and Luse," Azoun added. "Stay with them as much as you can. And you can put my lasses into spell-sleep for a year if you deem it needful—just *don't* let them run off!"

The war wizard bowed again, looking grave.

* * * * *

Though it was dark enough in the shadow of the Hullack Forest to foil the eyes of most humans, it seemed that there were more trees around Lord Prester Yellander's hunting lodge this night than usual—and that some of those trees were *moving.*

A patient eye would have eventually identified those extra dark trunks as the torsos of bodyguards. Many, many bodyguards, standing staring out into the night and listening intently for sounds of anyone approaching.

Those veteran swordjacks could hear nothing from inside the thick log walls of the hunting lodge, despite the relative quiet of small night sounds in the forest and their own breathing, because the three men inside all wore multiple magecloak magics on their persons. Enough to foil even the most intent war wizard scrying.

Which was a good thing, because every word of their converse was dark treason.

Chapter 7

HIDDEN DRAGONFIRE

So much magic lies hidden in Cormyr
That I scarce know where to begin.
Darlock's six tasked spirits
The Crown of the Slayer
The Hunting Blade
The Door Into Nowhere
The wandering cloaks of wyvernshape
And dead Emmaera Dragonfire
Who left so many silent flying swords
To guard her enchanted bones
And I've but begun the list.
There are all the tombs of the nobles, yet.

Sebren Korthyn, Sage of Elturel
The Realm of the Dragon:
Cormyr In The Time of Vangerdahast
Volume 1
published in the Year of the Bright Blade

The table between the three lords was small. If it hadn't been for the metal goblets between them, their knuckles could easily have touched.

Lord Maniol Crownsilver stared across that small distance at Yellander and Eldroon, and said quietly, "I believe all Cormyr knows *my* very good reason for hating the Knights of Myth Drannor and wanting to see them meet swift and brutal dooms. Lords, may I know yours?"

The two lords across the table exchanged glances, Yellander gave the briefest of nods, and Lord Blundebel Eldroon leaned forward to explain calmly, "We're furious at the Knights for shattering a means of income that brought us each more than a thousand-thousand golden lions a year."

Crownsilver blinked. "Might, ah, I know how *any* noble of Cormyr manages to make such sums without all the realm knowing about it?"

"Smuggling," Eldroon said simply. "Scarce or banned goods that command high coin, and upon which we pay not a copper thumb in taxes. The scarce wares include certain wines and scents much sought-after by many nobly born—and even more avidly by the wealthiest merchants of Suzail; those desperate to show the kingdom that they're either worthy of ennoblement, or are wealthy and powerful enough that they can have what we nobles have."

"And the banned goods?"

"Poisons and certain drugs prohibited under Crown law. Thaelur, laskran, blackmask, behelshrabba—that sort of thing."

"I have heard of thaelur, and that it has something to do with pleasure," Lord Crownsilver said slowly, lifting his eyebrows in a clear request for information.

"Thaelur comes from the beast-cities of the South," Eldroon obliged. "It gives a sensation of intense bodily pleasure, and short-lived freedom from pains in the joints, but each dose does damage. Frequent users lose years off their lives. Hence its illicit status."

"We concern ourselves not with the uses to which others put goods, but merely with the business of moving such goods around," Lord Yellander put in. "Untaxed and expensive goods in, and certain shipments out—which is to say shipping done for those who pay us highly enough."

Crownsilver frowned. "Slavers?"

"Nothing so crass, man." Eldroon's drawl held irritation. "Dealers in pickled cadavers and body parts, thieves who want jewels they've stolen from nobles out of the realm in a hurry, that sort of thing."

"The Knights fought from end to end of our warehouse in Arabel. What with all the Zhentarim, war wizard, and Purple Dragon scrutiny since, our business—which flowed through that building—is in shambles."

Crownsilver frowned. "Can you not use another warehouse? It's not as though you haven't coins enough to buy dozens of them!"

"Coins don't move a portal elves created long before there was a Cormyr," Eldroon grunted, "and it's that portal in that warehouse—with its other end on the far side of yon mountains—our wares move through."

"By the way," Yellander purred pleasantly, lifting a fluted decanter to refill all three goblets, "speak of this to anyone, Maniol, and you'll die." He took up his own full goblet, sipped appreciatively, and added matter-of-factly, "*Very* slowly, and screaming in agony. We have the poisons to make very sure of that."

Crownsilver stared into Yellander's gentle smile, then took up his goblet and sipped as his host had done—and doubled over in sudden sharp agony, as something caught fire in his throat and gut.

He couldn't breathe, couldn't. . . .

The world spun, he slid helplessly out of his chair, everything going oddly green—and Maniol Crownsilver found himself on the floor, writhing and gasping, staring up helplessly into Yellander's tight smile and cold, cold eyes.

His host unhurriedly produced another goblet and poured some of its contents into Crownsilver's mouth—a flood that brought cool relief, coursing through him in a racing flow that banished his pain as if it had never been.

"Always keep antidotes handy," Yellander said brightly, reaching down a hand to help Crownsilver to his feet. "Sound policy for every poisoner."

Settling thankfully back into his seat, Maniol Crownsilver shook his head in disgust. "That demonstration was *not* necessary."

He waved his hand as if to banish all memory of what had just occurred, and said, "What I don't understand is why you two don't own all Cormyr—Obarskyrs, war wizards, Purple Dragons, stinking Marsember and all—already! You could have been sending long caravans of loaded trade-wagons, or mounted, weapon-gleaming armies, through that portal!"

Eldroon shook his head. "Listen not to minstrels' tales. Portals will never replace caravans for overland trade. Even if the way you're using is free of some fell and ancient evil watching over it in the belief that all who use it are their rightful meals, the ways themselves occasionally 'drink' or melt away things taken through them."

" 'Things'?"

"Coins, swords, trade goods. Anything you're wearing or carrying."

"Which is why," Yellander put in smoothly, "you can step through a portal in your best armor, waving your sword—and arrive at the other end naked, with your sword hand empty." He sipped from his goblet. "Something of a crestfallen disaster for your mounted, weapon-gleaming armies."

"So our trade has been well and truly disrupted," Lord Eldroon concluded. "Wherefore we want the Knights of Myth Drannor and particular war wizards and Zhentarim dead, and their corpses missing or reduced to scattered dust—so not even beyond death will they be able to tell anyone about certain things they may have seen in our warehouse."

"Which, by the way," Yellander added, "also contains many legitimate wares, stored for other traders."

Eldroon nodded. "We only need six-and-twenty or so slain, but they must be the *right* six-and-twenty."

Crownsilver frowned. "Adventurers, war wizards, Zhents—so you're going to start a war in the streets of Arabel? *How*, exactly, without dragging every war wizard in all the realm—and half the Purple Dragons too—down on our heads like so many hungry war-dogs?"

"No," Yellander snapped, "not Arabel. We're not *dolts,* man."

"Halfhap," said Eldroon.

"Halfhap?"

"Walled town, well on the way to Tilver's Gap, going eas—"

"Yes, *yes,* I know it. Why Halfhap?"

"It has a lure we can use. With your help."

"All right," Lord Crownsilver said warily, "suppose you tell me first how *my* help is a key to this cunning scheme. Then you can tell me the cunning part, and all about this lure."

Yellander smiled thinly. "Well said, Maniol. Here 'tis then, bluntly: you're being watched."

"By?"

"The war wizards, who else? They're *very* interested in you right now, expecting you to either take your own life or more likely work treason in a rage against your recent losses. So, upon our signal, you will bait our hook by hiring a few bullyblades and gathering your most able servants for a little run to Halfhap—telling said servants why of course, so they can tonguewag it all over Suzail—to find and seize Emmaera Dragonfire's magic for your own."

"Ah. That's your lure."

"Indeed. The persistent local legend of the hidden, never-yet-found magic of Emmaera Dragonfire. More properly Emmaera Skulthand, but minstrels prefer her nickname, of course. Long dead, cloaked in many wild bards' tales—just the sort of thing adventurers, Zhents, and our ever-meddling war wizards all find irresistible."

"So given that very irresistibility, why hasn't someone plundered Emmaera's magic long since?"

Yellander shrugged. "Perhaps they have. It certainly isn't in Halfhap, so far as we can tell."

"And given that the war wizards undoubtedly know that too, how exactly do you expect the lure to work?"

Lord Eldroon smiled. "You cover ground the two of us have argued over a time or two before. Let us share our conclusions with you."

"Please do."

"Well, if we make sure the Knights of Myth Drannor and particular Zhents—and, once our favorite adventurers have reached the Oldcoats Inn in Halfhap, certain war wizards too—overhear news that the dead woman's long-lost spellbooks, wands, and all have been discovered behind a false wall in the deepest cellar of the inn, *but* that no one dares approach them because a ring of floating, magically animated swords guards them—"

"Swords that blaze with all-consuming dragonfire," Yellander murmured.

"Guardian swords that blaze with all-consuming dragonfire," Eldroon agreed. "The Knights and the war wizards are sure to race to claim such a prize. As the rumors we spread and the hook-baiting your hurried preparations and travel serve to make that 'sure' even more certain."

Crownsilver nodded. His face seemed to be getting used to wearing a slight frown. "And how will that help you? Once they discover there's nothing there, won't they all just leave again?"

"Ah, but there *isn't* nothing there. There's a spell Dragonfire cast, an illusion of her spellbooks, wands, and baubles. The war wizards have searched that old decaying barn of an inn dozens of times, and banished her spell, too, but it keeps returning. It was *her* lure—and one of the reasons we bought the inn some years back."

"Her lure, you say? So where is her magic, really?"

"No one knows, and we've never wanted to waste coin, time, and lives finding out. The inn cellars serve us as way-storage, and the new keeper serves us, sending us coin that the rooms above bring—the rooms that aren't full of our bullyblades."

"So the Knights go down into the cellar . . ."

"And we pounce." Lord Eldroon smiled. "Or rather, our bullyblades do, using all the back passages and curtained-off corners in the cellars; crossbows that fire bolts tipped with our poisons, and that sort of thing. They can bring war wizards down dead just as easily as they can foolhead adventurers."

"And when it's all done," Lord Yellander added, sliding aside the top of the table between them to reveal a velvet-lined storage niche that held a string of cheap-looking beads and a note that read *Caution: necklace of fireballs*, "this will provide a blast-the-bodies pyre to thwart war wizards spell-prying into dead brains."

"And how will you get there in time to use it?"

Yellander smiled softly. "By means of the other reason we bought the inn. The portal into its back pantry. Yes, another portal; the realm's riddled with them."

* * * * *

Old Ghost drew the last three runes of the spell in his mind, silently and emphatically thinking of the words that ended the incantation as he did so, in deft and exacting sequence.

And the swirling, building spell-glow rose into a bright fist, trailing sparks, that opened to him and flooded over him with a rapture sweeter than he'd ever felt in his long existence before.

He'd now mastered every one of the ancient Netherese spells! *At last!*

Gleefully he soared up out of the roofless "haunted" ruin in the hills of upcountry Amn he'd been using as a spell chamber and raced through the dark tangled wood like a howling storm, darting through the gaps of a badly boarded-over back window into a tavern storeroom, and thence out into its smoky bustle like a half-seen, streaking arrow—that plunged right into a human host. He had every exultant intention of riding the man mercilessly.

The hitherto fat and lazy master of the Bright Mare Fine Tavern, best (and only) drinking-house in the rural Amnian village of Darthing, suddenly flung himself across a littered card table, viciously punched a warrior twice his size in the throat, snatched out the gargling, strangling man's short sword and slashed that same throat open, and then bounded up, howling.

The taproom of the Bright Mare was as crowded as usual—and every jack and lass in it stared in open-mouthed, dumbfounded astonishment as Tavernmaster Undigho Belarran waved the short sword around and around his head, laughing and hooting in wild, loud incoherence as the blood flew from it to spatter faces and tables all around—and then lurched forward and butchered a staring cobbler, right in front of the man's shrieking wife.

Then Belarran became a fat, panting whirlwind, racing here and there across the taproom and back, wildly and recklessly slashing and stabbing. Men swore, fumbled for daggers and belt-knives—and died, hacked and pinioned by a man no one believed could move so fast, even as they gaped at him doing so.

Belarran's wife and his favorite ale-maid toppled over in their blood. The old miller's dog was laid open from jaws to haunches. Then the wild-eyed tavernmaster slashed open the throats of two cowering guests in one huge swing of the blood-drenched sword in his fist and made it to the door.

He tarried not to trap and stalk the two wounded but feebly crawling guests still left alive, but burst out onto the main street of Darthing.

Villagers turned to give him greeting, frowned at what they saw, and then died as the tavernmaster rushed at them, hacking and slashing, hurling himself forward recklessly to chop at knees and wrists and ankles.

Folk screamed and shouted in fear, and some men came running with shovels and picks and the rusty swords of old wars, to try to ring the madman and slow his wild butchery. They failed.

Thrice the tavernmaster hewed down armed men who faced him, rushing this way and that at rolling-eyed random, so that none dared strike at him from behind for fear they'd suddenly be kissing his blade as he whirled to face them. Another Darthingar fell, and another, until the village blacksmith shouted at them to all strike at once, rushing in from all sides.

Two more died in that fray of clanging blades as the grunting, flailing-armed tavernmaster lashed out faster than ever—but it ended with Tavernmaster Undigho Belarran spitting blood and sagging to the ground with seven swords thrust through his body, like a large crimson pincushion.

"Well," the smith said to Darthing's chandler at his right shoulder and harness-maker to his left, "that's tha—"

Something like gray-white smoke raced up out of the dying man at their feet and plunged right through them—chandler, smith, and harnessmaker—and the three Darthingar clutched their chests, reeled, and fell on their faces, dead.

The smoke-thing raced on down the village street—and it was *laughing.*

As villagers shrieked and stared, the mirth of what they could now see was a human-shaped wraith, its arms and legs trailing off into ragged wisps, became a howling guffaw.

The folk of Darthing turned and fled, pelting down stairs into their cellars to cower, panting, as Old Ghost veered through a few more of them, stopping their hearts as he plunged through the sobbing, running humans.

He soared on, gloating aloud in triumph, his voice a raw and terrible hissing. "The spells are all mine at last! I can snatch power enough to destroy Hesperdan! To destroy *Manshoon!*"

He chortled as he raced on, sweeping east out of Amn faster than any racing hawk.

The old Netherese spells were poorly written. The incantations awakened stresses in the flowing and rebounding energies of the

Weave they called on. A wizard could handle two active spells at once, but trying a third one tore that wizard apart every time. So had perished many wizards and sorcerers of Netheril. Yet only corporeal casters stood in peril. Old Ghost could survive having six working at once, perhaps more!

And what spells they were! Slow but titanic, they literally melted away land—rock and soil, energy flows, *everything*—into energies that Old Ghost—and only he!—could control, by directing their flows into the Shadow Weave rather than the Weave. He was getting good at doing so, now, and the beauty of it was that Mystra attributed the slight weakening of the Weave to Shar, but Shar couldn't even sense his work.

Or so it seemed. If he was wrong, he might soon face the wrath of two angry goddesses . . . *if* he was wrong.

He'd noticed the castings also stole energy from portals, causing a marked increase in what sages of the Art termed "portal drink"—non-living items that vanished from creatures traversing portals. But what of that? Only creatures who lived and breathed and grasped after food and drink and each other had need of coins or clothes and such!

Casting another spell whenever he needed more strength, he would become one of the mighty. Ever-stronger, even able to rise up again like mist if "destroyed," as long as creatures used portals anywhere in Faerûn.

Old Ghost raced toward Cormyr, bellowing triumphant laughter.

* * * * *

As she trotted through the wet Arabellan night, Pennae was breathing hard and starting to limp as her leg stiffened.

Someone's dagger had sliced her arm, and a Zhentish sword had more than nicked her leg. She'd slain both Zhents who'd wounded her, but that didn't make their little gifts to her throb any the less, and if she lost her agility, her career—gods, her *life*—went with it.

Wherefore she'd left that happy little fray of Zhents and Knights of Myth Drannor butchering each other in the stables, and hurried a few streets across sleeping Arabel to here.

Dark, empty, and dripping Crownserpent Towers. The boarded-up mansion of a minor noble family that to her certain knowledge was extinct, unless undead could sire or bear living offspring. It was old and massive, with air-vents large enough for a skilled sneak-thief to crawl through, and doorposts a child could scale. Decaying moldings and crevices everywhere, and the sort of genteel decay that seeping water, rats, and birds caused.

All of which made it the perfect place to hide healing potions until they were needed.

Such as now, for example.

The rain was slackening, and the mansion was boarded up as tightly as ever. Good; she wasn't in the mood to fight a street gang—or the servants of a new owner, for that matter.

She climbed up a doorpost, along the ornate stone cornice to a corner, then onto a wide stone windowsill adorned with a fresh duskfeathers nest. The bird sitting on it cheeped once in its sleep as Pennae's foot came down softly beside it. From there, a long, aching stretch led to the lip of the roof-carving. She dug in fingers like claws, because everything was wet and it could be a killing fall from here.

Up and over, and there was the vent cover.

It slid off as readily as ever, and Pennae lowered herself cautiously down and in. Along the attic air-vent to the moot of six vents, down—

Hand on a precious vial, she froze. Murmurings. Voices. Mens' voices. Crownserpent Towers, it seemed, was empty no longer.

Chapter 8
More Confounded Scheming

No fight nor foe of Cormyr ever angered me.
I had no wrath to spare, for it was twice or thrice
daily provoked by all the confounded *scheming*.

Horvarr Hardcastle
Never A Highknight:
The Life of a Dragon Guard
published in the Year of the Bow

Thrusting the precious vial she'd come for into her seldom-used throat pouch, Pennae crept along the vent-passage as stealthily as she knew how, until she was peering down through a grating at a sudden glow in a bedchamber that should have held only darkness, cobwebs, and mold.

It was a cold radiance, bright blue and glimmering. Magic.

A glow that came from an orb on a neck-chain, held on high by the robed and hooded figure that was wearing it.

A second, similarly garbed man held up a second orb, clearly in response to the first. "With both of these at work," he said, his voice sounding male, Cormyrean, and old, "not even Vangey's magic can see or hear us. Well met."

A man who also sounded like a native of Cormyr, but slightly younger, echoed that dry greeting even more sarcastically, and then asked, "Is the time to strike come at last?"

"Not yet. Soon."

"When?"

"When all the alarphons are dead—that is, they believe you to be dead—and Laspeera's dust, and Vangerdahast is weakened or preoccupied, or both. I'll write 'Leak here' on the wall at the bend in the Long Passage, to let you know when the time is right. If anyone sees it, they'll dismiss it as a steward's message to the Palace masons."

Pennae frowned. The alarphons were the internal investigators among the war wizards, the watchers who kept all war wizards honest. Or *supposedly* upheld honesty, by the sounds of this.

In the bedchamber below, the first man lowered his orb. "And then?"

"Set the traps on the crystals. When ready, you write the same phrase on the opposite wall of the passage, facing mine, and I'll know to send word to Vangey that the princesses are imperiled."

"And he'll come running, and—blam! What then?"

"The same lure should work just as well on Azoun. Mind you rig something physical—stone, falling from above, perhaps—to disable him in case his shields are strong enough to defeat your spells."

"Yes. I'd not want to end up facing him blade to blade."

"Indeed. Kill him, but keep the head. We may need it."

"We must all get a head in this world."

"Ha. Ha. We'll arrest Filfaeril for treason, accusing her of Azoun's murder—we can say we found the head wedged down the shaft of her private garderobe. Tana we marry off to our puppet, Alusair we keep in hiding as our backblade, in spell-thrall—and then, regrettably, the traitor Filfaeril is killed by our spells while trying to escape."

"Not smooth, but—"

"It doesn't have to be. Many grumble about us, day in and day out, but how many dare to denounce or even challenge their war wizards? Remember: 'Leak here.' "

" 'Leak here.' And if someone tries to check on the princesses before we're ready?"

"Leave that to me."

The two men exchanged deep, dry chuckles, and then parted. As one—the one who sounded a little younger—turned away, Pennae caught sight of his face in the light of his orb.

It was not one she'd seen before, but she'd know it again. White hair at the temples, framing a handsome, commanding face. Imperious nose, hard eyes.

Pennae remained absolutely still until the other man, his hood still hiding his face, was quite gone. And then she crawled back the way she'd come, not even daring to whisper a curse.

* * * * *

"You'd think all this rain would've washed enough of the smell of blood off us," Semoor complained, tugging on the reins that his snorting, head-tossing horse was threatening to drag right out of his hands.

The other three Knights of Myth Drannor were all too busy to reply. The rest of the horses were just as agitated. It had been some time since the four had seen a living Zhent, but Florin had been missing just as long, though Pennae—who kept vanishing and reappearing, a flitting shadow in the night—insisted his body was nowhere to be found in or near the stables.

She was gone right now, leaving just four Knights struggling in the deepening, still-raining night with horses enough for everyone, plus two remounts Pennae had insisted in taking from the stables "because the queen would want to see us properly equipped."

The four were bruised, soaked, and cold. They were too tired to be scared any longer, but they were *very* nervous, and growing ever more so—expecting more misfortune at any moment. Either another Zhent attack, or the arrival of Dauntless and dozens of grim, armed-to-the-teeth Purple Dragons, to arrest them.

It was Doust who sighed and said, "I remember a day rather less damp than this one, and a herald proclaiming our names and the thanks of King Azoun, as the crowds cheered and—"

"Sounds nice. Wish I'd been there," Pennae said laconically, from just behind him. She grinned as a startled "Eeep!" burst out of the priest of Tymora, as he jumped a little, hands shaking, and then whirled around.

"Pennae, if you *ever* do that again—"

"You'll make that same charming sound? I await it with fond anticipation," the thief said smoothly, patting his arm. She set down a sack almost as large as she was, with the clangor of many things made of metal shifting inside it. "Daggers," she explained. "I've been plundering Zhents too dead to resist me."

"A habit learned in festhalls?" Semoor asked; the darkness hid the rude gesture she made in reply, but he saw enough of the shift of her shoulders to know she was making it. "You wound me," he said.

"Not yet, Light of Lathander," she murmured, her voice heavy with promise. "Not yet."

Then she spun around, hand streaking to a sheathed dagger. A sword glimmered suddenly, its flat coming down on that hand in a gentle slap.

"Please don't," Florin said wearily, from the other end of that sword. "I'm growing a little tired of facing sharp war-steel this night."

Pennae nodded. *"That's* not your sword. What befell you, and where have you been?"

"Aye, I wish I still had my own blade. This one's old, good steel—and so it should be; I had it from a princess!—but badly balanced, too small for me, and heavier than it should be."

"Oho! A princess, hey?" Semoor asked. "What *else* 'had you' from this fair royal flower? Or are we speaking of a festhall 'princess'?"

"We are not," Florin said. "We are speaking of the Princess Alusair Nacacia, whom I met with on the roof of yon temple, by merest chance. A Zhent almost slew her, but I was able to defend her—until too many Purple Dragons appeared for me to dare tarry. Unfortunately, neither did the princess, who used some sort of magic to vanish rather abruptly. I doubt those Dragons are all that pleased with me, just now."

"I'm not surprised," Jhessail said. "This being Arabel, they probably have their hands full of truculent madmen already. An Obarskyr princess, standing around on a rooftop, in *this?"*

"Belike you met someone who *told* you she was Alusair the princess," Doust said, wrestling with two less than happy horses, "to avoid getting in trouble for being on that rooftop. She was probably a temple-thief, or hoping to be, until the gods sent you into her lap."

"Friends," Florin said, "I've seen both princesses a time or three while we were at the Palace, and this *was* the Princess Alusair."

"Ah," Semoor said, "you had time to examine her properly, checking all the birthmarks, did you? *My,* but the Obarskyrs will be glad to see us go! Right into fresh-dug graves, if you start dallying with royal daughters!" He tossed the reins of the largest horse to Florin, and added sharply, "Nice to know you keep your brains in your codpiece. Pity it isn't larger, so you'd have a hope of carting a little more of them around with you!"

"Semoor," Florin said heavily, "our meeting was *not* like that, and was none of my doing—"

"So," an all too familiar voice came out of the night behind them, "do I add molestation of a personage royal to horse-theft, in my reasons for having all of you flogged to death? Or have you some crimes more inventive yet to add to your confessions? Take your time, and leave nothing out of your reply. We Purple Dragons tend to be all too starved for entertainment."

Half a dozen lanterns were unhooded in unison, and the Knights of Myth Drannor found themselves staring into the mirthless smile of Ornrion Dauntless—at the head of dozens of grim, armed-to-the-teeth Purple Dragons. Most of whom held loaded hand-bows, aimed at the faces of the Knights.

"Falconhand speaks truth," said someone grimly, from just behind the ornrion's shoulder. It was Laspeera of the war wizards. "I very much hope he continues to do so, as I ask this of him: what's become of my fellow war wizard, Melandar Raentree, who was assisting you at the stables?"

Florin shrugged. "He bade us farewell there, departed—and we were promptly attacked. By many Zhentarim. Swordsmen, led by a wizard. Who was torn apart in a spell-blast . . . or so I believe."

"So he's gone, all his Zhent blades lie dead, and the Princess Alusair is gone too!" His tone of voice made it abundantly clear that Dauntless believed not a word. "Well, now, isn't that *all* just so convenient?"

"Dauntless!" Laspeera's rebuke betrayed the fury she was swallowing.

She gave the Knights a long, level look and snapped, "Let's get you out of Arabel before anything *else* happens."

* * * * *

"Lathalance blundered," Sarhthor reported, "and it cost us the mageling Neldrar, who had showed some small promise."

Manshoon, Lord of the Zhentarim, turned from lighting the last of the tall bedside candles to smile sardonically. "Lathalance's blunders are part of his charm. Make his death serve us some useful purpose."

Sarhthor nodded. "I've ordered him to Halfhap."

"And in that flourishing metropolis he'll prove useful to us how?"

"The adventurers who were just given the Pendant of Ashaba by the Blackstaff will reach there on the morrow, on their ride to Shadowdale."

"I quite see. This may prove amusing. Leave us now."

Sarhthor bowed, turned, and went to the door. When he opened it, he found himself gazing into the darkly beautiful face of Symgharyl Maruel, The Shadowsil, Manshoon's current favorite. It was a face widely feared among the Zhentarim—in particular when it was wearing the little catlike smile adorning it now.

The Shadowsil lifted an eyebrow in unspoken challenge as their eyes met. Sarhthor carefully kept a faint, polite smile on his own face, and his eyes on hers. Her black robe was hanging open, and she was bare beneath it.

In smooth silence he bowed and stood back to wave her in through the door. The Shadowsil slipped off her robe, handed it to Sarhthor, and strode into Manshoon's bedchamber, clad only in high black boots.

* * * * *

"At least the sarking *rain* has stopped," Semoor muttered, peering up at the bright moon riding high above them, in a sky full of stars and a few tattered clouds.

"Hush!" Jhessail hissed, from beside him. "The gods will hear! And we'll have hailstorms, or worse!"

"I'd like a rain of gold coins," Pennae said, looking up into the sky. "Of respectable mintings, slightly worn from use, that no treasury's missing." She waited, hands outspread, but nothing happened.

"I think the gods believe they've rewarded you more than enough," Islif grunted, "coming through that fray without a scratch—leaving the dead heaped in your wake."

"That," Pennae replied flatly, "was my doing, not any achievement of the gods."

Doust and Semoor cleared their throats in unison, and she turned and laid a finger to her lips in a "be quiet" admonition. Semoor used one of his fingers to make another sort of gesture in reply.

The Knights were trotting their horses cautiously along the moonlit Mountain Ride, heading north-northeast out of Arabel. They were making good time, and talking in low tones about all that had unfolded.

"How will we even find Shadowdale?" Jhessail murmured, looking at the dark forest, and the soaring mountains beyond.

"This road leads there," Doust told her, "so if we don't stray off it in Tilverton or elsewhere . . ."

Pennae turned in her saddle, teeth flashing in a grin, to unbuckle the saddlebag behind her left leg. Flipping it open, she plucked something forth with a flourish. A map, splendidly drawn—as they could all see by the magical glow that awakened across its drawn surface, the moment she unfurled it.

Doust blinked. "Where'd you get *that?"* Without pause for breath he added gloomily, "As if I didn't know."

"Stolen," she replied cheerfully. "Speaking of which—"

With a more elaborate flourish, Pennae flipped aside her half-cloak and drew forth something from behind her back.

It caught the moonlight as she reversed it in her hand: a well-used, splendidly made sword. She handed it to Florin, who hefted it appreciatively. Before he could ask, she said, "Now Officer Dauntless has a place to store his blinding temper. Inside his empty sword-scabbard."

Florin groaned. Semoor whistled in appreciation. Jhessail snapped, "You *didn't!*" Doust and Islif turned in their saddles to look back at the road behind them, for signs of pursuit.

Pennae shrugged. "I did. And War Wizard Laspeera saw me, and said not a word. She was too busy winking, I guess."

* * * * *

In the darker streets of Arabel, it was not unusual to see the few folk of wealth and importance who walked around by night inside a protective ring of bodyguards.

In this particular street, this night, a drunken merchant came reeling out of an alley-mouth to stumble against the foremost bodyguards in one such ring. One bodyguard roughly slapped the drunkard aside—and then stiffened, whirled around, and took a swift step to clutch at his master, walking in the center of the ring; a wizard of the Zhentarim.

Who in turn stiffened, even as the other guards wrestled their fellow bullyblade back from him.

They saw the wizard's eyes glow eerily. "Release him," he ordered them curtly. "No harm was done."

The bodyguards stared at their master suspiciously, for both the attitude and the manner of speech were unusual for him, but his wave to continue on was emphatic, even angry. They obeyed, leaving the drunken merchant slumped on the cobbles in their wake.

A few steps farther on, the wizard suddenly crumpled.

Bodyguards snarled curses and reached for him. Their curses turned to shouts of fear and horror when they felt the light weight in their arms—and saw they were holding little more than bones shrouded in skin. They let the lifeless husk fall to the cobbles and fled in all directions.

None of them saw the cloud gathering in the darkness above the nigh-skeletal wizard. It thickened, whirling, as Horaundoon mentally pawed through the memories he'd just ripped out of the wizard's mind.

None of the bodyguards were left to hear him murmur, "So

Lathalance is out on the Moonsea Ride . . . for a very *little* while longer. Ah, Lathalance, *you'll be first!*"

* * * * *

"True, Horaundoon," Old Ghost muttered, arrowing through the moonlit night, high above the Mountain Ride. "But you won't be the one to claim him. When you arrive, you'll find me."

He began the plunge that would end in Lathalance's unsuspecting body. The Zhentarim was galloping hard along the road ahead, not caring what he was doing to his horse. He had no intention of slowing until he caught sight of the Knights, whereupon he'd begin trailing them more stealthily, to Halfhap.

Duthgarl Lathalance was as cruel and capable as he was handsome, a Zhent swordsman and mage who obeyed his masters with unhesitating efficiency, coolly slaying scores at their behest. His magics shielded him against arrows and the like, and would even protect him if his hard-racing steed fell and hurled him down. He was crouching low and enjoying the ride.

Until something hurtled down out of the sky into him, causing him to arch his back and gasp.

Lathalance swayed in the saddle, eyes glowing red . . . then gold . . . blue . . . then returned to their normal brown.

Slowly his worried frown faded, and he smiled a wolfish smile.

* * * * *

Dauntless hadn't been back at his desk long enough to feel truly dry—and they had to bring him *this*.

He glowered in the lamplight at a darkly handsome young lad, perhaps fourteen summers old, that he was certain he'd never laid eyes on before—who beamed back at him, despite standing clamped in the none-too-gentle grip of two hairy, burly Purple Dragons.

"Sword-brawls, wizards blown to spatters, what *next?*" Dauntless snarled. "Well?"

"Says his name's Rathgar," one of the Dragons said laconically.

"Says he was expected, by whoever dwells inside the window we caught him climbing through."

"Oh?" The ornrion's voice fell into soft tones that dripped sarcasm. "Does he carry it around with him, this window, or was it part of a building I might know?"

"The widow Tarathkule's house, on the Stroll."

Ornrion Dahauntul stared at the boy, who gave him a merry wink and said brightly, "She's insatiable! Worth coming all this way for!"

"Lad," Dauntless said heavily, "she's seen ninety-odd winters, walks with two canes, is as deaf as yon wall, and looks about as handsome as this desk. *Try again.*"

"Ah. Well . . ." The lad who gave his name as Rathgar looked at the Purple Dragons on either side of him, one after the other, and then peered past Dauntless as if seeking spies in the gloom beyond the desk. He tried to lean forward, but the Dragons hauled him firmly back, so he settled for lowering his voice into a confidential whisper. "I got lost on the way to my tryst with the princess. I said the Tarathkule tale, first, as, well, ah, one doesn't like to stain a lady's hon—"

"You *got lost*—stay! *Which* princess?"

"Ahh . . . Her Highness, Alusair Nacacia Obarskyr. She'll vouch for me."

The Dragons looked expressionlessly at Dauntless, and he looked back at them. None of them bothered to roll their eyes.

Silence fell, and stretched, until the ornrion grew tired of the view, and turned his head to peer harder at the handsome lad.

"Lad," he growled, "I don't know what your name is, except that it's not Rathgar. I don't know your game, but you lie like a sneak-thief. I don't believe you for the time it takes me to draw *one* breath, and all I really know about you is that you come from Westgate—your speech tells me that—and that you own"—he squinted at what was lying on the older Purple Dragon's palm —"three thumbs, five falcons, and a dagger too big for your hand. Which means you can feed yourself in this city for about five days, if you eat in the worst places, drink nothing that doesn't come out of a horse-pump, and sleep on the streets. So, d'you want to be turned out of our gates? Or are you looking for work?"

"I don't particularly want to be a sarcastic, bullying ornrion," the lad replied, as his stomach rumbled loudly, "but if the job lets me keep my vow to lovely Aloos, I'll accept your kind offer."

Dauntless gave him a glare, and then smiled grimly, turned away, and snapped, "Jar him for the night. And give him something to eat. Leave the dagger here."

"It starts with a dungeon inspection?" the boy asked impishly, as the Dragons lifted him off his feet, turned him, and started marching away. "Or does she want me in chains? She didn't mention such tastes, but . . ."

A heavy door slammed behind them. Shaking his head, Dauntless turned back to his reports.

Chapter 9

A NIGHT UNSUITED FOR SLEEPING IN SADDLES

> Then the king spake the last words
> he ever said to me: "When you hear
> the wolves, lad, it is unlikely to be
> a night suitable for sleeping in your saddle."

Horvarr Hardcastle
Never A Highknight:
The Life of a Dragon Guard
published in the Year of the Bow

When Dauntless looked up again, just before dawn, the dagger was gone from atop his papers—and a key was lying in its place.

A cell key.

His eyes narrowing, the ornrion looked up at the key-board, clapped his hand to his belt—and swore horribly.

His purse was gone, its lacings neatly cut and dangling.

Striding heavily and breathing like a winded horse in his anger, Dauntless snatched up the key and headed for the door to the dungeons. With his luck, the lad had locked both Glarth and Tobran in the cell, wearing signs reading, "Kiss me, I'm the Princess" or some such.

Little rat.

But how by the blazing Dragon Throne itself had he known about the Princess Alusair being in Arabel this night?

Laughing, Horaundoon plummeted down out of the night like a striking hawk, plunged into the hard-riding Duthgarl Lathalance of the Zhentarim—and swirled right back out again, shrieking in pain.

"Yes, Horaundoon," the Zhent said coldly, the voice clearly that of Old Ghost, "we meet again. You can burn this worm to ash in a day or three, if you want, but not now. And if you cross me, I'll burn *you*—and the Realms will hold one fewer Horaundoon. I can. Believe me."

"What . . . what d'you want of me?" Horaundoon gasped.

"Absolute obedience, all the time the Knights of Myth Drannor are in Halfhap. If you don't give it, I'll destroy you. If you serve me well, you can have Lathalance and your freedom in a few days. I'll even help you destroy Manshoon."

"Manshoon? You know?"

"Oh, stop *gasping*, man. *How* high did you rise in the Brotherhood?"

✦ ✦ ✦ ✦ ✦

The War Wizard Gorndar Lacklar flung open the door and rushed inside, gasping, *"Sorry* I'm late, Ghoruld! Gods, what a night! Off to Arabel with the queen's new blades, then back here again to see to the Andamus matter—and then Sarmeir tells me I'm to report to you again for another jaunt to Arabel! Queen's own orders, he says! What's up?"

"This," Ghoruld Applethorn said sweetly, ramming a wand into Lacklar's mouth and speaking the word that triggered it.

Even before the back of Lacklar's head had finished spattering all over the old cloaks he'd pinned ready on the ceiling, Applethorn had laid hold of his underling's slumping body and whirled him aside, into the glow of another waiting portal.

He'd be back before Lacklar's brains started to drip onto the floor. Damned disloyal young war wizards—who'd have thought it? Better call in the best of the alarphons to investigate. Good old Applethorn.

Dragon-damned right he'd be back. There was Sarmeir to butcher before this night was out. And if Gorndar Lacklar, Sarmeir Landorl, and good old Applethorn, too, all went silent, Vangerdahast would *have* to send Laspeera to investigate. With whoever else she thought she'd need hurrying along right beside her.

Right into the trap he'd prepared in Halfhap, and thereafter, oblivion.

✦ ✦ ✶ ✦ ✦

The sudden shrieks of pain were far behind them, but were certainly clear enough.

The Knights of Myth Drannor grabbed for their weapons and asked each other, "What was that?"

A wolf howled then, nearby in the trees off the road to the north, and the horses became *very* uneasy.

The Knights held their reins in firm hands and made gentling sounds and speech until their horses slowed again, and Semoor dared to answer their shared question: "Someone screaming in agony, obviously. It didn't last long."

"So much killing," Florin muttered. "It goes on and on."

Semoor nodded. "I'll confess I was glad we were leaving Arabel, earlier, and gladder still that the rain stopped, but now . . ."

"Oh?" Pennae asked. "Is the stern and oh-so-certain Light of Lathander actually changing his mind?"

"The changing of my mind," Semoor purred back at her, "is the best evidence *I* know for proving I've got one. Unlike certain barb-tongued present company."

Doust managed the feat of rolling his eyes and yawning simultaneously—and so impressed himself that he promptly repeated the yawning part.

"Don't go to sleep and fall out of your saddle," Islif told him, spurring her mount near enough to take hold of his elbow. Doust looked at her with heavy eyes, and she told him crisply, "Listen to the splendid entertainment Semoor and Pennae are providing, and *stay awake."*

Ahead of the battling tongues Islif had just heralded, Florin scowled into the night like he wanted to slay it. Jhessail frowned at him and asked gently, "What troubles you just now, Florin?"

"Narantha," her friend told her. "We're just riding away from her, leaving her unavenged, and every time I try to think of her and make peace with myself, someone else comes at me with a sword and snatches the time away from me again, and . . . and. . . ."

He set his teeth, and shook his head. Jhessail put a hand on his thigh, looked up into his hard stare, and murmured, "I understand, Tall Sword, and I'll do my best to see to it that you get plenty of time to think of her in days to come."

He nodded curtly, and they rode on. After a time Jhessail hissed, "And to you I swear this: I will give all aid I can to help you deal with those who drove her to slay herself, when the time is right."

Florin brought his hand down to cover and then clasp hers, where it rested on his leg, and managed a smile.

"I thank you," he said, "which should mean that 'tis now time for someone else to attack us."

Jhessail smiled thinly. " 'Tis certainly starting to seem that way, isn't it? This life of adventuring is not what I dreamed of it being, back in Espar."

"No," Florin sighed. " 'Tis . . . dirtier."

No sudden menace came at them out of the night, so Jhessail risked a look back over her shoulder. The horses were faltering, plodding now as often as they trotted, and their riders all reeled and yawned in their saddles. This fighting and riding all night wasn't the splendor-glory minstrels made it out to be! When they reached Halfhap—hah! *If* they reached Halfhap—it would be high time for all, humans and horses alike, to rest. Being Knights of Myth Drannor or carrying said Knights across the wide Realms, it seemed, were similarly wearying professions.

* * * * *

The young prisoner wasn't in his cell, of course, but neither were the two Dragons who'd put him there. Evidently the lad had picked the lock and let himself out after their departure.

Thinking darkly murderous thoughts between persistent urges to just blow out the lamps and seek his bed, Dauntless trudged back to his desk—and came to a sudden halt at what he saw awaiting him. Watching Gods Above, what deep sin had he committed, without even remembering doing so, to be so amply rewarded this night?

The Lady Lord of Arabel herself stood waiting for him, leaning on his desk with her hand on her hip. She was in full armor—the leathers that clung to her so interestingly, not her battlefield coat-of-plate—and no fewer than four senior Purple Dragon officers were standing behind her, similarly garbed. Everyone wore swords.

"Do you leave this desk unguarded often, Ornrion?" Myrmeen Lhal asked mildly.

"No," Dauntless told her. "Only during jailbreaks."

"Oh? Who's missing?"

"A young lad, a thief, from Westgate, who was caught climbing through a window not his own, but insisted he was here to tryst with Princess Alusair—who *was* in Arabel this night. He gave his name as Rathgar."

"And stole your keys, by the look of it," Myrmeen added, looking pointedly at his belt.

"And stole my keys," Dauntless agreed. "I take it worse matters have arisen whilst I was inspecting an empty cell?"

"You take it correctly. I understand you were earlier this night given the responsibility of escorting the adventurers known as the Knights of Myth Drannor out of the city?"

Dauntless managed—just—not to sigh. "They were attacked by some Zhentilar at the stables used by the war wizards, and upon hearing reports of the butchery, I gathered some Dragons from the barracks and made haste to arrest them. Laspeera appeared, rode with us, and commanded me not to detain them, but rather to assist her in conducting them out of the gates. I obeyed, and they were off up the Mountain Ride by the time the rainclouds fled and the moon came out. Whereupon Wizard of War Laspeera took herself—I presume—out of Arabel by magic, without a word of farewell."

"I see. Constal Raskarel, explain to the ornrion here what befell Lord Ebonhawk this night."

One of the officers stepped forward, fixed Dauntless with a frosty look, and announced flatly, "The younger Lord Ebonhawk—Lord Duskur Ebonhawk—had much to drink this night, and so was out late, unsteady on his feet, but within a walking ring of bodyguards who had imbibed nothing. They were traversing an alley hard by the stables as the fray you referred to was abating, and one of these Knights of Myth Drannor—a woman who goes by the name of 'Pennae,' we believe, and who steals for a living—encountered the young lord, cut away his purse, sprang up onto a nearby balcony, and thence climbed a drainpipe to the roofs, and got away."

Dauntless nodded, completely unsurprised. "That wench," he said, "is so low she could put on a tall helm and stroll right under a slithering viper!"

"And so?" another officer—an oversword—snapped.

"And so . . . what?" Dauntless asked. "An interesting tale, but the miscreant is now out of my jurisdiction, transported thus under Crown orders, and—"

"And so," Myrmeen said gently, "I find myself needing to return this miscreant to the jurisdiction of my most capable ornrion, who stands most experienced in dealings with these particular adventurers. I'm temporarily relieving you of your engaging duties here, Dauntless, and ordering you to ride after the Knights of Myth Drannor, with however many Dragons you feel you'll need, and recover all that this Pennae stole from young Lord Duskur Ebonhawk."

"But—"

"These orders are effective right *now,* Ornrion Dahauntul!"

"Uh—yes, Lady Lord Lhal. I go." Swallowing his curses, Dauntless turned and headed for the garrison stables, snapping the names of five Dragons he wanted riding with him over his shoulder.

"What," Myrmeen Lhal asked mildly, "not the princess?"

✦ ✦ ✦

It was a chill morning of drifting mists as the two shivering guards pushed open the creaking western gates of Halfhap.

Old Pheldarr stared out and down the empty road as far as the curling mists allowed—the length of a good bowshot, no more—spat thoughtfully onto the cobbles between his worn and split boots, and announced, "First watch is yours, Rorld. I'll get the stew hot."

No sooner had he lumbered slowly into the gatehouse, still shivering, than a man in a splendid doublet, with breeches and boots to match, stepped out of a deep doorway across the street and strolled over to join Rorld—who had squared his shoulders and posed himself against the gatepost, spear placed in one rest and shield propped in another, so that from more than a few strides away it appeared as if he were wearing the one and holding the other at an unwavering angle. Then Rorld devoted himself to practicing his spitting.

"Our deal stands?" the well-dressed man murmured, coming to a stop beside the gate-guard.

"It does. When d'ye expect these adventurers, Velmorn?"

"Right about now," was the reply, accompanied by a lifted, pointing finger.

Rorld peered into the mists, and beheld a weary line of riders, swaying in their saddles atop even wearier mounts. "Hunh. *They'll* be going no farther soon."

"Indeed," Velmorn agreed, stepping a careful pace farther out into the road. He stood watching the adventurers approach in gently smiling silence, until just the right moment. Whereupon he nodded greeting to Pennae and Florin and observed, "Long ride."

"Long enough," Pennae agreed. "You look like a man paid to stand awaiting wayfarers and recommend an inn."

Velmorn grinned. "This being the flourishing many-spires realm-seat of Halfhap, you'd be right about all except the 'paid' part."

Pennae smiled. "Well?"

"Well, you have the look of adventurers, and that means you'll find a proper welcome only at one place inside our walls. The Oldcoats Inn. Turn right at the fork ahead, then left immediately, and when that road bends north again, it's the black half-timbered building on your left, with the arched gate for its stableyard. It has a signboard. You can't miss it."

"Thanks, friend," Florin said appreciatively, as he passed. Velmorn and Rorld nodded pleasantly to them all: the thief and the ranger; the little lass—no, she was a little older than that, just small; the two priests; and the watchful warrior-woman bringing up the rear.

"Lathander and Tymora," Rorld commented on the priests' holy symbols, as they watched the travelers turn right where the street forked. "Adventurers."

Velmorn nodded. "Adventurers."

The gate-guard casually held out his hand. "They're the ones, hey?"

"They're the ones," Velmorn replied, spilling a clinking stack of Lord Yellander's gold coins into Rorld's palm.

✦ ✦ ✦ ✦ ✦

The Purple Dragons who guarded the Royal Palace in Suzail were neither young nor inexperienced. They knew their duties very well—and when to call upon reinforcements.

"Just *here,* sir," the grizzled old first sword said with a puzzled frown, pointing at the floor. Something small, round, and blackened was lying right in the angle where the floor and two walls met, nigh a door. A ring. "You smell it too?"

The lionar nodded and bent down to peer at the ring. He started to reach for it, and then caught sight of several human hairs standing straight out from the wall where they'd been spattered—and then partially melted—against it.

By some sort of explosion.

He carefully straightened up again without touching anything, and ordered, "Go get the War Wizard Laspeera. I'll stay right here. Tell her, and anyone—*anyone*—who tries to stop you that nothing at all in the realm matters so much as her getting her here, right quick, to see this. If you can't get her, get Vangerdahast."

"The—the Royal Magician?" The guard gulped visibly and then added, *"Yes,* sir!" He flung open the door and raced away down the passage beyond, his speed surprising for his age.

The lionar closed that door, drew his sword and his dagger, and placed himself carefully against the wall across from the ring.

After a moment he stepped hastily away from the wall, whirled to stare at it suspiciously, and then slowly moved to the center of the passage, where he turned slowly all around, blades raised, looking for a foe.

✦ ✦ ✦ ✦ ✦

The Oldcoats Inn was a large, sagging place with a swaybacked roof. It was cloaked in black paint, broken briefly here and there by rows of small white-painted medallion ornaments, like lines of stars in a moonless midnight sky. The doors were black, the yard fence and arch were black, the porch pillars *and* floorboards were black—even the shakes on the roof were black.

Yet stablelads trotted out to take their mounts cheerfully enough, and the innkeeper's smile was affable, his welcome ringing true.

"Ondal Maelrin, at your service whilst you're under my roof here at Oldcoats," he told them. "We're an old house, but a good house."

His words fell into a soft, waiting silence: the stout tables and chairs of the dark common room were all empty, with not a living guest to be seen or heard. That seemed to bother Maelrin not a whit as he accepted a gold lion per Knight from Pennae's purse and carefully entered them in the ledger ("Knights of Myth Drannor, adventuring band, Royal Charter Cormyr: Florin Falconhand; Islif Lurelake; Jhessail Silvertree worker-of-Art; Pennae; Doust Sulwood anointed of Tymora; Semoor Wolftooth anointed of Lathander").

Four of the Knights peered around at the dim silence a little uncertainly; what afflicted Oldcoats, to leave it this dark and empty? Pennae stared at Maelrin's writing intently, and Jhessail studied Maelrin. He was of middling years, jet black hair, easy smile, wearing a leather vest over an immaculate tunic and black breeches; as quiet and graceful as the servants in the Royal Palace. As if aware of their scrutiny, he looked up, flashing a bright smile.

"A tankard of mulled cider and house soup each, to your rooms in a trice—all food and drink after that costs more coin," he announced. Taking up one of the two low-trimmed lanterns on the bar that he was using as a reception desk, he led his guests up the flight of stairs that ascended out of the center of the common room, the stairs down to the cellar right beside them.

Upstairs seemed no more populated.

“Are we the only guests, just now?” Pennae ventured to ask, as the innkeeper produced two large room keys with a flourish, offered them to her, and bowed, indicating the first doors on either side of the passage, at the head of the stairs.

“Just now,” Maelrin replied, “but word has been sent ahead of a few more who’ll be joining us before nightfall—and a large caravan’s expected, coming down from the Moonsea, this night or the next. When it arrives, we’ll have folk sleeping out in the stable loft.”

The rooms were as dark as the rest of the inn, but were clean, furnished simply with massive wooden wardrobes and rope-and-straw mattress beds; the straw was fresh, and the Knights nodded and smiled acceptance.

Maelrin lit the rooms’ oil-lamps and departed, taking his lantern with him. The moment they heard his boots descending the stairs, the men trooped across the hall to confer with the lady Knights, yawning hugely.

“Three coppers one of us is asleep before those tankards arrive,” Pennae suggested.

“No takers,” Doust muttered. “My thighs and backside fell into slumber well before dawn. Could we possibly arrange to have adventures that *don’t* involve riding horses, from now on?”

“Doubt it,” Islif said cheerfully. “And what do the intrepid Knights of Myth Drannor think of the dark and haunted inn, hmm?”

“Certainly looks haunted,” Semoor agreed.

Jhessail shot a look that had daggers in it at Islif. “Have my *deepest* thanks for mentioning that. Now I’ll—”

“Be snoring in a trice like the rest of us,” Semoor said. “Good thing the doors have foot-wedges; I doubt any of us could stay awake on watch.”

“Ah,” Pennae murmured, “but are the doors we see the only ways into these rooms?”

Everyone glanced around, and swiftly agreed that thus far, each room in the Oldcoats they’d seen looked like the sort of place where every wall, floor, and ceiling had sliding panels, and secret passages behind them.

Pennae grinned at that and started toward the nearest wall, but Islif and Florin both grabbed her by the forearms and growled, *"No."*

Islif added, "See if you can get through one night—just one—without prowling anywhere, getting into trouble, or stealing from anyone."

Pennae lifted her chin defiantly.

"For the novelty of it?" Semoor suggested.

Pennae rolled her eyes, and handed him his own purse.

Semoor looked down at his belt where it was supposed to be—and wasn't—and then back up at her, dumbfounded.

Doust touched the back of Pennae's neck. He sprang back as she whirled to face him and snapped, *"Catch* her, Florin!"

Florin shot out one long arm and got hold of Pennae's shoulder as her spin turned into a topple. She was senseless, eyes wide and staring.

"You used magic on her," Islif said.

Doust nodded, yawning. "I'm too tired for her nonsense just now."

Islif gave him a cold look. "So am I, as it happens, but I think you and Semoor are going to sit down with the rest of us and have a long talk about any of us using magic on each other without agreement aforehand."

Semoor frowned. "Oh? What about her?" He pointed at Jhessail.

"She," Islif said, "isn't an idiot. You two, I'm increasingly not so sure about."

"Well," Semoor observed with a bright smile, *"that's* reassuring."

Chapter 10

All Nine of the Hells Break Loose

The Realms tremble whenever
The last six or so of the Nine Hells
Break loose again
To spill their latest bloodshed
Any fool can scream and die then.
The trick is to notice, earlier,
When the first few Hells silently gape wide
Dark smiles heralding the doom to come.

Aumra Darreth Vauntress
One Bard's Musings
published in the Year of the Wanderer

Laspeera rose with the ring in her hand, face expressionless, and told the lionar and the first sword quietly, "You were right to summon me."

"Someone was spell-blasted here," the lionar said grimly.

She lifted a finger to tap her lips and warned him, "You didn't say that, and you won't say that again. Anyone who hears you might just be the one who decides it's necessary to silence you forever."

"Does—does the ring identify who died?" the first sword asked. "There can't be *that* many unicorn-head rings like that."

The lionar gave him a sharp look. "There aren't. They're worn by all alarphons in the war wizards."

Laspeera nodded. "Of whom, it seems, we now have one fewer in the service of the realm."

✦ ✦ ✦ ✦ ✦

"*Three* fewer, actually," Ghoruld Applethorn purred into the glow arising from his scrying crystal, "but who's counting? Any moment now you'll remember I'm the senior alarphon, and should know where all the others are. Idiot novices like Lacklar included."

He turned to look at the row of fingerbones in the open coffer behind him, and added with a crooked smile, "And as it happens: I do."

✦ ✦ ✦ ✦ ✦

Tarnsar's Platters was one of the better dining-houses on the Promenade—good food, attentive staff, and pleasant decor, without the breath-robbing prices of the truly haughty establishments. As a result, it was always crowded to the doors, and nigh-deafening with the chatter and clatters of hundreds of excited Suzailans.

Two men having the appearance of middling years and wealth pushed and sidled patiently through the crowded passages of the Platters, seeking a certain back room where strangers off the street seeking to dine weren't customarily seated. They knew two young war wizards were wont to dine there, in a curtained-off back alcove of that room, and enjoy a quiet post-prandial game of lanceboard.

Reaching the archway they sought, they slipped through door-curtains enspelled to quell all sound, into the dimly lit, seemingly deserted room beyond. Then they padded as quietly as they knew how—which was *very* quietly—to the booth nearest the alcove, and settled down to listen.

". . . and this Elminster had written in the margins!" a young voice murmured indignantly. "Right in His Majesty's book! The *gall* of the man!"

"He's legendary for that," a voice that sounded as young, but more nasal—and calm—replied. "What did he write?"

"Well, I copied it out, to study and make sure 'twasn't a code, or some such. He wrote: 'The death of an old hero, gone toothless, is not tragic. It may seem so, but the tired old bones are at peace, in pain and loss no more. The bards and minstrels and those who spin tales in taverns have been handed the freedom to make the hero what they want him to be, glowing giant or otherwise, unfettered by such inconveniences as the truth.' I mean, how trite! Does he think no one but him has ever thought such thoughts before?"

"You've never taken Alaphondar's 'High History of the Realm' classes, have you?"

"No! Crashing old bore! Why?"

"You would have heard that Elminster wrote that over twelve hundred years ago, for the eyes of King Duar, when Duar was but a lad and grieving over the passing of various grand old lords at Court. If you flip through some of the other volumes that used to be Duar's, you'll find some far more, ah, *fascinating* advice."

"Oh? Such as?"

"How and when to get royal heirs—and how *not* to. The arts of pleasuring others, and the best ways to refuse without offending."

"You're jesting! Old Nastyspells giving advice on *wenching?"*

"Huh. If *that* makes you incredulous, picture him doing so to a young and callow Vangey!"

"Mystra spew! Gods Above and Below! I . . . I . . ."

There followed a tapping sound that might have been a fingernail on a hard-polished lanceboard, and the other war wizard chuckled and added, "I suppose this is as good a time as any to point out that your seneschal is imperiled by *both* of my champions."

What? *Tluin!* Armandras, you sly *bastard!"*

"Why, Corlyn, you credulous ramhorn-head!" Armandras sounded amused. *"Such* endearments!"

The two listeners looked at each other, nodded, and retreated to the doorway as quietly as they had come. The moment the two war wizards fell silent again, they advanced down the room once more, pushing past some chairs noisily.

"In here," Harreth stage-whispered to Yorlin, as they headed straight for the curtain. "No one can overhear us in here."

The two agents of Lord Yellander took a table just the other side of the curtain from the one that must be hosting that customary game of lanceboard, where the hidden war wizards couldn't help but overhear them.

"Right," Yorlin said excitedly, leaning forward across the table. "This is private enough, so out with it, man! What's this so-secret news?"

"Ever heard of Emmaera?"

"Who?"

"Better known as Dragonfire. Long-dead, practiced her magic around Halfhap? No?"

" 'Dragonfire' I heard once or twice, years back . . . something about animated swords, I think. A legend, not anything Vangey found useful."

"*That's* the one! Well, the swords *are* real—and they've been found! What's more, they're guarding Emmaera's treasure, all her spellbooks and wands and such, that've been rumored in Halfhap to lie hidden here, there, and everywhere for *years!*"

"So who's the lucky finder, and when will he show up to blast us all to feast-meat?"

"Well, that's just it: *no one* has all the magic—yet. Y'see, there's this old inn in Halfhap, the Oldcoats Inn, and it has the usual old, damp cellars. Well, some of them, on one side of things, have been getting a lot damper. So they wanted to dig out more space, for storage, over on the dry side. Which is when, about a tenday back, they found that one of those old cellar walls was just a single stone deep."

"Someone threw up a wall across one end of a room to hide its back half."

"Exactly! Well, behind that wall are a heap of chests and coffers and spellbooks and cloaks and wands and I don't know *what* all—but no one can get close to them."

"Some sort of flesh-eating field? Or a spell that fills the air with hungry snapping jaws when you try to step forward?"

"No, better than that! That's where the swords come in! Emmaera Dragonfire put a ring of flying swords around her treasure to guard it, and the swords burn with all-consuming dragonfire! The innkeeper paid his pot-boy to put on armor and try to get to the treasure, and the swords cut through it and his body under it like he was smoke! He *was* smoke, too, in less than a breath! A little ash on the floor was all that was left of him!"

"So the likes of Vangerdahast might be able to stroll in and pluck this treasure, but the rest of us—"

"Are like to be kissing death, right quickly! Not that such fears're stopping the local adventurers! They're hurrying down from Tilverton just as fast as horses can bring them—and dying just as fast!"

"No real wizards among 'em, then?"

"Not yet. Or rather, hadn't happened when the trader who told me left for Arabel. I heard it yestereve, from him and two others after him, who'd all been on the same run, straight through Arabel to here. Yet surely if someone snatches it, we'll hear all about it! If things fall quiet, it's a hoax or too deadly, or—"

"Or our gallantly watchful and protective war wizards have rushed in and hushed it all up," Yorlin said heavily. "*Well*, now. This bears thinking more on—over a good deep drink. Or three. Let's go get us some thirstquench."

"The brilliance of your plan overwhelms me." Harreth chuckled, as they rose and hurried out, not daring to wink at each other until they were beyond the door-curtains.

Leaving two war wizards staring excitedly at each other across a forgotten lanceboard—and then springing up to return to work early from their highsunfeast for the first time in their professional lives.

"Of course not," Duthgarl Lathalance agreed, giving the innkeeper a smile of cold promise. "Dissatisfaction on my part would prove to be . . . unfortunate."

Maelrin's own smile never wavered. "If you'll just follow me . . ."

"Of course." The handsome Zhentarim dropped a hand to his sword hilt as two rings on his other hand glowed briefly. If the keeper of the Oldcoats Inn saw those things, he gave no sign of it as he lifted his lantern and led the way up the stairs.

Lathalance peered around the room and then nodded.

Maelrin bowed. "We customarily serve newly arrived guests with a light repast, at no charge. Shall I have something sent up to you?"

"What sort of something?"

"Ale, zzar, or clarry, and soup, stew, or venison or fowl pie?"

"Mulled ale and a pie. Venison."

Maelrin bowed again and withdrew, leaving the Zhentarim standing alone in the room staring at the window.

The moment the innkeeper was gone, Lathalance went to the window, took down its bar and threw open its shutters, and discovered an outer set of shutters rather than any glass. He opened them, looked out over the three-man-height drop into the stableyard, and replaced everything as before.

Then he went slowly around the room, peering at walls, floor, and ceiling before half-smiling, and taking up the lone chair in the room. He moved it to the empty center of the room, turned it to face the closed but unlocked door, sat down in it—and was asleep in moments, a sleep that lasted until a floorboard creaked ever-so-slightly in the passage outside his door.

By the time the two serving-jacks knocked politely at that door, Lathalance was wide awake, on his feet, and striding confidently forward to greet them.

"Is it him?"

Maelrin smiled thinly. "He's a 'he,' yes. If you mean 'is he the Zhentarim?' the answer is—undoubtedly. I saw their sigil on his dagger hilt. He's a wizard *and* a warrior; he could probably fight us all at once, just with blades, and prevail. So it's the nauthus and the nutmeg."

The cook nodded and uncovered a platter that had been pushed to the back of his bench; the undercook took it up on a paddle and thrust it deep into the massive stone oven.

The cook unstoppered the nutmeg vial and stirred a generous handful into the mulled ale warming on the iron rack above the oven vent. Separately, they were harmless, the nutmeg a spice and the nauthus a fatty thickener for gravies and cooked sauces. Together, they acted as a deadly—and swiftly virulent—poison.

The Lords Yellander and Eldroon loved poisons. And as everyone on staff at the Oldcoats Inn now worked for them, the loves and desires of Yellander and Eldroon reigned, as Lathalance of the Zhentarim was about to unfortunately discover.

Lathalance sipped appreciatively. The mulled ale was *very* good. He sipped some more, and turned to the venison pie only reluctantly. It was steaming hot, and smelled—ahh, yes . . .

It tasted even better than it smelled, and he had to stop himself in mid-forkful to avoid burning his gullet.

And then a different sort of fire bloomed inside him, racing up and out his nose, and—

Lathalance convulsed, slowly went purple—like a bright over-ripening fruit—and slumped over in the chair, staring wide-eyed at nothing.

After a time, the fly that had come into the room with the food got tired of walking all over the half-eaten pie and the rim of the tankard, and buzzed over to Lathalance, where it walked daintily to and fro over his staring eyes.

✦ ✦ ✦ ✦ ✦

"Has it worked, yet?"

"Long since, if he ate any at all. Unless he has some sort of magical protection."

"Huh. If he had that, he'd be down here trying to hack us all apart already! Torence, Orban—trot up there and see if our Zhent guest's deep silence means what I think it means."

"And if he's as right and bright as a spring day, and tries to kill us?"

"Wear the rings. His spells will be hurled back from you and his blades will pass through you harmlessly, and you'll have a wonderful story to tell in taverns."

The two serving-jacks gave Ondal Maelrin sour, disbelieving looks, but they'd been bullyblades in the service of Lords Yellander and Eldroon for long enough to know what would happen if they disobeyed Maelrin. Like every lass and jack in the Oldcoats Inn, they served Yellander and Eldroon in matters shady and sinister. At least at this inn, playacting meant regular meals and a roof over their heads and ale and wine whenever they felt thirst.

Wherefore they donned the rings, nodded curtly to Maelrin, and went up the back stairs with their swords drawn.

✦ ✦ ✦ ✦ ✦

It had been more than a tenday since the secret panel in the back of the wardrobe had been used, and its hinges squealed.

"Bane's brazen boll—" Orban snarled, ere a glaring Torance slapped him fiercely across the throat to silence him.

Like two black shadows the serving-jacks came out of the wardrobe and crossed the room to the man slumped in the chair. Torance leaned forward to peer into the Zhentarim's staring eyes from less than a finger-length away, and then nodded.

"Dead, right enough," he told Orban. "Glorn hasn't dug the grave yet—Old Ondal wants it big enough for five or more, not just this one—so for now we'll have to put him under the hay in the end sta—"

The dead man's hands shot up to sink fingers deep into Torance's throat, and squeeze, hard.

The startled serving-jack fought to raise his sword and draw breath, kicking and flailing—but the dead man in the chair ignored his frantic hacking and throttled him all the harder, standing up suddenly to haul Torance off his feet and swing him.

The dying man's boots caught the fleeing Orban across the back of the head. The dead Zhentarim let go of Torance to let him sail across the room and crash into a wall. Lathalance sprang forward to pounce on the fallen Orban, pinning him to the floor with both knees, and brutally twisted his head.

The moment that thick neck broke, Lathalance was up and across the room again, to serve Torance the same way.

Bleeding copiously from the deep cuts Torance's sword had inflicted, the dead Zhentarim then picked up the two men he'd just killed, stumped to the wardrobe with them, and shouldered through it into the servants' passage beyond.

As he dragged the two dead serving-jacks down the back stairs, Old Ghost made the body he was animating grin hugely. Ah, but he was enjoying this.

Frightened faces gaped at him as he passed the open door of the staff ready-room with his limp burdens. He gave them Lathalance's best grin—or as good a grin as a purple body streaming gore from where one side of its head was largely sliced away can manage—and went on down the cellar stairs, to dump them.

In his wake, staff bolted in all directions, some seeking weapons, others a place to hide, and a few the portal, to report to their masters and plead for much armed aid—and swiftly.

Lord Yellander and Lord Eldroon strongly favored teamwork and plentiful reinforcements.

* * * * *

On her hurried trip through the Palace to Ghoruld Applethorn's chambers, Laspeera ordered the two Purple Dragons back to their duties and collected a trio of on-duty war wizards. Her words brought stern excitement to their faces and the wands at their belts into their hands. She set a brisk pace, and let them scramble to keep up with her.

Applethorn's office door was closed, and she smiled wryly at the words on the card in its placard-slide: "All inquiries to Laspeera of the Wizards of War."

It was written in Ghoruld's hand, right enough. She raised her left hand, calling up the powers of the ring on her middle finger—and then stopped and frowned, throwing up her other hand in a quelling warning to the younger mages behind her.

The door bore the usual spell-lock, and the trap magic that would hold immobile anyone passing through the doorway without the lock spell being properly ended. Both usual war wizard practice. Yet there was something more . . .

The ring winked in warning as she attuned it to ignore the lock and the hold, and seek that additional magic. Behind her, the other three war wizards waited patiently.

It was . . . something hostile, of course, but why the *emptiness?* Laspeera wondered The . . . oh, Mystra! It must be a feeblemind trap! Very dangerous to all mages, and so very much *non*-usual war wizard practice.

"By all Nine of the Hells," she murmured. "That it should come to this. . . ."

And then she shook back her sleeves and began to cast counterspells with her usual unhurried, cautious care.

✦ ✦ ✦ ✦ ✦

Jhessail yawned, groaned in sleepy protest, and turned over in the bed for perhaps the twentieth time, kicking at the linens that enshrouded her.

"Can't sleep?" Islif asked from beside her, throwing out a long arm to gather her close. "Try remembering all the things we did together in Espar, dreaming of being adventurers. *That'll* have you snoring soon enough."

"I'll try. Can't you sleep, either?"

"Not until Pennae here stops waiting for us both to nod off, so she can get up and go creeping around the inn. I don't want to have to spend far too much time, later, searching for her body."

"You," Pennae murmured in the darkness, "worry too much. They have to catch me first."

"It won't take them long if you haven't figured out by now that this place is one big waiting trap for the likes of us."

"You hayteeth backlanders persist in using the wrong words when you speak. Say not 'trap,' but rather 'challenge.' "

"Right. One big waiting challenge. I'm *still* staying awake."

"Mother hen."

"Black sheep."

Silence fell again, until Jhessail filled it with a sudden snore.

Chapter 11

Treasure in the Cellars

I know of more than a few strings of words
that shine with excitement, but should be
treated with the darkest of suspicion.
One of these is any variation on the phrase
'These very cellars hold a treasure yet unfound!'

Onstable Halvurr
Twenty Summers A Purple Dragon:
One Soldier's Life
published in the Year of the Crown

Touch *nothing*," Laspeera said, "and stay together, here with me."

Cautiously they peered around Ghoruld Applethorn's offices.

The man himself was missing. On his desk lay a scroll-tube labelled "Map: Halfhap." Its end cap was off, and it was—Laspeers bent and peered inside—empty. The entire desk glowed faintly, as if reflecting the flames of a distant fire.

"What spell is that?" Roruld asked from behind her, waving at it.

"No spell," Laspeera told him. " 'Tis wildsnarl powder. Very rare, and priced to match. Used to defeat most divination magic." Her eyes narrowed. This was all just a trifle overdone. "Go get Vangerdahast," she ordered.

"Well met," said the Royal Magician of Cormyr dryly, from just behind them.

As they stiffened, blinked, and whirled to face him, he snapped, "Roruld, go now in haste and seek Ghoruld Applethorn in the Garden Wing. Alais, the same search; Palace staterooms. Morlurn, likewise, but 'tis the Royal Court for you—and mind you don't miss the cellars!"

The three war wizards nodded, still blinking, and hurried out. Leaving Vangerdahast and Laspeera facing each other in the empty office.

"Odd, indeed," Vangey said. "I'm beginning to think I should collect those unicorn-head rings. Baerauble made them just a bit *too* useful."

Laspeera nodded. "Applethorn's will prevent us magically tracking, farscrying, and detecting him, but what about mind-prying; will it stop *your* spells?"

"Yes. Everyone's," the head of the war wizards said shortly, turning away. "And Ghoruld knows that. The question is: Who else does? Are we chasing Applethorn, or someone working with him—or someone who put a dagger through his ribs and took his likeness?"

He strolled across the room, one hand raised and the rings on it winking restlessly, before shaking his head and adding, "No one's scrying us right now, at least."

"I know of a dozen unicorn rings, all worn by alarphons," Laspeera said quietly. "Are there more I should know about?"

Vangey turned. "In case *I* go missing on the morrow? No, just twelve. That I know of. And no master ring to control them or overcome their protections, though Baerauble may have enspelled them in a way that let him shut them down by means he kept secret, that died with him. There'd be no point in using them at all, to try to keep their minds hidden and protected from all magic, if a way to defeat them could be seized and worn by just anybody."

"Of course. I—"

Running feet made a brief thunder in the passage outside, and two war wizards burst breathlessly through the door, gabbling about Emmaera Dragonfire and swords and inns and treasure, long-lost magic and adventurers converging on Halfhap.

Vangerdahast and Laspeera listened until Corlyn and Armandras ran out of excited things to say. They then politely thanked and dismissed the pair, who went out again peering at the two highest-ranked war wizards a little doubtfully, evidently wondering if the Royal Magician of Cormyr and the Court Underwizard of the Realm had heard them correctly.

When they were well out of sight and hearing, Vangerdahast turned to Laspeera. "Just a bit obvious, isn't it?"

Laspeera nodded.

"Well, take a dozen or more of our best with you—and have them conduct themselves with caution. Even when you know what you're striding into, a trap's a trap."

* * * * *

The rapping on the door was insistent, and Florin came awake reaching for his sword.

When he opened the door, blade at the ready, the man on the other side of it also held a drawn sword. And a worried, wary, but not hostile expression.

"What news?" Florin asked quietly, as Doust and Semoor sleepily joined him.

"Grave news," the man replied, a distinct whiff of horse coming from him as he grounded his blade. The innkeeper Maelrin and a serving-jack stood behind the stablemaster, facing in either direction down the passage. They, too, had drawn swords in their hands.

"Item the first. There's a killer on the loose. Here in the Oldcoats Inn."

"Oh?"

"A trained Zhentarim slayer, a sword and spell man. He's in his room now, but he killed two of us—of the inn staff—while all of you were sleeping, and neither poison nor being hewn to the bone with a sword seems to have stopped him. He is, in fact, walled in with us."

"Walled in?"

There was a brief commotion behind Ondal Maelrin as the door across the passage opened and an alert and fully dressed Pennae and Islif peered out.

"Item the second," the stablemaster began, but Maelrin put a hand on his arm and he fell silent.

"There's more," the innkeeper said, looking from the lady Knights to the men. "Your horses have all been taken."

"Taken?" Jhessail snapped, before anyone else could, as she pushed past Islif, looking almost child-sized beside her tall friend—but far from a child indeed in her clinging shift.

The three Oldcoats men stared at her, and then quickly looked away. Jhessail folded her arms and waited, withering glare at the ready, for them all to surreptitiously glance her way again. "Taken?" she repeated.

"Uh. Ahem, yes," the innkeeper said, clearing his throat. "Confiscated, I should say, by the local Purple Dragons. Who came here looking for the Knights of Myth Drannor, with intent to take *you.*"

"I'd say Laspeera didn't overlook your little theft," Jhessail snapped at Pennae. "I'd say she kept it as a reason to go after us, *after* we were safely out of lands where they have to keep to Azoun's law. Or is there something else you did, that you perhaps forgot to tell us?"

" 'Take' us?" Pennae asked the master of Oldcoats, ignoring Jhessail.

"Arrest you. 'Take' is what they always call it. As you can tell, we thwarted them."

Islif patiently made a circling gesture with her hand, urging him to say more. Maelrin nodded to her and added, "We lured them back out of the inn by saying you'd all gathered in the stables to do something you wouldn't tell us about, except that we were to stay away. Of course they couldn't resist all dashing off to the stables—whereupon we activated the Dragonfire magic to keep them out of Oldcoats proper. Er, that is to say, this building we're standing in."

"And what," Semoor and Jhessail asked, almost as one, "is the 'Dragonfire magic'?"

"Later," Pennae snapped. "I'm sure all the arcane details are fascinating, but first tell us, Master Maelrin, what's befalling *now.* I don't care so much—yet—what this Dragonfire is, so much as what it *does.*"

The innkeeper looked at the stablemaster. "Druskin?"

Stablemaster Druskin looked from the lady Knights to the men and back again, sighed, and said, "I used to keep the Dragons' stables, here in Halfhap. I know how they work. I can't see through the magic, but I'm as certain as if I could that Oldcoats is surrounded by Dragons right now, while they wait for the war wizards they've called for to get here. The Dragonfire magics are like a huge wall all around this building—and *just* this building—to keep everyone out."

Islif frowned. "And us *in.*"

"Can we get away over the rooftops?" Pennae asked quickly. "Or the cellars? I suppose you'd better tell us a little more about this Dragonfire magic."

"The rooftops, no," Ondal Maelrin replied. "Not unless you can live happily with a dozen-some Purple Dragon war-quarrels through you." He hesitated. "The cellars, yes, but there's a little problem."

He fell silent, looking less than happy. Islif stepped forward until she was towering over him, so close they were almost touching, and said firmly, "That you're going to tell us all about. *All* about."

Maelrin sighed again. "Where to begin? Well . . . our cellars flood. From the stable side, and not often, but—we need more dry cellar space. So we started digging on the other side, toward the front of the inn, and soon enough we found a cellar wall that was only one stone deep; a false wall thrown up across the end of a larger cellar."

"Long ago, to hide treasure," Pennae added. It was not a question.

The innkeeper nodded. "So we believe, though we haven't dared go near it. We can see it, and an old tunnel that leads into the cellars of other shops along this street is supposed to be just the other side of it, but . . ."

He waved his hands in exasperation. "There's this legend, here in Halfhap. Years ago, a famous mage dwelt hereabouts; a lady called Emmaera Dragonfire. After she died, no one ever found her magic. Well, we have—at least, we can see wands and chests and thick books with runes on them, a big heap of it all. The tales all say she guarded herself with flying swords that flew at her command, and that she left them guarding her treasure. A ring of flying swords that strike at all who venture near. Well, the ring of swords are down there right now—and right enough, they strike at anyone who goes too close!"

Pennae's eyes gleamed. "Which way to the cellars?"

Jhessail rolled her eyes. "Can I put some clothes on and *eat*, first?"

✦ ✦ ✦ ✦ ✦

Yassandra Durstable was by far the best-looking war wizard ever to wear the unicorn-headed ring of the alarphons. Tall, shapely, and possessed of a tumbling fall of glossy black hair and eyes that were both large and dark, she had devastated many with her frowns—and many more with her crooked, catlike smiles. She was frowning now, but Laspeera Naerinth was unimpressed.

"No," the alarphon answered, "I know nothing at all of where Melandar, Orzil, Voril, and Ghoruld Applethorn are, or what they're up to."

"Really?" Laspeera's tone of voice and raised eyebrow made her disbelief clear.

Yassandra's frown deepened, and she deliberately slid off her unicorn ring before replying, "Really." Receiving only Laspeera's reluctant nod by way of reply, she asked, "Why? What's this all about?"

"All four men are missing," Laspeera told her, "and now you know as much as I do. You have your battlebook with you? And spells at the ready?"

Yassandra's frown abated not a whit. "Yes, and yes."

"Good. Come." Laspeera strode right at the solid wall beside her, and vanished through it without disturbing it in the slightest.

The alarphon followed unhesitatingly, and found herself in a spell chamber she'd visited only once before—a dark, bare, dirty chamber with a lofty ceiling lost in cobwebs, several thick candles burning, each on its own head-high wooden stand, a large circle chalked on the flagstone floor, and more than a dozen war wizards standing and shuffling tensely from boot to boot. Yassandra knew all of them: Brors, Taeroch, and old Larlammitur well; Alsketh from Marsember and Cordorve of High Horn slightly, from working with them twice or thrice; and the rest merely as veteran war wizards, faces and names no alarphon had yet seen need to know better.

"I've chosen you all for a little task that is very likely to involve both danger and spell-battle, I'm afraid," Laspeera said, without greeting or delay. "Please enter the circle."

Everyone stepped inside the chalk, Laspeera included, and three more war wizards promptly appeared, stepping through another stretch of apparently solid wall. This elderly, white-whiskered trio received Laspeera's nod, nodded back to her expressionlessly, and began casting a mass teleport in perfect unison.

The spell was crafted without incident, everyone in the circle vanished, and the oldest war wizard gave a satisfied grunt, turned on his heel, and trudged back through the illusory wall he'd come in by.

The other two lingered. They were both very familiar with the kept-empty-for-this-very-purpose room, in the southwesternmost of the two gate-keeps of Halfhap, that they'd just sent all their colleagues to, but the youngest of the three elderly war wizards was very curious as to why Halfhap, just now. "What's the grave emergency threatening the very survival of the realm *this* time?"

The other war wizard shrugged. "Laspeera's getting like Vangey. 'You've no need to know, so I'm not telling you.' Something about exalted rank always takes their wits that way."

"Hmm, yes," the younger one agreed. "Yet, somehow . . . I've a grave feeling about this."

"And so you should," his fellow war wizard replied approvingly.

And blasted him to ashes before turning away.

* * * * *

Standing in the common room of the Oldcoats Inn, at the head of the cellar stairs, the Knights of Myth Drannor traded glances with each other.

"Ready?" Florin asked quietly, and started collecting nods. They were all rested, fed, watered, armed, and in armor. Everyone nodded.

"Right," he said, and he started to head down into the cellars. Pennae sprang past him, turned on the stairs to give him a reproving look, and then led the way, lit lantern in hand.

The innkeeper watched them go. When they'd all descended and were clear of the cellar steps, Ondal Maelrin made a hand-signal to a maid upstairs, who darted to the door of a guestroom next to the one rented to the lady Knights, opened it, and repeated that signal.

At the open window of that room, a serving-jack nodded, waited for her to close the door again, and then leaned out the window and blew a hunting-horn.

A serving-jack walked softly across the common room to join Maelrin in peering down the cellar stairs. "Well?"

"Well, it's worked thus far," the innkeeper murmured, "and we herded them down into the cellars like starving men eager to swarm a feast. We'll just have to see how long we can keep them believing in their horses gone, Purple Dragons surrounding the place, and all this Dragonfire nonsense."

"Your acting was peerless," said the serving-jack. "And they were trusting enough to not even try to go and check on their horses. They mustn't have been adventurers for long."

"Nor will they for much longer," Ondal Maelrin said with a soft smile. "Gullible fools."

"That's more or less what Lord Yellander called them. Lord Eldroon just laughed."

"It will be as well for us," the innkeeper muttered, "if he goes on laughing."

* * * * *

Folk all across Halfhap lifted their heads and frowned as a horn-blast that was quite different from the war-horns used by the Purple Dragons rang out across the town.

"Who's that, d'ye think?" a cooper asked the vintner across the yard-fence, as they both tossed out discarded casks to be chopped up into kindling.

The vintner straightened up. By the look on his face, he was thinking hard. "Someone with a hunting-horn, down center way. Oldcoats, or near there."

"Someone in a hurry to signal something."

They nodded, stared at each other, and then shrugged in unison. Either they'd never know, or the taverns would ring with various wild tales about who'd winded that horn, and why.

Not far from the cooper and the vintner, two local "oddwares" traders who bought and sold goods for costers and factors in distant cities—but whom no one in town had the slightest idea were agents of two nobles of Cormyr, the Lords Yellander and Eldroon—smiled knowingly at the sound of that horn-call, and turned in their strolling toward the door of a particular shop.

Baraskor's Brightwares wasn't an establishment either Horl Bryntwynter or Jarandorn Vantur visited often, but it was one they wandered through from time to time, looking for items to interest their far-off contacts. It would not have flattered Ordaurl Baraskor to know that they were choosing to tour his shop, at this particular time, because he was widely considered to be Halfhap's worst gossip. But then, neither of them intended to tell him that.

The two traders began to chat as they drifted through Baraskor's doors.

"Aye, the Dragonfire magic's been found at last!"

"No! Horl, are you *sure* this isn't just another of Traulaunna's wildtongue tales?"

"Well if it is, lots of folk were a-telling it before Traulaunna ever heard it. Though she'll burnish and adorn it, right enough! So hear truth from me now, before she gets the chance: Emmaera Dragonfire's leavings are a heap of magic. Rings, wands, rods—the lot! And her spellbooks too!"

"Ho!" Jarandorn exclaimed, raising both his eyebrows as he peered at some tall, fluted glass bottles from Turmish. "That'd make it everything legends have glowingly described, all these years!"

"It is!" Bryntwynter ran a critical finger over the inlaid flank of an ornamented jewel-coffer, ignoring the hovering, watchful presence of Ordaurl Baraskor at his elbow, and added, "Yet I doubt any of us will get to see any of it! Adventurers just arrived from Arabel have camped in Oldcoats and are keeping everyone away with their swords—and spells too!"

"Everyone? Purple Dragons of the grasping Crown, too?" Jarandorn stopped in front of a display of belts and pouches, to peer and stroke his chin and consider.

"Well, not yet," Horl told him through the shelves, "but they're probably plodding over there right now! You know how word gets around in *this* town!"

"So who are these lucky swordswingers of Arabel? Rebels who'll use the Dragonfire treasure to challenge the king? Or outlanders who'll rush off to Westgate or Waterdeep or Amn to sell it all, as fast as they can fall over each other?"

"The Knights of Myth Drannor, they call themselves! There's talk of them all over Suzail. They must be the ones Queen Filfaeril bedded—with them in full armor all stained with monster-blood too!"

Without lifting his gaze for a moment from the shelves of glittering coffers in front of him, Horl Bryntwynter became aware that the shopkeeper had stopped oh-so-patiently awaiting a moment to break into their chatter with an offer to assist him in selecting this coffer or that, and receded smoothly from anywhere Bryntwynter might happen to notice him. He was listening avidly to the converse between the two traders.

"What?" Jarandorn chuckled. "Do you *believe* that sort of gossip? I mean, how now? The Ice Queen, bedding *anything?*"

"Ah, but who called her the Ice Queen before the rest of us? Suzailans, that's who. Who sees more of her than all the rest of us unwashed upcountry louts? Suzailans. So if they can believe such talk, I can believe it, too!"

Vantur chuckled. "You mean you *want* to believe it, for the sheer fun of picturing such sport."

Bryntwynter moved on from the coffers, passing over a selection of hats and bound presses of parchments to a squared, rough-hewn pillar decorated in a selection of ornate hasps and latches. "Well, yes," he laughed. "You have me there!"

"Well, folk seem fair crazed up in Suzail," Jarandorn said dismissively. "It's we of Halfhap, good and bad, as I have to live with, every morn to every dusking. So how're they taking all of this down at Oldcoats? Or have these adventurers turned them out, slit their throats, or locked them all in the wellhouse?"

Bryntwynter snorted. "Vantur, you spend entirely too much time listening to minstrels' fancies. Nothing so wild-bold, to be sure! Maelrin's fair gnawed away all his mustache already, for fear they'll sword him *and* all his staff, and blast the Oldcoats to dust around his dying ears—but they've not *done* any of that, yet, and they'd be fools to do so, with the Purple Dragons marching down to see what they *are* up to." He sighed. "Well, I see nothing here to impress Suzailans. Fine wares, but nothing . . . you know; *gleaming.*"

"I know, and am finding much the same. Good wares, but Suzail's awash in good wares *and* bad, and so's Athkatla. We'll have to check again in good time, of course. Have you heard from Turrityn yet?"

"No," Bryntwynter said mournfully, sighing an even bigger sigh, "and that's beginning to concern me. What's Faerûn coming to, that a . . ."

He nodded to the shopkeeper with the vacant smile of a polite man whose mind is now on financially graver things, and strolled back out of Baraskor's Brightwares, Jarandorn Vantur drifting along in his wake.

As if as an afterthought, and with an apologetic smile for not buying anything, Vantur turned briefly upon the threshold to give the proprietor a farewell nod of his own, and then turned again and was gone.

Ordaurl Baraskor calmly returned that nod, but after the weighted front door of Brightwares glided gently shut again, he hurried into the back to snap excitedly at his wife, bidding her leave her cooking upon the instant to take over the shop.

Before she could reply, he was out the back door and hastening down the alley. Certain local ears must hear of the Dragonfire treasure and of these Knights of Myth Drannor.

Zhentarim ears.

* * * * *

"What's that?" Jhessail asked sharply.

Pennae flung back a scornful reply without turning her head. "Rats. *Quiet.*"

The thief raised her lantern, waiting until Florin had come up on her left and Islif on her right, and then advanced, slowly and cautiously.

More rats scurried; Pennae saw Islif's frown, and nodded. Yes, she agreed silently, it *was* unusual for an inn to let quite so many rats run hither and yon in the cellars where they presumably stored their foodstuffs.

Unless something was there to draw them. Something like . . .

The light of the lantern fell on an unmoving human hand. A man's hand, fingers spread on the uneven stone floor.

Fingers that had been nibbled.

Grimly Pennae took another step, lifting the lantern higher.

There were two dead men on the cellar floor of the Oldcoats Inn, one draped over the other. Their slack faces would have been staring at her if the rats had left them any eyes to stare with, but the Knights of Myth Drannor knew their faces and their uniforms.

They were staring at the corpses of the serving-jacks who'd brought soup and cider to their rooms, upon their arrival at the inn this morning.

Chapter 12

When the Killing Starts

Too many nobles and young officers alike
Share the affliction of spitting insults,
Shouting denunciations, and snarling orders
Only to vanish like shadows before full sun
When the killing starts.

Onstable Halvurr
Twenty Summers A Purple Dragon:
One Soldier's Life
published in the Year of the Crown

"So what, by the holy light of Lathander, is *going on* in this inn?" Semoor demanded, staring down at the eyeless bodies of the serving-jacks. "Does the innkeeper not *know* these corpses are down here? Or did he herd us down here so he can 'find' us with the bodies and blame their murders on us?"

Islif shrugged. "The rest of us know how to ask questions too. 'Tis answers we're short of providing." She lifted her head to gaze warily around into the darkness. "Doust, fetch down that lantern—on the pillar by your head, there. We need it lit. There are rooms ahead of us and behind us. The stairs are the only way we know to depart these cellars, so we must guard them, but otherwise stick together, as we master what's where in these cellars, and who or what can harm us down here. I dislike surprises."

"Really?" Semoor murmured. "You surprise me."

"Whereas you," Islif murmured, "utterly fail to amuse me with such pointless witticisms at this particular time. Florin?"

"I've always hated having foes or the unknown behind me," the ranger said slowly, "but this time, for some reason, I very much want to go on. Straight ahead, in that direction. If these bodies were left for us to find, they might have been intended as a 'turn back from here' warning, to keep us from proceeding . . ."

Pennae nodded, walked around the bodies to the bare floor beyond them, and murmured, "Then let's go this way. This is a large room to leave empty. With open stairs down from the common room, I was expecting to see a dozen kegs or more, right here at the bottom of the stairs. Or empty chests or potato bins or *some*thing. The running of this inn seems strange."

Doust nodded. "D'you think that man at the gate was waiting for us, to send us straight into a prepared trap?" Under his careful hands, the lantern flared smokily into life.

"Huh-uh," Pennae disagreed. "We're not *that* important, that every town and village we ride into will have a trap ready-waiting for us. Let's go find this treasure." Her fellow Knights nodded, and they started to move.

"Ah," Semoor asked, "but what if it's a trap for all unwelcome visiting adventurers, not the Knights of Myth Drannor specifically?"

No one answered him.

"Keep together," Florin reminded everyone, as they walked cautiously into the darkness.

"Doorway," Pennae murmured, almost immediately. "Nothing else except . . . yes, a few old barrels and crates that look like they've been rotting down here for years, over in yon corner."

"Lead on," Florin urged. "Islif?"

"I'll guard our rear," she murmured, "alongside our holynoses. Where did all those rats run *to,* I wonder?"

"Rooms beyond rooms we haven't found, yet," Pennae replied, lifting her lantern to peer at the massive ceiling-beams overhead. Black with thick-shrouded cobwebs, they sprouted uneven rows of rusty storage-hooks that should have supported bulging nets of onions and garlic, or rotting arnark boughs sprouting fistfuls of kitchen mushrooms, but instead were all empty.

"Every one," she murmured, half to herself. "No guests, no food—is Doust right? Did they open this inn just for us? The stables seemed busy enough, but . . ."

She went cautiously to the open doorway and peered through, half-closing the shutters of her lantern to make its light a beam she could aim into the darkness beyond. She checked the floor and ceiling just past that door-opening, then to left and right, hard by the door, to make sure no one—or *thing*—was lurking to stab or pounce on any Knight of Myth Drannor bold enough to step through.

No lurking foe, and no fallen door nor any sign the opening had ever been fitted with one. The room beyond was crowded with kegs in wooden cradles, and crates of food. Onionskins were strewn across the floor, and here and there she saw the beady gazes of rats peering back at her.

In short, all of the clutter Pennae had expected to find at the foot of the stairs. There was a faint glow coming from the far end of the room. She turned aside her lantern, and made sure of it. Yes, another doorway, or door standing open, and coming through its gap, a soft, steady golden glow.

"What we're looking for may well lie just ahead," she murmured, without looking away from the room through the doorway. "Come and see."

The Knights pressed in close around her, and she opened the lantern wide again.

"We're guarding the rear," Islif reminded Doust. "Keep your lantern and your eyes facing back *that* way. We'll have plenty of time to see this next room when we're in it."

"Tymora bids me take chances," Doust told her with dignity, but whatever else he might have gone on to say was lost in her reply.

"You're adventuring. I'd say that's more than chance enough," Islif said. "If you want your life to swiftly grow more chancy, just ignore my bidding again, and I'll see that it does—with an alacrity that's *certain* to please Lady Luck."

"How many places are there where you think an armed man could hide from us, amid those casks and such?" Florin asked Pennae, waving at the room beyond the doorway.

"Six at least . . . four more, perhaps," she murmured. "I'll know better once I'm over the threshold. Stay close to me, but when I look right, down the room, be sure you face left and watch sharp."

Without waiting for a reply, she lowered the lantern and stepped through the doorway. Florin scrambled to follow. The rest of the Knights leaned forward to watch. Islif had to disgustedly take hold of Doust's shoulder and firmly turn him around to face back the way they'd come.

"I'll 'Tymora' you, see if I don't," she muttered fiercely into his ear.

Behind them, Pennae and Florin had found no foes, and were already down the crowded cellar room to that far doorway, and peering cautiously around its edge, lantern entirely hooded, to try to see the source of the glow.

Then they gasped softly, in unison, at the sight of—

Treasure. Golden treasure—a long, low heap of rods and scepters and wands and thick spellbooks, coins spilling out of chests and gems glittering inside open coffers, a harp and a sword and something that looked like a shield with horns and fins of metal filigree projecting from it. The golden hue bathed everything, and came not from the heap itself—a pile about as long as two Jhessails laid end to end, and about as high as her head, when she was sitting on the ground—but from the guardian ring of swords that hung in the air above it.

Four-and-ten . . . no, six-and-ten swords, all identical, with long slender blades, black hilts and black, hooked quillons, floating silently in the air point-down, that steady golden glow running down the sides of their blades and thrusting like the beam of a spell from their points, lighting the air golden as well as Emmaera Dragonfire's treasures beneath.

"This, Florin, is why one goes adventuring," Pennae murmured. "The favor of kings and the kisses of princesses and noble ladies are well enough, but they fade or are swept away with the passing days and years—whereas gold and magic endure, gleaming and unchanged."

"We'd best go tell everyone," Florin murmured. *"Don't* go touching it, now! Not one bauble!"

Pennae crooked an eyebrow at him. "With that many swords hanging there waiting for my blood? Not likely!"

They turned and hastened back through the room of casks and crates. "We found it," Florin told the waiting Knights. "Just as the innkeeper described it. I—"

" 'Ware!" Islif snapped. "Weapons *out!*"

Everyone turned to stare where she was looking. Past the stairs that had brought them down here, into the darkness where a broad and sudden blue glow was just dying away—and eight hard-eyed men in robes were standing, in a spot that had been dark and empty a moment before.

"Knights of Myth Drannor!" one of them boomed. "In the name of King Azoun, fourth of that name, who signed your charter, I command you to down weapons! In the name of Queen Filfaeril, who granted your knighthoods, I demand your ready obedience. We are war wizards, of the fair kingdom of Cormyr, and we would have peaceable speech with you."

Florin and Islif both grounded their blades, putting their sword points to the floor.

"Florin Falconhand am I," the ranger announced, "and I have every intention of obeying the Crown of Cormyr. Yet words are spoken easily, and I have only this handful of yours to say that you speak with royal authority—and it is that very same royal authority you invoke that allows us to bear arms within the realm. Is your royal authority somehow better than mine? Moreover, we do not now stand within the Forest Kingdom, but in a border protectorate. What laws and authority apply at all? I desire no dispute with any of you, and so seek to know more, that I may best decide how to proceed. I have given you my name, Lord Mage. Might I now know yours?"

"Taeroch am I," the wizard replied, "and I am not accustomed to having to repeat clear and reasonable orders. Sir Florin, I say agai—"

During the converse, one of the war wizards had quietly stepped back from the line of cross-armed, expressionless mages, and half turned away. He whirled back to face the Knights again, with a wand in his hitherto-empty hand—aimed at his nearest fellow war wizard.

He fired it, moving it to blast not just that man, but the next and the next. As he drew a second wand with his other hand, to unleash smiting magic in the wake of the first.

Those three wizards stiffened as their shielding spells flared and were swiftly overwhelmed. Even before they could turn and shout, they were staggering and falling, blasted where they stood.

The Knights stood aghast as the mage with the wands turned to serve the other four the same way.

They were fast, and were already striking at him with wand-blasts and ring-beams of their own—but even before his mantle-spell collapsed in a roiling chaos of short-lived black stars, the Knights saw the wizard's eyes go dark and empty, and something like a wraith rush out of his soundlessly screaming mouth.

By the time the renegade war wizard was being torn apart by four magical dooms lancing into him at once, the wraith-thing had plunged into the face of the nearest of the four remaining war wizards.

He turned stiffly to point at the Knights and scream, *"They're* doing it! Their magic—in my mind! *Stop them!"*

Doust and Semoor gaped in utter astonishment, but Florin and Islif were already racing forward, and Pennae promptly hurled her lit lantern into the accusing face of that war wizard and yelled, "Scatter!"

The Knights scattered, as men with swords and daggers in their hands came charging down the common room stairs—and plunged into the war wizards, thrusting and hacking.

"Brors!" a war wizard shouted as Florin reached him.

The man Pennae had just struck staggered past, screaming and clawing at a face whose beard—through the blood spilled by the many shards of glass—was flaming and shriveling, and the wraith-like thing started streaming out of him again.

Jhessail slashed at it with her dagger, but found herself slicing nothing more tangible than smoke, and hearing horrible whispering laughter in her ears that seemed to say, *See, Old Ghost? Horaundoon does know how to obey!*

The air around the stairs erupted in a sudden rain of bright fire that left many men shouting in pain and sagging back, as the wizard Brors hurled a spell intended to drive Florin and Islif away from his colleague.

A dagger came whirling down the stairs, flashing harmlessly past the war wizard's head. In its wake, the thunder of boots on the stairs announced the arrival of a second wave of bullyblades with swords and daggers—and as they sprang down to join the fray, these reinforcements roared, "Zhentarim forever! Zhentarim *triumphant!*"

* * * * *

Lords Yellander and Eldroon stood in the darkened, tapestry-hung private dining room with Yellander's crossbowmen, all of them listening intently to what could be heard through the half-open door into the common room of the Oldcoats Inn. Behind them, the cold blue fire of their portal flickered almost hungrily.

As the Zhentarim war cry rang back off the common room rafters, Yellander turned and snapped, "Now! Quickly!"

He waved his waiting crossbowmen past him, toward the door. "Before anyone gets the upper hand! Use poisoned tips! Kill wizards first!"

The crossbowmen streamed past him and banged through the door.

The two nobles grinned at each other. "Why, I *do* believe it would be highly prudent to be elsewhere about now," Yellander drawled—and ducked back through the portal, Eldroon hard on his heels.

Eldroon's rearmost boot was just vanishing into the throbbing blueness when a tapestry across the room was thrust aside.

The hand moving that worn and none-too-clean cloth belonged to Laspeera of the war wizards—who strode across the room with a purposeful cluster of veteran war wizards right behind her, and plunged through the portal after the two noble traitors.

The wizards followed in smooth haste; Andabral, Torthym,

Larlammitur, Alsketh, Cordorve, and the least battle-experienced, Yassandra, last.

At least, that was the intended order. Yassandra, bringing up the rear, smiled crookedly at the shimmering blue portal in front of her—and whirled away from it to head across the ground floor of the Oldcoats Inn.

Toward the cellars.

• ✦ ✶ ✦ •

"It is good," the dead, purple lips of Lathalance mumbled, before Old Ghost billowed out of him to tower over Horaundoon. And smile.

Behind the two wraithlike spirits, as they raced out into Halfhap, the Zhentarim's abandoned body lolled limply in the chair at the center of his rented inn room.

Old Ghost and Horaundoon scudded along alleyways and over rooftops like one wisp of smoke chasing another, eager to possess local Zhentarim and draw them into the fray at Oldcoats.

It seemed the mageling Tantarlus hadn't thought about chimneys when casting wards around his home, so two unwelcome—but utterly unnoticed—guests curled like lazy smoke along the bottom of tapestries as he yelled excitedly to the mouth inset into the center of his corner table, "This is a Bane-bestowed chance to slaughter many war wizards! Send as many of the Brotherhood as you can through my portal!"

"All right, Tantarlus," the mouth said, "you needn't *shout*. Some of your fellow magelings—those you trained with at the Citadel—will shortly be arriving in your parlor. They will need to be directed to the inn. See to it."

The mouth closed and faded into dark, carved immobility. Tantarlus covered it reverently with the cloth that customarily concealed it, put the oil lamp back in its usual place atop that cloth—and stiffened as Old Ghost plunged into him, possessing him with far greater care than Horaundoon had used on the war wizards.

But then, Old Ghost had no intention of burning out this useful host yet. He turned to Horaundoon. "Keep hidden from the arriving magelings," he ordered. "They will be all too eager to blast anything that interests them."

"And you are?"

"Off through the portal in the other direction, to Zhentil Keep. Where Tantarlus of the Zhentarim will eloquently exaggerate this skirmish into something that demands an even larger response."

"Will they listen to a mere mageling, stationed as local eyes in Halfhap?"

"Yes, if that mageling speaks forcefully enough of great magic to be gained, a chance to break the strength of the local war wizards, seize control of Halfhap, butcher the Purple Dragon garrison, and provoke Cormyr into sending forth an army that can then be blasted at will."

Dauntless glared at the streets and hovels of Halfhap as if they personally affronted him—and would serve all Faerûn better if they were hurled down before the next nightfall. Weary and stubble-chinned, he was sore from riding through the night, and not even snarling at the gate-guards until they openly cowered had given him any satisfaction.

At least they'd reluctantly imparted the information that the Knights of Myth Drannor had reached Halfhap and been directed to the Oldcoats Inn, though Dauntless had felt the silent contempt of his five picked Purple Dragons, boring into his back, all the while he'd bullied the two guards.

He was beyond caring. He just wanted to arrest the Knights, clap them in the dungeons of the Halfhap keeps, and get some sleep. They could be questioned as to the whereabouts of Lord Duskur Ebonhawk's belongings—a lot of coin, in a cloth-of-gold-covered metal purse with the black hawkhead family badge on its clasps—later. Now, Halfhap wasn't *that* big, so this sagging black-painted dump before him had to be the Oldcoats Inn.

A man and two maids were standing together on its front steps. The wenches were dressed alike, with matching vests over their gowns—inn staff. By his manner, the man was their master, and had the look of an innkeeper, though less stout than most.

Dauntless halted his tired mount in front of them, and looked down from his saddle at the man. "Is this the Oldcoats Inn? And are you master here?"

The man looked up at him expressionlessly. "I am, and this the Oldcoats Inn. Fitting lodgings for Dragons of the Realm. Ondal Maelrin, at your service."

Dauntless didn't bother to nod. "You have adventurers staying here who call themselves the Knights of Myth Drannor, I believe?"

The innkeeper shrugged. "We have guests, yes. I haven't heard that grand title before, no. You can examine my lodging ledger, of course."

Dauntless glowered. Maelrin stared back at him.

"Well," the ornrion snapped, "get it, man! The duty of all good citizens is to obey Dragons and officers of the Crown without hesitation or dispute!"

Maelrin's eyes went cold, and he snapped right back, "You're mistaken, soldier! I have this from the lips of the King himself: the duty of all good citizens are to watch those who govern them like hungry hawks, and to defend whoever needs defending!"

"His Majesty was a young lad when he said that; an adventurer!"

"So he's changed the brain in his head since then, has he? I must have missed *that* proclamation!"

Dauntless snarled in wordless anger and swung himself down from his saddle, pretending not to hear a lone snicker from the five Dragons at his back. Wincing, he strode stiffly past the innkeeper.

Who said, without turning his head, "Ledger's on a table at the bottom of the cellar stairs. They descend from the center of the common room, which you'll be standing in when you pass through the front doors."

Without replying, Dauntless and his five men stalked into the inn.

Maelrin turned to smile frostily at their backs ere murmuring to the maids, "Time to get up there and plunder the Knights' belongings, lasses. Then out the back and gone. They'll soon be hurling spells that'll blow this place into the sky even before it gets burned to the ground!"

Chapter 13

Dauntless goes a-brawling

Oh, I am proud to be a Dragon loud
There is no higher calling
We swagger along, villains a-trawling
And merchants and maids a-mauling
But be ever so bad, there's nothing we do
To blacken the Crown, to match the rue
Of high nobles who start a-bawling
When Dauntless goes a-brawling.

from Dauntless Goes A-Brawling
street-song of the Purple Dragons
in Arabel (composer anonymous),
popular circa the Year of the Spur

Yassandra Durstable went down the stairs like a gloating shadow, the blue-green fire of the two wands in her hands still crawling away from her in a deadly, staggering wave of struggling crossbowmen dying on their feet. The only living war wizard she'd seen in the cellars had gone down into a silent heap of protruding bones in her first wand-burst, but these magnificent brutes were still fighting her magic, clawing at the air as it rode them and cursing their inevitable doom.

She'd blasted them all from behind, of course. Why tempt the gods to hand any foe a chance?

Now the last crossbowman was down, and with him the last dying flames of wandfire, leaving but one sound ahead of her in this dark and cool cellar. From the only light here in the cellars, a little way down the room, came the faint sizzling of cooking flesh.

One of the war wizards—and she couldn't see all of their corpses; some could well be very much alive, and lurking in other cellar chambers ahead of her—had blasted a Zhentilar warrior with a spell that had left his body burning like a hearthfire.

A fire in a hearth that had a good chimney—it made very little smoke but a lot of racing, flickering flames. The corpse-light wouldn't last long. Smiling grimly, Yassandra advanced past him cautiously, wanting to get out of the view of anyone standing at the top of the cellar stairs with a wand or a crossbow, before she cast light magic of her own.

Doom fell on her—hard—without the slightest warning.

Pennae swung down on the war wizard from above and behind, arms trembling from the strain of bracing herself between two rusty hooks. She hurled herself out of the inky darkness in the lee of a ceiling-beam and scissored her legs viciously around the wizard's head, swinging hard to the left and kicking upward as she did so.

Yassandra's neck broke with a horrible wet crunch—and Pennae put all her might into a frantic shifting of herself forward, so as to pass over the lolling head and down on the wizard's arms from above, rather than ending up with her feet pointing at the ceiling, head-downward with the dying woman toppling back over onto her.

She had to gain control of those wands—*had to!*

Pennae was still clawing at the air and a swinging beam-hook for balance when Yassandra sobbed the words that set off the wands, blasting the ceiling above with more blue-green fire.

"Tluin," Pennae announced calmly, as the spraying magic shook the dying body under her, driving it back just enough that she could overtop Yassandra and reach down the war wizard's failing, spasming arms.

Hopefully before hungry blue-green fire thoroughly cleaned Pennae's teeth—and throat, and her gizzard and whatnots beyond it too—for her.

* * * * *

Dauntless and his Dragons were halfway across the deserted common room, swords singing out of scabbards and striding hard, when the floor to the angry ornrion's right, just behind him, burst upward in a splintering roar and flood of blue-green flames.

Shattered floorboards erupted in a deadly spray, hurling two Purple Dragons bodily up into the ceiling above.

With a roar almost as loud as the wandfire, Dauntless launched himself at the cellar stairs in a furious rush, the three remaining Purple Dragons right behind him. They were pounding down the steps even before the bloody, broken remains of their two comrades peeled free of the riven ceiling and fell wetly onto impaling splinters below.

* * * * *

Pennae struck the wands out of Yassandra's weak hands as they fell, and the wandfire abruptly stopped.

They hit the floor together, hard, the war wizard's body slamming down atop the wands, and out of long habit Pennae slashed Yassandra's throat open; for who knew what sort of spells a war wizard might have, to snatch herself back from the sword-edge of death? Mute mages hurled fewer spells.

Fearful and angry shouts rang out, deeper in the cellars—and no wonder; a sleeping man could have heard every instant of the wandfire! Pennae rolled hastily over to lie still among the bodies, dragging the dead war wizard atop her.

Feigning death was wisest until she knew who held sway down here. There! In the flickering corpse-light she could see a few crossbowmen coming cautiously into the room from somewhere deeper in the cellars, peering around with their poisoned-quarrel-loaded bows held ready.

Some jagged shards of wood fell from the torn ceiling, and a startled bowman fired a quarrel at their noise. It flashed past Pennae and down the room, thudding hard into an unseen wall . . . a wall of thick, damp wood, by the sound of that strike.

Heavy boots suddenly thudded across the ceiling overhead, moving in a hurry, and came charging down the cellar stairs.

Suddenly all the crossbowmen were firing.

* * * * *

Crossbow quarrels came leaping up out of the darkness as Dauntless and his Dragons plunged down the stairs; the ornrion scarcely had time to curse and fling up one armored forearm to shield his face before the swordcaptain beside him blurted out a sudden, wet snarl and fell over backward, a quarrel in his face.

Thrumming viciously, quarrels slammed into Dauntless, twice—thrice—if they'd been longbows, he'd be full of arrows already and likely dead. Another of his Dragons grunted, behind him; staggered but not transfixed by a striking quarrel.

"Down!" Dauntless roared, *"In the name of the King!"*

These foes would have to be taken down before they could reload and fire again; if there were more with loaded crossbows ready, it'd be just too bad for an ornrion called Dauntless.

Wherefore he flung himself recklessly down into the darkness, caring nothing for footing or dignity, sword reaching out. The crossbowmen would have to crank their windlasses like madmen to recock their crossbows, a noisy task that took time no matter how strong and fast they were, and then slap quarrels into firing-channels.

They knew they hadn't time enough, and flung down their crossbows to claw out daggers and short swords, even as the ornrion hurled himself off the stair to crash bodily into two of them and bear them to the cellar floor, bouncing hard.

"Murderers!" he roared. "In the name of the king, Azoun the Purple Dragon, I—urrkk!"

The punch across his throat temporarily silenced Dauntless, but the man who dealt it started dying an instant later, when the ornrion drove a dagger into his eye with brutal ruthlessness and rolled hard to his left, fully onto the second crossbowman he'd borne to the floor. By then, the other crossbowmen were coming for him with swords and daggers drawn. His Dragons rushed past to meet him.

"Aye," a crossbowman snarled, "that's just what we've been doing: murdering war wizards! And we should have no trouble at all with a few Purple Dragons!"

Then blade was clanging on blade, and the hollowness of that boast was swiftly apparent. The crossbowmen were fast and mean—but the Dragons were veterans of many an Arabellan alley-brawl, trained to work together in battle. They were bigger, stronger, and far more heavily armored. One Dragon grunted in disgusted pain as a sword slid through the leathers covering the joint above his left forearm, but that slight wound was the only harm the three soldiers suffered before the crossbowmen broke and ran, leaving four of their fellows dead.

Dauntless pounded after them, barking a command over his shoulder that left the wounded Dragon tarrying to slice all the bowstrings he could see. The ornrion caught another crossbowman before the staggering man could get out of the room with the stair, hewing him down from behind and trampling him without slowing.

The crossbowmen fled right at—and *through*—an apparently solid stretch of dark, cobwebbed stone wall. Dauntless plunged after them, right on their heels and hacking the air wildly on all sides to try to foil any slayers waiting for him.

There was a moment of tingling darkness as he passed through the illusory magic that cloaked the unseen doorway, and then he was in a lamplit room where startled crossbowmen fought desperately against other, hard-faced men with better swords and daggers, who'd been . . . yes, plundering the bodies of dead war wizards!

"You *dare?*" Dauntless bellowed, smashing his way right through a hapless crossbowman to get at the nearest of these new foes.

"Ha!" that man laughed, striking aside the ornrion's sword with the ease of a veteran swordsman. "Of course we dare! We dare anything for the glory of the Brotherhood! *Zhentarim triumphant!*"

One of the crossbowmen kicked the man's feet out from under him and stabbed him brutally as he toppled. Dauntless rewarded the slayer with a slash that half-severed his head and left it lolling as the dying man let out a wet, burbling squeal and collapsed atop the Zhent he'd just slain.

Dauntless ducked under the wild slash of a halberd—what sort of fool tried to swing such a weapon, in cramped chambers like these?—as Zhents and the crossbowmen—and whom did *they* serve, hey?—enthusiastically killed each other all around him. He saw one of his Dragons lay open the halberd-wielder's throat with a mighty, off-balance slash, and snarled, "Try to take one of the idiots who used the crossbows on us *alive!* I need some answers!"

"Commanded," First Sword Brauthen Haernhar growled in the usual Purple Dragon acknowledgment that an order had been heard and understood. He kicked a Zhent hard enough in the cods to lift the man off his feet, into a helpless plunge forward onto the Dragon's waiting blade.

The crossbowmen were all dead now, killed with swift ease by Zhents who were obviously disciplined, well-trained warriors. They must be Zhentilar at work here without their customary armor and spears, so as to avoid raising an alarm that would bring Baron Thomdor riding hard into Halfhap with several hundred mounted Dragons at his shoulders.

Which meant that whatever the fate of Lord Duskur Ebonhawk's plundered riches or the Knights of Myth Drannor, and regardless of Lady Lord Lhal's orders, Ornrion Taltar Dahauntul *must* survive this fray and get alive back to Arabel or to a moot with one of Baron Thomdor's patrols, so the Warden of the Eastern Marches swiftly learned of these Zhents. If the Zhentarim were in Halfhap, then they were in Arabel, too, or soon planning to be . . . and if ever Arabel fell to the Black Brotherhood, all northeastern Cormyr would become a lawless battlefield of marauding monsters unleashed by Zhents, orc and goblin hireswords let loose on every steading and hamlet, and all—

A Zhent lunge came within a shrieking bladewidth of finding the gap in his armor—and Dauntless found himself forced to lean into that lunge, almost embracing the steel seeking to slay him, as he parried a teeth-jarringly hard cut to the side of his helm, and needed room to interpose his own sword or risk decapitation.

He managed to avoid both blades somehow, reeling back out of that tangle of swords in time to see First Sword Brauthen coughing his way to the floor with a sword in his guts, clawing at it vainly and desperately as the Zhent wielding it laughed in triumph.

He should turn and flee, alone now in this room of Zhentilar, but Brauthen deserved to be avenged—for what good is a glittering kingdom, if it lifts no finger to help or seek justice for every man who dies for it?—and he was damned before the gods if he'd turn away when it was so *easy,* with Brauthen grappling the Zhent's blade, to spring to the side and slash open that laughing face as he did so.

So Dauntless killed that man, and the next, winning himself time to flee and turned—to discover the illusion of solid wall was in force on this side of the hidden doorway too!

He could not be sure where it was, and the blades reaching for him even now would give him no time for any sort of a search.

Then Swordcaptain Darasko Starmarlee, whom he'd left behind, wounded, to disable crossbows, burst suddenly through seemingly solid stone gaping in astonishment, with blade held high—but not high enough to properly parry the vicious swing from the Zhent who'd been charging to block off the ornrion's escape.

Starmarlee's jaw and throat exploded in gore, and the swordcaptain reeled helplessly forward, past Dauntless and under the knees of the Zhent leaping after him. Which left only Starmarlee's slayer between Dauntless and the way out.

It was a matter of swift and burning satisfaction to butcher that Zhentilar and charge past him, still hot with rage, back out into—

Utter darkness. There must be doors in the common room above that could be swung down over the stairs, and that thrice-cursed innkeeper must have closed them!

Locked them, too, no doubt, dragged a weight atop them, and gone to fetch weapons with which to greet the face of an ornrion straining to heave things aside and gain freedom. Well, his belt axe was a puny thing, meant more for kindling and smashing locks and hasps than for fighting, but if he had to hew through doors—or the cellar ceiling, elsewhere—he would. After killing every last Zhentilar down here, of course.

Dauntless had already stepped aside along the wall, out of sheer warriors' instinct, and turned to make ready to deal death to Zhentilar in the dark. Strike the first man down from one side, then get across to the other to await the second.

There! He thrust hard and low at the faint gleam in the darkness, and was rewarded by a snarl of pain and the heavy thud of a man falling precipitously to his knees. He drove his blade down into an unseen back, twisted it, and vaulted over the now-screaming man to the far side of the unseen door.

The second Zhentilar came through in a rush, with the third just behind him, both men veering sharply aside, in different directions, as they burst into the darkened room. Which meant one ran right onto the ornrion's waiting blade, and Dauntless was able to swing the impaled man around as a shield against the other. The man whirled at the sound of his comrade's sobbing gasp, charged toward the sound, stumbled over the Zhentilar Dauntless had already felled, and came blundering into his impaled fellow, whom he hacked and stabbed enthusiastically from behind. Dauntless waited until a deep slash left the man's sword stuck deep in the ribs of his dying fellow, and then stepped nimbly around to drive his dagger into the man's neck.

The man groaned loudly, as the last Zhentilar—unless there were more beyond those Dauntless had seen in the room—hurled a blazing leather glove through the illusory wall, and followed it with lit lantern in one hand and sword gleaming in the other. This let Dauntless see him well enough to act before the man caught sight of Dauntless behind the dying Zhentilar—or the two Zhentish swords Dauntless had just thrown at him.

The Zhentilar struck one blade aside with his lantern, but the second one broke it, plunging the cellar into darkness for the space of a breath or two, ere the warrior of the Brotherhood started to burn. Spitting curses, the Zhentilar staggered back, wildly waving one blazing, doused-in-lamp-oil arm in a vain attempt to extinguish the licking flames.

Dauntless devoted himself to plucking up and throwing every weapon he could find, a storm of tumbling steel that the raging Zhentilar struck aside with his own sword, roaring as the pain went on clawing at him, until he turned to stagger back through the hidden door, clawing at the fastenings of his own leathers.

Whereupon Dauntless bent, picked up the last sword, and brutally swept the Zhentilar's ankles out from under him, hurling the man head-first onto the cellar floor. The ornrion pounced and stabbed. He cut away a big piece of leather, laying bare the dying man's shuddering back and giving himself a torch of burning-edged leather cloaking the tip of his borrowed blade.

He retrieved his own sword from the Zhentilar he'd left it buried in and strode grimly around the room. Dare he try the stairs? Or should he seek another way out of these cellars? He gave the stairs a teeth-bared glare, then peered around at all the bodies and the—

There! Hanging from the back of the stairs! A lantern . . . two lanterns. Well-made, almost new candle-lanterns with sliding shutters and hot-hoods, the candles as thick as his wrists and shielded on three sides with bright-polished steel. Dauntless lit them both from the burning scrap of leather and thankfully let it fall to the stone floor.

Well, these made him a target, but bought him the chance to explore down here. And he'd best be about it. He hung one lantern from a ceiling-hook to light up the room, adjusted the other to shine a directional beam, and started past all the bodies, shaking his head at all the dead war wizards. Vangerdahast would blast this place clear over the Thunder Peaks when he found out.

Unless he didn't find out in time, and this end of Cormyr was all Zhentarim territory by then.

Which, again, meant one Ornrion Taltar Dahauntul *had* to get out of here and report back to Arabel. "*This* Ornrion Dahauntul," he muttered aloud. "There is no other."

He stalked past body after body, never noticing the lone eye watching him from under the sprawled and gory Yassandra Durstable, heading for whatever else awaited behind the stairs, besides lanterns.

There came a sound from overhead, of something heavy being dragged aside, and heavy footfalls. At the top of the cellar stairs.

Dauntless set down his lantern carefully, turned and raced back to the one he'd hung up, hooded and shuttered it but left it hanging, and raced back to the lantern on the floor. More bumps from overhead, as things were flung aside.

He shuttered the second lantern and hunkered down just behind it amid the bodies, shielding his face with one forearm and hefting his sword before letting it rest ready in his lap. Hopefully he looked dead.

If not . . . well, he'd die fighting a breath or two from now.

Whatever had covered the stairs was flung back, and light flared, floating down the stair in eerie silence. Dauntless peered over his arm.

A glowing ball of light—bright-glowing air, not flames—floated down into the cellar as silently as a falling feather, flying off into a far corner of the room, as boots struck the stairs. Lots of boots, belonging to dozens of Zhentilar warriors in full black battle armor, drawn swords and axes gleaming in their hands and one—no, three—Zhentarim wizards striding in their midst.

Gods bedamned above. Wizards!

He was going to die here. He was going to die now, or a breath from now. Well then, gods, Dauntless thought, see that *you* save Cormyr.

Chapter 14

Dead Wizards Dancing

Call up your mightiest spells, archmages,
For I would see stern high castles riven
Great dragons fall in flames from the sky
And dead wizards dancing.

Tethmurra "Lady Bard" Starmar
from the ballad
Raise High My Cup of Dreams
published in the Year of the Crown

The cellars end here," Jhessail said, running one slender hand along a dark, damp stone wall. "So unless you know a way to blast through solid stone . . ."

"This is it," Florin agreed. "We fight and die right here." Abruptly he put an arm around her, swept her against his chest, and kissed her cheek.

Startled, Jhessail looked up at him, heart quickening. She lifted her face to offer her lips for a real kiss, but he gave her a fond smile instead, let go of her, and murmured, "Come. Our holynoses need our aid. They're hurt worse than I'd thought."

Frowning, Jhessail did as he bade, silently turning to join Islif in binding torn strips of Doust's formerly grand tunic around the worst wounds Zhentish blades had dealt Semoor and Doust.

The two priests lay pale-faced and silent on the floor, staring up at the dark ceiling. Above them, Islif dripped blood on their chests from a wound of her own, but shook Florin's hand off impatiently when he reached for her. She'd stripped off her armor-coat so as to be able to move quietly, and her under-leathers were dark with welling blood.

"We," Doust husked, from beneath their working hands, "are a mess."

"A valiant mess," Semoor corrected him, faintly.

"*Next* time," Islif said grimly, "we go not chasing cellar routes so swiftly as to leave our healing potions up in our rooms."

"Next time, she says." Doust coughed, closing his eyes and shuddering as Islif's probing fingers found a broken rib in the gore all down his side. "Is Pennae still alive, d'you think?"

"That lass could steal the gods' undergarb right off their loins and get away clean," Islif said. "Worry not a whit about her."

Then she lifted her head sharply, listened, and hissed, "Not a sound! Someone's coming!"

The Knights were lying or kneeling in the dimness behind and below the golden heap of Dragonfire treasure with its ring of guardian swords, where the cellar floor fell away in two broad, descending steps, to end in a dark and mildew-reeking recess.

They fell tensely silent, hands stealing to weapons, as a lot of someones stealthily approached the heaped treasure from the other side. Someones that brought their own steady, unwavering light with them.

There were gasps of wonder, and muttered oaths of awe.

"Touch *nothing*," a man snapped, speaking with absolute authority, his cold voice startlingly loud and near. "This treasure's mere illusion—all of it—but the swords are real enough, and they fly and slay more surely than our best spells."

Jhessail was on her knees crouched over Doust, right at one end of the heap, and now risked silently moving her head to the side just far enough to let one eye peer past the glowing riches.

She found herself staring at a sphere of light, hovering above Zhentilar warriors in gleaming black plate armor with swords and axes in their hands. There were too many of them for her to count, crowded together gaping at the Dragonfire treasure, and three robed men stood among them. Wizards. Zhentarim wizards.

"Just illusion," the oldest mage agreed. "We've searched and scoured this place a dozen times since I was posted here. There's nothing—"

The young wizard beside him stiffened, something like a wisp of smoke encircling his head. Then the smoke was gone—*into* him—and he calmly drew his dagger, turned, and drove it hilt-deep into the oldest wizard's nearest eye.

Everyone shouted, the murderous young mage crumpled as that smoke arrowed out of his eyes—leaving them dark and staring pits—and the old wizard shrieked as he started to topple.

Three blades thrust deep into the young mage before he hit the floor. The smoke raced right at the last mage, who batted at it vainly, shouting out words of warding that seemed to echo and roll away across vast distances, despite the stone walls and dark ceiling of the cellar. Zhentilar lifted their blades in a ring to menace him—and Jhessail bit her lip to keep from gasping aloud as she saw a lone warrior appear in the doorway behind the Zhents, lurching forward like some sort of monster.

He was purple-skinned, bloated, and wept spumes of dripping foam from his eyes, ears, nose, and mouth. He had a wand in his hand.

It flashed, blasting Zhents into tumbling ruin before they could even shout. The warrior aimed the wand and triggered it again, smiling crookedly beneath unseeing, foaming eyes as more Zhents died.

Duthgurl Lathalance hated to miss a good fray.

* * * * *

Pennae rolled the body of the war wizard off her as she tugged the end of Yassandra's belt free. It was hung so heavily with interesting and useful-looking pouches, keys, and magical-looking tools suspended on thongs that she'd have no way of carrying all this plunder if she didn't bring along the belt that held them too.

It took but a moment to buckle that slender leather loosely around her hips, turn to give the ornrion a warning glare across the heaped bodies—he lay motionless, still feigning death—and then creep across the chamber, to see where all the Zhents had gone.

Her fellow Knights were somewhere beyond that doorway, and they'd need the help of all the Watching Gods to handle *three* Zhentarim, to say nothing of a small army of Zhentilar warriors—

From the other side of the doorway, men shouted in sudden, angry alarm, swords clanged, and there was a loud *whoosh* that sounded like magic. Someone screamed.

Pennae snatched up a fallen dagger from the floor and started to run. If she could hurl it at a Zhentarim wizard from behind, and mayhap stop him from crisping Florin with a spell—

She stopped in the doorway, stared open-mouthed in astonishment at what she saw, and then hurled herself back and aside, out of the way.

It was too late for a hurled dagger to save anyone.

✦ ✦ ✦ ✦ ✦

The ring of Zhentilar staggered back from the last wizard standing as a battlestrike blossomed from his fingers, its many glowing missiles leaping like darts to plunge sickeningly into their vitals.

Several of them turned to join the rush at the purple-skinned man with the wand, but others struggled forward again, determined to hack down the mage who'd commanded them mere moments ago.

He fed them another battlestrike, the searing magic missiles sending them reeling helplessly once more—but a hurled axe bit deep into the wizard's head and sent him staggering.

The Zhentilar who'd flung it sprang after it, pouncing viciously on the mage and bearing him to the floor, where the Zhentilar slit his commander's throat ere sawing at his neck. He didn't stop until the mage's head rolled free.

Over that Zhentilar's head the purple-skinned man's wand flashed repeatedly, spitting death at Zhent after Zhent as they charged desperately at it, the Dragonfire glow flaring to gloriously blinding brightness whenever wandfire touched it.

Zhent after Zhent toppled, but the wand-blasts suddenly waned into more feeble strikes, and a Zhentilar sword managed to reach and bite into the wand.

It burst in a small star of brief sparks, and the singing shriek of that sword exploding into shards.

Shards that butchered the Zhentilar who'd wielded it, the lacerated body tumbling apart in bloody cantels, and diced Lathalance's arm to the elbow.

Zhentilar roared in triumph and leaped forward, slashing and thrusting at the undefended purple warrior.

Seemingly heedless of pain, as blade after blade sliced into him, that lone warrior doggedly drew his sword and started to stab and hack them right back.

Jhessail winced more than once as the ruthless butchery unfolded. The purple-skinned warrior seemed heedless of his own doom, and dealt much death before he was overwhelmed, and swarming Zhentilar hewed his rotting body apart.

A wisp of smoke curled up from it like a rearing serpent, and out of long habit the Zhentilar drew back, for in the Black Brotherhood magic was not to be trifled with.

A second wisp arose from the remains of the beheaded Zhentarim commander, rearing up in like manner.

The two serpentine plumes of smoke seem to regard each other for a long moment, as if in converse—and then, as one, they turned and raced through the doorway, to arrow up the cellar stairs together.

With a ragged roar, the surviving Zhentilar charged after them.

* * * * *

As the last Zhentilar warrior—there were a dozen left, no more—pounded back up the cellar stairs, Pennae rose from among the old barrels and crates, darted along the wall, and slipped through the doorway, keeping low and moving fast.

Despite knowing what she'd find, the Zhent bodies were piled and strewn in such profusion that she almost overbalanced skidding to an abrupt halt. Beyond the heaped corpses the Dragonfire treasure glowed in unaltered splendor.

Pennae gave it a wry smile. Deceptive and deadly, like so much else in Faerûn.

Then she picked her way carefully past all the dead men, keeping to the walls and wending her way as quietly as possible, until she could round the far end of the treasure and see—

A sword, leaping at her face!

"Hold *hard,* there!" she hissed, springing back.

Islif gave her a level look from the other end of the sword. "Next time, *warn* me. We still have ears, you know."

"Yes," Pennae hissed, "but we're not the only ones still alive down here, even now! That cursed ornrion from Arabel is here! Alone, I think."

"Spew of the gods!" Florin growled. "He *does* love us, doesn't he?"

Pennae nodded sourly, and then peered more closely at all of the Knights. "Will our holynoses live, d'you think?"

Islif shrugged. "If we could reach our healing potions, I'd feel a lot happier answering that."

Pennae regarded her fellow Knight expressionlessly for a moment, and then tugged open her leathers to reveal her dethma of soft, well-worn leather. Her fingers sought something beneath the swell of her breasts, and tugged it forth: a gleaming steel vial, cork-stoppered and wax-sealed, with the shining sun symbol graven on it. One of the healing potions they'd gained from Whisper's hoard. She held it out to Islif.

Who frowned. "Where did you . . . ?"

"*I* don't go into battle without essentials," Pennae murmured.

Islif regarded her for a moment in silence, and then said, "Thank you."

Pennae shrugged. Then she looked along at the Knights again, nodded slowly, and asked, "Florin? If Jhess and Islif are enough to tend and guard the stricken, care to join me in trying to find a way up out of these cellars?"

Florin looked at Jhessail, and then at Islif, collected two slow nods, and said, "Yes." He hefted his sword. "I take it things have quieted down out there, in the rest of the cellars?"

Pennae grinned mirthlessly. "You could say that."

* * * * *

In the seemingly deserted common room of the Oldcoats Inn, Old Ghost and Horaundoon floated lazily in the shadows of the rail at the top of the cellar stairs, waiting for their next prey.

Not that they had long to tarry idle. Eleven wild-eyed Zhentilar warriors charged up the stairs, waving swords and axes and thinking of nothing more than getting away from whatever strangeness had just slain so many of their fellows—and three rather capable Zhentarim wizards to boot.

Old Ghost and Horaundoon slid into the foremost pair of Zhents as they gained the top step, made them smile at each other in grim satisfaction, and then compelled them to turn and strike at their fellows.

Amid shouts of fear and anger, battle broke out on the stairs. Zhentilar frantically hewed fellow Zhentilar, to avoid being penned into the cellars, and Old Ghost and Horaundoon darted into one warrior after another whenever anyone shouted for calm and "down swords!" Three Zhents died before the fray boiled up into the common room and across it, chairs and tables suffering greatly.

In the midst of all the shouting, screaming, and clashings of steel on steel, Ondal Maelrin and one of his maids came dashing down the stairs from the floors above, their arms full of steel vials, and raced across the common room, dodging furiously fighting Zhentilar.

"Our potions!" Pennae hissed, from her cautious vantage point partway up the cellar stair. "That thieving boar-pizzle of an innkeeper is stealing our potions!" She sprang up the stair, drawing her sword to keep company with the dagger in her other hand. Florin frowned, flourished his own sword, and charged up the steps after her.

Pennae went around and—with the aid of a handy table and a deft leap—over the black-armored Zhentilar, but Florin found himself under attack almost immediately. He struck his attacker's blade aside, kicked an inn chair up into the man's face, followed it with a hard punch to the cods that drove all the breath out of the man and lifted him back to a hard seat-first arrival on an inn table, and then struck the man's neck with a deft backslash. Then he was past, outrunning another Zhentilar to follow Pennae through a doorway on the far side of the common room into a room hung with tapestries, that held the shimmering blue fire of a magical portal.

In front of which the hastening innkeeper and maid had just come to an abrupt halt because someone was stepping through it, toward them.

Someone female, wounded, and alone, whose limp was unfamiliar to the Knights, but whose face was not.

Laspeera of the war wizards looked bleakly at Maelrin and the maid, and then past them at Florin and Pennae. Her face was as white as bone.

* * * * *

The coach rattled through the streets of Halfhap like a whirlwind. Its white-faced, shaking coachman whipped his galloping horses to go ever faster, despite merchants and shoppers diving and stumbling back out of the way, and the shouts and screams that soon had Purple Dragon patrols bellowing and waving at the coachman to stop.

The whip came down again, the trembling coachman now weeping in fear, as the coach smashed its way along the front of a fresh greens shop, baskets splintering and produce flying—and its burly proprietor made a furious grab for the hand-bars, to swing himself aboard.

The hard-faced man riding beside the coachman snatched a wand from his belt and coolly blasted the shopkeeper's red face to flying shards of bloody bone. Then he served two Purple Dragons, who were clawing at the bridles of the horses, the same way.

As their bodies tumbled under the racing hooves of the horses, the hard-faced man stood up, aimed carefully, and immolated the rest of the Purple Dragon patrol, one by one—as the coach raced on, heading for the Oldcoats Inn.

Inside the speeding coach, Zhentarim were being slammed from side to side, crashing into each other bruisingly.

The eldest wizard watched one of his younger fellows bite his own tongue—the third one to do so—and shook his head wearily. He had long since hooked one arm around a wall-rack to keep himself in one place, and was repeatedly using his feet to kick those about to slam into him away. As the curses and moans around him reached deafening heights, he snarled, "Oh, get down on the floor, all of you! Why the Brotherhood tolerates dolts such as you I *don't* know!"

The potion had been divided carefully between Doust and Semoor, who had both promptly gone to sleep, but gained color, looking more like living men lying on their backs and less like sprawled corpses. Jhessail had stopped frowning down at them and was now studying the glowing Dragonfire treasure and murmuring tentative incantations.

Islif watched her darkly, sword drawn, and murmured only one thing: "Just *don't* set those swords to striking at us."

Now, as Jhessail sat back with a weary sigh, shaking her head, Islif caught sight of movement on the far side of the glow, and fell into a crouch, sword drawn back to strike.

There came the sound of a lantern being unhooded, and then its light, moving slowly to where they could see it, well back out of sword-reach.

The lantern was lowered until they could see the grim face of Dauntless above it.

"Truce," he greeted the Knights. "I come in peace."

"Well," Islif replied warily, lowering her sword a trifle, "I guess there's a first time for everything."

Laspeera took two slow steps forward—and toppled like a felled tree, falling right on her face.

The innkeeper juggled vials for a moment so as to draw his dagger, hefted it flashing in his hand to turn it for stabbing, and bent down to slay this unexpected guest.

Then Ondal Maelrin made a wet, surprised sound as Pennae's dagger opened his throat from behind. He kept right on bending, down into his own face-first meeting with the floor.

Vials bounced and rolled as the maid threw up her hands and started to scream. Florin snatched one up and forced it into Laspeera with brutal haste, rolling her over and away from the innkeeper's spreading blood.

Pennae backhanded the maid across the face, ending her screams but sending her running wildly and clumsily to a tapestry, and through it and a banging door beyond. As the thief-Knight started scooping up potions, Laspeera started to cough and shudder under Florin's hands—and the pulsing blue portal flared brightly as more men in leathers, with swords and daggers in their hands, stepped through it.

"Gods, guts, and garters," Pennae cursed, "is there no *end* to them?"

Florin lowered Laspeera's head gently to the floor and sprang to meet these new foes—who were already trotting forward with unpleasant grins on their faces and swords reaching for the Knights. Six—no, seven . . . eight of them.

Pennae kicked the empty potion vial under the boots of the foremost bullyblade, who started to slip and flail his arms—and weapons—wildly, almost striking the man right behind him, who arched back and away with a curse. So when Pennae sprang at them both and then ducked down to strike their ankles in a swift and hard roll, they both toppled helplessly, entangling a third bullyblade and causing him to fall too. The fourth and fifth onrushing men crashed right into their fellows, with loud and startled curses, as Florin stabbed downed men as swiftly as he knew how, slashing those trying to scramble away across the foreheads to try to blind them with their own blood.

A breath later he was forced to leave off killing to deal with the sixth and seventh bullyblades, who'd rushed around the tangle to come charging at him from either side. The ranger ran at the one on his left, using his longer reach in a vicious slash that struck the man's parrying blade and spun him half-around—to where he tripped over a crawling Laspeera, and toppled helplessly into bouncing and rolling potion vials, as Florin launched himself back at the seventh man.

The man knew how to use his blades, and almost slew Florin thrice in the first few frantic instants of sword-strife. The ranger was only dimly aware of Pennae stabbing the eighth bullyblade in the stomach and then turning to slice open the throat of the only entangled man Florin hadn't dealt with, who'd struggled half-upright from under the bodies of his fellows. Then Pennae hurled her dagger at Florin's foe. It struck the man's neck hilt-first and bounced away without doing damage, but startled the man into an awkward sidestep. He turned his ankle, staggered—and ended that stagger staring and spitting blood, impaled on the point of Florin's sword.

Laspeera finished downing her second potion. Wiping her mouth, she looked up at the two Knights and murmured, "The queen chose well. You Knights are capable indeed. In a sword-brawl, at least."

The portal flared again, and Pennae groaned, "Oh, *no!*"

Laspeera lifted her hands to cast a spell—and then let them fall again as more men came crowding through the portal. More bullyblades—foes beyond counting!

Laspeera hastily started snatching up potions, and Florin sprang to join her.

"To the cellars!" he gasped, waving at the common room. "Stairs down—behind desk!"

Laspeera nodded and sprang up, moving as if completely healed and re-invigorated. She proved able to run almost as swiftly as Pennae, and so was in the lead as the three burst back out into the Oldcoats common room, with bullyblades hard on their heels, shouting for their blood and waving swords and daggers galore.

Wisps of smoke sped to meet those bullyblades, and two in the lead suddenly spun around and stabbed those just behind them. Amid screams and startled shouts, the running men stumbled over the falling bodies and crashed to the floor.

The few black-armored Zhentilar still alive in the common room turned to gape at these new foes and then moved grimly to engage them—as Laspeera and the Knights plunged down the cellar stairs.

Bullyblades roared defiance and sprang to meet the Zhentilar, who sneered and hacked at them, in a great crashing and clanging of war-steel.

A clangor that was echoed by a larger, louder crash that made the combatants blink and turn in suddenly bright, flooding daylight.

The front doors of the inn had just been blasted off their hinges and were tumbling across the room, shattering tables and then running bullyblades alike.

Outside, the astonished Zhentilar could see a wrecked coach on its side, with wheels still spinning and struggling horses shrieking.

Striding past it and up the inn steps into the room, through the huge hole where the doors had been, were nine Zhentarim mages. They were smiling cruelly, their hands already shaping spells.

Chapter 15

Sarhthor's Mightiest Spell

No mage should hesitate to use the right spell
No matter if it slay or diminisheth him.
Neither did Sarhthor, on that day
When wizards converged on Halfhap,
And a realm needed saving.

Baraskul of Saerloon
One Sage's History
published in the Year of the Tankard

The glow of the scrying crystal cast pale shadows around the dark room, and across Ghoruld Applethorn's watching face.

A face that was slowly acquiring a look of profound disgust.

"Just kill Laspeera," he murmured. "Is it *really* all that difficult?"

✦ ✦ ✦ ✦ ✦

"These thicknecks serve a few scheming Cormyrean nobles," the oldest Zhentarim wizard sneered, his left hand raised so as to keep all nine mages safe from hurled weapons behind his greatshield. He waved contemptuously at the bullyblades with his other hand. "Eliminate them."

He watched castings unfold around him, and at the right moment dropped his shielding. Spells lashed out from all eight of his fellow mages, howling across the common room in a bright, fell flood to rend men limb from limb, melt their flesh away from their spasming bones, hurl them into tables and pillars with shattering force, and cause their brains to explode bloodily out of their heads.

A few rushed desperately back toward the portal, only to stiffen and fall as they were struck by more than a dozen pursuing bright bolts each. A handful ran the other way and made it down the cellar stairs before they could be slain.

Up out of the foremost of those, arcing back up into the common room as two large, bright streamers of eerily glowing smoke, came Old Ghost and Horaundoon.

"What by the Nine Hells—?" one Zhentarim cursed, the rings on his fingers winking into life as he called up hasty wardings.

"Stop those—" the oldest wizard snapped, but that was as far as he got ere Old Ghost plunged into his chest and Horaundoon slid into the ear of the Zhent mage beside him.

Both men stiffened, rearing back—and then spun around and hurled the swiftest slaying spells they had at their fellow wizards.

Ghoruld leaned forward to peer intently into the crystal, anger and alarm flaring into warfare with each other across his face. "There it is again! What's *happening?* Someone's controlling those fools, yes, but who? And *how?*"

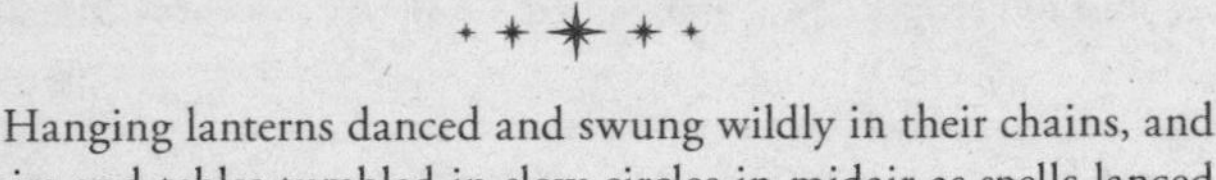

Hanging lanterns danced and swung wildly in their chains, and chairs and tables tumbled in slow circles in midair as spells lanced and sizzled, stabbing and flickering across the common room of the Oldcoats Inn.

Zhentarim wizards hurled spells not in power-duels or wary attempts to cow foes with a minimum of destructive Art. Rather, they struck to slay. Two of them did so uncaring of their own safety.

Wherefore Harlammus of Zhentil Keep, heart-high with the excitement of his first real Brotherhood foray, found himself lying dazed and blinking against a wall, with the splintered ruins of the table he'd just been hurled through on top of him, and a welter of broken legs and riven wood that had been its chairs tangled on top of that.

Trapped, barely able to breathe, and just beginning to be aware, through crawling numbness, of agonizing pains in his legs and gut, Harlammus frantically cast the new spell Eirhaun had taught him, the one that would alert his teacher that something had gone badly wrong in Halfhap, and the Zhentarim he'd sent there needed aid. Urgently.

"Master," he mumbled, when the spell was done, eyes refusing to focus on the splintered table leg standing up out of the bloody ruin of his gut, that rose and fell with his every gasp amid bloody bubblings, "Come swiftly, or . . ."

Then numbness claimed him. He never finished that thought, as he sank slowly into a nightmare world of racing wraiths and Zhentarim wizards turning on their fellows, of sinister cowled figures turning suddenly to grin at him with cold, ruthlessly gleeful faces out of nightmare, of beholders floating in the distance watching over everything and laughing . . . always laughing. . . .

* * * * *

The chamber was dark. It was always dark, save for temporary radiances of awakened magic. Magic was awake there now, a robed wizard lounging back in his chair studying spells in a tome.

Glowing runes floated in the air above the open pages of that book, runes that turned slowly and changed hue as he stared at them and murmured, seeking to understand them and shift them to his will. Their power aroused little crackling radiances, that danced and played along the edges of other tomes stacked nearby.

Sarhthor of the Zhentarim slowly rose from his lounging, leaning forward more and more intently as he started to understand this magic at last. Three seasons he'd struggled to master it, understanding four constructions of the Weave at once so they could be shifted and fitted together in combination—*thus*—and—

There came a chiming behind him that broke his unfolding glee and collapsed the spell in bright chaos above its pages. Sarhthor murmured a curse—just which one, he never knew—and leaned forward again, fighting to regain that fourfold understanding, that visualization that was just so, with every—

The chiming came again, shattering all and leaving Sarhthor blinking at the stack of tomes as the one he'd been perusing started to sink down, its floating runes fading. He cursed again, loudly and fervently, and spun his chair around to see what neglected duty of the absent Eirhaun had disturbed him *now*.

The teacher-wizard's desk bore a row of crystal balls, each resting on its own black cushion.

Except for one, that had winked into life and risen off its cushion, glowing and pulsing as it spun slowly. As he beheld it, it chimed again.

Sarhthor glared at it. Then his eyes narrowed and he rose suddenly up out of his chair like a storm wind to snatch up his untidy belt of wands. Buckling it briskly around his waist, he strode across the room to firmly shove the errant crystal back down into place—it chimed again, and then went dark—turn, and wink out, leaving the room entirely empty of wizards.

Thus abandoned, the books all went to sleep again.

* * * * *

The floor of the cavern glowed with runes Eirhaun would never have been able to conceive of. He stared at them hungrily as the beholders—tiny monsters, none of them larger than his own head—rose from crafting them to hang in the air and gabble and hiss among themselves, glaring at him from time to time.

He knew how contemptuously the eye tyrants regarded humans in the Brotherhood—all humans, probably even Lord Manshoon himself. These "little manyeyes" were doubtless little different than dogs. The small, yapping sort were always the most aggressive. And the most insecure.

Yet Eirhaun hurried not at all. He'd been invited to work this magic with them so that he could learn, and he had no intention of their rushing things to a conclusion so they could later dismiss him as "deficient of wits" when he couldn't work this spell himself under their coldly sneering scrutiny.

Ah, so *that* was how such power was leashed, and then twisted to achieve this rather than that. He nodded, trying to sear the runes into his memory, seeking that mental stillness inside himself wherein he could be certain of remembering all, and—

A chiming sounded within his head, startling him out of all concentration. No! Not now! Not when he was so close to—

The chiming rang again, loud and cheerful and insistent. Eirhaun clenched his teeth and growled out wordless anger, trying once more to frame the spell.

Abruptly he became aware that a beholder was hanging in the air right in front of him, glaring at him with its central body-eye. "Go," it hissed coldly at him. "You are summoned. Shirk not your tasks: Go."

Eirhaun opened his mouth to protest that another Zhentarim had been left on duty to respond to such a summons—and another chiming sound rolled out of it, loud and bright.

All twelve of the human-head-sized beholders were staring at him now. *"Go,"* they hissed in unison. "If you are loyal to the Brotherhood, go."

Eirhaun sighed, nodded, and murmured the word that would whisk him away.

Lord Eldroon set down his goblet. "Something's awry," he said firmly. "They were to report right back. We've been waiting now far too long."

Lord Yellander glared across the table. "You think I've not noticed? What's *taking* those dolts?"

Eldroon shrugged, rose, looked at Yellander, and went to the silently flickering portal. Yellander hastened to join him. They looked at each other, then drew their swords.

Together they stepped through the cold blue flames—and together gaped in astonishment at what they saw through the common room door.

Unseen men shouted, and a surging magic of tumbling velvet night shot through with roaring sparks flooded across the common room. They saw it wash over some support pillars and melt those stout timbers away.

Chairs and tables sighed into nothingness as the dark magic passed through them, rolling right on through back pantries, off to the left.

In its wake, daylight flooded the riven room, leaving them gazing at distant roofs in Halfhap.

With those pillars gone, the ceiling began to loudly groan and sag.

Yellander and Eldroon exchanged astonished, fearful looks—and hastily retreated back through the portal again.

* * * * *

Eirhaun found himself standing in the sunlight on the top step of the entry stair into the Oldcoats Inn, in Halfhap, staring through a blasted-open hole that had presumably recently been its front doorway. And blinking in astonishment.

Had all of the Brotherhood mages he'd sent gone *mad?* They were leaping around the room they'd obviously destroyed, hurling spells at each other! Well, he Bane-be-damned knew what would happen the moment they noticed him; they'd all turn on him. No one likes a ruthless, devoted-to-humiliation teacher.

But then, he'd never liked any of *them,* either. His shielding was singing around him now, fully up and working.

So Eirhaun allowed himself a smile of anticipation, raised his hands, and quietly and precisely cast the most powerful battle-spell he knew.

Had there been no spell-chaos roiling and grappling in the room in front of him, they'd probably all—or all but the two or three most accomplished, perhaps—perished as that spell smote them.

As it was, one burst apart like a rotten fruit, another burned like a torch, howling in helpless dying agony—and the others all staggered, turned with hatred in their eyes, recognized him, and started casting their strongest remaining battle-spells.

Eirhaun called up a magic in his mind that should slay one of them. He was still debating which one he should fell when half a dozen Zhentarim spells howled into his shielding.

And the world around Eirhaun briefly vanished.

His shielding flared into blinding radiance, searing whiteness that faded into rainbow hues. He was still struggling to peer through them when his legs started changing, bulging and flexing into amorphous bonelessness, all at once. The pain made him sob involuntarily, it was . . . so great, so horribly . . .

His shielding was going wild around him, as spells fought for supremacy within it. It was clawing at him, and he was still changing, barbed wings sprouting from his breast in a sickening struggling of knees and elbows that shouldn't be there, but were bursting out of him, sliding *through* his ribs . . . it was agony, it was terrible . . .

As he sank to his knees, or rather collapsed into wriggling tentacles, his ribs and all twisting into snakelike *things* that he stared at with revulsion, Eirhaun became aware that one of his eyes was growing very large and thrusting forward out of his face, while the other stayed its usual self and stared in horror. He also became aware that someone was shrieking in agony, long and raw howls and wails of agony and terror.

Then, at last, he became aware that the shrieking someone was him.

Which crystal had chimed had told Sarhthor where the trouble was. He had teleported to his favorite tower in Halfhap, intending to use magic to locate the precise location of the summons, but one glance across Halfhap had told him the Oldcoats Inn was the place to be.

Or rather, not to be. Frowning, he'd teleported again, to a spot he knew, right behind the hotel desk. He'd taken care to arrive crouching, and that thoughtfulness had served him well.

It seemed his arrival hadn't been detected, and his personal wardings had thus far passed unnoticed as he crouched in hiding behind the hotel desk—and warring Zhentarim blasted most of the Oldcoats Inn down into sagging, perilously hanging ruin in front of him.

He'd watched them, thrusting two tendrils of his shielding around the edges of the desk to serve him as eyes, and seen Eirhaun's arrival—and their unison attack on him. He harbored no love for Eirhaun—no one in the Brotherhood did, not that any Zhentarim dared allow friendship or kindness to weaken their schemes for an instant—but this . . . this was madness.

Something was afflicting these magelings, who hitherto had smoldered in waiting maliciousness, not daring to hurl their every spell as they were doing now. Something was forcing them to dare this much.

Wherefore that something had to be hurled out of the Realms, to protect all mages everywhere. If it cost the Brotherhood every last one of these ambitious magelings, what of it? Faerûn bred no shortage of ambitious magelings.

Frowning, Sarhthor spun a particular ring around on the middle finger of his left hand, until its customary display was beneath, and its band uppermost. He kissed that band, carefully murmured a word, and kissed it again.

Whereupon the ring spat itself off his finger, into his other (waiting) palm, and became a shield-shaped, rigid scroll. He touched two of its many runes in the right sequence to awaken it to life and make its words appear; when he could see them, he slowly and carefully cast the spell laid out before him.

Ere long his words boomed and rolled, forcing a hush over that battling room by the sheer weight of their power. Sarhthor spoke on, his body starting to shake from the power racing into and through it, streaming out into a roiling *something* that became a darkness in the air, a waiting, reaching darkness that plucked at the startled warring Zhentarim.

Then he finished the spell, completing the last gestures with nary a tremble. It was done, now, and the howling darkness of his creation snatched all of his fellow Zhentarim out of the shattered room before him.

The Abyss would take them; they would be whirled away into it, there to fend for themselves, hopefully taking that cursed something that was afflicting them with them.

The darkness was roaring now, hungrily, whirling away wild-eyed and shouting Zhentarim, and wispy wraiths that came clawing up out of the eyes and mouths of two of them too. Then Eirhaun, struggling to grow a tail and fins to go with his mismatched, feebly-flapping wings—was whirled up and away with a name on his lips.

"Sarhthor, curse you!" he cried. *"Ar auhammaunas dreth truarr!"*

And to his horrified and helpless fury, Sarhthor felt himself plucked up from behind the desk and snatched across empty, crackling air into his own waiting darkness.

The Abyss opened many-fanged jaws and hungrily swallowed them all.

* * * * *

Azuth, Mystra, and *fire in the Weave!*

It was the only curse Ghoruld Applethorn could remember in his blind agony.

His scrying crystal had burst in front of him, spraying his face with deadly shards.

He roared in pain, spewing out thick, choking blood as he reeled back, blinded and sliced open in a hundred places.

His limbs trembled uncontrollably; it was all he could do to stay on his feet. He shook from shock and pain, he knew, but also from fear.

Fear of the doom he'd so narrowly escaped. That awful pull of the Abyss . . . the bone-melting tugging that awakened yearnings he'd never thought he could feel, never dreamed of.

He could have been mind-ruined, or worse: snatched away to the Abyss forever, fair Cormyr and all his schemings lost to him in an instant, even the knowledge that he was Ghoruld Applethorn, and could work with the Art, torn from him.

He fumbled for the healing potions on their shelf, found them, and—wishing some of them were strong drink instead—started frantically uncorking and quaffing.

* * * * *

"What's going *on?"* Jhessail hissed, as the Knights cowered. Everything above them shook as if angry gods were beating on it with great clubs. Another shower of dust and small stones pelted down on and around them.

Florin shook his head, having no answer to give her. Pennae and Laspeera clung to his arms as he crouched over them, trying to shield them and knowing how useless his gallantry was. If the ceiling came down, they'd be entombed together, to gasp out their last breaths in the crushing dark . . .

The air around them felt *alive.* Crackling with unseen sparks, slithering and coiling restlessly.

"Magic," Pennae muttered, sounding disgusted. "But whose? And what?"

"Orders, Lady?" Dauntless growled, as if seeking reassurance. Tight-lipped, Laspeera merely shook her head.

As they all felt a sudden, horrible *tugging,* a compulsion that clawed at them and awakened a yearning to rise and drift up, up—Doust arched his back under Islif's hands, and groaned like a man lost in lust—a restlessness raged inside everyone, that made Jhessail whimper, and Pennae and the ornrion whisper soft curses.

All around the Knights, the darkness started to glow, radiances that outlined doors and formed great nets and curtains, like sparks frozen in the air.

"What—what is it?" Dauntless mumbled, eyes wide in wonder.

"Magic—all the magic that's down here, old wards and preservations and portals, too—shining forth," Laspeera said slowly. "But what could . . . ?"

She fell silent in startled awe as lights kindled deep in the stone walls around them, illuminations to match the Dragonfire illusion before them.

Nine swords, vertical with hilts uppermost, were glowing deep in the rock . . . and drifting soundlessly forward, *through* it, out into the air above them.

And from the illusory treasure, the nine glowing guardian swords drifted to meet them, right above the heads of the crouched and kneeling Knights.

Met, and then the illusions slowly faded into the nine swords that had come out of the stones. They promptly brightened into dazzling brilliance.

Laspeera, Dauntless, and the Knights of Myth Drannor all gaped up at this magnificence—deadly though it probably was—a mere handspan above their noses.

Then there came a great groan from overhead, a deep, thunderous complaint that heralded doom. As they tensed, huddled together, the Oldcoats Inn slowly, ponderously, and inescapably . . . collapsed onto their heads.

Chapter 16

The High Price of Entertainment

Some kings delight in seeing traitors die
Writhing in torment as the realm watches
And many subjects cower, not daring to decry.
Some wizards delight in enspelling all foes
Bringing down the nastiest dooms they can hatch
Twisting men into monsters in agonized throes.
But wise bards and sages turn away, grim
From such gloating; for the unfolding past tells
The high price of such entertainment a-glim.

Ambauree of Calimport
The Vizier and the Satrap:
Twenty Tales of Foible
published in the Year of the Highmantle

Many a shocked and staring eye in Halfhap saw the great black whorl erupt out of the walls of the Oldcoats Inn. Spitting black lightning, it spun slowly, like a gigantic drain of black swamp water being emptied, carrying the upper floors of the inn atop itself like a great cracked cap before it started to spin faster and faster, tightening in on itself until . . .

It vanished, the upper floors of the inn crashing down upon the ravaged ground floor, so that all collapsed into tumbling, smoking rubble.

The very air above Halfhap tingled, winking with half-seen sparks and shadows that echoed the turning of the vanished whorl for a few long, silent breaths ere fading.

Leaving the town gaping in stunned silence at the heaped rubble that had been the Oldcoats Inn, a great cloud of dust hanging thickly above it.

They did not have to regard unadorned rubble and slowly drifting dust for long.

There came a flash of white light, a winking that left in its wake a stout, bearded man who bore a great gem-headed staff. His robes were black, with a great baldric of interlaced purple dragons, and his face was grim and terrible.

Vangerdahast stood in the heart of the rubble and turned slowly, peering all around. Then he laid the fingers of one hand over the dragontail ring he wore on the other and called, "Laspeera? *Laspeera!*"

Silence fell; he cloaked himself in it and awaited an answer.

That did not come.

After a long and silent time the Royal Magician of Cormyr shook his head sadly and said to the empty air, "I fear we've lost her, Beldos. She's under half a building, right in front of me, and not moving or answering."

He threw back his head, and the watching folk of Halfhap could see that his face was wet with tears.

Suddenly someone else appeared, standing in the street in front of the Oldcoats front arch, on cobbles that had been empty a moment earlier.

The few Zhentilar who'd been standing uncertainly around a wrecked coach stepped hastily back, straightening to attention with terror on their faces. Ignoring them, the tall, darkly handsome wizard impatiently waved a hand and murmured something—banishing the cloud of dust in an instant.

Vangerdahast whirled around, black robes swirling, and the staff he raised glowed with threatening magical fire. "Begone!" he thundered. "This is Cormyr. You shall not prevail here! Get you hence, Lord of the Zhentarim!"

Manshoon merely sneered at him, causing some of the Zhentilar to chuckle—but their lord went abruptly expressionless when a long arm sent Vangerdahast staggering aside, and the owner of that arm stepped forward.

Few in Halfhap had ever seen Khelben 'Blackstaff' Arunsun, but there was little doubt as to who they were staring at, when they beheld a wizard as tall as a black pillar, with what could only be *the* Blackstaff floating upright in the air above his head, pulsing menacingly.

Khelben glanced at Vangerdahast. "Put that toy away," he said quietly, lifting a finger to indicate the gem-headed staff.

Without waiting for a reply, he turned to Manshoon. "Well? We both know you're a fool, but here and now you can answer a question you and I have both been pondering for some time: Just how *much* of a fool are you?"

Manshoon raised his right hand—and a ghostly arc of beholders appeared above his own shoulders. The watchers all gasped, though they could clearly see sky through the gently writhing tentacles and bodies of the floating eye tyrants.

"I guess," the Master of the Black Brotherhood said silkily, "we're just going to have to see."

There came a sudden thunderclap of magic that shook the sky, staggered Manshoon and Khelben—and made the folk of Halfhap gasp anew. The Blackstaff, the ghostly beholders, and all the staring Zhent warriors were simply . . . gone.

"So it's come to *this?*" a disgusted voice asked, from just behind Manshoon. "Spell-slinging in the streets?"

The Lord of the Zhentarim hastily sprang away from that voice and spun to face it—in time to see Elminster shaking his head, and wearing the face of an elder priest saddened at discovering novices indulging in sinful foolery.

"Spell-slinging in the streets," Elminster added sadly, "is *my* style, gentlesirs. *Ye* are all supposed to be 'grander,' more puissant, more mindful of the implications of what ye do, more . . . mature."

"Pah! Goddess-lover!" Manshoon hissed, fear and hatred making his words spittle.

Elminster shrugged and hissed back in perfect mimicry, "Lover of none but self!"

Khelben had been gaping up at the empty air where the Blackstaff had been. He now lowered his gaze to ask Elminster in a voice more dumbfounded than angry, "How did you *do* that?"

Elminster acquired an impish grin. " 'Tis called magic."

Khelben glared at him. "Where is it? I can't feel the link! *Where's my staff?*"

"Waiting for ye at home," Elminster replied mildly. "Ye should join it."

"Leave, all of you!" Vangerdahast cried, stepping forward and brandishing his staff. "*I* hold sway in Cormyr, and this soil is under the protection of the Purple Dragon! Leave! Depart! This—this is not done!"

Khelben, Manshoon, and Elminster all regarded him with silent scorn, and Vangerdahast swallowed, shrank a step or two back, and cowered.

"We'll speak of this later," Khelben said coldly to Elminster—and vanished.

As if that had been a cue, Manshoon strode forward. "One Chosen of Mystra flees the field," he sneered. "Does the other self-styled servant of the Goddess—such empty titles may scare children, but they are naught but words, old man, and you know it as well as I do—care to match spells with me?"

Elminster regarded the fingernails of his left hand, and said mildly, "Ye have thirty-nine spare selves in stasis, but two are damaged. If ye inhabit them, ye'll go insane, trapped in a body that obeys ye not, and leaves mastery of any magic beyond ye." He looked up. "Two chances, out of thirty-nine. Ah, but which two?"

Idly stroking his beard, he started to stroll closer to Manshoon. "There's no way for ye to tell, without stepping into the abyss that awaits ye."

He was almost within Manshoon's reach now, and still stepping closer. "Or shall I change those odds? Damage another—or another dozen? Or all of them?"

"You bluff!" the Zhentarim snarled.

"No. I promise." Elminster unconcernedly turned his back on the tall Master of the Black Brotherhood, and started to stroll away again. "Just as my title is not a fiction, Manshoon, neither is what I say of thy clones. It alarms ye that I even know their number. Shall I now recite exactly where each is hidden—whilst my Art carries my words to the ears of every last Zhentarim and Banite of thy Brotherhood, from the High Imperceptor to the novice Brother Thanael, who trembled through his blood-oath to join ye but two nights ago? Shall I tell Fzoul the wordings of thy pacts with the eye tyrants—*all* of them, even that which involved thy mating with—"

"Enough! Speak no more! Be still!"

"Easily enough done, *if* ye quit this place and work no magic nor scheme directly against Cormyr, its Royal Magician, its rulers, or its territory. Seek to subvert or bring about the death of an Obarskyr, Manshoon—or do anything more in Halfhap—and I will deal with ye. Permanently."

He turned to face the Zhentarim once more, smiling, and added softly, "Thy schemes entertain all Chosen, but we can find others to afford us such entertainment. Mystra can show us *everything*. So think on this calmly, and as the merchants on thy own docks say: 'consider well, and cut thy losses.' "

Manshoon snarled wordless fury, spat in Elminster's direction, and vanished.

Leaving Vangerdahast and Elminster looking at each other.

"What . . ." The white-faced Royal Magician of Cormyr swallowed hard, ere he managed to whisper, "What dare I say to you?"

Elminster lifted one bristling eyebrow. "Ye could try the two most appropriate words in all Faerûn, lad: Thank ye."

"Thank ye—you," Vangerdahast whispered, so softly that his voice was almost soundless.

Elminster clapped him on the shoulder like a kindly old uncle. "Now, was that so hard? Ye'd best leave this place and get back to work: ye have a worm in thy bosom to find and slay. Ah, before 'tis too late, as the bards say."

"A—a worm? *You know who the traitor is?*"

" 'Traitors are,' " Elminster corrected kindly—and vanished.

Leaving Vangerdahast to stare at where the Old Mage of Mystra had been standing and let loose a string of heartfelt oaths that made the Purple Dragons now hastening up to him grin in admiration—and the wealthiest Halfhap merchant's wife hurrying up behind them drop her jaw in scandalized outrage.

She was just drawing breath for her first blistering words when the Royal Magician's gaze fell upon her.

"Later," he snapped, before she could say a word. Then he, too, was suddenly gone.

* * * * *

A raging Manshoon appeared at the center of the magnificent dark star carpet in his bedchamber, strode across the room like a storm wind, and slammed his fists into the splendid wood panelling beside the door as if trying to batter it right through the stone wall behind it, out into the passage beyond.

"Entertainment?" he roared. *"I'll* show him entertainment!"

Whirling around, he stalked back across the room to his spellbooks, viciously backhanding The Shadowsil out of the way as she came hurrying through a side-door, worry on her face and a wand ready in her hand.

Snarling, Manshoon jerked down one heavy tome, and then another. They thundered down onto his polished desk, he flung them open—and stepped back in horror as a body appeared out of nowhere, sprawled faceup atop them.

Though it had the semblance of an intact corpse, The Shadowsil's gasp told Manshoon he wasn't imagining what he'd just noticed. The dead man's head, torso, arms, and legs were all neatly arranged, in their proper places, but were in fact severed, separate pieces, all slowly oozing dark gore all over his most precious grimoires. He'd already recognized the face. Himself.

As Manshoon stared down at his clone, its lips moved and Elminster's voice issued from them, saying, "Aye. Entertainment."

* * * * *

The air was thick with dust, and the coughing, choking Knights, Laspeera, and a tattered and dusty Dauntless all lay in a heap, entangled with each other. The ceiling no longer groaned and shivered into shards—but it now hung just above them, nowhere more than waist-high, held up on the points of nine floating, glowing swords.

Pennae eyed the Dragonfire swords longingly. They were so close that she could easily have stroked the golden sheen of three of those blades from where she lay. Yet it was obvious that trying to take even one might well cause a collapse, and death for everyone.

She sighed. "*Now* what?"

Half-pinned beneath her, Florin lifted a long arm to point down their low-ceilinged prison at one of the doorways that had been outlined in sparks by the awakening of the Dragonfire magic. It was the only portal not now walled away by rubble, and it continued to twinkle, wavering slightly as they stared at it.

"We take the only way out," the ranger-Knight said, "and hope for the best."

Jhessail shuddered. "And if it leads into somewhere alive with snarling beasts? Or wizards hurling spells at us?"

Florin shrugged. "I haven't avenged Narantha yet," he said softly. "So I *cannot* die. Wherefore, if you keep behind me, you should be safe."

Jhessail stared at his eyes and shivered.

Florin looked up and down the tangle of Knights and Crown folk, and pointed again at the portal. "I say again: we chance the portal. Now."

"And we don't even *touch* any of those swords," Islif added, looking at Pennae. "Not one, and not even for an instant. So shift your selves carefully. Let's *move.*"

"Our holynoses?"

"Drag them. Gently."

Semoor groaned theatrically. "Oh, yes. 'Drag me. Gently.' *Wonderful.*"

"Upon second thinking," Islif said, "bring Doust and leave the noisy one behind to guard these valuable magic swords. We should be able to return in a year or so. He won't lack for entertainment, nor starve; he can chew on his own words."

"Drag me *please,*" Semoor pleaded, quickly.

"Aye, I'll drag you," Dauntless growled. "Lady Mage?"

Laspeera had seemed senseless, but her eyelids fluttered as he shook her gently. "Lady Laspeera? Lady of the war wizards?"

She gasped, opened one eye, winced and gasped again, and finally murmured, "I-I'll be all right. My *head* . . . someone just cast spells, up above us, that smote my head like a hammer."

"Oh?" Semoor asked brightly. "You've been smitten with hammers before?"

"Yes, Holy Wolftooth," Laspeera replied, "I *have.* If it's a sensation you're seeking to know firsthand, I'm sure Ornrion Dahauntul can oblige you, when we reach a place that has a hammer."

"And room enough to swing it," Dauntless grunted, as they crawled down the chamber, clambering through the rubble until they could pass—one by flaring one—through the waiting portal.

Dauntless found himself at the rear of this undignified journey, with his leathers in tatters and all trace of anything that might have been deemed a Purple Dragon uniform all but gone. Though he was behind everyone, Laspeera turned in front of the portal, frowning, and waved him through.

He hesitated. "Lady? Is this wise?"

"Disobeying my orders?" she muttered, eyes catching fire. "No, not wise at all, Ornrion Dahauntul!"

He nodded, bowed his head wordlessly, and crawled past her into the waiting, silent fire.

Laspeera sighed and shook her head. It was by merest chance she'd happened to remember the potions. Gods above, was this the beginning of getting old?

No matter. *That* could be worried about later. Right now, she had to crawl back, paw around in the rubble to find them, and bring them along.

"Doing what is needful and best for the realm," she murmured, smiling wryly. "Just as I do every day." She winced her way over some knee-jabbing fragments of stone. "Well, 'tis a life."

With one arm cradling potions, she turned once more to face the waiting portal, crawled a little way, and then stopped and looked longingly up at the nearest Dragonfire sword, floating so near, its glowing point so close overhead.

Upon a whim she silently reached for one. Its glow blazed up as if in welcome as her long fingers got close . . .

Then Laspeera of the Wizards of War shrugged, smiled, shook her head, drew her arm firmly back, and used it to crawl steadily through the portal.

✦ ✦ ✦ ✦ ✦

Lord Prester Yellander stood at the back door of his hunting lodge, and stared out into the depths of the Hullack Forest, at a wild and familiar beauty that didn't seem to hold any answers.

Ignoring the questioning looks the swordjacks guarding the door were giving him, Lord Yellander hauled the door shut, dropped its bar into place for good measure, and turned back to face Lord Blundebel Eldroon.

"I *still* don't know what to do now," he snapped, waving an angry hand. "So speak. 'Confer with me worriedly,' as the writers-of-plays say. *Everything* seems to be going wrong."

Lord Eldroon said, "I have little comfort to give. You saw what I saw."

The two nobles exchanged grim looks. Both of their Halfhap portals now opened into sagging, splintered-wood ruin. It seemed the Oldcoats Inn had been destroyed. Purple Dragons wading in that rubble had seen and shouted at the bullyblades Yellander and Eldroon sent through the portals to learn more. Those blades had hastily returned, but there was no telling how soon Purple Dragons might—would—come flooding into the hunting lodge through those portals.

"We must put this all behind us, or our heads and shoulders will soon want for each other's company," Yellander muttered. Then he clapped his hands, drew himself up briskly, and went back to the door.

"Brorn, Steldurth: Bring *all* the lads in here! At once!" he barked. To Eldroon's silent, questioning look, he murmured, "Later."

When his four-and-ten surviving bullyblades were assembled, Lord Yellander crisply directed them to heap the furniture in the room into two long barricades well out from the walls, facing the two portals both before and behind.

"Poisoned bolts," he commanded. "You are to await and fell anyone coming through these magical ways except Lord Eldroon or myself—or anyone with us, *if* we tell you to refrain from slaying them. Keep at this duty in shifts, until I order you to cease, even if that's a tenday or more hence. Use the other rooms to sleep, eat, and cook. Keep hidden behind the barricades when in this one, and keep all doors closed. If Purple Dragons come to the outer doors, you know not where I am, and are guarding these portals—which just appeared, startling myself and the Lord Eldroon very much—for the safety of the realm, awaiting our return with war wizards to deal with them. You've never been through them, you don't even want to go near them, and you don't know where they lead."

Collecting their nods of obedience, Yellander nodded curtly back at his men and turned away, tapping Eldroon's forearm in a silent direction to walk with him.

Together they strode through the door that led into a retiring room, and thence to Yellander's bedchamber. As the door swung shut behind them, Yellander silently directed Eldroon to help him lift and set into place its inner door-bar, as soundlessly as possible.

Then he hurried into the bedchamber, turned immediately through a door to enter the adjoining jakes, and turned again to pass through a small door into a wardrobe. Eldroon followed silently, following Yellander down a dark row of hanging cloaks, breeches, doublets, and boots, to a sliding panel at its end that flooded the wardrobe with cold blue light. There was just room in the cubicle beyond for them both to stand, breast to breast, without touching the portal itself. Yellander slid the panel closed again.

"Where?" Eldroon whispered, jerking his head at the cold blue fire so close to them.

"Suzail. Where we've been these last two days, engaged in the longest and most fascinating game of castleboard either of us has ever played."

"Ah. Are we off to slay Crownsilver?"

Yellander lifted an incredulous eyebrow. "While he can still play the guilty traitor responsible for all? Far from it!" He inclined his head toward the panel they'd just come through and murmured merrily, "Truly, 'tis amazing, in a realm so well governed and so strongly held, the sort of thieves, ravagers, and blackguards that so swiftly infest the private hunting-lodge of even the most upstanding noble in their absence, and work lawless deeds so evil as to verge on treason!"

Eldroon smirked.

Yellander's reply was a shrug and the words, "Or so my tale runs, as I stand staunchly behind it!"

The portal swallowed him, then did the same to Eldroon an instant later.

Wherefore neither lord heard the door of Yellander's bathing chamber open in the next moment, and a fully restored Ghoruld Applethorn step out of it, wearing a crooked smile.

"Yes, you oh-so-clever conspirators," he murmured. "Run to your spies at court, to see how many war wizards have fallen. And so present yourself to Vangerdahast as the traitors he's looking for. And while he's gloating over you . . ."

He grinned broadly, strode across the bedchamber until he was as far as he could get from Yellander's private portal, and teleported away.

Chapter 17

The Knights Go to War

Oh, but the realm should tremble
If ever the Knights go to war.

Ilmdrar of Zazesspur
Dreams of a Dark Future:
A Sage's Visions Regarding Fair Tethyr
published in the Year of Shadowed Blades

"Keep moving," Florin murmured, as Dauntless strode out of the blue fire, found himself in a dank, utterly dark stone passage somewhere underground, and faltered. "Two paces. That should give Lady Laspeera room enough not to run into you."

Dauntless growled agreement and took his two paces. He could tell by the warm ghost of breath that someone was standing near him. He wrinkled his nose, breathing in leather and a faint whiff of sweat. She-sweat, coming from someone as tall as him. Islif. "So, where are we?"

Islif said not a word, but Semoor offered brightly, "Somewhere underground and dark." His voice sounded as if he was slumped against the wall a few paces on. Or lying on the stone floor.

Dauntless growled again, letting a little of his anger into it.

"Somewhere utterly unfamiliar to us," Jhessail said quickly, from beyond Semoor. "I can give us light, but Lady Laspeera's magic may be far better than—"

The cold blue fire flickered again. Laspeera stepped out of it, stopped, and asked calmly, "Where are we?"

"I was hoping you might be able to help us with that," Florin said, from beside her. "Jhessail can give us light to see by, but if you've a spell that would serve better . . ."

"No. Jhessail, please do."

The casting was simple, and when it was done two spheres of flickering light appeared above Jhessail's palms. She willed them to the ceiling—damp, of large fitted stone blocks, and low overhead—and sent them past herself a little way, showing them all a long, straight passage lined with well-dressed stone. Then she sent them bobbing past the Knights in the other direction, veering around either side of the portal and on, to illuminate more of the same.

"Very exciting," Semoor commented. "Not quite the thrill the inn became, but—"

Laspeera handed him a potion, and another to Doust. "Your healing potions," she murmured. "Drink, everyone who stands in need."

When Islif shook her head, the war wizard's voice sharpened. "In the name of the Crown of Cormyr, Islif Lurelake, I *order* you to drink one of these. Stubborn heroes are usually soon too dead to accomplish anything."

Islif nodded, took the proffered potion, and drank.

"Still dark, dank, and utterly unfamiliar," Doust commented, looking down the passage. "So, where are we?"

An instant later, Florin snapped, "Pennae, *get back here!*"

Behind their backs, beyond the portal, the thief-Knight had been softly walking away down the passage, but at Florin's command—and the approach of Jhessail's dancing lights that followed—she stopped, turned, put one hand on her hip, and gave Florin a look that wasn't quite expressionless. "And you became my keeper *when?*"

"Pennae," Islif said, "we've talked about this. When we know not where we stand, we stay *together* until we're agreed on what we'll do."

Dauntless chuckled, and Pennae favored him with a withering look.

Laspeera smiled. "Pennae—no, all of you Knights of Myth Drannor; I'm well aware of your charter and your oaths that accompanied it. Yet I must hear truth from you, here and now: Are you loyal to the Crown of Cormyr?"

"Lady," Florin replied, "we are."

"I know your loyalty well, ranger," Laspeera replied, "but I have yet to be convinced as to that of some of your fellows. You, thief-lass?" Her eyes were steady upon Pennae. When Pennae's gaze became a challenge, Laspeera let her eyes drop meaningfully to the things that had been Yassandra's, now hanging from Pennae's belt, and then stared up into Pennae's eyes again.

"I have sworn an oath," Pennae said stiffly, "and I stand by it."

"Good. Priests?"

"Forgive me, Lady Laspeera, but my first loyalty is to the divine," Doust said, "and my second to my fellow Knights. My third is to the Crown of Cormyr."

Semoor added, "Those words are mine, too."

Laspeera nodded. "Honestly said. Wherefore I'll not try to arrest or thwart you, Knights, and instead tell you we are standing in what's called the Long Passage, a way that runs under the courtyard between the Royal Court and the Palace, linking secret passages within the walls of both buildings. It is guarded at both ends, at all times, so you'd best stay with me—and Ornrion Dahauntul."

"You step into a bare stone passage, and know where it is?" Semoor demanded suspiciously. "Or did you know all about the portal we just came through?"

"I did not. I can, however, feel the wards all around us, and they are as familiar to me as your childhood homes undoubtedly are, to you. The portal is part of them, so long unawakened that I was not aware of its existence. It is fading back into invisibility already. See?"

They all looked, and saw.

"So we're in Suzail," Doust mused, "somewhere between the Palace and that huge stone pile of offices and audience chambers and more offices that stands in front of it. And presumably we're in trouble for not staying out of the realm." He looked up the passage, and down it again. "So which way is the Palace, and which way is the Court?"

Laspeera pointed in the direction Pennae had been heading. "Palace."

Jhessail's dancing lights moved smoothly a little way past the thief-Knight, farther down the passage Laspeera had pointed along than they'd been before, revealing to the Knights that there was a bend in the passage . . . and something written low down on the wall there.

Something fresh.

Pennae hastened to it, peered hard at it and then at the wall across from it, and said, "Oho." Then she turned and started trotting back to rejoin the Knights.

Laspeera smiled. " 'Oho,' indeed. Yes, Pennae, the treasury vaults are somewhere behind us. Before you race off in search of them, know this: the guardians of those vaults were old and wise a thousand years ago, and they can destroy any of us with casual ease."

Semoor looked interested. "Even the Royal Magician?"

"If he's not careful. Just now he's being *very* careful: he's hunting *you*. Now, have I your word that you'll peacefully accompany me to where I can translocate all of you safely to Shadowdale, right now, or am I going to have to—"

Pennae launched herself into the air, hurling herself right at the war wizard. Dauntless stepped forward to clutch at her, but she kicked his hands aside—and slapped Laspeera's face as she hurtled past.

The war wizard reeled, threw up her hand to the spot of blood now welling up on her cheek, and murmured a little sadly, "Poison?"

"Sleep venom," Pennae said tenderly, lifting her hand to display a fanged ring on the inside of one finger.

Laspeera nodded—and toppled over. Florin caught her, even as Dauntless cursed and clawed out his sword.

Pennae sprang back at the ornrion, and did a handstand right in front of his reaching blade to arch over in the wake of his swinging steel and kick him in the face.

Shaking his head and growling, Dauntless grabbed at her knee to haul her down.

Pennae slapped twice at his hand as he hauled at her, but he twisted away to protect his face and managed to kick her arm aside, winning himself room enough to pluck her up by breast and back of knee—and charge her hard into the passage wall, putting his shoulder into her.

Pennae gasped as something snapped wetly—Jhessail shuddered—and the ornrion ground her against the unyielding stones. Half-hidden behind his bulk, the thief-Knight sobbed.

"You little bitch," Dauntless growled, waving his sword wildly to keep the other Knights at bay. "If you've harmed Lasleeer-aaahhh . . ."

As his voice trailed off into gurgles, he sagged down the length of Pennae's body to the floor. By the time he reached her boots, he was snoring.

Pennae kicked herself free of him and went to Laspeera in Florin's arms, wincing as she bent over to snatch the last few potions from the war wizard's belt. Drinking one, she thrust the others through her belt.

"Pennae," Florin snapped, into her sweating face, *"what have you done?"*

"Won us a little time to rescue the princesses!" Pennae blazed back at him. Then she looked from Knight to Knight, and raised her voice. "Listen! There's a conspiracy to kill Lord High-and-Mighty Vangerdahast and the king, *and* the queen—and I'm beginning to think all the war wizards except Vangey are in on it! See that?"

She pointed down the passage, at where the words were written on the wall.

" 'Leak here,' " Semoor said slowly. "Doesn't look as if anyone's obeyed it yet . . ."

"Ha-ha. Look yon, across from it. Any writing there?"

"No."

"Good. This side is one wizard saying he's ready. If there were another 'Leak here' yonder, it would mean the other wizard was ready, too, and to start it all by grabbing the princesses. Well, we've got to stop it! You heard Laspeera: Vangey's hunting us. Well, the Royal hrasting Magician doesn't hunt with dogs or riders in the forest: he hunts with *spells*. I want him off my well-rounded rump *now*—and henceforth. You saved the princess! That ought to be worth *something*! If we can get to the queen and get her to order Vangey off our trail and work with us, mayhap we can stop this treason."

"It'll be one more order he disobeys," Semoor said sourly. "That man is a law unto himself."

"Well, then," Pennae said angrily, "isn't it time we were too?"

✦ ✦ ✦ ✦ ✦

Faerûn holds many deep, dank stone chambers.

Chambers beyond counting, most built by hands now forgotten and crumbled to dust, many for purposes now unregarded. A man may spend a lifetime just visiting the rooms that are safe to enter, free of hauntings and monsters, and those not guarded by the jealous vengeance of kings and rich merchants, who regard every visitor as a thief bent on stealing what they have hidden down there.

Even an elder elf or a tireless dwarf may exhaust their days before seeing and counting all such chambers, even if they limit themselves to those no more deeply buried than the buildings most men dwell in rise above that ground.

Yet Faerûn is large enough to hold them all, without complaint and with very few murmurs.

Consider just one such chamber. This one had a war wizard in it, rushing around alone. He is working, placing crystal balls on black stone waist-high plinths and chalking circles around them, which he then links back, with carefully chalked lines, to a central circle. And as he works, in the way of many wizards who trust no one but themselves—and perhaps not even that—he is talking to himself.

"First Vangerdahast must fall," Ghoruld Applethorn murmured aloud, carefully touching up a ragged edge of his latest chalked line. "And then the Obarskyrs."

"Alaphondar and half a dozen Highknights have come to consult with me," a sharp, exasperated male voice announced suddenly from the empty air above his head, "and I can't get away to write 'Leak here' on anything. So take it as written. Do it now!"

"I hear!" Ghoruld replied loudly, and he glanced over at the one crystal that was awake.

A bright scene was shifting in its depths. He strode over to it, folded his arms, and watched.

"Yes," he said, murmuring to himself again, the smile that was growing across his face repeatedly threatening to twist into a sneer. "Vangey's closing his net around them now."

He turned away and went to the door, letting the sneer take hold. "Gloat over them long enough, Old Goat," he told the door as he swung it open, "and my spell will be ready. And every scrying crystal in all Suzail will explode, and behead anyone looking into it, upon my signal. It's a pity your self-importance demands you surround yourself with eight or nine crystals. There won't be enough left of you for them to find and bury."

Pennae raced down the Long Passage like a storm wind in a hurry to catch up with its gale. The rest of the Knights pounded after her.

"So just where are we heading?" Islif demanded, putting her shoulders down and really starting to move.

"Well, if Laspeera was honest with us and the Palace *is* this way," Pennae panted, racing along just ahead of her, "we have to get past the guards and up out of its cellars into the Palace proper. The royal wing is at the back and on the east side, overlooking the gardens."

"I was, ah, talking with one of the maids, once," Semoor gasped, "and—well—aren't all the secret passages inside the Palace guarded too?"

"Yes," Pennae said sweetly.

"We'll have to change *everything,*" Lord Yellander muttered, a step ahead of Lord Eldroon as they hurried along the hallways of the Royal Court. "There's no way we can take shipments through Halfhap with every jack and brat in the town crawling all over the inn ruins, gawking."

"True, true," Eldroon agreed, nodding and wagging his forefinger as if it were a sword. "The heart of it for us right now, though, is how much do the war wizards know about us? That's what Ruldroun'll know—but we've got to get in and out fast, in case old Thunderspells already has them all looking for us!"

Yellander nodded grimly. They ducked through a door, stopped in the side passage beyond immediately and faced another door on their right, opened it, and stepped into the usual gloom.

"Ruldroun?" Yellander said into the darkness. "The raven hunts at twilight."

All around them, darkness fell away in a sudden blossoming of bright white, magical light, showing them a large, thronelike chair with a matching footstool. Rising from it was a bearded and all-too-familiar man in robes, who offered the two noble lords a wintry smile.

Vangerdahast's teeth positively gleamed. "I'm sure Ruldroun will be fascinated to learn the habits of ravens—in a decade or so, when I let him out of the deep cells. Old Thunderspells, traitors, at your service!"

"Naed," Lord Yellander spat, and whirled to run.

There was no door behind them any longer—only a thing like a fleshy wall, of many staring eyes and silently screaming mouths and clawlike fingers, looming up over them like a great, crawling darkness.

Vangerdahast smiled gently and said in a voice as soft as silk, "Do try to run. Please. We haven't fed the gravewall for days."

✦ ✦ ✦ ✦ ✦

"You *promised,"* Lord Maniol Crownsilver hissed.

"And I'll do it," Wizard of War Ghoruld Applethorn said, holding the trembling lord by the shoulders. "Your Jalassa will live again. This very night. There's just one thing you have to do for me first."

"What?"

"Run to Vangerdahast—right now, and getting past anyone who tries to stop you. Tell them you bear an urgent, private message to him from the king, that's for Vangey's ears only. If he happens to be with the king, then say the message is from me. Anyroad, the moment you're alone with him, tell the Royal Magician I've captured the princesses! You heard me gloating, but then I vanished right in front of your eyes, and you don't know where I've gone!"

"What?"

"That's all you have to say—just that! *Go!* And Jalassa will be in your arms again tonight, alive and loving!"

Lord Crownsilver blinked, shook his head as if to clear it, and rushed away, sideswiping a table in the process.

The war wizard watched him go, and grew a slow smile that wouldn't have looked out of place on a wolf.

Hearing that news, Vangerdahast could hardly help but look into a crystal ball—or teleport into the Dragondown Chambers.

And either way, headless Royal Magicians make poor powers-behind-thrones.

"Hold! Who are you?"

The end of the Long Passage was indeed guarded, and the Purple Dragon hailing the hurrying Knights sounded angry. His spear flashed as he turned to menace them. It bore a collar that supported a ring of eight more spear tips, all pointing at the Knights, and seeming to fill the passage, all by themselves.

Beyond him, in a little ring of glowing light, another six—or more—Dragons readied their own weapons, one of them turning toward an alarm gong, and fumbling for his dagger to strike it with.

As Pennae skidded to a halt, panting hard and clawing at the wall to slow herself before she came within reach of all those sharp points, Florin snapped, "Stop the one at the gong!"

Doust and Semoor nodded and stepped grandly past him in almost perfect unison, raising their holy symbols. Waving their free arms in flourishes, they fixed the rearmost guards with flashing eyes, calling upon divine power, and commanded: *"Fall!"*

And those two guards crumpled, the gong unstruck.

"Eight in all!" Pennae cried. "Two down!"

"For Cormyr!" Florin roared as he charged. "That the king may live!"

"Forget not the queen!" Islif shouted, springing to join him as he struck aside the unwieldy Crown-spear and kept running, hurling its wielder back into the Dragons behind. Islif did the same, ducking and parrying so the spear menacing her went past her shoulder and she could simply run in along it, drive her sword between her Dragon's legs, and bring the flat of it up as she kept running, thrusting him off his feet and back into more Dragons, behind. They in turn stumbled over their two fallen comrades, just behind them, and went over on their backs in a confusion of wildly kicking boots.

The Dragons were all shouting now, as they fell into a confused tangle. Pennae sprang forward and swarmed into it, slapping faces with her ring as she danced, ducked, ran up arms, and vaulted sagging bodies.

She slapped the last guard standing three times, leaving him shaking his head, glaring at her—and then bringing up his spear in slow menace.

Pennae danced back, waved the hand with the ring at her fellow Knights, and sighed, "Out of venom, I guess."

"Ah," Semoor responded, wading through the heaped bodies. "Well, then."

The spear swung around at him, but he clawed up the shaft of a fallen spear from the tangled fallen to block its point, and then thrust it aside. "I do most humbly beg your apology for this indignity," he said to the startled Dragon, as he pulled his way down the spear-shaft to reach the man, "but the needs of bright Cormyr compel us all, and in this particular case, that means—"

He tugged with all his strength on the spear, the snarling Purple Dragon kept hold of it but overbalanced and came staggering forward—and Semoor lifted his knee to take the man under the chin with devastating force.

As the man crumpled, Doust picked his way past all the fallen Dragons.

Islif gave him a look. "What're you doing, holynose?"

"Seeing if I can take this gong down—*without* sounding it—so we can take it with us. They'll find it a little hard to ring it if it's missing, no?"

"Yes. Or no. Just be *care*ful."

"I don't *like* this," Jhessail hissed. "Fighting loyal Dragons of the realm, courting banishment or worse at our every step!" Her voice rose, trembling—as her light spell wavered and then failed. "What're we *doing?"*

"There, there, Jhess. Greet a little calm," Semoor told her. "We're the heroes, remember? This will all end happily."

Jhessail glared at him. "But what if it *doesn't?*"

Florin put an arm around her shoulders. "Ah. Then, lass, it's not really the end."

Chapter 18

WHEN REVELS GO ALL WRONG

Be ready, O thou minstrels
To raise thy cheerful song
For blood will stain the carpets
When revels go all wrong

Orammus 'the Black Bard' of Waterdeep
from When Revels Go All Wrong
a ballad contained in Old Or's Black Book
published in the Year of the Scourge

"I *like* these guards' glowstones," Doust commented, lifting the one in his hand to peer at yet another moot of ways, in the dark maze of passages they were now lost in. "They beat lanterns all hollow."

"Use it, don't admire it," Pennae snapped, pointing Doust down the way she thought was right. "Some urgency *does* ride us, you know."

"Ah," Semoor said dryly, as they all started to run again. "That would be why you poisoned Lady Laspeera and the ornrion, and why we're running along fighting every loyal Purple Dragon we see. I *knew* there had to be a reason."

Pennae gave him an exasperated look. "We're looking," she said, not slowing, "for some linked rooms called the Dragondown Chambers. It would be good if we could find them before some of the guards wake and start striking that gong." She shook her head. "I *still* can't believe they reinforced it with adamantine wire. What sort of see-to-all-details courtiers *do* that?"

"Cormyrean ones," Doust offered.

Pennae snarled something dirty at him, then snapped, "Just remember: we need to find the Dragondown Chambers."

Semoor peered at the passage wall he was trotting past. "I'm not seeing any handy signs," he said.

"Pray harder," Pennae suggested.

"The *next* guards we meet, we ask," Jhessail said. "*Before* we send them off into dreamland."

"Or they put their swords through us," Semoor added.

Doust threw up his hand and waved the glowstone to warn all the Knights to halt. When they joined him, he wordlessly pointed with the glowstone. They were standing at the junction of six dark, apparently identical passages.

"So, which way?" Florin asked.

Pennae frowned, raised her hands to indicate two adjacent passages that angled off slightly to her right, seeming to diverge only a little from each other, then shrugged and dropped one hand, to leave the other pointing. "That one. The Chambers must be a fair distance on, yet."

"Huh," Semoor said, as they started to trot again, on into the darkness. "Just like the treasure that was supposed to start showering down on our heads, never to stop, when we gained our charter."

"You," Islif told him, "can be replaced."

"*Oh*, no," he replied, holding up both hands in mock dudgeon. "I don't *think* so. An Anointed of Lathander willing to rush around the realm taking down Purple Dragons, fighting your many-gods-bedamned robed and belted wizards of your fabled Black Brotherhood of Zhentil *sarking* Keep, while inns tumble down around his ears and lady war wizards lecture them on ethics, to say nothing of being told what to do by their armed companions, many of whom seem like reckless dolts—I'm trying to be polite, here—would seem to me to be a rare breed. A *very* rare breed."

"Behold, Watching Gods, our Wolftooth speaks truth," Jhessail observed with a wry smile. "For once."

"Just how blazing big *is* this Palace?" Doust asked, puffing along. "Or do its cellars and underways underlie a good bit of Suzail?"

"They do," Pennae and Islif answered together—ere each giving the other a frown and asking in unison, "and just how is it that *you* know that?"

Semoor rolled his eyes. "Crazed-wits, all of them. And I'm trapped down here with them."

"Florin," Islif inquired, "would it be a breach of our agreement if I drove the toe of my boot forcefully into a certain Wolftooth backside?"

"Just one boot?" Florin replied. "No."

Then he chuckled. A few running strides later, he chuckled again. Then he threw back his head and roared with laughter. Almost immediately, Islif and Doust joined in.

And so it was that the Knights of Myth Drannor were laughing like madfolk as they came rushing out of the darkness at the next astonished Purple Dragons they were fated to meet, four full-armored soldiers standing deep in boredom around a painted Purple Dragon on the passage wall.

A guardpost. This one, thankfully, had no gong.

* * * * *

The younger Zhentarim was breathing hard as he came through the door.

"I got them all back here—*just* in time. There're more Purple Dragons riding hard to Halfhap right now than I thought Cormyr could muster!"

"Local Dragon commanders shrieking about Lord Manshoon and the Blackstaff and Elminster blowing up an inn in town will do that," the older Zhentarim said, rising from a desk littered with librams, grimoires and scrolls.

"Huh. Morelike old Vangerdahast got the scare of his life, ran home with his tail between his legs, and shrieked hard in his king's ear. And Azoun was so awestruck at his oh-so-haughty Royal Magician babbling in fear that he called out all his armies!"

"Perhaps so, indeed. So we're well out of it, and can thank Lord Manshoon for the continued good health of our necks."

"You mean he got the same scare?"

"Careful, Mauliykhus, careful. One never knows what words *he* might hear, or how he might take them. 'Tis best not to speculate as to his thinking; he frowns on those who do. Deeply. All I know is, from now on, we're to stay out."

"Just that? 'Stay out'? Aumrune, where did you hear those words?"

"Orders. From the top. I hear the Lord Manshoon doesn't want any of us near when the envoy from Silverymoon is welcomed at Court with all the pomp and glitter Suzail can mount. It seems some of the sorceresses she travels with like to hunt we of the Brotherhood—and they have something that links them all together, and makes them far more deadly than a mere handful of nosy women with a taste for the Art, each working alone. If they sniff us, Manshoon said, Harpers will just flood into Cormyr and trammel us for years, hacking at our backsides whenever we turn around."

Mauliykhus blinked. "Ah. Well. Put that way . . ."

"Exactly." Aumrune reached for a decanter, pointed at two goblets in a silent command to Mauliykhus to fetch them, and sat down at his desk again, sweeping glowing written magic aside with a careless wave of one arm.

Turning a ring on his finger that awakened a singing in the air—a singing Mauliykhus had long suspected shielded against scrying—the older Zhentarim added in a lower, softer voice, "None of which forbids us to discuss points of interest in this matter that obviously had nothing at all to do with Lord Manshoon's decision. Like the disappearance of one of his most trusted mages, Sarhthor. And a few treasonous nobles whose trade routes and dealings—when they're soon jailed or beheaded—we may be able to make a little *private* use of. Oh, and talk of something called a hargaunt. And the wraithlike things seen plunging into and probably possessing too many loyal Zhentarim, to make them turn on fellows in the Brotherhood. Or the possibility that the Dragonfire magic, lo these many years passing, just might be more than mere illusion and minstrels' fancies, after all."

Mauliykhus smiled as he set the goblets down, and took a seat across from his superior in the Brotherhood. "Ah. Good. I've been struggling not to ask over-many questions about all those things, but they've been burning inside my head these last few days."

"I've noticed," Aumrune commented, his voice drier than Mauliykhus had ever heard it before. He poured until the goblets were full to the brim.

"Just make very sure that talking and watching is *all* you do, until we receive orders otherwise. For now, we stand back and let nobles doom themselves with their little treasons, and Ornrion Dahauntul snarl and roar like a boar in rut, and these Knights of Myth Drannor stumble around like the naive fools they are. If Bane smiles on us all, their blunders will reveal more to us of the true nature of those wraiths and what the Dragonfire magic really is, before . . ."

"Before we need to pounce on these Knights of Myth Drannor?"

"No. Before it's too late."

✦ ✦ ✦ ✦ ✦

"Peace, loyal Purple Dragons!" Florin cried, waving his open and empty hand. "We serve the king and queen, and bear their charter! We have no quarrel with you, but must in haste find the Dragondown Chambers!"

He broke off with a sigh. Faces hardening, the soldiers had already spread out, drawing their swords—and revealing a door behind them, out of which another four Dragons were hurrying, swords and maces in their hands.

"Peace? Parley?" Islif snapped.

"Surrender!" the oldest Dragon ordered, gesturing sharply at the passage floor with his drawn sword. "Down on your bellies, and toss your weapons aside!"

"That's the fastest way to the Dragondown Chambers?" Pennae asked impishly.

"Hoy, now!" one of the Dragons said in pleased surprise. "Some of 'em are *women!"*

"Fancy that!" Jhessail said sarcastically, looking down at herself. "All these years I'd not noticed, until now."

"Awake at last, Dragon?" Islif asked that Purple Dragon archly, smashing aside his sword with her own and twisting her blade to send his clanging and skirling from his hand.

The Dragon beside him thrust his blade at her throat, shouting, *"Surrend—"*

That was as far as he got ere Islif ducked past his sword point, and her free arm caught hold of his sword arm and tugged sharply. Her other hand, still gripping the hilt of her sword, crashed hard into his chin as he fell helplessly forward. He sighed, rolled his eyes up into his head, and crashed to the floor like a full, wet sack of grain.

Beside her, Pennae danced across in front of three of the Dragons, blowing them a kiss—and then flung herself at their ankles, rolling hard and sending them toppling forward over her. As they landed, amid startled curses, Doust leaned forward and carefully rapped each one on the back of the helm with his mace, counting like a child at play in the street, *"One* Dragon. *Two* Dragon. *Three* Dragon!"

"What madness is this?" the Purple Dragon officer snarled. "What're you *doing?"*

"Searching for the Dragondown Chambers!" Florin said. "Can you help us?"

The officer flung up his weapon in a dramatic pose. *"Never!"*

Semoor swung his mace. It slammed into the man's helmed forehead and sent him reeling. Pennae promptly ducked behind him, going to her knees—and he tripped backward over her and crashed down onto his behind, roaring in pain. Thoughtfully she turned and hopped, landing with both knees on his armored chest and driving the wind out of him.

His head snapped up as he struggled for breath. She smiled sweetly at him and backhanded him across the face, ringing his helmed head off the stone floor.

"Then kindly drift off into dreams and get out of our way!" she snarled into his face. "We have a kingdom to save! *Yours!*"

* * * * *

"No, Torsard, *not* the jeweled blade. *No* magic, remember?"

"But—but—"

Lord Elvarr Spurbright sighed. "Did we not discuss this? Have you not been instructed in Court etiquette for lo these dozen years now and more?"

"But Algranth Truesilver will be wearing his best sword. It has quillons made to look like spread eagle wings! Why will *he*—"

"He will *not,*" Lord Spurbright interrupted. "Vangerdahast may—with a frown—allow the Obarskyrs to wear weapons that bear magic to a revel, and just perhaps not rend the visiting envoy of Silverymoon limb from limb in front of us all for daring to do the same, but neither of us are royalty. Which is why your Lady Mother won't be wearing her tiara that chimes, nor your sisters those glowgem pectorals they're so proud of. It may be a high-handed rule, it may be irksome, but Vangerdahast's duty is to protect the Crown, he is doing so, and he worked to make this particular rule stone-solid long before you were born. You've grown up with it as something that 'is,' just as your noble standing 'is.' How can you accept the one without the other?"

Torsard Spurbright's lip curled. "Forgive me, Father, but our proud lineage is scarcely to be measured against an arbitary, some-occasions-only detail of Court etiquette!"

"Oh? Are not our noble privileges matters of that same Court etiquette? The Crown can strip them away at a whim, can they not?"

"Aye, the Crown," Torsard said. "The *king,* not some jumped-up wizard!"

"Well, that particular jumped-up wizard, daily and in truth, rules the realm more than king and queen put together, and happens to do so right now! So take hold of your temper, do off that blade, and choose one without enchantment!"

"And what if some outlander or hired adventurer storms into the revel and menaces the fair Obarskyrs? What then?"

"Then all the watching war wizards will hurl their spells at such menaces, and the sorceresses who pose as Lady Summerwood's maids will do the same," Lord Spurbright replied. "And if there just happens to be anything left of those menaces afterwards that half a realm's worth of Purple Dragons seem to need aid carving up, your *non-magical* blade may prove useful!"

"But—"

"Now, are you a Filfaeril-favored Knight of Myth Drannor, or perhaps a murderous outlaw? *Or a loyal noble of Cormyr, whom his father can be justly proud of?*"

Torsard snorted, threw up his hands in exasperation, and turned on his heel to stalk out of his father's study. Only to spin around again, frowning. "Look you, why before all the gods do we have to get dressed up and mingle with every commoner who can afford a bath and a decent tunic?"

"We don't. We can stay right here and take no part in this reception. I'll not be surprised if the Bleths and Illances do just that; they oppose closer ties with Silverymoon."

"Huh. Want all the gold their ships can bring them, in ever-more trade with the Vilhon, don't they?"

"Precisely," Lord Spurbright said. "Though I'd *also* not be surprised if the young Bleth and Illance men sidle in with masks on to enjoy the revelry, even if their fathers forbid them."

"Oh? A revel for an outlander envoy? Of some elf-loving, backwoods Sword Coast city that freezes every winter and river-floods every summer? *Why?*"

"Your vast knowledge of Silverymoon overwhelms me, son. As to your 'why,' well, they say the Lady Summerwood is almost as beautiful as High Lady Alustriel herself."

"Ah, yes, fair and fabled Alustriel," Torsard said. "One of those silver-haired polearms of women who bed everyone within reach and claim to be the daughter of a goddess. If you reached through the spells they use to make themselves so beautiful, to actually touch them, I daresay your fingers would find near-skull faces and wrinkles and warts and all the other delights old hags have to offer."

"Oh? Think you so? Well, my all-knowing heir, my fingers *have* gone on that adventure you so sneeringly refer to—well before I took your mother to wife, I might add—and I found Alustriel to be very fair. Very fair, indeed."

Torsard stared at his father. Lord Elvarr Spurbright's voice had gone both soft and rough, and his eyes were gazing at something far away and long ago. Eyes that seemed suspiciously bright—until Lord Spurbright turned his back on his son, and said gruffly, "Well? Just how long is it going to take you to fetch that blade? The revel's *today,* look you!"

✦ ✦ ✦ ✦ ✦

"We seek the Dragondown Chambers," Semoor said, shaking the battered-looking Purple Dragon by the throat, their noses almost touching. "Where are they?"

"I'll never tell!" the guard snarled. "Cormyr forever!"

Semoor backhanded the man across the face, ringing the man's helm against the stone wall behind him. Then the priest grinned and told his fellow Knights, "Hey, this is fun! I've *years* of being clouted by soldiers to make up for!"

Florin turned away. "*Must* we do this?"

Islif laid a hand on his shoulder. "Easy," she whispered. "I'll not let it go on much longer."

"Now"—Semoor smiled into the guard's face—"let's try this again. The Dragondown Chambers: where are they? How do we reach them from here?"

"I'll not tell you, false priest!" the Dragon spat.

Semoor's punch had real force behind it this time, and his smile had vanished. "You insult Lathander more than you do me, man," he snapped. "Now, are you—"

Islif took hold of Semoor's arm and hauled him to his feet, away from the guard—who promptly launched himself into a frantic run that lasted for only a single stride before Islif's deftly outstretched leg sent him sprawling.

Pennae landed on the Purple Dragon's back, bounced hard, and drawled, "I wonder how he'll look after a little slicing?"

She let the man see the knife before she cut the rear strap of his codpiece, and was rewarded with a whimper and a frantic attempt to escape that ended, this time, with Florin hauling the man to his feet—and then off his feet and up against the wall, kicking helplessly with Florin's hand around his throat.

The ranger said to the guard, "We serve the Crown of Cormyr just as you do. The king himself signed our charter; the queen knighted us and gave us her blessing. We're trying to save the realm right now. We need to get to the Dragondown Chambers, where as you well know there will be war wizards aplenty, who will promptly and firmly stop us if they judge us disloyal. We need directions. Please give them."

"Or I'll continue," Pennae added lightly, "with this." Lifting the armored Purple Dragon codpiece aside, she pressed the point of her knife against the revealed leather beneath, just enough for the man to feel it.

"I—uh—don't let her! Ah—"

"My arm," Florin informed the guard, "is growing tired. There will soon come a time when I let you fall. And then—"

Pennae swiftly moved the knife to press upward beneath bulging leather, where it could be felt. Its owner swallowed and then said in a rush, "Take the passage with the spyholes to the second way-moot! Turn left there, and go to the end. There's a cross-way and two doors. Either one opens into a Dragondown Chamber!"

"*Thank* you," Florin said gently. "It's been a pleasure talking with you, saer."

"Go to sleep now," Jhessail whispered, and cast the spell that would send the Purple Dragon into deep slumber.

Florin lowered the man gently to the stone floor. "So, which passage is the one with the spyholes?"

"This one," Pennae said, starting off into the darkness. The rest of the Knights rushed after her.

"So this is being a hero," Doust muttered, as he started to pant again. "None of the minstrels ever sing about all the *running!*"

"How'd you know the right passage," Semoor called to Pennae. "Or *do* you know the right passage?"

Pennae gave him a grin back over her shoulder. "Of course. See those?" She pointed at a few tiny glows along the passage wall ahead.

"Glowfire paint," Islif murmured.

"Aye. Marking little swivel-panels that can be swung aside to look through a spyhole; there must be a room on the other side of this wall that the war wizards or Highknights have occasion to watch folk in. The ladies' baths, perhaps."

"I see," Islif said. "And how is it that you recognize these spyholes at a glance, hmm?"

As she ran on, Pennae started to hum an oh-so-innocent little tune by way of reply.

Chapter 19

When hungry vultures gather

And at the looked-for death of kings
When hungry vultures gather
Look you for the most reluctant to retire
And you'll see the proudest titles,
The most gleaming gems
And the brightest fangs.

Anglym Warlar
One Bard's Book
published in the Year of the Firedrake

The Calishite wizard yawned. "Merchant Haerrendar, *never* try to threaten me again. Or should I call you Bravran Merendil?"

His host went as white as winter snow. "You know!" he gasped.

"Of course. It is the business of Talan Yarl to know such things." The wizard's smile was jovial as he stroked his scented, immaculately trimmed beard, but his eyes were ice cold.

"Moreover," he added, "your threats are unnecessary. When Talan Yarl is bought, he stays bought. You have blundered; pray refrain from doing so again. You intend a little regicide at this revel, do you not?"

The man Suzail knew as Ostagus Haerrendar, dealer in barrels, kegs, and pipes, stepped back, shuddering. It was some moments before he swallowed and said faintly, "It seems to be your business to know *all* things, no matter how secret or dangerous to know."

"It is more than my business; it is my life, or rather, the reason I still have one. Yet that does not mean I ever approach knowing all, merely that I like to know who I'm truly dealing with. Doing so, I find, saves excess spilled blood."

The Calishite looked down at the still form on the table between them. "This would be Rellond Blacksilver, known to many young noble ladies of your realm as 'Rellond the Roughshod' for his crude and impatient lovemaking. A rake and a wastrel I expected to see dead and buried long ago, with some angry noble father's sword having relieved him of both his life and what fills his codpiece. Yet I see that he lives. Drugged or enspelled. *This* worthless braggart has something to do with your cunning plan?"

"Drugged," Merendil said stiffly. "And there's no need to mock my cleverness—or lack of it. I'm paying you *very* well."

"That is true. Your gold should be sufficient to make me contentedly accept any idiocy you might offer, I'll grant. Yet humor me, Merendil. Unfold to me your scheme. I *really* want to hear it. Truly."

"If your magic is sufficient to accomplish control of this man's mind," the nobleman said carefully, "Rellond Blacksilver will . . . do the deed. Stabbing the King of Cormyr during the dancing. Outraged, you will then reduce him to ashes—regrettably too late to save Azoun, but—"

"I will do no such thing, idiot. If I am using a spell to control your dupe, the war wizards will detect it before he or I am anywhere near the king, and we shall both be imprisoned and later mind-reamed and executed."

"Ah, but you won't be using a spell on Blacksilver!"

"Oh? How, then?"

"There's a mindworm in his brain. You've heard of them?"

"I have indeed." Talan Yarl looked thoughtful. "I know of only one mage who uses them successfully—and he had to flee Halruaa and go into hiding in Turmish to keep his life, after word spread. Is this his work?"

"I know not. The mage who did it—name unknown to us, but we believe he was an outlander—first placed a worm in a young noble lass, who in turn infected Blacksilver and some others. He has since disappeared. We believe Vangerdahast's pet war wizards got him."

"So how did you learn of this worm?"

"Though the mage—again, we believe—never knew it, he was being spied upon by War Wizard Sarmeir Landorl, who was working with me."

"A war wizard. So I am necessary how, exactly? Are you and Landorl seeking a scapegrace? A dupe to be blamed for your villainy?"

"No! I need you to do this, because, well . . . Landorl's disappeared."

"Vangerdahast's war wizards again?"

"We—we think so."

" 'We'? Who is this 'we'? You and—?"

Merendil reddened. "My mother."

"Your *mother?* Oh, brave conspirator, to make war on kings with your agéd mother? What is she—fivescore years old, by now? A bedridden bag of bones, or a grave you stand over and murmur questions by night?"

"I am not quite either of those things, yet," a sharp voice said from just behind Talan Yarl's ear. "Just as the poison on this dagger you're feeling hasn't entirely faded away either. Now, are you with us? Not that I'm sure how much of a choice you have, O Yarl who stays bought. I very much doubt that we can let you walk out of here, knowing what you now know."

Talan Yarl had stiffened at the first touch of the dagger point, eyes widening in utter astonishment. *Nothing* should have been able to approach him unawares, let alone pass through his shielding spell without him even noticing. He took great care not to move, though he wanted very much to see the Lady Merendil.

"Why, great Lady," he said now, the sudden sheen of sweat on his brow belying his smooth manner, "this puts quite a different complexion upon the matter. Consider me enthusiastically and steadfastly with you. Upon my honor."

"I'm utterly uninterested in your honor, mage. I want your blood-bond, sworn in a magefire pact. I want to *know* your blood will boil in your veins if you betray us. I find such mutual knowledge builds such stronger trust than honor."

Swallowing, Talan Yarl managed a shaky smile. "That it does."

* * * * *

Kahristra had been her personal maid these nine years, and to a lass who had seen little more than fourteen summers, that is a lifetime.

Wherefore Princess Tanalasta regarded Kahristra as a friend and a confidant, not a servant to be ordered around—nor someone she needed to act the dignified, glacially expressionless royal heir in front of. Wherefore she now pouted openly, as Kahristra finished dusting her with powder, until Kahristra stepped back, put hands on hips, and asked, "Tana, what's wrong? Why this mood?"

The princess sighed. "I'm displeased that some *stranger* is sitting out there while I'm getting dressed. Can't you send her away?"

Kahristra shook her head. "I can't give her orders. *She* gives *me* orders."

"What?" Tanalasta's head snapped up, her brows drawing together in the frown that would always make her plainer than most women—and the very echo of her father the king.

"Yon woman," the maid explained, lifting a finger to indicate the door that led out of the robing room into the retiring room beyond, where they both knew the unwelcome guest was sitting, "is a war wizard, and she's here on your royal father's orders."

Tanalasta's eyes widened in a mockery of incredulity. "So much I had guessed, but *why?*"

Kahristra sighed. "There are certain suspicions that you might be endangered at this revel, if you aren't protected."

"You mean Vangerdahast is acting mysterious," Tanalasta said disgustedly. "Again. *He* is the one who has suspicions."

"Well . . . yes," her maid confirmed, trying—not entirely successfully—to hide a grin.

"That man," Tanalasta said, "is impossible! I wish someone would turn him into a frog, or a dragon would swallow him, or—or—*something* would happen to just take him out of all our lives!"

Kahristra shrugged. "In unfolding time to come, you just might get your wish. You can't say plenty of folk haven't tried. One of them is bound to succeed, some day."

* * * * *

"You do realize," the young man with the blazing yellow eyes said calmly, poised naked and magnificent above her, "that if we succeed in this, we must inevitably end up as foes."

"Oh?" The hands of the lady merchant of Marsember tightened

on his hips. "Does your Cormyr so firmly embrace fair Marsember, then?"

"As firmly as I'm embracing it now," Terentane gasped, yielding to her hungry tugging.

"Well, now," she snarled under his riding, through clenched teeth, "I suppose we will, at that. Years hence, I hope."

"I hope so too," Terentane panted—in the instant before the bed broke, beneath them, crashing to the floor.

Which groaned ominously, and started to cant, oh-so-slowly tipping as a worm-gnawed post gave way. Together, laughing wildly, the young man so powerful in his Art that Vangerdahast feared him, and the wily merchant twice his age who'd built her wealth into a rival of the Crown treasury, dashed out of the doomed room and down the stairs.

"*Must* we use your rotting old boathouses for our trysts?" he protested, as they fell into each other's arms again on a heap of old ropes at the bottom of the stairs, rats squealing and fleeing in all directions. Loud crashing through the wall beside them heralded the arrival of the shattered bed—piece by piece—onto the oar closet floor. Together they waited for the neatly racked oars, jarred loose, to topple . . . one, two, and then in a thunderous rush, many.

Between giggles, Amarauna Telfalcon told her newfound lover, "I—I thought it would be more romantic!"

He burst out laughing, and mirth conquered passion for a time.

They were oddly matched: an energetic mageling, rejected when he tried to join the war wizards by a Royal Magician awed by the strength of his untrained mastery of the Art and mistrusting his loyalty—and a ruggedly attractive, ruthless merchant shipper, owner of twenty cogs and caravels, a dozen warehouses in Suzail, and twice that many here in Marsember, who harbored no dream more burning than the desire to see Marsember free of Cormyr again. A Marsember ruled by its merchants—hard-working master merchants like the Telfalcons, meeting in council—rather than by corrupt nobles or sneaking, spying wizards.

When Terentane, the first man to look at her in a score of summers as anything more than a dupe to be fleeced or a rival to be shattered, reached for her again, Telfalcon playfully slapped his hands away.

"*This* is supposed to get me ready to play at being this Yassandra? So just what, exactly, do lady war wizards *do* all day?"

"No, this was supposed to stop me getting nervous, and brooding over what could go wrong; remember?"

Amarauna turned a wooden cross-latch to let a door in the wall fall open—and oars come spilling out in a wooden flood. "Is it working?" she asked innocently.

Terentane's sudden roar of laughter was so strong that it took him some time to master himself enough to pounce on her.

"Oh, you *rogue!*" She laughed, as he caught her and whirled her around and down. "Come here."

"Demands, demands, demands," he growled, in a steadily more muffled manner.

So skillful was his tongue in the moments that followed that Amarauna finally relaxed, purring, eyes closing as she enjoyed the moment.

Then she heard a singing in the air that shouldn't have been there, something quite different from the lapping and creaking of the boathouse, and her eyes snapped open.

She could not help but gasp. There, hanging in the air above them both like golden icicles, were nine glowing swords, long and keen, their points close enough for her to reach up and touch. "Terent?" she dared, trying to keep her voice from quavering.

"Nice, aren't they?"

She managed not to shiver. "Yes." When he made no reply, she asked, "You called them here?"

"Willed them here. Watch, but don't move a muscle."

Whatever reply Amarauna Telfalcon might have thought of making was lost in the hissing of blades as they sliced the air, falling *just* beside her bared skin, flats rather than edges touching her—two down each side, another two either side of her ankles, and the last—

"You young *bastard!"*

"You old bitch," he said affectionately—as the blades all slid silently skyward again, lifting in magnificent unison. "Let's go kill war wizards."

✦ ✦ ✦ ✦ ✦

"Halt!" the war wizard ordered, as three Purple Dragons stepped out of darkened doorways to stand in front of him, drawing their swords.

The Knights kept on running.

"Get out of the way, in the king's name!" Islif ordered, her voice firm and deep.

"I speak for the king here!" the wizard snapped. "I say again: Halt! Throw down your weapons, and yield yourselves!"

"We seek the Dragondown Chambers!" Pennae shouted. "Where are they?"

"I gave you an order!" the war wizard thundered.

"I ignored it!" Florin roared back, with a violence and volume that startled everyone. "In Azoun's name, wizard, I order you to stand aside! In Filfaeril's name, I order you to assist us! Defy these orders *at your peril!"*

"Nice," Pennae said, as Florin's bellow echoed away down the passage.

And then the Knights reached the Purple Dragons, and the wizard barely had time to howl, "We *will* not!" before swords were ringing off swords. Pennae rolled like a ball under a guard's boots, and the Dragon fell helplessly on his rear, bouncing hard and sending the wizard staggering back.

Pennae launched herself into the air with a firm boot planted in the fallen Dragon's stomach and her arms spread wide.

As Florin's mighty swing numbed a desperately parrying Dragon's sword hand and sent him staggering aside, and Islif did the same to the third Dragon, Pennae struck the wizard's chest with one knee, driving him over backward. He received her grin and kiss just before he struck the stones hard enough to know no more—which was about the time Doust and Semoor tore off Islif's Dragon's helm and together ran him head-first into the passage wall and oblivion, and Florin's solid punch felled his Dragon into similar unconsciousness.

"Oh," Jhessail murmured, standing over the bodies shaking her head, "we are going to be in *such* trouble."

Florin looked up, rubbing his knuckles, and growled, "I am beginning not to care."

* * * * *

Seven more swords appeared in a winking whirl of drifting sparks to join the nine already hanging in the air. Terentane struck a triumphant pose that would have looked far grander if he hadn't been young, pale, on the bony side, and stark naked. "Behold the Dragonfire swords, lost for so many years!"

Amarauna smiled. "Or rather, your counterfeits, crafted this last tenday."

"Indeed." Terentane dusted his hands briskly. "So. The gods themselves granted that I was in Halfhap. Two dead war wizards I managed to get out of the ruin of that inn with my spells: Yassandra Durstable—that's you—and Brors Tamleth—that'll be me. They're in that family vault you use for smuggling right now, where they should be just fine unless some misfortune strikes that house and they decide to trundle the dear departed all the way over the mountains to the vault—before the revel's over."

"Hardly likely," Amarauna granted. "Yet something we should remember. Sembians with that much coin have their family vaults spell-shielded, but it *is* in Cormyr—and war wizards, like brigands, poke their long noses into *everything*." She grinned, then, and added, "Hmm. Like some young prodigies-at-Art I could name."

Terentane rolled his eyes. "So let them poke. They can hardly do so in time. My spells will make us look like Durstable and Tamleth, and we rush to the Palace to triumphantly show them to Vangey. We only now won free of the Oldcoats wreckage, but look what we have!"

"And our act should get us through the war wizards on guard duty?"

"Yes, because all the important and powerful ones will be in the hall that's hosting the revel; by the time we get to them, we'll be close enough that I can let the swords 'go wild.' I'll drop our disguises when we're out of sight somewhere, and start killing war wizards—just striking at anyone who launches a spell. I can do that by feel, sitting in some back room far from all the screaming and Purple Dragons running around shouting and waving their swords at nothing, trying to protect the royal family. I only want to kill war wizards—Vangerdahast, of course, and as many more as possible—and should soon be able to win a position in the war wizards, what with scores of them dead and because I'll then stand forth dramatically and hurl a spell before all the gawping Court that will dramatically destroy these deadly blades, saving the realm for everyone to see!"

Amarauna Telfalcon reached out her arms. "Whereupon you'll help me make Marsember slowly and softly more and more independent, and Cormyr's rule there weaker and weaker, as the years pass?"

Terentane strode over into her arms and kissed her with a fierce, impatient tenderness. "Of course," he said. "You have my word on it!"

Bravran Merendil snarled and waved his hand again, "Phaugh! That wizard's well gone, but his stink remains! *Why* do Calish—"

"Bravran, that will do! His scent may not be *all* he left behind."

"Yes, but—"

"Not a word!"

"But—"

"Not a *word*, Bravran!"

Lady Imbressa Merendil had indeed seen fivescore summers, but magical potions had held back much of the ravages of age. She looked like many a wealthy matron of sixty summers, painted here and there to cover the worst of the wrinkles that could no longer be held entirely at bay. Her eyes flashed dark fire, her wide mouth looked always eager to laugh, and even an observer seeing her but fleetingly and for the first time knew at a glance she was no fool. She cast a strong shielding spell with the same swift expertise that had so impressed the departed Calishite in working the magefire blood-bond. Elegantly frail she might be, but her Art was as strong as many a veteran war wizard's.

Her fretting son tried to speak again when the shielding was done and singing in the air around them, but she put a sternly reproving finger to her lips and worked another spell, this one a scrying-ward that rose within the shielding to wall out the world in steel gray mists.

"*Now* you can speak freely, my son. In the brief time left to you before you must cease to be Ostagus Haerrendar for a time, become Dorn Talask, and get yourself to the revel."

Dorn Talask was a Palace courtier whom Bravran Merendil happened to closely resemble. He would, if Lady Merendil's agents failed her not, very soon be taken and slain.

Bravran nodded impatiently, and then burst out, "Mother, what if Blacksilver stabs Azoun but doesn't manage to kill him? The king's known to be a great warrior!"

"A mere scratch will do. The dagger blade is poisoned."

Her son did not look reassured. "But Azoun is protected against so many venoms, by spell and antidote and deliberate dosing exposures!"

Lady Merendil smiled. "Not this one. It's a Chultan distillate my best poisoner devised for me before he died." Her voice turned wistful. "Ah, Laerakkan."

Bravran Merendil waved away those last words he didn't want to hear, an expression of distaste on his face, and snapped, "What? But you didn't tell me this!"

"Of course not. The Calishite would have read it in your mind. He was reading you like a bright unrolled scroll, all the time he was here. It was all I could do to deflect his probes away from what you know about me—see the sweat on my brow? We can't let him know about the poison."

"Why not?"

"For two reasons. First, he'll want it enough to slay us both and take it, rather than taking part in our risky venture at all. *He* needs no revenge on the Obarskyrs, remember. To him, all of this seems ill-planned madness."

"And the second reason?"

"The very same poison is going to be on your blade, and you are going to stab him with it. Calishites are blackmailing serpents, given a chance, and I'm not about to give this one anything."

Chapter 20

The Grandest Disaster of the Season

In any land crammed with coin-hungry merchants
Wizards, and young fools seeking more power
Or social glory, there will be many
Only too eager to do Grand Things
To get noticed. And from Grand Things,
Every season, there springs with utter inevitability
The Grandest Disaster of the Season.

Heldurr Blackoun, Sage of Neverwinter
Blackoun's Book Of Tired Wit
published in the Year of Flamedance

There came a sudden rumbling in the dimness. The rushing Knights slowed, peering this way and that—just as a wall of old, black, and massive iron came crashing down out of the ceiling right in front of Florin's nose.

Which meant that—

"Pennae?" he bellowed. *"Pennae?"*

"I'm still alive," the ranger heard her cry faintly, from the other side of the great barrier.

Florin slammed his fist against the wall. It was solid, all right.

"Lady in your Forest!" Florin implored. "Deliver me from this *damned* Palace with its damned neverending gods-be-DAMNED passages!"

As if in reply, there came another rumbling boom, this one laced with Islif crying out in sharp warning and Jhessail letting out a little shriek—as another wall slammed down behind him.

Leaving Florin standing alone in utter darkness, with no company but a sudden heavy grating of stone beside him, the cool, gentle caress of moving air, and a rough, very deep voice saying, "In the name of the king, intruder, lay down your arms and surrender. Or, of course, die."

As he fought his way out of the crowds and past hard-eyed Purple Dragons to hasten through the servants' door of the Royal Court,

Bravran Merendil found himself sweating hard in Dorn Talask's clothes and trying even harder to forget how Talask had yielded up those clothes. It was still a long walk to the Palace proper, where he was supposed to find some chamber called the Dawnlurdusk Room, and report to Skeldulk Maumurthorn, Master of the Red Passage.

Dodging among throngs of excitedly scurrying servants, he found the right hall and started the trudge to the Palace.

Only to fetch up, almost immediately, against a balding old courtier in all-black finery—ribbon-trimmed hose, a puffed-sleeves doublet, fine gold chains at wrists and throat, a matching black throat ruff—who was regarding him what seemed to be barely leashed fury.

"Talask, I thought you went home to bathe and change into finery!" this unexpected obstacle snapped. "*This* is finery? The same clothes, only torn here—look!—and dirtied there?"

Bravran swallowed, catching himself on the very point of snarling, "Well at least Talask didn't bleed all over it, when they took him down!"

For a moment he almost thought he'd said it aloud, the courtier was giving him such an odd look.

The old man took him by his ruffed collar and shook him. "Dorn, *Dorn!* Come out of it! 'Tis *me,* Rolloral! Don't look at me like you don't know me!" He frowned. " 'Tis a lass, isn't it? Bathe in *her,* you meant, you rogue!"

Abruptly, Rolloral broke into a grin and clapped "Talask" on the arm. "Good lad! Hah, to be your age, again! Tell me *all* about it, mind—on the morrow! Right *now,* we've the gods' own list of things to do, and precious little time to do them in! Maumurthorn's been summoned to the Dragondown Chambers for a jawing, and left us with all his inspections to do, before he comes back and does them again and thunders at us for how we did them; *you* know. Come *on!*"

"Dorn Talask" shook himself once more, felt again inside the grand barrel-front of his jacket for the reassuring heft of his dagger, and came on.

✦ ✦ ✶ ✦ ✦

When Wizard of War Ellard Duskeld got to where imperious royal lips had ordered him to go, he stopped. And blinked.

The Dragondown Chambers were in an uproar. Senior courtiers, a few hulking Purple Dragons in polished-to-gleaming armor, and robed war wizards snapping orders and, looking grim, were striding purposefully everywhere.

And at the heart of it all, Vangerdahast, Court Wizard of Cormyr and Royal Magician of the Realm, stood conferring with an ever-changing ring of younger war wizards, deploying them hither and thither in the Palace to accomplish the security concerns of the moment.

"Of *course* we need a man in the Royal Gardens!" Old Thunderspells said gruffly. " 'Tis the best way to get a large armed force—or a dragon, for that matter!—up to the very windows of the Palace without fighting through guard after guard! You think mere helmheaded Purple Dragons can stop a dragon? Or one wizard riding any sort of wingéd steed? Do you *want* this day to turn out to be the grandest disaster of the season?"

Ellard Duskard swallowed, drew in a deep breath, and marched purposefully across the room, almost colliding with no fewer than three hard-striding war wizards moving in other directions, and in the process collecting one glare and two disdainful looks. He had to force his way shoulder-first into the ring, where he bowed deeply in greeting, straightened, and awaited a chance to speak.

"Not *now,* Khalaeto!" Vangerdahast dismissed a short, bespectacled war wizard who looked like a clerk-of-coins; the man scuttled hastily away with scrolls and quill in hand. The Royal Magician of the Realm turned a little, like a weary Purple Dragon moving a crossbow along to aim at the next target, fixed his eyes on Ellard, and snapped, "Speak, man! And don't shuffle so."

"Uh. Ah. Ahem, yes. The princess begs leave to speak with you."

"Which one, lad?"

"Uh . . . oh! Tanalasta, saer."

"Well, *bring* her!" Vangey's growl was impatient.

"She . . ." Ellard Duskard reddened to the roots of his tangled hair, uncomfortably aware that the Royal Magician's glare was practically shouting, "What is it with younglings, these days, and their hair? Have they no combs? Nor dressers to draw them water? Or did they all *like* the feel of lice wriggling around their heads all the time?"

"She—she wants you to come to her, Lord Vangerdahast," he managed to blurt out. "Says it's a royal command." Then, sinking into misery, he shook like a storm-flailed weed, fearing the inevitable.

Astonishingly, Old Thunderspells smiled. "Did she, now?"

He turned away before adding, "Look you, lad! Do I seem to you to have time to spare to kneel before spoiled little girls at time or two, just to indulge their ever-changing whims, right now?"

"Ah . . . *no,* saer.'

"Brilliant boy!" Vangerdahast said. "No, saer, indeed. You've captured it right off! So go you back to Princess High-And-Mighty Tanalasta, and tell her it took you forever to find me, and when you did I changed into a bat and flapped around you by way of answer, and you don't speak bat so you don't know what reply to give her, and so you've come back to her to ask her what she wants you to do now. Oh, and tell her you last saw me flapping off across the Royal Gardens with her father's best state crown hovering above me. That'll give her something to puzzle over!"

Wincing, Ellard Duskard turned and hurried back the way he'd come, slipping out the door a breath too soon to see two war wizards appear in a doorway clear across the largest Dragondown Chamber, with their arms full of golden-glowing swords and eager smiles on their faces.

Vangerdahast frowned at the sight of them, plucked his staff from the war wizard who'd been patiently holding it for him, and aimed it at them as he snapped, "Yassandra? Brors? You're dead, so *who are you, really?*"

That shout brought down a hush over the Chambers—in which the false Yassandra and Brors flung their swords at the Royal Magician of the Realm, and fled. Sixteen golden blades raced across the room like a volley of speeding arrows.

Vangerdahast roared the command that triggered his staff.

And the air in front of it exploded.

* * * * *

"In the name of the king *and* the queen," Florin replied, sword raised against the darkness, "stand aside and let me try to save the realm. I *must* reach Vangerdahast without delay! I have no desire to fight you or anyone else, believe me."

"I obey the orders I am given," the unseen guardian replied. "Cormyr would be a fairer place by far if more folk did. *Aramadaera.* You, on the other hand, have defied the orders of loyal Purple Dragons, just as you defy mine, now. So you must now yield or die."

As that deep voice spoke the lone word unfamiliar to Florin, there arose a faint, brief singing sound in the darkness, and the ranger-Knight now perceived a glimmering across the chamber, a glimmering that swiftly kindled into a glow bright enough to show Florin that it emanated from a helm—an open-face helm worn by a mountain of a man.

Well, a mountain at least. This Palace guardian was half again as tall as Florin, who was used to being among the tallest men in any gathering, and his arms and shoulders would have put any two oxen to shame. Grotesquely corded muscles rippled under a webwork of scars that bared throbbing veins here and highlighted knife-sharp tendons there. The guardian did not so much wear armor as have battered fragments of armor strapped to him and bolted to each other, in a great coat muffled from clangor by ragged leather hides affixed between the shifting metal plates. The man's bracers bristled with outthrust sword blades, one hand ending in a greataxe and the other hefting a short, very broad sword that ended in a trident of horns like those of a bull. As the glow of the helm strengthened, it became apparent that its magics had been crafted to illuminate the air out in front of the man, so that for twice his sword-reach, wherever he was looking, foes were illuminated.

"Mielikki forfend!" Florin gasped.

The man-mountain nodded as if he had heard such reactions far too many times before. "They call me the Dread Doorwarden," he announced, gloomily rather than triumphantly. "Or sometimes, the Stalking Doom."

Florin shuddered, recalling those names spoken by retired Purple Dragons telling horrific tales on sunny days back in Espar—a place where he'd far rather be, just now, than facing death in the dark passages under the Palace of the Purple Dragon. Those stories had been gory horror-yarns about men, sent on errands, who strayed into the wrong passages in the darkness, and were diced and eaten raw under the Royal Palace in Suzail.

"I was told tales of you as a lad," he said slowly, staring up at the hulking mountain of flesh, "but I never believed them."

The Doorwarden grunted wearily as if he'd heard such words a thousand times before, and trudged ponderously forward. Florin moved hastily aside to avoid being trapped in a corner.

One great arm swung, and the ranger flung himself into a roll on the floor to get under those three horns. They sang slashing past overhead. He was barely up again before that axe crashed down, striking sparks on stone just behind his heels.

"You still *are* a lad," that deep voice rumbled. "Believe in me now?"

Florin ducked and dodged again. This time those three blades passed so close he could feel them and hear the whistle of air along their blades.

"Yes," he whispered, "but I don't want to." He ran to get behind the guardian and lashed out at one huge elbow with his own sword. If he could get to where he could hamstring—

No. The backs of the Doorwarden's knees were protected with overlapping, flared arcs of armor. No wonder the man moved ponderously.

Florin flung himself to the floor again to avoid weapons slicing down at him from two directions—both of those massive arms, coming down from full stretch to converge—and then saw his only chance.

The Doorwarden knew this room well, and had never given him safe room to get past, and out the way the guardian had come in by. So Florin would have to take an unsafe way. He came to his feet running, as if to circle along the walls again, but as the Doorwarden turned and sidestepped to prevent him racing past, Florin changed direction and ran right at the man, hurling himself forward sword-first like a great dart—between those armored legs.

And then up and on, panting in frantic haste, ribs aching from the sideways kick the Doorwarden had managed to land while trying to close that gap. Florin darted through where he knew the opening was, sword up, fleeing blindly into the darkness.

"Fool," a cold voice said out of the darkness right in front of him, as an unseen blade rang out of a scabbard.

✦ ✦ ✦

The staff's blast shattered a few of the blades, shards spinning away amid showering sparks. It flung the others aside, but slowed them not a whit. They swerved to converge once more upon the Royal Magician of Cormyr, who hurled down the staff to cast a swift and desperate magic.

Those racing points almost reached Vangerdahast, three of them looming up right before his eyes, before his spell erupted out from him in all directions, a blast of ravening force that shook him as it sprang from his skin, his mouth, and his very eyeballs, a horrible roaring that—ended as swiftly as it had begun, the Dragondown Chambers falling into a deathly silence broken only by the brief tinklings of broken swordblades finding the floor.

Vangerdahast gazed bleakly all around, turning slowly to view the devastation. He was alive and unscathed, but of the dozens of war wizards who'd been so busily rushing around, nothing was left but bloody smears on the walls and pools of gore on the floor.

Whoever his blast hadn't butchered had been felled by whirling, ricocheting blade-shards.

That was the problem with that spell; to rend enchanted weapons, it must needs destroy wards and shieldings. In saving himself, he'd doomed every other war wizard in the Chambers.

Not for the first time.

Vangerdahast felt sick. "Forgive me, Mystra," he whispered, watching his ruined staff smouldering at his feet.

An excited voice suddenly blatted at him from the empty air in front of his nose. "Lord Vangerdahast! The guests are pouring into the Palace now, and among them we've—Jarlandan, Garen, Costarr, and me, that is—recognized the Calishite mage-for-hire Talan Yarl among the folk pouring into the Palace. He's disguised as the Turmish envoy who was expected, and so may well have done something to that man. What should we do?"

Durward, of course. The fool couldn't handle an open-yon-door assignment without asking for assistance.

"Royal Magician? Do you hear? This is Durward, and I ask again: what should we do?"

Vangerdahast threw up his hands in exasperation. "I'm *coming!*" he snapped. Looking grimly around at the red slaughter once more, he growled, "No time to try to save any of them. No *time!*" Then he marched out, face gray and old.

"I'm getting too old for this," he muttered, striding hard along passages where Purple Dragons saluted hastily. He swept past, ignoring them.

✦ ✦ ✦ ✦ ✦

"Florin!" Islif yelled. "Pennae?"

Her voice echoed back to her off unyielding black iron in front of her nose, and down the long, dark passage behind. If anyone answered, none of the Knights heard it.

After the silence had started to stretch, they all looked at each other and shrugged.

"Right," Semoor said, "*now* what?"

"We decide what to do," Jhessail told him, "and do it."

"Well, *that's* simple enough," Doust agreed sarcastically. "Glad you came along, Jhess. Without you, we'd have been lost!"

"We *are* lost, holynoses," Islif snapped. "Try to think of useful things to say, while we—as Jhessail said—try to decide what to do."

Doust shook his head. "All we *really* know is that Pennae told us there's a war wizard conspiracy to slay Vangerdahast and the king and queen, and that we have to get to the Dragondown Chambers as quickly as we can. She didn't even tell us why, though I'm guessing it was to find and tell Vangey. Only guess, mind. And now our way there is blocked, we're lost under the Palace—and we've lost Florin and Pennae." He looked up, spreading exasperated hands. "Have I missed anything?"

"Plenty," Semoor told him, "but your aim is getting better."

"Belt up!" Jhessail snapped. "Just . . . be still! You're not funny, you're not helping, and—and I'm trying to *think.*"

"Yes, of course," Semoor murmured. "I can see how hard that must be for you."

Islif cuffed the Anointed Light of Lathander across the back of the head even before Jhessail snarled and kicked him in the shins. Semoor hastily withdrew into a protective ball, holding forth his holy symbol in front of him—and beside him, Doust threw up his hands in an "I'm innocent, pray strike me not!" gesture.

The two lady Knights disgustedly turned their backs on the priests, put their heads together, and after a few swift murmurings Islif turned and said briskly, "Right, we've decided. Doust, you'll lead, with the glowstone out. I'll be just behind you, sword at the ready, then Jhessail, then Semoor. Your job, Semoor, is to look behind us—all the time, mind, not once or twice and then forget about it. We'll turn back from this barrier to the first cross-passage, take it, and at our first chance we turn back in the direction we were heading in this passage. Once we think we've gone far enough to outflank this barrier, we try to head back this way until we find the other side of this barrier, and search for Florin or Pennae."

"Still with you," Semoor murmured, his voice quiet and serious.

"Good. Now, if we don't find them soon, we turn instead to seeking a way up, into the rooms of state, and try to find a high-ranking Purple Dragon who might believe us about the conspiracy. We can trust no war wizard except Vangey. Any questions? No? Right, let's move!"

With Doust walking in the forefront with the glowstone, they turned their backs on the iron barrier, retraced their steps down the passage to the first cross-passage, finding it closer than they remembered, and turned along it.

Almost immediately, they saw a radiance in the distance, growing to sudden splendor as it rounded a corner and came out into the passage, then bobbing as it came rapidly toward them.

"Hide your glow," Islif murmured in Doust's ear, and then turned and hissed, "Over to the side, everyone, and right in behind me."

The light came closer—a glowstone held by someone in a hurry. Hastening toward them came a frightened courtier, in a grand barrel-fronted jacket that looked a little torn and dusty. He saw them and hesitated in his anxious trot, stiffening for a moment, but then looked away and started to rush past.

Which was when Islif stepped away from the wall and took his arm, just above the elbow, in a grip of iron.

He let out a little squeak of fear, and thrust his free hand wildly into the front of his jacket. Islif let him draw the dagger she'd expected clear of the garment—and then deftly punched the point of his elbow with her free hand, and sent the dagger clanging away along the passage.

"Well met, courtier," she said heartily. "Have you by chance seen a ranger named Florin? Or a lady in leathers, who goes by the name of Pennae? Or anyone at all down here, who shouldn't be here?"

"Y-you," the man stammered.

Islif shook him. The Knights heard his teeth rattle. "Anyone *else?*"

"N-no."

"Where's the nearest way up into the Palace floor above us?" she said.

He gestured mutely, pointing with fervor somewhere diagonally through stone walls. Suspecting this meant along the passage and then turning the right corner to find stairs, Islif kept hold of the courtier's arm and told him flatly, "Take us there. Now."

"My . . . my dagger . . . my mother'll *kill* me if I don't come home with it . . ."

"And I'll kill you right now if you try to go and get it," Islif told him pleasantly. "Does that make your choice easier?"

He nodded, clapping a hand to his mouth and staring over it at her with wide, fearful eyes.

Then those eyes rolled up into his head and he fainted in her arms. Disgusted, Islif let him fall to the passage floor in a heap.

Chapter 21

Letting the Madwits Out

Well may dragon roar
And dying captains shout
For the fields are red with gore
And they're letting the madwits out.

Tethmurra "Lady Bard" Starmar
from the ballad
Trust Only In Your Sword
published in the Year of the Crown

"Florin?" Pennae called softly. "Florin?"

She waited, but he did not shout again. After standing still and silent in the darkness for a long time—in case the iron barrier rose as suddenly as it had descended—Pennae shrugged, turned, and set off alone down the passage.

She could see nothing at all except very faint light a long way ahead, but her fingertips trailed lightly along the stone wall, the passage floor was smooth and level, and there seemed to be nothing standing between her and that distant light.

So Pennae strode on, quickly and confidently, her soft-soled boots making little sound, and was soon approaching that light.

It was leaking around the frame of an ill-fitting door, the first of a row of closed doors; the rest were dark. As she slowed to think about what to do next, the door suddenly opened—giving her a momentary glimpse of an untidy office stacked high with scrolls and coffers—and a tall, black-robed man strode out to face her, pointing at her as he did so.

A war wizard, his eyes unfriendly—tall, thin, and wart-covered, his face was homely and entirely dominated by a great ravenbeak nose. "You," he snapped imperiously. "Wench! What're you doing here?"

"Seeking Vangerdahast," Pennae replied calmly, striding steadily nearer as if she had every right to be walking along this passage, and was mildly surprised at both his presence and his question.

"Why?"

"My business, I believe," Pennae told him. "As you seem suspicious, perhaps you'll take me to him."

He shook his head. "I'm very busy—the revel. No, a cell will keep you just fine until this is all over. Thieves and hired slayers are just what we're here to thwart. You look the very picture of one, and you might well be wanting to get to Royal Magician Vangerdahast so as to *slay* him! Or distract and delay him whilst someone you're working with manages something nefarious! *Oh*, no, you'll not be distracting—"

A bare two paces away from him, Pennae quelled her sigh and deftly stripped off her leather jack, baring herself from the waist up with the allure of long practice, leaving her leathers dangling from one wrist.

The war wizard's eyes bulged, he started to stammer something unintelligible—and she glided forward, gently took his hands, and guided them to her breasts.

"Like them?" she murmured, looking hungrily up into his eyes. "Ahhh, war wizards . . . I admire you all so much. I wanted Vangerdahast, but . . . you're here, and so commanding . . ."

She let her eyes half-close, and moaned as his cold fingers, trembling with excitement, moved inexpertly over her. He drew in a sharp, ragged breath, and she whispered, "May I . . . kiss you?"

"Uh, ah, well—" War Wizard Lhonsan Arkstead ran out of things to say, and settled for swallowing. Hard.

Her mouth was parted and reaching for him, so temptingly close below him. Arkstead was not a handsome man, and had never learned the arts of being pleasant. No woman's mouth had ever been so offered to him.

"I shouldn't be doing this," he muttered, as he bent his head to hers. "This is . . . less than wise."

Abruptly leathers whirled over his head, blinding him, then were thrust into his mouth, muffling his cries—and the very hard pommel of a dagger struck Arkstead in the throat, robbing him of breath and voice, and then on the side of the head, robbing him of all Faerûn.

"You were quite correct," Pennae told his senseless body, as it slid down her legs into a crumpled heap at her feet. "Loins-driven idiot. But then, I seldom do wise things either."

She reached down to retrieve her jack—and three Purple Dragons came rushing at her out of the darkness, blades stabbing.

Pennae spat out a curse and sprang back, abandoning her leathers. There was no place to flee to. She snatched out her dagger and crouched behind the war wizard's body, hoping they'd not trample him, and so give her a little room to move.

She was wrong. The soldiers charged right over him, maintaining their unbroken line three abreast. Pennae sprang to one side, to try to cut down on the number of blades that could reach her, and parried desperately.

One blade, then two, clanging aside in a skirling of ringing steel—and the third burst past her little steel fang.

Despite her desperate twisting and arching, it darted in, snakelike, and slid like icy fire into her side.

Islif slapped the courtier's face briskly, then pinched the skin of his throat between her fingernails, and finally rolled back an eyelid and put a fingertip to his staring-at-nothing eyeball. He never flinched in the slightest.

Exasperated, she rose from him and snapped, "Come on! We haven't time to try to get this fool awake and talking!"

The Knights rushed off, Semoor plucking up the man's fallen glowstone as he passed.

The moment they were out of sight the courtier sat up.

"What do you know?" Bravran Merendil said aloud in wonder, managing a shaky smile through the drug-sweat that was suddenly drenching him. "Mother's deadsleep proved useful at last!" His smile of disbelief grew. "Who'd have thought playing dead ever helped anyone?"

He pulled another glowstone from his codpiece, used it to find his fallen dagger, sheathed it back inside the grand barrel-front of his courtier's jacket—and then smotes himself on the forehead, and gasped, "Talan Yarl!"

He launched himself down the passage, sprinting hard and thanking the gods that woman and her ruffians had gone in the other direction. "Suddenly," he muttered wryly to himself, "playing dead sounds like a very good idea indeed!"

* * * * *

"A fool? Aye, I've never denied that," Florin replied, rushing forward and waving his sword rapidly back and forth right in front of him. It struck that unseen blade with a glancing clang, and then he was past, and turning in the darkness to face whoever it was, but backing away as he did so.

He was backing into the unknown, and facing a foe with a drawn sword—a woman, unless he was mistaken about that cold, arrogant voice—whom he couldn't see, but he'd managed to get her between him and the Doorwarden.

He became aware of a faint glow in front of him, a thin line that he was sure hadn't been there before, a line that was moving, sweeping around—'twas her sword!

Its glow was growing slowly but steadily stronger, now, as it swung at him, Florin steadily backing out of her reach. He had to win time for that glow to grow until he could see it better, and to move away from the Dread Doorwarden, hopefully to and through a place too narrow for him to follow.

He could see a face—female and human, and bone white in hue—behind that blade now, as their swords met again, hard, ringing off each other and striking sparks. It was not a kind face, and it did not wear an expression even a fool would have termed "friendly."

Not even this fool.

"Who are you?" he asked, giving ground again—as heavy breathing and a ponderous footfall told him that the Doorwarden was striding up behind the woman with the sword.

"One evidently doomed to chase cowards who won't cross blades with me," came her terse reply. "Who are you?"

"One who doesn't want to fight any stranger for a reason he understands not," Florin replied, "and would much prefer to be allowed to continue the king's business without being attacked in his very Palace!"

"Do you *dare* to accuse *me* of disloyalty to Cormyr?" Her voice sharpened into real anger. "Know, man, that I am a Highknight, personally sworn to King Azoun himself, and am accounted one of the deadliest blades in all the realm."

She lunged, and Florin sidestepped and backed away again, without replying. With a hiss of exasperation she pursued him, adding, "The king creates very few female Highknights. I am one of them."

Florin bowed his head. "Well met."

"Do you mock me?" she snarled, gliding forward to launch a flurry of thrusts and slashes. He fell back again, parrying energetically, and as she pressed him, worked his steel faster and faster, until sparks were raining down.

He was stronger, and the weight he was putting behind his sword swings must be numbing her arms. Yes, her attack was lessening. He gave ground more slowly now, and there came a time when her arm grew tired and her attack openly faltered.

He listened to her swift breathing, stepping back again. Her pursuit this time was plodding, no longer a furious whirlwind.

"No," Florin replied, his voice low and respectful. "I do not desire to mock you or give offense. I, too, have been honored by the Purple Dragon. King Azoun himself sponsored our adventuring charter, after I saved his life in the forest."

"Ah. Then you would be . . . Florin Falconhand. Ranger of Espar. So why this treason, Florin?"

"No traitor am I," Florin told her, "nor are any of us Knights. We're here to protect the king and queen—and the Royal Magician, too—from a plot to slay them all, this day!"

"Ah, no, that's *our* task and duty," she replied, the sneer loud and clear in her voice. "Anyone running around down here with weapons, who I don't know about, is a traitor."

She lunged at him again and, when he parried, mounted another furious whirlwind of cuts and thrusts, pressing him back once more, the glow of her blade mounting to a white brightness. Their blades rang numbingly as the Highknight threw all of her strength behind her blade, starting to trust in his defensive bladework that never thrust back at her, nor offered her the slightest menace of steel.

Florin stood his ground, this time, and after a while the fury of her attack faded again, and he found himself listening once more to her swift breathing. The Doorwarden loomed right behind her, now, like a patient mountain.

When she spoke this time, her words came in rushes, between gasps. "However, just for purposes of entertainment, why don't you tell me a little more about this plot?"

"No, Lady Highknight, I fear not," Florin told her. "Treason among war wizards is involved, and I know not how far it spreads. I will speak with Vangerdahast and no other—or if I reach the king or queen, I will defend them with my body."

The Highknight sighed then, and murmured, "I weary of this."

As Florin backed away from her again, she undid a pouch at her belt, plucked out a large chestnut, and threw it at him.

The previously cracked-open nutshell fell apart in flight, to let a delicate glass vial tumble out. Florin sprang at it desperately, caught it a fist-width above the stone passage floor that would have shattered it, and hurled it back in her face.

She closed her eyes as it shattered across her nose, and then chuckled as its tiny shards fell away. "It doesn't affect we Highknights, fool, but it will affect *you,* if I—"

She struck his blade aside with a deft strike of her own and leaned close to him, grinning mirthlessly.

Trying not to breathe, Florin punched her as hard as he dared, spinning her head around and hurling her limply back into the armored shins of the Doorwarden. Then he turned and ran.

He didn't risk a look back until his outstretched blade found a doorframe too narrow for the Doorwarden to pass through. Her blade was still bright, but Lady Highknight was sprawled senseless on the passage floor, with the man-mountain of a guardian frowningly poking her with his fingers and growling at her to "Wake! The man flees! *Wake,* stlarn ye!"

Florin shook his head, stepped through the doorframe—there seemed to be no door, any more, just the marks of abandoned hinges—and cautiously went on into ever-deeper darkness, feeling along the stone passage wall to his left with his fingertips, and keeping his sword raised and thrust out before him in his other hand.

His fingers found a door, and it proved to be unlocked. He opened it and felt cautiously into the utter darkness it opened into. Nothing met his timidly reaching fingertips, but when he used his sword more boldly, it immediately struck smooth metal. Florin tapped and probed cautiously forward and then up and down, and discovered that the door seemed to open into a laundry shaft. There was no floor and no ceiling, but merely smooth metal walls with holes in them that seemed to be grab-holds. They had metal a little way within them, and more than one had what felt and smelled like sweat-reeking underthings—dethmas and clouts—caught on its lip.

Eventually he dared to sheathe his sword and reach out a hand to one of these unseen openings. He took hold of it—a rolled lip, seemingly meant for human hands to grasp—felt for another, and then bent down and felt for lower openings to thrust his boots into.

He found them, and a breath later was climbing the chute, going up in the darkness and feeling warm air coming down into his face from above. After only a little climbing the chute started to bend, becoming a nigh-horizontal slope that ended suddenly in a room where three descending chutes met, and there was an access door with handholds beside it—and a spyhole in it!

The door had no lock that he could see. It was held shut by a small metal drop-bar latch, on his side. The bar dropped into an angled metal iron against the wall. He must be a floor higher in the Palace.

Florin peered through the spyhole, and found himself looking into a little room crammed with a table piled with linens, and two men. One held a glowstone and wore the barrel-chested jacket and livery of a Palace courtier, an anxious expression, and copious sweat. The other wore the grand robes and sashes of a Turmish envoy, and looked furious.

"You weren't supposed to get anywhere near me!" the Turmishman was snarling. "What're you *doing,* fool?"

"Well, *you* weren't supposed to follow Blacksilver around like a dog, always six paces right behind him. If all of the courtiers in my passage noticed—and they did!—the war wizards *certainly* noticed."

"Listen," the Turmishman hissed, and then uttered words that made cold black rage blossom in Florin, so suddenly and strongly that he almost whimpered. "The mindworm has eaten a lot of his brain. There's not much left to control him *with.* I have to stay close, or he becomes little better than a striding zombie. They'll notice *that,* to be sure."

The courtier was trembling violently now. "I—uh—ah—yes," he stammered. "Of course."

"Good," the Turmishman snarled. "Now get back to your post or to doing whatever it is that you're supposed to do, and leave me be. As it is, I'll have to chase down Blacksilver and not be seen doing it! *Go!"*

The courtier bolted out of the room, and the seething Turmishman pounded his fist into his palm and growled, *"Hrast* that Merendil bitch and her blood-bond! Without that, I'd slip away now and let that idiot puppy rush to his doom all by himself! This is going to be messy! So messy!"

"You bet it is," Florin whispered to himself, face white and eyes blazing, as he flipped up the drop-bar, wrenched the door open, and flung himself through it, sword and dagger singing out.

Striding out of the linen room, the Turmishman reached a dimly lit passage beyond, and spun around.

Florin charged, roaring, "For Narantha! *You bloody murderer!* For Narantha Crownsilver!"

The man paled and stepped back, raising one hand like a claw. From his fingers streaked the bright magical missiles of a battle-strike, lancing into Florin almost before they had time to fly.

Florin groaned at their searing pain, staggered, and struggled on despite rising agony. Reaching the Turmishman, he started hacking.

The man struggled to draw a dagger and to spit out an incantation, but Florin cared not. He sliced and chopped and hewed ruthlessly until fountaining blood stung his eyes and blinded him. Then he went on hacking until there was nothing still standing in the slippery passage but himself.

Panting above a heap of what looked like clumsily butchered meat, in a passage now awash with blood, Florin burst into tears.

"Narantha!" he wept. "This won't bring you back, but I avenged you! *I avenged you!"*

* * * * *

The ready-room had been crowded not so long ago, but all the guards were out at their posts now, leaving behind two bored Purple Dragon lionars.

They were bent over their littered desks, rather wearily writing out duty rosters for when this cursed-by-all-the-gods revel was over, when Florin's distant shouts arose. The older one looked up and frowned at the din. "Are they letting the madwits out to join the revel too?"

The other lionar shook his head, flung down his quill, and drew his sword. Together they hastened out into the passage.

* * * * *

Amarauna Telfalcon knew two things: she was more frightened than she'd ever been in her life before, and she couldn't run much farther. She suspected one thing more: that her magical Yassandra the war wizard guise must have melted away. Surely there was no way Terentane could maintain the spell, gasping as they both were, pounding along Palace passages and hallways, running hard past the occasional startled servant.

They'd begun by racing up a long staircase. It alone had left Amarauna's chest burning, and that had been a long time ago.

Or so it seemed. "Just a little farther, 'Rauna!" Terentane gasped, from close behind her. "Keep going!"

They were heading for a room he knew, where he could cast a teleportation unobserved, and whisk them back to Marsember. Yet every corner could bring them face to face with Purple Dragons, or a real war wizard, and—

"Turn here! 'Tis just ahead!"

Blindly Amarauna Telfalcon obeyed, racing past a tapestry with her lover right behind her.

Neither of them noticed the eyeholes in that tapestry, nor the eyes behind them that watched them run past.

And neither of them heard the voice from behind that tapestry that then sneered, "Bumbling novices."

Chapter 22

Take her alive

Among the orders we hated most
As they always meant greater peril
And more of our blood spilled,
Was any command of, "Take her alive."
In my years, I learned hard, sharp, and often
That no woman wants to be taken alive.

Onstable Halvurr
Twenty Summers A Purple Dragon:
One Soldier's Life
published in the Year of the Crown

Pennae staggered, sobbing with pain, and one of the Purple Dragons laughed, "Ha! *This* shouldn't take long."

The oldest of the three shook his head, and waved his sword at his fellows, directing them to spread out, to come at the wounded woman from three sides. "None of that! Disarm her, Strelgar! I want to know just what a lass is doing running around down here half-naked, felling war wizards! A hired slayer, or did we just interrupt a love-quarrel? Or something in between? I want some answers from this one, and so will Vangerdahast, so take her alive!"

Strelgar growled, obviously not liking these orders—and he liked them even less a breath later, when Pennae raced at him, hurled herself at the floor when he slashed viciously at her, rolled in against his shins, and stabbed upward. Hard.

Her blade darted under the edge of his chain mail shirt, up through the leathers beneath, into Strelgar's belly and the hairy chest above it ere it flashed away again. He shrieked, writhed in pain, and staggered forward, getting in the way of the other two Dragon's blades as they thrust at Pennae—who'd spun around against Strelgar's ankles and past him, out of the trap closing in on her.

Both of those Dragons fully expected her to flee, and jostled their ways past Strelgar to give chase, but Pennae whirled around behind Strelgar to stab him low on the seat of his leather pants, and sprang sideways across the path of the rushing Dragon commander, parrying his reaching blade.

Their swords tangled together as he charged on, but Pennae trailed one leg rigidly behind her, catching his running feet at just the right height to collect some severe bruises, and to send him sprawling.

The third Purple Dragon, also running too fast to do anything adroit, ran right over him, tripping and swearing and ending up hopping and staggering awkwardly. Which gave Pennae time enough to land with both knees on the commander's back and slash his neck open, and then spring up again to deal with the moaning, doubled-over Strelgar. She dealt his temples two furious blows with her sword hilt, and watched him sag senseless to the floor over her shoulder as she finally did what was expected of her: turned and ran down the passage, not taking the time to try to retrieve her leathers from beneath the Dragon commander—and his slowly spreading pool of blood.

The last Dragon gave pursuit, smiling as he saw the running lass ahead of him falter, put a hand to her side, and bring it away dripping with blood. She'd not last long, and then the glory of her capture would be his.

Ahead, she turned a corner, reeling now as if she could barely keep her feet. His grin widened, and he started to hurry.

Aye, Telsword Bareskar of the Palace Guard would win the day! Recognition at last! Recognition finally beyond mere war wizards' disapproving looks whenever he slouched at a post, or traded saucy words with a passing maid. Oh, this would be—

Rushing around the corner, his ankles met something hard, thin, and sharp, that shrieked against his metal-shod boots as he toppled helplessly into . . .

A bone-jarringly hard meeting with the passage floor, bouncing with the wind slammed out of him and his helm tumbling away across the floor. He fought to keep hold of his sword, suddenly aware—with deepening fear—that the wench must have tripped him with her sword, and would probably be coming at him right now! He hoped not; he hoped she'd broken her stlarning arm trying that trick on him, but somehow the gods would have to smile on him far more widely than they'd been doing lately before he'd expect—

Hoy! Desperately he flung up his sword and struck away the blade reaching for him. She *was* trying to slay him, and if he didn't move right swift-like—!

That blade came at him again. He parried desperately, staggering rather dazedly to his feet and discovering his left ankle hurt like tomb-fire, trying to beat back this lass while he got his wits and balance back.

Steel met steel again, right in front of his eyes, and his parry was a shade too slow. Her sword leaped over his to slice along his forehead like *real* fire.

Bareskar roared in startled pain; he'd made telsword without ever suffering so much as a scratch, let alone—

That cursèd sword was coming at him again!

Dripping his blood, too, it was! He struck it aside savagely and backed away, suddenly blind. Something wet and stinging was in his eyes, was—he wiped at it, desperately, and found himself looking at blood, running from his fingers. Tluining *hrast!*

A door banged, nearby, and then another. Bareskar wiped the back of his hand across his brows, to try to see what—

She'd slashed open his forehead, stlarning near blinding him, and now she was tearing open door after door along the passage! What by all the Watching Gods was she doing?

She rushed at him again, bare chest bobbing distractingly. Bareskar wiped at his forehead again so he could see it—uh, her—better, hefted his sword, and prepared to meet her charge.

He parried her first thrust with surprising ease, grinned at her shocked expression, and thrust back at her. She gave ground, one arm waving wildly as she fought for balance, and Bareskar's grin widened as he pressed her, striking her sword aside once—twice.

They fenced, swords clanging and rebounding in a ringing fury, and the telsword saw his half-naked foe holding her side again, pain creasing her face as they fought, as her sword started to waver.

Aye, *this was it!* Bareskar blinked away stinging blood again, wiped his face frantically, and charged at her, hacking and chopping as she staggered back. They were hard by the doors she'd been opening, now; she'd strike the passage wall if she retreated farther. He knew he was grinning as he wiped at his forehead again, then lunged—

Suddenly there was no half-naked lass in front of him, only darkness, and there was no floor under his right boot.

Pennae shook her head as she kicked the Purple Dragon's backside as hard as she knew how, and watched him plunge helplessly down out of sight with a shout of fear and pain, riding the laundry chute she'd found down into deeper cellars.

Such an overconfident dolt, to swallow her sudden oh-so-wounded act, and believe his bladework was suddenly so superior, after she'd just wounded him at will. Some fools will believe *anything.*

Yet there was a kingdom to save, and she would fall over if she went on running around and bleeding for long enough. She had to get gone, *now.*

None of these doors had held stairs leading upward, but there were a lot of doors she hadn't tried yet.

Pennae sprinted down the passage to the next few. Darkness. Locked. Locked. Darkness; crowded room, not stairs. Locked. Locked.

She ran out of doors, flung up her hands in exasperation, and ran on, around another corner, seeking more doors. Not that she expected to discover any shortage. They seemed to positively *love* doors in this Palace. Locked ones, in particular.

✦ ✦ ✦ ✦ ✦

"I should just run away," Bravran Merendil sobbed to himself, cowering in the darkness of another Palace linen cupboard. "Just run from all this, and let Yarl get himself killed and Blacksilver get hacked down while I'm far away—and then go back to Mother and tell her it all failed. At least I'll still be alive."

Then a cold and all too familiar voice spoke in his head, sharp and clear and seething with fury.

"If you do that," Lady Imbressa Merendil told her stunned, terrified son, "don't expect to live for a day longer than it will take me to breed you with some suitable wench. I need Merendil *heirs,* not spineless worms."

Bravran Merendil thought it a very good moment to faint again, and did so. This time, he didn't even need a vial of deadsleep.

* * * * *

"Nine Hells afire!" The Purple Dragon bearing the glowstone swore in amazement as much as anger, and broke into a run, his five fellows drawing their swords and hastening after him.

Two Purple Dragons were sprawled on the passage floor, amid much blood.

"I *thought* I heard battle-din!" the Dragon with the glowstone exclaimed, peering all around for any sign of a foe.

Nothing. Just a swordcaptain lying facedown in a pool of blood, and this—Strelgar moved a little, then, and moaned.

"Sword!" They snapped at him, seeing his rank but not knowing his name. "Soldier! What happened?"

The wounded Dragon groaned again, eyes fluttering, and drooled blood as they gently tugged him up to a sitting position, cradling his shoulders to keep him from sagging back. "What's your name?"

"Strelgar am I," Strelgar mumbled slowly, and groaned again, retching blood. "Hurt. Hurt bad."

The lionar with the glowstone had seen sorely wounded Dragons a time or two before. He looked up at the five men under his command and shook his head in disagreement. This one just *thought* he was "hurt bad."

"What happened?" he said, more loudly and firmly. this time.

Strelgar groaned, and then managed to mumble, "Well . . . uh . . . there was this lass, see . . . half-naked she was . . ."

* * * * *

There were times when Wizard of War Tathanter Doarmond hated the good looks and superbly impressive voice the gods had gifted him with—and this was one of them. Even the comforting banter of his best friend and fellow war wizard Malvert Lulleer was doing nothing to quell his nervousness. Grand Court events were always headaches, and matters weren't helped by racing gossip insisting that someone had already managed to butcher dozens of war wizards, leaving the Dragondown Chambers looking like a slaughterhouse, and that someone was probably running around somewhere under Tathanter's feet right now, hurling spells even Vangerdahast couldn't quell.

And none of the bitter "well, well, you haughty-robes finally got yours" chuckles from various Purple Dragons were helping, either. Tathanter was finally starting to understand why the soldiers were all so surly. Once the fighting and running around started, it would be fine—provided he wasn't blown apart or maimed, right off—but this hrasted *waiting* . . .

He and Malvert stood in the Longstride Hall, with its high, beautifully painted ceiling, just outside the doors of King Duar's Hall. Until further orders arrived, they were apparently guarding a rather splendid pair of arched, gilded double doors.

Doors that stood open, with their fellow Purple Dragon guards' shoulders keeping them that way, to allow seemingly endless droves of glittering-gowned ladies and their splendidly attired escorts to parade grandly in and out of the ballroom, gossiping—and laughing, and occasionally shrieking with malicious mirth—their scented and primped heads off.

There were more than thousand of these early arrivals in the hall already, and more were arriving in stlarning droves with every passing breath. Some idiot servant had decided to start serving them wine, which meant the hurling and fights and bodices being torn off and all of that would be starting *just* about the time the newly arrived envoy from Silverymoon was formally received. As the Dragon guards had already sourly noted.

"Always get someone's sick all over my best uniform, at one of these," Telsword Torlgrel Dunmoon growled. "Hope their High-n'-Mightynesses like the smell of it."

"These hrasted revels always go wrong, one way or another," Tathanter said, adjusting his jet-black-with-silver-trim uniform for the thousandth time.

"Of course," the oldest Purple Dragon murmured. "So just watch and enjoy and wait for the disaster—and then enjoy *that.*"

"Tath, if you don't stop fiddling with that codpiece, the hrasted thing's going to fall off," Malvert warned.

"Don't tempt me," Tathanter muttered.

* * * * *

Florin had tried three of the faint, dim glowstones before he found one he could wrench out of its iron cage, high up on the passage wall. Its glow was feeble indeed, but it was all he wanted. He sought light enough to see by, not the making of himself into a bright beacon.

He hurried along passages, glowstone in one hand and drawn sword in the other, seeking stairs up, or some sign of the other Knights.

Instead, he found the passage he'd been traversing for a long time suddenly ended in a short flight of steps going down.

For a moment he hesitated, thinking he should turn back, but there was light ahead, down there, and that probably meant a better chance of finding stairs and servants—and a way to reach Vangerdahast. As well as returning him to the same level of cellars where he'd been separated from Pennae and the others.

So he hurried down the steps. The light proved to come from oil lamps burning in a servants' room that looked recently vacated—by many folk, no doubt bearing things the room had held up to rooms of state somewhere overhead—but not far beyond it Florin found other things.

First he came upon many bootprints, stark on the stone floor. Prints that had been made with fresh blood, and trailed back to a large pool of gore. Right beside it was . . .

Florin rushed forward and plucked it up, hoping he was wrong.

He wasn't. He held Pennae's leather jack—yes, there was the hooked slice in it that some foe's dagger had made, long ago. This was hers—and it was soaked with blood.

Blood that still dripped from it in streams. No woman could lose that much blood and yet live.

"Oh, no," Florin sobbed, there on his knees staring at what he was holding up—and watching Pennae's blood drip to the floor. "No."

"Pennae," he whispered, as tears flooded up to choke and overwhelm him. "Pennae!"

He was dimly aware of shaking his head as he bowed it, trying to deny all of this. "Pennae . . . Narantha . . ."

He'd been holding black misery at bay for so long, and now was suddenly swallowed up, in the midst of it. Falling, falling with no hand to steady him, to comfort. "Martess . . . even Agannor and Bey, damn them!" The faces of the dead were swimming up to loom over him—laughing obliviously at least, not staring at him accusingly. He couldn't have borne it if they'd been doing that.

It wasn't glory and laughter and parading grandly across the lands, being bowed to by farmers and Purple Dragons alike. It wasn't gold coins in heaps in one's hands, or high titles. He'd known that, back in Espar, known that death lurked impatiently always, waiting . . .

Yet there was knowing and . . . knowing. By the gods, he hadn't even the *words* to grieve properly!

"Mielikki," he cried. "Lady, aid me!" For if ever I've needed my goddess, I need her now. . . ."

He seemed to smell wet forest moss, then, and hear the rustle of leaves in a green, growing forest, see dark trunks and a glow of power behind them, a glow he was rushing toward . . . just around this tree . . . just . . .

Then he was around the tree, and the light was full and gloriously bright before him, and he stared at—

Islif, with her arm around Jhessail's shoulders. Doust smiling at him in greeting, and Semoor giving him that familiar wry, sly grin too. His fellow Knights of Myth Drannor.

His Knights. Still alive, still his family, still needing him.

Always and ever worth fighting for.

Just like Cormyr.

Both needed his sword, and the little he could do to aid and save them. The fallen were the fallen, but the living . . .

"Are still mine," he managed to croak. "My problem, my burden."

He sprang to his feet, then bent down again to pluck up Pennae's bloody jack from where it had fallen from his hands.

Drawing in a deep, shuddering breath, he threw back his head and whispered, "*Thank* you, my lady."

He shifted the dripping garment into the hand that held the glowstone, hefted his sword, and went on.

"Lady of the Forest," he murmured as he walked, "aid me ever."

Once there was a kingdom, and it needed saving . . .

✦ ✦ ✦

The moment of chill blue sparks faded and fell from them, leaving Terentane and Telfalcon standing together blinking at the familiar decay of the boathouse around them.

Amarauna drew in a deep breath. "Well. Safe back in Marsember, at least."

"There'll be another day, and another way," Terentane told her. "Patience will keep both our heads on their shoulders."

Then he turned, grabbed at her clothing, and started to tug it off.

"What're you—?" she asked, laughing. "*Now?*"

"Well," he replied calmly, his fingers busy on her laces, "we could both be dead tomorrow."

✦ ✦ ✦

"Hreldur, you're so full of naed 'tis coming out of your mouth now, not just your ears!"

"No, I'm *not* lying, Drel! I *swear!*"

"I swear, too, and my teeth gleam when I do! Now just *away* with it! There're sneak-thieves and cutpurses by the hundreds all over the Palace right now, and half a hundred women I'd like to get a better look or three at, too, and most of 'em are wearing things that'll *let* me get those looks I want, and more." Drellusk waved an exasperated hand. "So my head's full of all this, and you are spewing wild and wilder tales of some stlarning *nude* sorceress and expecting me to *believe*—"

"Ho, Drellusk! Ho, Hreldur!"

"Ho, Lhaerak!" the two Purple Dragon telswords replied in chorus. Lhaerak was their lionar, and had come out of a side passage striding along even faster than they were. They started half-trotting to keep up.

"So, what's all this I'm hearing about this sorceress?" he growled.

Drellusk waved a dismissive hand. "Just another of Hrel's fancy-tales, mi—"

"Well if it is, Hrel's managed to get himself clear out to the front gates of the Royal Court to tell the lads there all about it. Which is passing odd, because as I recall, the two of you were just now stationed at either end of the north Palace guardstands, yes?"

"Yes," Hreldur replied. "See, Drel?"

Drellusk nodded. "I yield me, and offer sorrows."

"Taken," his friend replied with dignity, and then turned his head excitedly and told the lionar, "A nude sorceress, they're saying! All alone, but her spells animate a dozen swords to fight for her! She's butchered dozens of war wizards and a few of us soldier-lads, too, and is still on the loose in the cellars!"

His words had brought the hastened trio of Purple Dragons to the room they'd been seeking in such haste: Hawkinshield Hall. One of the older, shabbier rooms of state at the north end of the Palace, it was where Vangerdahast was now trying to rally the war wizards he had left, and re-establish some security, with thousands of guests already flooding into the Palace.

Hreldur fell abruptly silent as he became aware his words fell loudly into a tense silence, and men were glaring at him.

Many men, all of them war wizards and high-ranking Dragons, and all of them clustered in a great ring around the Royal Magician of Cormyr.

Who now turned his head to give them a severe look and confirmed, "There're reports—as you've just heard from Telsword Hreldur Imglurward, here—of an unclad sorceress running around the Palace cellars.

If you should happen to see this almost-certainly fanciful lass, take her alive and bring her to me. There'll be a reward."

He waited for the predictable chuckles to arise from the male war wizards in the room, and didn't bother looking to see how the handful of females reacted. Paying overmuch heed to the feelings of others was a luxury neither the Court Wizard of Cormyr nor the Royal Magician of the Realm had much time for—and being both, Vangerdahast had even less.

"One thing more," the wizard growled. "The revel also seems to have attracted thieves, hired slayers, and adventurers here to the Palace this night. If you should happen to meet with anyone desiring urgently to reach the king, the queen, or even me, treat them with *great* suspicion. Even weapons-out hostility would not be seen amiss. Better far to safeguard the living, than guard corpses at a royal funeral, hmm?"

Chapter 23
WHEN COMMANDS CLASH

For good men go down in smoke and ash
When tempers fail and commands clash

Dathglur "the Roaring Bard"
from the ballad
Swords And War And Sorrows
published in the Year of Embers

Waving his gigantic, roiling-with-fat forearms about as wildly as any juggler, his face growing redder and redder, Master of the Kitchens Braerast Sklaenton looked more than ever like a gigantic, angry flameshell crab standing on its hind legs.

"No! Not a goblet goes out of this room that I don't see put on a tray! And not a tray gets out that door without its carrier submitting to the spells of our war wizards! Can't you dolts remember simple orders for longer than it takes you to say your own names? Darthin! Harlaw! *Get back here!*"

Jowls quivering, the head cook pointed the two serving-jacks across the busy kitchen to its far doors, where already-exhausted war wizards were slumped in chairs, their pale faces showing the sweating strain of mind-probing every passing servant to seek out would-be poisoners and assassins. "March your lasses yonder! And mind they *stop* in front of the spellhurlers and get themselves checked, good and proper!"

The way to those mages was an everchanging tangle of rushing, shouting scullery maids, cellarers, and carvers rushing this way and that with steaming dishes and various sharp forks, cleavers, and knives in their hands, too busy to even notice that the highfront black gowns of the serving-lasses proceeding so deftly among them went clear down to halfway along the upper curves of what Master Sklaenton would have called their "carvable rumps."

The war wizards noticed, though, and managed faint smiles of appreciation that made the young lass of a mage who was Vangerdahast's designate as their superior for this task frown disapprovingly, and tap the wand in her hand into her palm in irritation. A moment later, she flinched so wildly, it could almost have been termed a jump.

The cause was a sudden bellow from Master Sklaenton, almost in her ear. "Lankel! Where are the cakes?"

"Here, Master!" The faint shout came from an adjoining kitchen.

"Well, what good are they in there? They need to be *here,* right now, in the hands of these wenches!"

Undercook Lankel was seven summers beyond learning better than to argue or explain. "Yes, Master!" he cried, sounding eager.

The Master of the Kitchens nodded in broadly smiling satisfaction—ah, but they still jumped when he ordered them to—and turned away, ignoring War Wizard Varrauna Tarlyon's glare. Sixteen thousand tarts awaited his attention, and he wasn't moving as fast as he once did . . .

There was a brief commotion, then, as one of the servers stiffened and reared back from War Wizard Markel Dauren in his chair, hurling her tray of drinks into his face and spinning around to flee.

Only to halt in an instant as the wand in Varrauna's hand clapped across her throat and paralyzed her. Markel shook his head to rid himself of some of the wine streaming down his face, but old Brasker in the chair beside him went right on probing serving-wenches as if trays of wine goblets were often hurled around.

Standing beside the quivering, wild-eyed lass in the backless gown, Varrauna touched the buckle of her belt and murmured, "We've found one, Lord Vangerdahast. Markel hasn't had a chance to say much, through the wine she threw over him, but he said something like 'Urlusk.' "

"The Merlusks," the grim voice arising from her belt replied. "Never numerous, exiled by King Duar, quiet for years—and since the ascension of King Azoun, they've become nigh the most energetic patrons of slayers-for-hire east of Amn. They send someone to almost every large Court event. I'm amazed they haven't run out of suicidal fools by now."

* * * * *

The blood was still welling out of her. More slowly, now, but that was probably because she'd lost so much already.

Grimly Pennae jerked open her thirty-fourth door, wondering how long she'd still have strength enough to open anything.

It swung open to reveal heat, the crackling of a fire—and two startled, sweating young men clad only in sweat, boots, and clouts.

They had long, heavy iron tongs and pokers as long as spears in their hands, as they straightened up to gape at her from busily rolling logs into place. They'd been feeding fires under the blackened flanks of what looked like huge water boilers. Now, however, they were staring in utter astonishment at Pennae, wavering weakly against the doorframe. A lass bare above the belt of her breeches, who held a bloody sword in her hand as if she knew how to use it.

Smiles of delighted disbelief broke across their faces, and they turned to look at each other, as if to seek reassurance that they were indeed both seeing the same thing.

Which was when Pennae exploded forward, her sword ready to ward away the nearest lad's poker—and slammed the hilt of her dagger against the side of his head with all the force she could still manage.

He fell, slack-jawed, but the pain of that jarring blow made her sob and stagger, blood pouring out of her sliced side with renewed vigor.

"What're you—?" The second lad was still so startled by her revealed upperworks that he could barely do more than stare.

"Like them?" Pennae gasped, to set him nodding.

He did, obligingly, and she struck him senseless the same way she'd served his fellow, falling atop him and riding his sweaty bulk down to the floor.

Well, not every Cormyrean is bred for his brains.

Their clouts were none too clean, but knotted together they were just long enough to go around her ribs, to try to hold her wound closed.

Wincing, Pennae reeled back out of that room leaning on a long poker—and, when she had to, on her sword, too.

Gods, but she was as weak as a bird.

A child's toy bird, made of glued-together feathers . . .

Rellond Blacksilver staggered stiffly along a back hall of the Palace, clutching his ornamental court sword as if it reassured him.

In truth, it did. For a long time now his mind had been a wallowing, swirling fog, betimes crushed beneath great cataclysms of bright lights and roaring sounds, but now . . . now bedeviled only by unsettling *gnawing* feelings . . . through which he fought to fling to the one thought that had been his for as long as his faltering memory served him.

He was here to kill King Azoun on sight.

"Highknight," a familiar voice rumbled, as a hand the size of a shovel shook her. "Lady Highknight."

Her jaw and neck ached horribly, and her head rang like a temple bell. That stlarning, grauling brute Falconhand! How *dare* he?

This was what came of Azoun's willful generosity. Though she'd benefited from it greatly—from that first tryst across his saddle to the training he'd made sure she got to the rank she now held—she'd warned him of it.

When he aided the disloyal, dangerous, and unsuitable, it was a weakness that could bring down the Dragon Throne.

Some backcountry thickneck of a ranger saves his life in a swordbrawl, and he gives the lad a charter, and a free hand at gathering the dregs of the countryside to go rampaging around with drawn swords, lording it over the law-abiding! Well, she'd put paid to *that* soon enough. Rangers tracked poorly when beheaded.

"Highknight?" the Doorwarden rumbled again, his shaking making her jaw shriek its pain through her skull. It must be broken.

She put a hand up to it to keep her talking from doing worse damage—could her jaw fall off, if she opened it too wide?—and managed to mumble, "My thanks, Baerem. Let me lie still for a bit. I must rise in my own way."

"Lady Tarlgrael, are you hurt?"

"No," she snapped, "I'm . . . all right, *yes,* I'm hurt."

It galled her to waste a precious healing potion on a broken jaw, but gods *above,* this hurt! Not that she'd felt pain all that often, since her training had ended. She was too good with a blade for that.

She fumbled at her belt, found the vial she'd need, teased it forth, and almost spewed her guts with agony when she momentarily forgot her injury enough to try to do as she always did: pull the cork with her teeth.

Fighting down nausea in a red mist of pain that had her curled up and mewing like a cat, and hulking Baerem rumbling anxiously over her, she managed to twist the cork off with her fingers and let cool, soothing relief trickle down her throat.

Almost immediately she felt better, good enough to sit up—gaining an approving roar from Baerem, bless him—and rekindle her anger.

She was going to have that ranger's neck—right now, not even taking the time to comfort Baerem or work with him at the winch to raise the dungeon door again.

The great iron barrier had split up the intruders but, so far as she could tell, crushed none of them, and its raising could wait until she'd downed Florin Falconhand and some or all of his Knights of Myth Drannor. She'd been told once which king had caused the barrier to be built, to wall off the lone way down into the Palace dungeons and prevent prison breaks, but there were no prisoners to keep safely penned up anymore.

There were just intruders stalking around the cellars of the Palace who should be prisoners, forthwith—or corpses.

Smiling, utterly unharmed now, the Lady Tarlgrael opened her eyes and held out her arms to Baerem, who reached down with that gentle deftness that still surprised her, to cradle her shoulders and ask anxiously, "Are you well again, Highknight?"

"I am, Dread Doorwarden of the Palace of the Dragon," she told him formally, eyes flashing fire as she stood up, stretched like a cat in her dark leathers, and added, "And I will be even better when I've slain the man who escaped us both. Florin Falconhand must die."

✦ ✦ ✦ ✦ ✦

War wizards were apt to be a snappish, sour lot, but this one was worse than most. The young wenches generally were; they all seemed to think they had to prove their cods larger than any man's.

First Sword Brelketh Velkrorn was interrupted in this less than happy thinking when the very war wizard he was measuring turned and glared back over her shoulder at him, fair tresses swirling. "Dragons," she snapped, beckoning imperiously. "To me!"

The trio of Purple Dragons kept their faces carefully impassive as they trotted forward, all of them privately wondering just what, here in the back halls of the Palace, could be so stlarned *exciting* that their presence was so urgently required—and why War Wizard Tarlauma Hallowhar felt the need order them around so dramatically.

"That man! He imperils the Crown! Look you, how he clutches his sword, his strange demeanor? Take him! I want him alive, mind!"

The veteran Purple Dragons looked along the line of her lancelike pointing arm at a lone man stumbling slowly toward them, down an otherwise deserted passage.

"Yon's Rellond the Roughshod!" Telsword Briarhult told her. "A peril to every lass who catches his eye, yes, but not to the king or Vangey—and I think even *he* has wits enough not to lay lecherous hands upon Queen Filfaeril!"

He shook his head, the three Dragons turning away as one, but Hallowhar put a firm hand on his shoulder and hissed, *"Look! Look now!"*

The Dragons sighed, turned, and beheld a courtier rushing up behind Blacksilver, calling softly, "Rellond! Rellond, there's a room I wanted you to see, remember? And I promised to polish your sword. Give it here and I'll get started on it, the moment we're settled."

Bravran Merendil's voice trembled. He hoped that's how a courtier would talk, because that war wizard and no fewer than three Purple Dragons were standing farther along the passage staring right at him. Somehow, he had to get Blacksilver—gods, the man must be little better than the shuffling undead by now, with the mindworms gnawing away but no one using them to compel him—turned around and locked in a storeroom somewhere until the revel was done. Thank the gods he hadn't gotten around to poisoning Blacksilver's sword yet.

"You," Blacksilver grunted, recalling Merendil befriending him and buying him drinks in a tavern. Drinks he was now certain—as much as this haze drifting through his head would let him be certain about anything—had been drugged. He drew his sword to give this Merendil pup what he deserved.

Bravran sprang back, plucking forth a dagger from within his jacket, and called, "Help!"

The three Purple Dragons exchanged weary looks and strode forward, War Wizard Hallowhar right behind them. Blacksilver stalked after the courtier, who was backing away, his face frightened and pale.

"Blacksilver!" Telsword Briarhult barked. "Sheathe steel, or face arrest!"

Rellond Blacksilver lurched around to face the Dragons, growling in anger.

"Enough, Blacksilver," the young mage said crisply, the self-important arrogance in her tone making the Dragons wince—and Rellond Blacksilver charge, sword sweeping up to hack and hew.

* * * * *

"Still no Florin," Jhessail said, clawing open yet another door. Darkness behind it; the silent dead darkness that meant a room that held no life.

"Not even a pinch of Florin here, either," Semoor said, letting his door swing shut. "Have you found any, Doust? Even a little piece?"

"*Enough* sour jesting, Wolftooth," Islif growled, from ahead. She was tirelessly plucking open doors and peering at the rooms beyond, while muttering more and more angrily about how much time was passing.

Doust considered a thought, and then shook his head and kept silent, judging it an inauspicious moment to remind Islif that each passing breath brought every mortal a breath nearer their last, and the inevitable waiting grave.

✦ ✦ ✦ ✦ ✦

With the unspoken ease of long experience, the three Dragons drew their swords and spread out, to face the enraged noble with a wall of parrying war-steel. They didn't expect War Wizard Hallowhar, having goaded Blacksilver into this, to do anything useful about dealing with him—wherefore they weren't disappointed.

As the fray of furiously clashing steel began, Tarlauma Hallowhar stood staring thoughtfully past it at the courtier, who had backed well away and was now sheathing his dagger inside his jacket, looking up at her rather guiltily as he did so.

Tarlauma frowned. Many courtiers openly bore small belt-knives, and were allowed to do so, but a dagger like *that?* Carried in concealment?

Shaking her head, she spread her hands and carefully started to cast a spell on the distant man, who had started to turn away. When he saw what she was doing, his eyes blazed—and then he launched himself down the passage at her, running hard.

Telsword Briarhult calmly stepped back and away from his parrying of Blacksilver, to stand between the war wizard and this onrushing madwits of a courtier, his sword raised and ready.

War Wizard Hallowhar finished her spell—a mindwalk, aimed at this courtier with the knife—and stared into the man's eyes to begin her plunge into his mind.

He seemed wild with terror, almost frothing as he sprinted down the passage, right at Briarhult's waiting blade. At the last moment he plucked and threw something else from within his jacket—a little cloth finger-bag, thongs dancing wide open the way he'd just pulled them—right into the Purple Dragon's face.

It burst on the bridge of Briarhult's nose, flooding the air with a cloud of black dust that had the familiar acrid smell of darkrun pepper.

Briarhult slashed blindly at empty air. The courtier flung himself aside, shoulders bouncing hard off the passage wall, and then stepped forward in the lee of the swinging sword and slashed at Briarhult's face, just catching his cheek.

Telsword Chorn Briarhult slumped bonelessly to the floor in an instant.

War Wizard Hallowhar gaped in astonishment at what she had just started to perceive of Bravran Merendil's racing thoughts: treason, on the part of this heir of an exiled noble house, with his mother smiling behind him . . .

That was as far as she got ere Merendil's knife slid hilt-deep between her ribs, and Faerûn whirled away forever.

* * * * *

Lady Tarlgrael idly sliced empty air with her sword as she stalked along yet another passage. She liked the heft and feel of favorite warsteel in her hand, and she was looking forward to using it. Soon.

Sound traveled oddly in these passages, but over the years she'd learned where some of the echoes carried. She slowed at one such place—and froze to listen intently when she heard faint murmurings, and a muffled bang. Then another.

Doors closing, and voices. Down here where there could quite likely be courtiers and servants conferring or stowing things, or even dragging forth extra chairs and tables—but not without someone contacting the duty guardian on this level. Her.

She stalked forward, knowing those sounds had to be coming from around *that* corner, up ahead.

"Lady Highknight," she murmured to herself, starting to smile, "may you enjoy good hunting."

✦ ✦ ✦ ✦ ✦

War Wizard Hallowhar crumpled to the floor like a discarded cloak, and the courtier who'd felled her turned in frantic haste and fled—less than an armlength beyond the Purple Dragon blade thrust out to bar his way.

"Kaerlyn, *get him!"* the ranking Dragon snapped, sweating under Rellond Blacksilver's swift and deft bladework. The rake had seemed but half alive when stumbling along, moments ago, but he seemed like Toril's greatest swordsman now! Gods preserve!

Frantically First Sword Brelketh Velkrorn caught Blacksilver's blade on the quillons of his own, the length of a finger away from its plunging into his face, and fought to hold it back. Blacksilver laughed coldly and then stepped back—and deftly drove his sword into an exposed-for-an-instant gap in the armor of the telsword trying to get past him and chase down the courtier.

Telsword Arnden Kaerlyn groaned, twisted in a vain attempt to parry as Blacksilver's blade pulled back, dark and wet with his own blood—and then went down with a startled squeal as the noble feinted at his face but then thrust in again at the same spot, far deeper.

Leaving First Sword Velkrorn staring over Blacksilver's shoulder at the distant figure of the courtier turning a corner, and vanishing.

"Damn you!" Velkrorn roared—as the noble's blade came back at him again, whirling and darting in a web of bright thrustings that had him parrying frantically. He threw himself to one side of the passage to force Blacksilver to turn, hoping to drive him into a stumble—and the moment the noble turned to engage him, he hurled himself back again.

The third time, it worked. Blacksilver swayed, waved his free arm wildly to try to keep his balance—and Velkrorn caught the noble's blade on his own, forced it to one side, got one boot around behind Blacksilver's leg, and shoved hard.

Well and truly tripped, Rellond Blacksilver went over backward, arms waving helplessly, and crashed to the floor. Velkrorn jumped on him, slamming both knees down hard, one on the noble's sword arm and the other in his stomach.

Winded, Blacksilver twisted in agony, straining for breath, his sword clattering beside him. Velkrorn punched him in the face and then in the jaw—twice—thrice, slamming the noble's head repeatedly against the passage floor until it finally lolled loosely, and he was sure Blacksilver was truly senseless.

The courtier was long gone. Disgustedly Velkrorn examined Telsword Kaerlyn. Also senseless and bleeding heavily—badly wounded but still alive. For now.

Briarhult, however . . .

"Dead," Velkrorn muttered grimly to himself. "From a scratch that shouldn't have even slowed him." The telsword's lips were bluish.

He turned to the war wizard. Stone dead. Her eyes were staring at nothing, her skin glistened with a sheen of sweat, and her lips were very blue.

First Sword Brelketh Velkrorn rose, trying to think of a suitable curse. Snatching up Blacksilver's sword, he hurried off to find the nearest alarm gong.

Chapter 24

In the Name of the King

There have been good kings, and careless kings,
sots and madwits and tyrannical bad kings,
yet all their villainies pale against the sheer number
of injustices and follies done by others
in the name of the king.

Mallowthear Stelthistle
Idle Notions of a Sage
published in the Year of the Mace

"Hear that?" Islif snapped, inclining her head toward a message-pipe. A faint thunder—the clamor of hundreds of excitedly chattering folk—was spilling from it. "The revel's beginning, or soon will be. We're running out of time."

"Before you ask," Jhessail said, "I haven't a spell to make us all fit in yon pipe and soar up it. If we're *ever* going to get out of the stlarned cellars, 'tis stairs we'll be using."

"Those stairs are still missing," Semoor said. "And the same paucity of relevantly helpful magic afflicts Doust and myself. So it's going to be the old way." He lifted one boot and waggled it, in case any of his fellow Knights had forgotten what "the old way" was.

By their weary expressions, none of them had. "We could open more doors," Doust said, "if Pennae—"

"*Yes*, holynose," Islif replied, a little testily. "And we could save the realm if the king and queen and Vangerdahast all came strolling up to us right now. But they won't. Waste not my time with 'ifs.' "

"That," a sharp and cold woman's voice said out of the darkness, "sounds like a herald's cue. I am none of the three you seek, but I know who *you* are: intruders. Throw down your weapons, in the name of the king!"

The woman striding down the passage toward them might have been a larger, more muscular version of Pennae. Her leathers and boots were glossy black, and her faced looked as sharp and forbidding as the sword gleaming in her hand.

Yet she was sleek, and moved like a tavern dancer. Set against to her grace and curves, Islif Lurelake looked like a man. A red-faced, work-stained farmer, with her smudged face and tangled hair.

"You invoke the king's name too?" Islif shook her head, taking a step nearer the approaching woman. "Why don't you throw yours down, at the same time, and we'll talk? I'm seeking the king, as it happens, and the queen too. Not to mention Royal Magician Vangerdahast and two fellow Knights of ours, who got separated from us down here by some sort of falling iron barrier—"

The woman in leathers lifted her voice to override Islif's. "I believe I heard myself give you a clear command, brigands!"

"Say not 'brigands,' but 'Crown-chartered adventurers and Knights of the Realm,' " Islif corrected her sharply. "And I do believe I heard myself offer you a suggestion."

They stared bleakly at each other in silence for a moment before Islif added calmly, "As far as I'm concerned—as you haven't bothered to identify yourself—your authority doesn't apply to us. I see a woman in leathers, alone, running around down here in the dark with a drawn sword in her hand; obviously a thief or hired slayer. So I believe I'll now command *your* surrender, in the name of King Azoun of Cormyr, fourth of that name."

"And Queen Filfaeril, our personal patron," Jhessail added, stepping to one side so as to cast spells freely.

"And have you proof of this patronage?" The woman sneered, putting a hand on her hip, among all the sheathed daggers and pouches there.

"Have you a name at all, to be asking us such things?" Semoor Wolftooth asked sharply. "We've met with Purple Dragons high and low—and war wizards, likewise—and seldom encountered such lofty arrogance. Being highnosed with strangers is *my* failing. You're not an Obarskyr . . . so who are you?"

"Rarambra Tarlgrael, Highknight of Cormyr," the woman with

the sword snapped, her eyes flashing fire. "Personally sworn to Azoun; a friend and more to me, not just my king."

"Behold me unsurprised," Semoor murmured. "Is there a woman south of, say, Jester's Green that Az—"

"Speak no treason!" Rarambra snarled at him. "And I say again, in Azoun's name, lay down your arms, Knights—if you *are* Knights—or I'll proclaim you traitors and treat you accordingly."

"Which would be . . . how?" Doust Sulwood asked, stepping forward.

In reply, Lady Tarlgrael gave him an unlovely smile and touched the gorget at her throat. There was a sudden shimmering in the air around her, that moved with her as she suddenly charged at Doust, sword flashing. "Let us see how enthusiastically Tymora aids you, Luckpriest!"

Doust retreated hastily, hefting his mace. She sneered, judged him, "Coward!" and lunged at him.

In the air, her blade was met and stopped short by Islif's longer, heavier sword with a ringing clang.

The Lady Highknight blinked in disbelief, then set her teeth and shoved, even though Doust had now backed well away. Islif's arm stayed where it was, as hard as an iron bar and utterly immobile, the locked swords quivering a little but not moving.

A breath passed, and then another, as Highknight Targrael struggled, Islif stood like a grimly smiling post, and the rest of the Knights watched.

They saw Lady Targrael's face grow dark with anger as she strained and shoved, then tugged her sword to try to dart it past, only to find it deftly caught and bound by Islif's blade . . . the silent contest of sword arms went on—until the Highknight suddenly snatched a dagger from her belt, to stab at her foe.

Only to find the wrist of her dagger hand gripped in midair, iron-hard, with Islif's gently smiling face behind it. The Lady Highknight stared furiously at that face, and saw contempt looking back at her.

"Traitor!" she hissed.

"I have found that word is flung around far too loosely," Islif replied, "by folk such as you, merely to brand anyone who stands against them. I'm growing tired of it." Her shoulders rippled, and she plucked her adversary up into the air by the hold she had on one straining wrist, and hurled the Lady Highknight across the passage, into the wall.

Lady Targrael thumped solidly against unyielding stone, well off the floor, slid down to meet it with a snarl of anger, and launched herself back across the passage at Islif, blade whirling.

"Knights," Islif commanded, as she stepped forward to meet that storm of steel, "go on opening doors. We can't let this woman delay us further. She could well be part of the treason!"

Jhessail and the two priests stared at her, and then hastened a little way along the passage, to where there were doors they hadn't examined yet, and started trying to open them.

"Well, Lady Highknight?" Islif asked, as their swords rang sparks off each other in a dazzling dance that let the woman in black advance not a stride. "Tired yet? Willing to consider a truce, that we can serve the realm together?"

"No!" the Highknight spat, starting to pant now. "*I* guard this level, and you *will* submit to my authority! Or I'll—"

"Or you'll what?" Islif growled, pressing forward and forcing her foe to give ground. "Sneer me to death?"

With a wordless grunt of anger and a toss of her head, the Lady Targrael sprang back, breaking off their blade play, and sprinted along the passage, heading for Doust's unprotected back.

Semoor barked a warning and Jhessail raised her hands to weave a spell, but Islif barked, *"Save our spells!"* as she ran after the Highknight. "Leave her for me!"

Doust whirled around, saw his peril, and sprang away from the door he'd just forced open, leaving it swinging.

"Find anything useful?" Islif called to him, merrily.

"Nay," he called back, trying to ignore the gale in black leathers racing down on him, sword and dagger flashing. "Nothing but a laundry chute! Goes down, not up!"

"That'll do!" Islif replied. "That'll do just fine!" And with a burst of speed she caught up to the Highknight, struck aside Lady Targrael's vicious attempt to stab her—and slammed into the running guardian, shoulder-first.

The Highknight reeled, almost falling, but caught her balance and whirled to slice Islif with sword and dagger.

The Knight ducked suddenly and kicked out, sweeping Targrael's feet from under her. She bounced on her behind, hard enough to make her shriek and lose her grip on both sword and dagger, but came up with another drawn dagger in hand and murder in her glare.

Islif was up, too, sword lashing out to force the Highknight to sway back and away or be cut open. Lady Targrael gave ground with a snarl—and then suddenly turned, dashed away, running raggedly but still at blinding speed, and scooped up her fallen sword, hard by the passage wall.

Whereupon Islif's drop-kick, with all her weight behind it, smashed the Lady Highknight's sword hand, shattering it against the stone wall.

Targraerl screamed in pain, her sword spinning away, and Jhessail darted in, slicing at the Highknight's belt with her dagger.

It sagged a trifle, exposing a little flat and sweating belly. Jhessail dropped her dagger, caught the bottom of Targrael's jack, and tugged straight up, pulling the garment inside out and up over the Highknight's head.

Then she planted one tiny fist in what she judged to be the face of that blinded head, only to back away, wincing and clutching her hand.

As Doust, Islif, and Semoor closed in, Islif starting to say that this should be left to her, Jhessail charged at the struggling Highknight, found that shattered sword hand, and punched it hard, slamming it momentarily against the wall.

Targrael shrieked and doubled over, sobbing, her furious struggles to be free of her leathers momentarily lost in writhing pain.

"Lathander defend!" Semoor muttered to Doust. "Remind me if we're ever captured: *don't* let them give me to the women!"

"Take over," Jhessail gasped to Islif, wringing her hand and retreating. Islif nodded, took one long stride to reach the Highknight, and delivered a solid punch to Targrael's shrouded head that bounced it off the wall.

The Highknight sagged, and Islif punched her again. This time, as the Highknight rebounded off the wall, she staggered. Islif took her by one shoulder and the back of her breeches, ran her a few steps along the passage, and thrust her head-first down the laundry chute.

Her descent was a short but noisy succession of bangs and slitherings that made the Knights of Myth Drannor grin at each other in satisfaction.

Their mirth would have been louder had they known that somewhere beneath them, a bloody and disheveled Telsword Bareskar of the Palace Guard had just revived. Bewildered, he was flailing around in seemingly endless dirty clothes, seeking to gain his footing and get out—when something fast, hard, heavy, dark-leathered, and very *sudden* slammed down atop him, smashing him back into the rather unpleasant dream he thought he'd finally escaped.

✦ ✦ ✦ ✦ ✦

"This way!" First Sword Brelketh Velkrorn gasped, winded from all his running. The war wizards, of course, had fallen well behind his fellow Dragons, but surprisingly, the duty priest—a cleric of Helm the Vigilant—was right behind Velkrorn.

Good, because his healing would be needed swiftly. Down this passage, turn at about where that hrasted courtier had gotten away, and . . .

Velkrorn slowed, cursing. The wounded and the dead were still sprawled in the passage, but Rellond Blacksilver was gone.

They rushed to the bodies regardless, peering, and gently rolled the blood-drenched Kaerlyn over for the Watchful of Helm to lay hands upon, and begin his prayer.

"Gone," Velkrorn said in disgust, "and all we have is this!" He hefted Blacksilver's magnificent sword in his hand.

It promptly exploded, taking that end of the passage and everyone in it to the gods.

✦ ✦ ✦

In the depths of her crystal, the dust and smoke hadn't stopped swirling, but the rubble had ceased to rain down. She could see enough to know no one was still standing.

Lady Merendil turned away from that chaos with a bitter smile on her face. "Witnesses are tiresome in the extreme," she murmured aloud. "Even corpses can be made to talk. Splattered blood and innards, now, thoroughly mixed . . . they can keep secrets."

Still wearing that crooked smile, she looked at Rellond Blacksilver, lying asleep on the table her spell had just brought him to. She ran a hand down his nearest hip and leg. And smiled.

"Physically magnificent," she said thoughtfully, "with a boorish reputation that will sour any revelations he might try to make, and just enough wits left to obey orders and use a garderobe without instruction . . . the perfect slave. And if anything happens to my dolt of a son, this walking meat can serve me in another way, and sire replacement Merendil heirs. So, Roughshod, lie you there and wait this revel out. Other days of glory await you."

✦ ✦ ✦

Pennae had never thought it would take such effort to climb a simple flight of stairs. If they hadn't been narrow servants' stairs, with rails on both sides for her to reel to and rest her forearms on, she'd never have made it.

Finding the stairs at last, it seemed, had been the easy part.

"Gods, I'm in bad shape," she mumbled. "No Purple Dragons, please. I need . . . I need . . ."

She'd had to abandon the poker down below, and slide her sword back into its scabbard. The din of all the revelers talking raged on all sides, which meant Palace staterooms were all around her. Dressed like this, covered in nothing but dirt and blood and sweat above her waist, she'd certainly attract attention . . . but to get a priest's healing, she'd somehow have to look like a revel guest, not some sneak-thief or pleasure-lass. So she needed a gown.

"But strike me if I have the strength left to take one off some passing lady," she whispered, leaning against a wall as a wave of weakness washed over her, leaving her feeling empty, weak, and trembling.

The stairs opened onto a moot of narrow and deserted passages, one running straight off to a distant curtain, and the other at right angles to the first, and lined with doors, the nearest one open and spilling light out into the passage. She was still in the realm of the servants, obviously, and she either had to go through that door or get past it unseen.

The door opened into just what she'd been seeking: a "ready wardrobe," of the sort most palaces and feasting halls kept, for the fashion emergencies of guests. It was a large room with chairs and tall, tilted dressing-glasses, lined with racks and racks of gowns, cloaks, sashes, and the like.

And of course, it came with a dresser. A maid, now rising from her stool by the door, looking at Pennae in startlement.

And no wonder. Pennae gave her a wavering half-smile, only too well aware of her white-faced, staggering, half-dressed state. "Well met," she husked. "In the name of the king—"

The maid shrieked.

Pennae winced. It sounded like a wyvern's scream, stabbing right through her ears. She snatched a garment off the nearest rack, as the wide-eyed maid tried desperately to sprint past and get out the door, and tossed it over that still-shrieking head, dropping her hands to catch hold of the maid's wrist, and hold on.

The terrified lass was still running hard; she dragged Pennae as far as the door, pivoting blindly around Pennae's hold, before running right into the doorframe.

Still running blind with a gown around her head, the maid reeled back into Pennae, her shriek becoming a moan.

When it promptly rose back to a sirenlike wail again, and the maid started running once more, Pennae sighed, took hold of her shoulders, and ran her hard into the wall.

Which she slid down in limp silence, to lie still in a heap on the floor.

"In the name of the king," Pennae muttered, *"shut up."*

Then it was her turn to groan, as the room started to move. It was turning slowly around her, now, and things seemed oddly dark . . .

Pennae clawed at the nearest rack of gowns, desperately seeking something that looked as if it would fit her. Twice she had to cling to the hanging-bar and rest for a moment, ere grimly clutching at gowns again.

This one! It looked like a fall of roses, and was a horrid blushing pink hue, but Pennae was long past being choosy. Slowly, moving as if in a dream with the room still turning slowly, she shrugged it on over her leather breeches and boots.

The floor seemed uphill, somehow, as she stepped cautiously out of the room . . .

Pennae managed three steps out and along the passage—and then fainted, falling on her face right in front of the boots of a startled Purple Dragon, who'd been rushing to the wardrobe with seven Palace Guards right behind him, to seek the cause of all the shrieking.

The shield-hung passages, magnificently paneled staterooms, and vaulted- and painted-ceilinged great halls of the ground floor of the Palace were all crowded now, and still the guests were streaming in.

All in their finery, gems and false jewelry alike gleaming and glittering on arms and down plunging fronts and a-drip from earlobes, great sleeves of shimmerweave and other exalted fabrics bright and flowing, men nodding grandly to each other and the women on their arms tittering and finger-waving and leaning their heads together conspiratorially to share the latest, juiciest gossip.

The din was incredible, overwhelming upon the ears. Goodwife Deleflower Heldanorn had gone from glowing-eyed awe and wonder to a look of worry and brow-furrowed, wincing pain; one of her hammering headaches must be coming on. Her husband patted her arm and tried to mask his irritation behind a soothing tenderness he did not feel.

Servers were everywhere, sliding deftly past with platters of cakes and decanters of wine, ensuring every guest was well supplied. Arbitryce Heldanorn could taste the faint bitterness under his tongue, and nodded sourly. The wine had been treated to make drunkards sleepy rather than angry or boisterous. Of course.

"I—I don't know how all of these people are going to fit into Anglond's Great Hall," Deleflower remarked worriedly, watching still more fellow guests arrive. "After all, it's only one hall, isn't it?"

Arbitryce Heldanorn, Master Trader In Spices, Scents, and Wonders, was one of the wealthiest merchants in Suzail, and had been in Anglond's Great Hall a time or two; he knew just how vast and many-balconied that chamber was. Yet he agreed with his wife, and was pleased. She wasn't going to say only silly things for once, after all.

A dozen Purple Dragons with the grand tabards of Palace Guards over their armor swept past, shouldering through the thronging guests swiftly with snapped orders of "Make way!" with a war wizard stalking along in their wake.

"Tryce, what's *happening?*" Deleflower Heldanorn gasped, eyes widening as she clutched his arm. "All these men with swords striding around—they look so stern!"

Arbitryce smiled and airily told his wife, "Ah, but think, my flower: there's nothing exciting about this for them. *They* do this sort of thing every day. See that one yawning? They're bored as posts, all of them. They'll probably welcome some pratfall or statue toppled over—or some such—just for a little excitement."

✦ ✦ ✦ ✦ ✦

Crouched over his crystal ball in the nearest ready room, a war wizard rolled his eyes. "Oh, *please,* Goodman!" he begged the oblivious image of the spice merchant. "Don't tempt the stlarning gods any more than they already have been, I beg of you!"

A Purple Dragon leaned his head in the door, peered around until he saw the wheat-sheaf badge that clerics of Chauntea used when on healing duty at the Palace, and called gruffly, "Saer priest? Healing needed, down by the ready wardrobe. Some lass in a gown has hurt herself."

"Gods, they've started already," another war wizard groaned, a little way down the line of crystal balls.

Chapter 25

Armed dispute and frantic runnings-about

Swordcaptains look to you, and dying shout
Who now stands for the Cormyr we die for?
Amid armed dispute and frantic runnings-about
You can find no answer save "Bleed some more."

Tarandar Tendagger, Bard
from the ballad
Bleed For Cormyr
published in the Year of the Howling

Florin Falconhand turned a corner. Was that light, ahead?

He quickened his pace, moving to the wall of the passage where, yes, a light was spilling down—down!—out of a break. Stairs at last?

Stairs at last. Growing a grin of relief, the ranger mounted the broad, steep stone steps in great eager bounds, hearing a faint din of voices growing swiftly louder. The grand Palace staterooms were before him at last, and—

Lamplight glinted on drawn steel, as blades were lowered to menace him. In the passage at the head of the stairs, seven full-armored Purple Dragons barred his way, swords or halberds in hand and stern looks on their faces.

"And who might you be," their commanding lionar asked, "racing up from the dungeons with sword in hand and someone's blood *soaking* that cloak in your hand?"

Florin drew in a deep breath, smiled with a confidence he did not feel, and announced, "I'm Florin Falconhand, Knight of the queen, and I must urgently speak with Her Majesty—or the king, or Lord Vangerdahast!"

The lionar scowled. "You were sent out of the realm, as I recall, and the lads up in Arabel were bidden to see you safely outside our borders. Now, I don't know what you did, you and your Knights of Myth Drannor, but by the Dragon we swear by, I'm letting you get nowhere *near* the three most valuable persons in all the realm!"

He leveled his drawn sword at Florin as if it was a crossbow, and snapped, "Now throw down your weapons and submit to us, or by the Dragon I'll put sword to you, here and now! You're an adventurer, and I don't trust adventurers as far as I can boot them with my toe up their backsides—and believe me, I've booted my share and more, down the years! Surrender, Falconhand! Surrender or perish!"

"Are those my only choices?" Florin asked, letting a little of his anger show as he started up the last few steps. "No taking me to your commander? Or conveying me to Vangerdahast under guard?"

"Not today, lad. Not with the Palace crawling with thousands of troublenecks, just like you, and we loyal blades stretched past our limits! Now throw down that sword, or die!"

"Do all of you read the same bad chapbooks?" Florin asked wearily, coming up the stairs to cross swords with five waiting blades—and slashing aside the two halberds that came thrusting for him.

Those halberds sliced at him from either flank, and he backed down a step or two, out of their reach, and carefully set down the glowstone and Pennae's jack on a lower step, keeping his eyes on the Dragons as he did so.

It was as well he did, because the two guards with halberds advanced down the steps to thrust at him again.

This time Florin rushed swiftly up between the halberds, past the heads, and clamped their shafts under each arm. He kicked out hard, hurling himself back down the steps—jerking both halberd-wielding Dragons off their feet into helpless tumbles after him.

Florin let the halberds fall with a clatter as he whipped off their helms and brought his sword hilt crashing down on the backs of their necks. The two sprawled guards quivered and then went still.

A roar of rage arose, and amid it three of the Dragons rushed him, swords gleaming. The ranger dodged to one side along his step and then swiftly back again, drawing the three hastening guards to converge—with clangs and jostlings—into each other's way.

As they stumbled, Florin snatched up a fallen halberd and drove its blade into one Dragon's ankles. He fell down the steps, shouting curses. Florin rushed after him, pounced, and struck him senseless with his sword hilt.

"Stop, you fools!" the lionar bellowed. "Break off! Get back up here!"

One Dragon turned to obey—and Florin's sword chopped his ankles out from under him. With a yell of pain he toppled, crashing and rolling all the long, painful way down the stairs with many bangs and boomings of metal on stone . . . to lie still at the bottom, senseless.

"O most mighty Dragons," Florin taunted, as he crossed swords with the last of the three Dragons who'd dared the steps. "Truly, your skill in battle awes bards and honest Cormyreans from end to end of the realm, and will be much talked of, in days to come! Behold: seven against one becomes three against one! Ah, but so bravely have those seven contended that no victory the like of theirs has resounded across the kingdom these ninety years past! No, not since—"

"Shut your *tluining* face!" the Dragon fighting him raged, hacking at the ranger wildly. "Just tluin yourself, you—"

Florin ducked, the man's wild swing cost him his balance, the ranger kicked his opponent hard behind a knee—and the cursing Dragon's knees slammed down hard on the edge of a step, ere sliding to a jarring landing on the step below.

The guard shrieked in pain, and Florin rang his sword hilt off the man's helm so hard he dented it as it bounded off the man's head, falling to clang and bounce its way down the stairs. The Purple Dragon fell sideways without a sound, out cold.

"Two to one, now," Florin said to the lionar and the lone Dragon still standing up in the passage. "Care to join the dance?"

The lionar smiled coldly, took a swift step aside from the stairs—and as the ranger started up to face the last Dragon, stepped right back into view with a loaded crossbow in his hands.

At a halberd's length away, he took careful aim down the steps at Florin.

✦ ✦ ✦ ✦ ✦

Slowly Pennae became aware that she was lying on her back on some sort of cot, with men standing over her, talking. Several men. She was still wearing her boots and breeches, but the weight of Yassandra's belt, with its wand and pouches, was gone. They'd taken the gown off, too—no doubt to examine her wounds—but laid it over her like a blanket.

She kept her eyes closed and her breathing slow, trying not to change the expression on her face, as gentle but work-roughened fingers flipped the thin garment aside, to touch her over her heart, the man's other hand going to her forehead.

"This healing will go more easily," a man's voice—a commoner, by his kindly tone—said suddenly, close above her, "if all of you fall silent for the short time I'll need. Hamper me, and you may soon be questioning a corpse."

Someone sighed impatiently. "Aye, Priest, do your wonders."

"By the will of the Great Mother," the cleric of Chauntea chided. "The wonders are hers."

He started to murmur words Pennae did not know. Gently, almost reverently, his hands moved—from her forehead to her lips, throat, and right breast, and from her heart to her left breast, her navel, and then under her tight breeches to low on her belly. Both sets of fingers then trailed along her, never losing contact with her skin, to the palms of her hands. The incantation ended—and Pennae fought not to gasp aloud in pleasure, as a sudden warm tingling arose and rushed through her, washing all the pain away. She thrilled to her very fingertips as muscles throbbed and relaxed, bruises and sprains vanishing and taking their discomfort with them, and she writhed on the cot, straining involuntarily up to thrust herself into those wonderful fingers. She wanted to grind against them, plunge into them, never be parted from them . . .

"She's awake!" a deeper, harsher man's voice snapped. "The little slut's aw—"

"No," the priest said firmly, his firm hand guiding Pennae down flat on the cot again. He feigned pinching her, hard. "See? I pinched her hard enough to make her shriek, and she moves not. What you saw was her body enthralled by Chauntea's divine magic, *not* an awakening." Those gentle hands withdrew, covering her with the gown again. "Let her lie undisturbed for a time; she'll waken soon enough."

"Priest," the deeper voice replied, sounding irritated, "we lack the time for such niceties! There's thousands of guests in the Palace right now, and more arriving with every breath! We're stretched past our limits! We've called in Dragons from out beyond the Wyvernwater, and *still* don't have enough! If we weren't all spread out at every last door and passage-moot and stairway, trying to keep all the gawkers where they belong and a few of His Majesty's sculptures and small portables where they belong, I'd parade this wench past every last Dragon here this day. If she's from Cormyr, there's bound to be at least one of us who'll know her."

"If you're so overstretched as all that," the cleric asked mildly, "why is it that there are *six* of you crowded into the doorway to question one wounded lass?"

"Holy man," responded a voice that was both higher and colder with authority, "you are duty priest on this shift, no more. Do not presume to tell the Purple Dragons of Cormyr how to do their work—just as we refrain from seeking to direct your devotions to the Earthmother."

"Of course," the priest agreed. By the sound of his voice, he was rising from beside the cot and turning away. "I am no expert in matters of war. Yet all holy folk are skilled in talking to and counseling the injured, and I do know much about that. I am also a loyal, lifelong citizen of Cormyr, and as such a taxpaying citizen, I am curious: why do you not merely call the nearest war wizard—there's one the other end of yon passage, as I recall—and have him do the questioning with his spells? Faster, and he'll know when he's hearing truth, and—"

"Something *happened* to many of our war wizards earlier today, which I'm not at liberty to discuss." The cold voice was now positively icy. "Wherefore they're . . . busy, and we've received orders that they're not sparing anyone away from scrying duty to deal with someone who's helpless and alone. The worst she might be is a madwits or a sneak-thief, not part of some plot or other, so she'll keep. Or so they tell us."

"So if she'll keep, why not lock her in here, let her sleep, and bring all your Dragons by to try to identify her after the revel's over?"

"Priest, stick to your herbs and greens-growing, and leave this to us, hey? She could be a sorceress just waiting for us to lock her in here, so she can cast spells at ease, in private, to bring this whole Palace down around our ears, and every last Obarskyr, war wizard, noble lord, and courtier with it! Now, *out* with you!"

"You're very welcome for the healing," came the mild rebuke, as the cleric of Chauntea departed.

"May the gods *save* me from such well-meaning *dolts!*" the deep-voiced Purple Dragon said with a sigh of relief whose volume meant that he was approaching Pennae; a moment later, a chair creaked right next to her. "Anyone know how to wake a just-healed lass?"

"Slap her," someone suggested.

"Climb on the cot with her," another voice said slyly, "and show her—"

"Telsword Grathus, that'll *do,"* the deep-voiced officer said sternly.

"Pour water down her nose," Grathus said quickly. "That always wakes Teln, here, when we're camped—"

The gown was plucked away from her, and silence fell.

"Nice," Grathus muttered appreciatively. "Should we remove the breeches too? She could have all sorts of weapons hidden—"

"I'm sure she doesn't," the officer growled. "No, I had her boots off earlier, and took out all the little knives she had strapped and sheathed so cunningly down there. They're on the table, yonder, thrust into all the extra loops and sheaths and the like on that belt of hers. An impressive arsenal. So numerous, in fact, that I doubt she carries yet more. She didn't look like a manacled prisoner shuffling along, remember, and with that much weight—"

"So, are you leaving the gown off to cow her into blurting out answers," the cold voice snapped, "or just to give us all a good look? I'd hate for this to be, say, a maid of Silverymoon, who'll swiftly tell her envoy what Cormyr's so highly regarded Purple Dragons did to her."

The gown was hastily returned—and gingerly smoothed over her too.

"She's gotten blood all over it," Grathus commented, "so she might as well keep it. She might need it, to keep warm in the cell."

"Har har har," another Dragon muttered. "I'm not easy about this. She doesn't look like a sneak-thief to me."

"Oh? And how many sneak-thieves have you seen, First Sword Norlen, to suddenly become so expert, hey?"

"Well," came the prompt reply, "there was 'Longfingers' Draeran, and the two sisters—Vaelra and whatever-the-gods-called-her—and Lethran Armantle, and Dharkfox, and Balantros of Westgate, and that young lad with the mask who called himself the Hand of Justice, and—"

"All right, Norlen!"

"—Zarmos of Essembra, and that Sembian with the missing fingers; Glathos? Klathos? Mrathos?"

"It was Drethlen Dlathos," Telsword Grathus said helpfully.

"Ah, thank you; it just wouldn't come to mind. Then there was Amglur the Amnian, Duke Hawkler who was no duke at all, and—"

"Enough, Norlen!"

"I—uh, sorry, sir. I . . . sorry."

"Forget it. We've got this one here, remember?"

"Forgive me, lionar," Grathus said quickly, "but we don't know she's a thief yet, do we?"

"Grathus," the lionar growled, "when I want your cracked copper's worth, I'll *ask* for it, and I *haven't* asked for it now!"

"He is, however, correct," the cold voice snapped. "Now put the gown on her, and get up out of that chair; I'll handle this."

"But—"

"Of the two of us, which is the lionar, and which the ornrion?"

"Yes, Ornrion Synond," the deep-voiced lionar said wearily, and the chair creaked again.

Rough hands lifted Pennae up to a half-sitting position. She played dead as best she could, head lolling and arms trailing limply, as the thin cloth was dragged over her face, bunching up around her shoulders, and then tugged down her body.

"Oh," First Sword Norlen said suddenly, in the midst of this process, "how could I have forgotten the one you chased down, lionar? Transtra Longtresses, remember? *She* was a looker, now—"

"Norlen," the lionar snarled, "shut up."

"Save the rest, thank you. Well done, First Sword. If I should need someone to *talk* this prisoner to death, I'll know who to call upon."

Telsword Grathus snickered, and the ornrion let that brief mirth die into silence before adding icily, "And if I should need someone to amuse her by playing the fool, I can lay hands on just the man for that, too."

Wisely, Grathus kept silent.

"Now, lass," the ornrion's voice said, close by her ear, "I'm sure you're awake after all that. Probably smiling inwardly at the thought of what prize idiots we all are too. I am Ornrion Delk Synond of the Purple Dragons, and I have the full authority to set you free, jail you for the rest of your life, butcher you here and now, or just cut little pieces off you and feed them, one by one, to the nearest hungry hogs—as you lie chained in their mud-wallow. Which I choose will depend upon your cooperation. Now, you can begin by opening your eyes, giving me a polite smile, and telling

me your full name. Then spell it, please, so the lionar here can write it down."

Pennae opened her eyes, thrust out a hand to stab Ornrion Synond in the throat with her rigid fingers—and then sprang up, vaulting over his choking, gagging body by planting a firm hand on his shoulder.

The door was open, all the Dragons were shouting, Grathus was backing away from her in fear and Norlen in frankly smiling admiration—and a pedestal table stood just ahead to her right, with the belt she'd taken from Yassandra displayed atop it.

She landed, ducked her hips aside to elude the lionar's half-hearted grab, snatched the belt, and whirled to menace them with the wand.

"Want to die, Dragons?" she hissed.

Ornrion Synond was struggling to try to breathe and shout something.

"See to him, Lionar," she ordered. "I think he may need his teeth knocked down his throat."

That earned Pennae startled blinks giving way to the beginnings of grins, around the room, and she added, "First Sword Norlen, we didn't hear all of the sneak-thieves you remember. Oblige us, please."

"Sorry, las—er, Lady! I—uh—well—uh—"

The lionar suddenly charged at her, so Pennae shoved the pedestal table under his shins and sidestepped to let him greet the wall face-first.

Then she plucked one of her little sand-bombs from her own belt pouches and hurled it in the telsword's face, its leaf-wrapping bursting satisfyingly. Grathus staggered blindly back from the door—and with Yassandra's belt flapping in her hand, Pennae plunged out into the passage, running hard.

* * ✦ * *

Florin ducked low and sprinted along the step, leaning to snatch up the glowstone and Pennae's jack.

The crossbow cracked, its quarrel shattering the glowstone into brightly cartwheeling shards, and Florin, staggering back a step with his fingers bleeding, heard the lionar curse and snap at the last Dragon, "Don't stand gawping! Get the other bow!"

Florin turned and dashed down the steps, as fast as he could. Behind him he heard an alarm gong sound, the lionar curse again, and then the high-pitched whizzing creaks of a windlass being used with frantic speed to recock the fired crossbow.

Florin hurled himself for the same corner he'd so enthusiastically rounded, and was in the air when the second bow fired.

Its quarrel hummed past so close that the tip of his right ear caught sudden fire.

Wincing, Florin ran on, clapping Pennae's jack to his ear and deciding it was his turn to curse.

Pennae pelted down the passage, buckling Yassandra's belt around her as she ran. The Dragons were shouting and pounding along after her; not quite on her heels yet, but closing fast. It'd be only a matter of time before she raced right into another guardpost, or ran out of passage.

She passed many dark, closed doors, and the crowd-din grew. She needed a door with that noise just the other side of it . . .

This one!

Gasping for breath, Pennae yanked down the front of her gown, letting it fall to hang around her waist, snatched open the door, and plunged into the brightly lit hubbub beyond.

The high tower room lacked windows to look out over the roofs and towers of Zhentil Keep, but hardly needed them. The glossy surface of the round table that dominated the dimly lit chamber had been worked into a great map of the lands from Tunland to the Vast, and the Moonsea to Turmish, inlaid in polished stones of many hues.

Behind that table stood a great chair, tall and dark and ornately carved. In it reclined Lord Manshoon, smiling slightly.

The Shadowsil sat beside him, in a lesser chair, arms crossed over her breast, wearing her little "I'll rend you" smile.

Sarhthor stood facing them, naked. His body was covered with dried blood and crisscrossed with great wounds. Some of his fingers, along most of his hair, were missing. His flesh had sprouted many clusters of little tentacles, but they hung lifelessly, looking very dead.

"You are *very* tardy in reporting back," Manshoon observed quietly, those great dark eyes steady upon Sarhthor, "and present a rather different appearance from your usual. So, tell me: What happened at the Oldcoats Inn?"

"Zhentarim fighting Zhentarim," Sarhthor replied calmly. "Not the usual betrayals, Lord. *Something* took hold of their minds and made puppets of them, burning the brains of some to ash, and working tyranny on all, forcing them to hurl spells at each other and at our Zhentilar. Eirhaun Sooundaeril was among them, Lord, and as affected as the rest. I saw no way to protect the Brotherhood but to cast them forth from Faerûn, using the mightiest spell I know."

"You sent them to the Abyss."

"I did," Sarhthor confirmed, unsurprised that Manshoon knew what his strongest—and hitherto most secret—spell was. "Eirhaun perceived it as an attack on himself, and worked a magic that dragged me along into the Abyss too. I encountered some difficulties, as my appearance should attest, in returning here."

"Eirhaun?"

"Also returned, though much weakened, and in the care of the priests right now."

"The others?"

"I slew most of them myself, seeking to eliminate the controlling presences I so feared."

"And did you?"

Sarhthor shrugged. "I believe so—and know I have returned untainted."

Manshoon raised an eyebrow. "And if I believe you not? And slay you now, in order to . . . protect the Brotherhood?"

"Do it, Lord, if you deem it needful," Sarhthor answered, a little wearily. "I cannot resist you, and desire never to defy you. I have served the Brotherhood well."

"What? No desperate flight? No plea for your life?"

"Lord, I never learned to beg. And if I go to my knees now, I fear I will fall on my face and never rise again."

"I believe you," Manshoon said quietly. "You may go, and see what the priests can do for you."

"Thank you, Lord," Sarhthor whispered. He bowed his head, turned to depart—and collapsed on his face.

"Symgharyl," Manshoon murmured, "use your magic to convey him, with all the haste that gentle handling allows, to healing. I would rather *not* lose him."

The Shadowsil crooked an eyebrow. "And may I . . . reward him?"

"Suitably? By all means. I want to know every last little thing in his mind."

"Yes. He said nothing at all about the swords of Dragonfire."

"Indeed. As it happens, I have that matter in hand. Yet it will be interesting to know his desires regarding them."

"You soon shall. So, what shall we do about what unfolds in Cormyr?"

Manshoon smiled, waved a hand—and above many places on the tabletop, sudden blue lights in the air announced the arrival from otherwhere of as many floating, glowing scrying spheres. "We watch—only that—and enjoy the entertainment, as mayhem unfolds at the revel in the Palace of the Purple Dragon, and war wizard slaughters war wizard. I expect much armed dispute, and many frantic runnings-about."

The Shadowsil smiled her catlike smile, and went out.

Manshoon stared silently after her lithe swayings, until the tapestry of many magics swirled closed behind her. Only then did he add calmly, "And while you pleasure loyal Sarhthor, I'll ride your mind and know all you learn from him. Just as I know all of your little treacheries. And the punishments they deserve, that you enjoy so much. Such a twisted little mind."

He shivered, just for a moment, and added in a whisper, " 'Tis why I love you so."

Chapter 26

WHO RISES AGAINST THEM?

The last Dragon dead, the campfire gone out,
Hungry goblins down from mountains do pour.
Who rises against them, to make ghostly rout?
It's the host of the fallen, again riding to war.

Tarandar Tendagger, Bard
from the ballad
Bleed For Cormyr
published in the Year of the Howling

They were crowded elbow to elbow in Baerauble's Back Bower—which despite its name, was a lofty-vaulted chamber of state whose soaring dark-paneled walls were crowded with old pikes, outthrust banners, and painted portraits of hunting and warring kings taller than most commoners' cottages. Hot, no longer desperately hungry or thirsty, for deft legions of platter-bearing servants had seen to that, they were not yet revelers, and increasingly unhappy about it.

"Well, *I've* heard that Anglond's Great Hall is clear across the Palace from here," a glass merchant brayed. "When are they going to let us in, I want to know?"

"And if they say there's too many of us," a sea captain splendid in swashbuckling green shimmerwave grunted, "and turn us away without so much as a look at the Silvaeren, who rises against them, hey? Will you be with me, then?"

The well-dressed horse-trader tossed her glossy fall of hair and snorted, "Outlanders! This always happens with outlanders! They take so long to bathe and dress, I doubt we'll be in there before nightfall!"

"I care not, so long as they keep these cheeses coming. And the cakes too! Huh; *almost* makes up for this cellar-swill they're serving us! Do they think shopkeepers of Suzail know *nothing* about wine?"

Some guests had discovered the sculpted delights of Blackhakret's Chamber, next door, and accordingly a little space opened up on the Bower's magnificent carpet, allowing guests to mill about.

That milling happened to bring a young and excitedly breathless jeweler's model—spectacular in a night blue gown that both supported and displayed the two magnificent reasons old Raskro the Jeweler employed her to display his best pectorals—face to face with a grandly monacled and bewhiskered man whose sash of intricately scrolled badges, each denoting a hamlet or farm annually taxed for a thousand golden lions or more, proclaimed him some sort of noble.

"Well met, Lord!" she said with shining eyes.

"Well met, lass," the grand personage replied kindly. "Enjoying the evening, thus far?"

"Oh, *yes!* I've met so many exciting people, and learned so much about the kingdom! Folk are so interesting, so knowledgeable!"

"Folk here? In this room? Child, if this is what passes for informed converse, the realm totters," the crusty old noble growled, glaring momentarily at a merchant in a fur-trimmed greatcloak before turning his fond smile once more upon the shop-lass. "What I hear around me, to my great chagrin, is but an admixture of floridly vapid discourse, mere furbelows—or, dare I jest, 'fur-bellows,' ah ha ha—uttered by fools so charmed by the unaccustomed sound of their own wits working that they—"

The deafening chatter all around them fell into a hush in an instant, the old lord among the silenced, as a young woman in a bloodied gown burst into the room, running like a hurrying wind across its carpet with Purple Dragons in hot pursuit.

Her gown was down around her waist, leaving her bare above; she wore no dethma. As she ran she cried, "Take your *hands* off me, you *beasts!* I don't care how heroic you've been, battling for the realm! Nor how magnificent and rampant Purple Dragons are, either! Nothing gives you the right to—"

All over the room, nobles flung down goblets and started striding forward, growling.

The shop-lass stared open-mouthed as the man she'd been speaking with stepped right into the path of the foremost Purple Dragons.

And drew his ornamented sword.

"I am Lord Cormelryn," he announced, in a deep roar that rang off the vaulting overhead, "and for fifty-two summers I rode with the Purple Dragons. No man under *my* command would ever treat a lady so—or even a lass who is decidely *not* a lady. Stand and explain yourselves!"

The soldiers skidded to a stop to avoid being spitted on that needlelike blade, and sought to duck around its wielder, for their hard-breathing quarry was clear across the room by now and fast on her way to disappearing.

Only to find their way barred by a taller, thinner, and slightly younger, but just as furious noble, who snapped, "Lord Rustryn Staglance am I, Dragons, and I stand champion for the fair damsel. You would despoil her before our very eyes, sirrahs? *What* have Purple Dragons come to, these days?"

Then half a dozen nobles were coldly barring the Dragons' way and disputing passage with them. At the far wall of the chamber, Pennae put her hand on the pull-ring of the door she most liked the look of; narrow and unmarked, it probably gave onto a servants' passage. The wrinkled old noble who'd been leaning against it to give his arms a rest from taking all his weight on two canes gave her a grin and shuffled aside, winking.

Pennae winked back, paused for a moment with hand on hip to give him a good look—and slipped through the door.

Good, she'd judged a-right, and was back in passages that might just lead her closer to the royal family or Vangerdahast.

She pulled her gown back up into place—it looked a ruin, and no wonder, but there was no helping it now—and then started to hurry.

On an impulse, she tapped the little inlaid eye in Yassandra's belt buckle, and whistled softly in appreciation when it shed a glow in front of her, like a glowstone. She tapped it again, and the glow went away.

By the noise, grand chambers of state full of guests were all around her, now. The center of this floor of the Palace should be *this* way, and surely she should soon find stairs up, to take her closer to the royal apartments, or at least meet with someone she might be able to trust. Perhaps this way, where the doors were most numerous.

She rounded a corner and found herself looking into a decidedly wolfish smile.

It was adorning the face she'd seen in Arabel, of the man talking treason, the man who had the "crystals trap." The man who now stood barring her way with arms folded across his confident chest.

"Who are you?" she asked, in the manner of a dazzled young lass.

"I am War Wizard Ghoruld Applethorn," he replied politely. "And you?"

"They call me Pennae."

"Well met," he said pleasantly, "you little scampering bitch. Prepare—as they say—to die."

Pennae rolled her eyes. "I always am," she told him, snatching open a door and plunging into another ballroom full of guests. "Can you say the same?"

* * *

"I am getting so sick of these endless passages," Islif muttered. "How big *is* this Palace, hey?"

"I heard some of the servants talking," Semoor offered, "and they said these cellars run for miles—out under the gardens, and in that direction under the courtyard, to link up with the cellars of the Royal Court across the way, and then even out across the Promenade!"

"*Thank* you, Anointed of Lathander. Such cheery aid you render."

"Always happy to be of assistance," Semoor responded.

Jhessail was wrinkling her nose. "If it goes out under the city, how do they keep everyone who's digging out a bigger cellar from accidentally or deliberately breaking into it, and then wandering around looting the Palace?"

"Guardians," Semoor said. "Lots of them. Magic guardians; striding suits of armor with swords, statues of stone, skeletons with weapons . . . that sort of thing."

"Thanks," Doust muttered, peering around a little nervously. "You lift my spirits so, that you do."

"But of course," Semoor said airily. "Think nothing of it. We faithful of Lathander delight in new opportunities, in the happiness of—"

"Belting up when told to," Islif snapped, reaching for Semoor's throat.

He gave her a startled look. "Have I done something wrong?"

" 'Thing'? No. Many things? Yes. Right now, however, you can tell me more about these striding suits of armor you were just gabbling about."

"Aye?"

"What do they look like, exactly?"

Semoor blinked. "Well, I've not *seen* one; I just heard the servants . . . why?"

Islif pointed down the passage. In the distance, a helm atop armored shoulders was turning silently to regard them. It was dark and empty, with no head inside it.

"That's why," she said.

"Oh, *tluin,*" Semoor said with fervor.

* * *

Ghoruld Applethorn murmured an incantation, clung in his mind to the noble lordling look he desired—tall, tip-of-the-chin white beard and bristling brows to match, flame-hued silk doublet, cods, and hose, *yes*—and waited for the tingling to die away.

Damn that hargaunt for disappearing when it had. He knew it was still in the Palace, slithering around somewhere nearby—but hrast him if he had the time to go seeking it now, what with Knights of Myth Drannor running all over the Palace, Vangerdahast roused and roaring, and dozens of Zhents and Red Wizards and worse in the rooms of state all around him, wearing their little disguises and pursuing their little schemes.

There was only *one* little scheme that mattered—and must prevail.

The tingling ended. "Behold another grandly dressed noble lord," he murmured. "Suzail, are you ready?"

Opening the door Pennae had disappeared through, he stepped boldly into the Hall of Archdragons, looking around for a lass in a bloodstained, wrinkled gown—or anyone trying to hide behind someone else.

There was a couple standing right in his way, a red-faced merchant with goblet in one hand and an armful of begowned goodwoman in the other. "And Kaylea—may I call you Kaylea?—the worst of it, these days, comes from all these Sembian traders with far more coins than good sense! Whenever they've made or imported more gewgaws than even Sembians will buy, they try to flood our markets their leftovers—from mock-dragonfeet footstools to glowfire doorknobs!"

"Oh?" Goodwoman Kaylea asked, looking up into his face with every indication of attentive interest. "Yet *try* to flood, you said. So who rises against them?"

Ghoruld Applethorn sidestepped, seeking to get around the two—and at that moment Pennae came whirling out from behind the obliviously chatting couple, caught hold of the wrist of his trailing hand in astonishingly strong fingers, thrust his hand back against the doorframe—and drove a dagger through it, pinning it solidly to the wood.

Agony stabbed through him, and Ghoruld Applethorn had to fight for breath enough to howl in pain. As he struggled, gasping for air, Pennae blew him a kiss and slipped back out into the passage, slamming him against the doorframe with her hip on the way past.

Even before he roared with pain, guests were staring and murmuring. He was in tears before he mastered his discomfort enough to tug out the dagger and free himself—and by the time he'd finished staggering and moaning, Applethorn knew she was long gone.

* * * * *

Hurrying along the passage, Pennae snatched open the first door she saw.

A laundry chute—but a big one, large enough to hurl a linen basket thrice her girth down. She shrugged, tapped her belt buckle to win the light she needed, stepped inside, pulled the door closed behind her, and let go of its ring.

Her fall was so swift, the shaft bending only a trifle, that she couldn't hold on to the ring of the door a level down. She stung her fingers trying, then threw her elbows wide and got them bruised against the sides of the shaft—but in doing so slowed herself enough to catch firm hold of the next door.

Clinging to it, Pennae grimly hauled herself up to its level, braced herself on the elbow-hold she knew would be there, and kicked it open, plunging out into the cellars again.

With a sigh, she spun around and carefully closed the chute door. Hopefully Applethorn was too busy with his treason to chase her any longer. Now all she had to do was find *another* way up into the Palace from this second cellar level down.

If there was one.

She set out at a trot, plunging through a doorframe that looked like it'd been missing its door for a long time.

Pennae went on past other doors, some of them huge, but all of them closed and rusting and looking as if they hadn't been opened in years. None of them looked in the slightest like a way up.

She had to keep hurrying. It was taking forever for this revel to begin, yes, but "forever" would come if she spent too much time.

When she rounded a corner and saw what awaited her, Pennae felt like crying.

An all-too-familar iron barrier, its massive wall blocking her way on. As before, she could see no way past, no winch to raise it . . . nothing. All that striving, just to end up *right* where she'd started.

Well, if the king and queen and Vangerdahast wanted to be rescued by the Knights of Myth Drannor, it seemed there'd be a lot of waiting involved, and they'd have to be very patient.

Shaking her head at that thought, she turned around to retrace her steps and seek another way, and found herself staring up at a man whose head brushed the ceiling, and whose bulk loomed over her like a mountain.

Huge muscled arms hefted an axe more than half as tall as she was, and a short, broad, horn-tipped sword. The giant wore a patchwork coat of battered, bolted-together armor plates and ragged hides, and a helm on his head that—brightening now, as she watched—threw a glow out before it like Yassandra's belt was doing, for her.

"Who by all the Watching Gods are you?" Pennae gasped.

"They call me," the man-mountain rumbled, spreading his weapons to block her way past him as he shouldered ponderously forward, "the Dread Doorwarden. Or the Stalking Doom. Which do you prefer, little doomed lass?"

✦ ✦ ✦ ✦ ✦

Mystra and Loviatar, it *hurt!* Cursing, and wondering if his disguise was wavering, Applethorn wrenched the dagger out of the doorframe, shouting at the pain.

He was free, sobbing uncontrollably and wringing his hand, blood spattering on his boots.

Other boots—lots of them—were pounding nearer in the passage, now. He managed to turn, clutching his hand but keeping hold of the dagger, as Purple Dragons came pounding up.

"*There* you are!" he blazed at them. "She's gone. Search the passage! Open every door!"

The Dragons frowned, and the swordcaptain leading them barked, "Surrender, saer! Drop that weapon!"

"I gave you an order!" Applethorn snarled. "Be about it!"

"Surrender," the lionar roared, drawing his sword. He jerked his head, and his men trotted out into a wide ring, as guests shrieked and shouted and hurriedly melted away into the back corners of the room, and drew their swords too.

"Will you *listen?"* Applethorn spat angrily, wringing his bleeding hand. The Dragons stared flatly at him as they stalked carefully forward, closing in.

With a snarl of exasperation the alarphon flung the dagger into the lionar's face, and managed to teleport away.

* * * * *

Pennae pulled down the front of her well-traveled gown. "I don't suppose," she asked hopefully, looking up at the hulking Doorwarden, "that you'd be interested in these?"

The monstrous echoing sound that answered her started like a chuckle, but sounded like a snort by the time the man-mountain was done.

"No," she sighed, "I rather thought not." Pulling up the sagging, bloodstained gown again, she drew two of her daggers, eyed that cleaving axe, and wondered how many breaths of life she had left.

* * * * *

An axe striking stone hard makes an unmistakable ring. Florin heard it twice, and then a roar, echoing faintly just ahead of him. Someone was fighting the Doorwarden.

He frowned and went to the nearest door to listen—in time to hear a faint cry of, "Never!"

He stiffened; had that been Pennae's voice? Florin flung the door open and found himself staring at a laundry chute. Of course.

The sounds were louder now; another ring of steel and the Doorwarden rumbling, "Stop *running,* little she-viper!"

Florin looked at the inside of the door he'd just opened. Aye, it had a pull-ring; the long-ago builders had obviously made all the doors the same. Which meant . . .

Holding his sword out in one hand and Pennae's blood-soaked jack in the other to slow himself against the sides of the shaft—it looked wide enough to take a large laundry basket, not just a person—he turned to face the doorway and stepped back into the shaft, stabbing out at its iron sheathing immediately.

His sword made a terrible squealing that made him wince at what he must be doing to it, but his shuddering shoulders met the challenge. He reached the door below moving slowly enough to grab at it with his jack-wrapped hand and cling.

It took him several tries to swing hard enough to thrust the door open into the passage with him hanging from it, but he managed it at last, rolling out and to his feet with the sounds of battle much louder and nearer, now.

Cones of light, like two flaring lantern-beams, were flashing and crossing yonder. Florin headed for them, hefting his sword. All Pennae could hope to do was run and run to avoid getting trapped, and to try to slip past the Doom, and he would know very well what she was trying. If the huge guardian got in just one solid strike . . .

Then he was upon them, the great axe coming into view on a backswing, and Florin bellowed, "Doorwarden! Turn and fight *me!*"

The great shoulders started to turn. Florin yelled, "Pennae! Get past—and keep running! There's a narrow place; get beyond it!" and launched himself at the guardian's gigantic legs, seeking to move in behind the Doom as the man-mountain turned.

"Florin!" Pennae almost shrieked. "Where have you *been?*"

"Touring the Palace," he shouted back, and then had no more breath for shouting. The Doorwarden knew what he was doing; he kicked his great boot sideways as he turned, smashing into Florin's hastily raised sword and flinging the ranger helplessly through the air.

Where was Pennae? She wasn't running past! Where—

The Doorwarden loomed up, sword and axe slicing down, one after the other, so that wherever he scrambled to avoid the first attack would be where the second weapon went hunting.

Florin launched himself forward, right at the Doom, seeking to get in between his legs where his own bulk would keep the Doom from seeing him properly to hack and slice.

The Doom backed away hastily, sword and axe swinging wildly to aid its balance—and Florin's mouth went dry as he caught sight of Pennae, rushing up the many seams and plates of the huge guardian's crudely cobbled-together boots to reach the back of his right knee, and thrust her dagger in under the plate there.

The guardian felt her presence, as she tried to saw at straps she could not see, and growled, bringing his sword fist down to slam into her. Pennae swung around right behind the knee, dangling.

"Run!" Florin yelled at her, from where he was right in front of the Doom. "Just drop and *run!*"

Pennae swung, kicked her legs high into the air like a juggler swinging from an overhead pole, and at the top of her swing let go.

Florin stopped watching; if he was to live, he had to get between the Doom's legs *right now,* and—

He managed it, fetching up on the inside of the guardian's left boot. There was a tempting split there in the overlapping hides and metal plates covering those huge feet, so he drove his sword into it, twisted, and then plucked the blade back out and kept running.

It was well he did. The Doorwarden roared in pain, deafening echoes rebounding off the ceiling and rolling up and down the passage, and stumbled, hopping awkwardly sideways, two huge boots moving through the spot where the ranger had been moments before.

Behind the Doorwarden, and with the way clear before him and Pennae watching anxiously from the distance, Florin put down his head and ran. If the Doom fell over . . .

"Run!" he yelled, the moment he had breath to do so. "Keep running!"

Pennae stood where she was, waiting for him.

"Run, hrast you!" Florin bellowed at her.

She started to move, backing so she could keep watching him and the stumbling Doorwarden—who'd gotten himself turned now, and was coming after them, shaking the passage in his angry haste.

"Pennae!" Florin roared in exasperation, as he came up to her.

She grinned. "I never was very good at taking orders," she said. "As I'm sure you've noticed a time or two."

"Just *run!"* he snapped as he pounded past, whacking her backside with the flat of his sword.

"Ah—such a greeting you give a lass!" She laughed, breaking into a run that kept her at his elbow.

Winded, Florin only nodded—and then, as she darted ahead, plunged thankfully through the doorframe after her and slowed, stumbling.

Pennae looked back as the Doorwarden roared his frustration at them, and then put out an arm and clung to Florin as he bent over, panting.

When he had his breath back, he straightened and held out her jack. It was blood-soaked, cold, and wet, but Pennae's eyes shone as if he'd been proffering the greatest treasure in all Cormyr.

"Thanks," she said, smiling widely, and tore the gown off over her head. Flinging it down, she took her jack and slipped it on, shivering at its clamminess.

"Come on!" Florin told her, clapping her arm. "I've uncovered another plot. Someone named Blacksilver is wandering the Palace, and—"

Pennae put firm fingers over his mouth to silence him, and then took them away a moment later to kiss him.

He blinked at her.

She smiled wryly. "Well, I had to shut you up *some*how. Now listen and heed, O mighty and valiant Falconhand!"

Florin nodded, gave her a rueful half-smile, and waved at her to "say on." "Nothing," Pennae told him, her eyes large and serious, "*nothing* at all, in all the Realms, is more important than finding our fellow Knights. Kingdom rise or kingdom fall, we're going through this together. I am sick unto death—or hrasted nearly was—of running around in these *stlarning* cellars, lost and alone! We find Jhess and Islif and our two chucklehead holynoses, too, and we *stand together*. Then we *all* go and seek out the king, the queen, and the hrasted Royal Magician Vangerdahast! Any disputes, faithful dog of a ranger?"

"None," Florin replied, his eyes shining. "None at all." Then he put a firm arm around her, and kissed her with fervor. And not a little valiant might too.

Chapter 27

Together We Stand

Together we stand against hosts
And prevail, glorious, victorious.
Together we rouse kingdoms
Gathering trouble as farmers reap turnips
Together we share laughter
And dig and remember each other's graves.

Velorna Jalaneth, Bard
from the ballad
Friends I Weep For You
published in the Year of the Adder

Applethorn swallowed, grimaced, and then shuddered all over and gasped, "Always hated the taste of these. Despite the relief—mmm, almost rapture—they bring."

Sitting in the dusty shadows of one of his secret places in the Palace, the alarphon restoppered the healing potion, put it upside down in the rack to remind himself later that it was now empty, and closed the cast-iron lid to keep the rats at bay. Nibbled corks meant healed rats . . . and doomed wizards.

One of the luxuries of a hiding hold was the chance to speak his thoughts aloud; he did so now, rather grimly.

"I can't spare any more time now for hunting down Knights of Myth Drannor. Vangey will check in with me soon. I must get back to my duties. Later, it won't matter a whit if he suspects, and comes for me—but not yet. Not quite yet. Not until his doom—as they say—is assured."

He chuckled, stepped through the sliding panel that would take him into the back of a wardrobe built into one of the long-disused apartments of the Northturret wing, still smoke-damaged from a minor fire of four decades ago, went via other panels into other wardrobes to emerge several apartments away, and hurried to the stair that would bring him down behind the pantries.

Healed and hale again, War Wizard Ghoruld Applethorn was his cold-eyed, smilingly alert self from the moment he stepped out into the back passage and started shooting looks at various war wizards that they answered with silent "all serene here" hand-signals.

Wherefore, when the expected gruff voice touched his mind and asked him much the same as he'd just been asking other mages, he was where he should have been, and in the mood he should have been. Vangerdahast imparted the mental equivalent of a supportive smile and broke contact.

Leaving Applethorn smiling softly indeed.

✦ ✦ ✦ ✦ ✦

"Semoor, I hardly think we're going to manage to *talk* it to death!" a sharp woman's voice—Islif's—rang out suddenly, from around a corner. "For the love of Lathander, *cast* your *spell!*"

Florin and Pennae exchanged delighted looks, and blurted out words at the same time: "The Knights!" and "We've found them! And they need us!"

Then they grinned at each other, roared "Charge!" in unison, and broke into a run, ducking around the corner with weapons out.

Islif and Doust were facing down a tall armored warrior—no, a suit of armor with no head inside its helm!

Jhessail stood with her back to Islif, and Semoor crouched behind Doust, causing Florin to frown and ask, "What're they doing, Jhess and Semoor?"

"Yon's a helmed horror, or similar," Pennae replied. "They can whisk themselves around from place to place like mages do—attack you from in front one moment, and behind the next!"

"Oh, *naed,*" Florin commented with a "what *next?*" grin, and charged between the busily parrying Islif and Doust to thrust his sword right at the emptiness inside the helm. The silent suit of armor parried with a swift, strong ease that astonished him, as if it had been waiting for just such an attack—but Florin had never expected anything less than a skillful parry, and had his dagger out even as he made that lunge. As his blade was blocked, he half-turned to bring his dagger full to the fore, and thrust it through the open face of the helm, into darkness.

A darkness that numbed his arm and shot sparks in all directions—in the fleeting breath before the armored guardian seemed to burst, armor plates (and Florin) hurtling in all directions.

The ranger screamed as he flew, scarcely aware of Islif and Doust smashed off their feet and tumbling along with him.

The fires of the gods—or so it felt—raced through him, searing his vitals, tongue, fingertips, and very eyeballs . . .

And then he crashed into something that gasped, gave, and curled herself around him, so they bounced bruisingly together, armor plates clanging and striking spitting sparks all around them, to roll and tumble and roll more slowly, finally to a stop.

Florin coughed. Then he blinked, and felt reassured that he could still do both of those things. He tried to move, to rise, and found that Pennae was wrapped firmly around him, arms and legs cradling him . . . and that she wasn't moving.

"Pennae?" he gasped, sudden terror rising in his throat.

"Ohhhh," she moaned, her mouth somewhere over his right shoulder. Then she moved weakly against him. "Great hero," she husked, "can we smite our next helmed horror in a different manner, d'you think?"

"I don't know if I *can* think, right now. Is it destroyed?"

"If you don't see armor plates flying back to draw together, yes. Which will doubtless annoy good Vangerdahast no end."

Florin chuckled, a chortle that built helplessly into a guffaw. Lying on his back on the cold stone floor, he roared with laughter, roars that echoed until he heard Semoor say archly, from somewhere not far off, "Well, *someone's* unhurt, I hear. Having a woman wrapped around you is obviously a tactic I must practice for our next fray. Islif? Jhessail?"

"Live in hope," Islif replied. They heard a clank of armor plate on stone, then a groan, as she rolled over and—unsteadily, swaying and trying to clutch at handholds that did not exist—stood up.

Across a litter of riven armor plate and sprawled Knights, Jhessail gave her a wan smile and used the fallen bulk of a grimacing Doust as a ladder to climb, hand over hand, up to a crouch. Pennae—

reluctantly, it seemed, her hands lingering on his shoulders and chin and then hips—drew back from Florin and sat up.

"Is everyone well?" Islif asked.

Semoor gave her a twisted smile. "As the immortal said to the dying man: I'll live—and you?"

A line of blood trailed down the side of his face and dripped slowly from his chin. Doust, too, bled from somewhere, though he rolled slowly over now, to flex his arms and then twist around to look for his mace. Semoor joined Islif and Jhessail among the standing, to shake their heads and kick at deadly shards of armor plate.

"The gods must have been watching over us, truly," Jhessail murmured, wincing at the sight of three long, swordlike fangs of riven metal. "We could all have been spitted like boar for a roast . . ."

The immediate growling from Semoor's stomach was more like a roar. "You had to mention food, didn't you?" he said. "Thanks, O most dainty of lady mages."

"Won't Lathander provide?" she asked innocently, spreading her hands like a preaching priest.

Semoor used his hands, then, to favor her with another sort of gesture.

Florin and Pennae joined them, reaching down to haul a grunting Doust to his feet. The priest of Tymora limped once, gingerly, then sat down again to adjust his boot, stood up to kick his foot back into its proper place, and pronounced himself fit.

"Unscathed, or nearly," Semoor murmured, ignoring the blood adorning him. "Truly, a miracle."

"Yes," Jhessail agreed, and turned to Florin to say severely, "Don't *ever* do that again! We might have been killed!"

He stared at her, struggled not to laugh—and then gave up and roared. One after another, the rest of the Knights joined in.

"Wha-why," he struggled to ask Jhessail, when his mirth started to abate, "didn't you blast it with a battlestrike or two?"

"I did," she replied. "Just once. It sent all of the little bolts right back at me. They *hurt.*"

"Hurt? I'm surprised you're still standing!"

"If I hadn't kept my healing potion in my boot, I wouldn't be. It's drunk now. That's why I demanded you not do that again."

"Is everyone all right?" Islif asked. "Truly, I mean?"

She gave ever-quiet Doust a hard look, then challenged Florin with her eyes. Both of them nodded, and there were mumbles affirming good health from all around Islif.

"Right," she said. "Then isn't it about time we got back to warning and protecting our king and queen and the formidable scoundrel who happens to be both Court Wizard of Cormyr and Royal Magician of the Realm—as well as holding a lot of other lesser or at least less savory offices too?"

"Quite a speech," Semoor replied. "Islif the courtier . . . hmm . . ."

"Semoor the battered corpse," she responded crisply. The Anointed of Lathander hastily stepped back out of reach behind Jhessail and said brightly, "As ever, your commands are an inspiration to us all, Lady Lurelake! Lead on! If you can find us a way out of these cellars before we're reduced to starving skeletons, I *will* obey you, right happily!"

"Then let's go!" Islif ordered, as loudly and firmly as if she'd been a veteran Purple Dragon lionar, and set off at a trot. When she was clear of the debris of the helmed horror, she started to *really* hurry.

Pelting along in her wake with the other Knights, Semoor complained to the listening Realms, "Somehow I *knew* this was going to involve running. Again."

• ✦ ✷ ✦ •

Lord Maniol Crownsilver gasped for breath. He'd been running through the Palace for a while now, his only falterings being his encounters with guard after wary guard. The last one had insisted on trotting along with him, until they turned a corner and came upon three burly, full-armored Dragons standing in a living wall across the passage. Each was a full two heads taller than the winded lord. They stood sternly gazing at him with their arms folded across their chests, not looking as if they had any intention of ever letting any lord of the realm past them.

There was an open door in the passage wall beside one of the three guards, and out of it stepped a fourth Dragon—this one only a head taller than Crownsilver, and wearing the badge of a constal on his chest. He gave the panting lord a tight, unfriendly smile, and asked breezily, "So, my Lord Crownsilver, what engenders such haste in you, this fine day?"

"I—" Maniol Crownsilver gasped for breath, furious that he once again was unable to seem grand and commanding. He fought for air until he managed to say, "I bear a message for the Royal Magician, of utmost importance for the realm!"

"Another one?" The Purple Dragon rolled his eyes and told the passage ceiling wearily, "Big state revels certainly bring out all the madfolk to join the parade."

"I'm serious!" Crownsilver sputtered.

"Aye, aye, of *course* you are. Wherefore we're going to take you into this handy little room here, where you can drop your hose and cods and fine doublet, and—"

"What?"

"Oh, 'tis the latest fashion at Court, Haven't you been keeping up, Lord? Aye, 'tis clothes off if you need whisper important things to Old—to Vangey. Orders of the king, of course."

Lord Maniol Crownsilver opened his mouth to say something, then, but nothing came out. He settled for blinking, once or twice, as firm hands towed him into a chamber lit by three braziers, with a bare table in it and half a dozen big, burly Purple Dragons who greeted him with welcoming smiles.

"The table warms up once you're on it, mind," a large-jawed, burly Dragon leaned over him to advise with fatherly joviality.

Lord Maniol Crownsilver shuddered, muttered, "The things I do for love of Cormyr," and firmly shut his eyes.

"Tell me when it's over," he snarled at the unseen soldiers around him, through clenched teeth.

* * * * *

"Well," Islif puffed, as they rounded another corner and ran on, "at least we're seeing passages we haven't been in before."

"Progress," Semoor added cheerfully. "Something every church supports!"

"Aye," Pennae agreed, "but *they* mean a little farther down the road to getting their own way in everything!"

Semoor grinned. "But of course! Isn't that what the word *means?*"

"There may come a time when we'll have the leisure to sit down and discuss such matters," Pennae replied. "I may even have learned patience enough to discuss them with *you,* by then. However—"

"However," Florin said firmly, "we're passing lots of closed doors, and I'm starting to hear folk talking behind some of them; should we open any, and look? We seem to be just running along bli—"

A door promptly opened, ahead of the running Knights, and a bearded Highknight in leathers peered out, gave the onrushing adventurers a startled look that fell into a glare, and shouted loudly, " 'Ware! Thieves!"

Doors banged open, up and down the passage. Purple Dragons stepped through them, both before and behind the Knights of Myth Drannor, who came to a swift halt.

In the sudden silence after their boots were stilled, there was a loud hiss as many swords were drawn.

* * * * *

Crownsilver kept his eyes closed as he was disarmed, stripped, and searched most thoroughly. At length, they helped him to dress again, asking him questions throughout, their voices becoming steadily more respectful.

In the end, the constal said gravely, "Lord Crownsilver, I shall be honored to escort you to the Royal Magician of the Realm."

"Good," Maniol Crownsilver said, not bothering to hide his sigh of relief. "Then let us go. I cannot help but think that urgency looms larger above us, with every passing breath."

Soon he was marching along passages with an escort, the constal calling out to guards they approached as to the whereabouts of Vangerdahast.

The lionar of the sixth such guardpost frowned and said, "He passed this way not long ago. By now, he's personally attending the Silverymoon reception, in Anglond's Great Hall."

The constal nodded, turned and opened a particular door, and started to run.

✦ ✦ ✦ ✦ ✦

"Stop!" Florin said sternly to the Purple Dragons who were forming a ring around the Knights. "We've no desire to spill blood here! We but seek the Dragondown Chambers!"

It seemed he'd said the wrong thing.

The ring of Purple Dragons around the Knights widened as every guard stepped hastily back, their swords rising to readiness.

The ornrions among them and the lone Highknight slapped fingers over rings they were wearing, and hissed into those rings, "War wizard aid! War wizard aid! Armory Shadowpassage! Armory Shadowpassage!"

✦ ✦ ✦ ✦ ✦

The two wizards standing in the Longstride Hall were just beginning to hope that their shift might somehow go off without a hitch, as day headed into evening, when the pendants they both wore under their splendid uniforms suddenly murmured, "War wizard aid! War wizard aid! Armory Shadowpassage! Armory Shadowpassage!"

"Oh, *tluin,*" Tathanter told the world feelingly, as that chanted summons continued. "What *now?*"

Malvert had already snatched a wand out of its chased silver scabbard on his leg; Tathanter hastily drew his too.

Dodging among curious guests, they ran to a particular panel in a tapestry-hung back corner of the hall, hastily clawed it open, and plunged through it.

"My," a bright young shopkeeper's wife, spectacular in a sheath of shimmerweave that covered her from throat to ankles—except where cutouts left both of her rounded hips bare—remarked to her husband, "it's just like in the tales—wizards running everywhere, doing urgent, secret things! Isn't it *exciting?*"

Her husband scowled. "No. Unless you change 'exciting' to 'frightening.' Then I'd agree with you."

" 'Frightening'? But surely not for you! You did your years in the Dragons!"

He nodded and replied curtly, "That's why."

✦ ✦ ✦ ✦ ✦

Lord Maniol Crownsilver was staggering and gasping for breath by the time they reached Anglond's Great Hall. Sweating and nigh-incoherent when he tried to speak, he clutched at a handy servant—who fought successfully to stand both still and expressionless—for support as the guards who'd escorted him laid hands on the magnificent door looming up over them, and hauled it wide open.

Crownsilver hastened inside, wiping persistent sweat from his brow, and stared around. He'd forgotten just how hrasted *huge* the hall was. It was heavily thronged with guests who were busy staring in all directions and marveling at the size and splendor of the hall and of each other.

Maniol Crownsilver took a few steps this way, and a few more that way, and then stopped, baffled.

He thought of Vangerdahast as a great looming figure, dark-robed and terrible, dominant at Court even when Azoun was on his throne. Yet it seemed that only in his mind was the Royal Magician of the Realms truly tall. Here, especially with all the thick-soled boots and high spiked heels being worn by guests desiring to make an impression, there were many folk who were taller than Royal Magician Vangerdahast. Many, many folk, some so tightly clustered together that movement among them was a matter of many bumped elbows and apologies.

In short, Vangey could be anywhere. And Anglond's Great Hall was big enough to hold a lot of anywheres.

Lord Crownsilver sighed and threw his head back to gaze slowly around at the heights of the long, rounded, high-ceilinged chamber. Not so much at that magnificent painted ceiling, with its gilded, relief-carved dragons, but at the tiers and tiers of balconies below it, that circled the hall in unbroken rings, four high.

Aye, a *lot* of anywheres. Crownsilver shrugged, let his gaze drift down again to the floor of the hall where he was standing, and starting hunting Vangerdahast.

* * * * *

"The wizards are coming," the Highknight announced, his voice startlingly loud in the tense silence that had fallen over the passage. "Maintain the ring of swords. Draw it closer. Two paces, no more."

Slowly and with care, the Purple Dragons closed in around the Knights, swords raised.

"Keep to the ring, even if they start hurling spells?" an ornrion asked.

The Highknight shrugged. "Kill them all if we must. The war wizards can always question their corpses."

Chapter 28

To Make Welcome Fair Silverymoon

Unbar and throw open your gate, burn off its bright rune
For the time is now come to make welcome fair Silverymoon.

Orammus "the Black Bard" of Waterdeep
from Alustriel Comes Calling
a ballad contained in Old Or's Black Book
published in the Year of the Scourge

I've had about enough of this," Jhessail snapped, and raised her hands to cast a spell.

Pennae whirled around and caught hold of her arm. "*No*. Try this, first. The firing-word's on the butt."

She snatched a wand from Yassandra's belt and slapped it into Jhessail's palm.

The red-haired mage looked at it, and then back up at Pennae. "Just which wizard is missing this?"

"One who's also missing her life—not my doing—and so won't be showing up to complain. I hope. Yet tarry a moment, before you start blasting." She lifted her head and snapped, "Knights, a ring around us both, please."

"Done," Florin and Islif said in perfect unison, steering the two priests by their elbows to form as much of a ring as four people could manage.

"Steady," the Highknight ordered the Purple Dragons all around them, from only a few strides away. "Continue to advance slowly and in formation. The man who charges will face my wrath."

"And my blade," Islif added mildly, earning herself a glare from the bearded Cormyrean.

Pennae had plucked something small from one of the pouches on Yassandra's belt, and hefted it in her hand. Now she held it up between thumb and forefinger—and threw it, hard.

It was a small black bead, and when it struck the Highknight's nose, there was a flash of blue light—and the passage was suddenly blocked off, blotted out by a black sphere of shimmering force that filled it, flickering wildly as it tried to expand farther than the distance between the passage floor and ceiling would allow. Purple Dragons cried out and struggled in its thrall, many of them fighting to back away—and were suddenly swallowed up in or behind the blackness, as the magic gave up trying to expand as a sphere, and flooded in both directions to seal off the passage entirely.

Pennae took Jhessail by the arm again, turned her around to face the other way, and gestured as grandly as any servant. "*Now* you may blast, please."

The Purple Dragons who'd crowded in behind the Knights were relatively few, perhaps two dozen in all. They backed warily away now, frowning, into a three-rank-deep living barrier across the passage, and more than one man turned to the ornrion among them and asked, "Permission to go and fetch our shields, sir?"

Whatever the ornrion might have decided was left unsaid, as Jhessail gave the massed Dragons a sweet smile and announced clearly, "*Clarrdathenta.*"

The wand in her hand quivered—and then spat bright blue-white bolts of magic like four battlestrikes all being cast at once.

The magical missiles sped home, just as she'd wanted them to, striking at every Dragon. Twice.

The Dragons reeled, and Jhessail fed them from the wand again.

Men went from staggering to falling, this time, and there were only a few weakly sliding down the walls when Florin said, "Come. Back through them, then start opening doors. Before all the gods, we are *going* to find those hrasted stairs up!"

The Knights charged, and the lone Purple Dragon to try to stand against them—the ornrion—fell on his face when Islif simply struck aside his sword and ran right over him, Jhessail and Doust right behind her.

Everyone started wrenching open doors.

"You'd not think it too much to ask, would you, to build a door that has stairs behind it?" Islif growled in rising exasperation.

Pennae grinned. "Was that your seven-and-tenth door?"

"No; score-and-sixth," Islif snapped. "Not that I'm counting."

"Praise Lathander!" Semoor crowed at that very moment. "Behold! Stairs ascending!"

Islif raced to the opened door that the Anointed of Lathander was so grandly indicating—and charged right up the stairs without pause, the rest of the Knights racing after her.

There was a dimly lit servants' passage running across the top of the stairs, and four guard-Dragons were standing in it, resplendent in large Purple Dragon tabards. They turned to peer at the Knights, frowning.

Islif and Florin ignored them, going straight to the two nearest doors in the passage wall.

"Hey! *Halt!* Halt and down arms, in the name of the king!" a telsword bellowed, from among the four Dragons.

Islif turned and snapped, "What room's on the other side of this door?"

"I said halt!" the soldier shouted, running up the passage and reaching for his sword.

Islif let him get it halfway out before taking hold of his wrist, ramming the weapon back down into its scabbard, closing her hand around the telsword's throat, and plucking him off his feet to touch noses with him and ask gently, "What room, valiant Dragon, lies on the other side of this door?"

There was a grunt and a crash from behind her, as another Dragon decided to turn and run to an alarm gong—and Doust threw his mace between the soldier's hurrying ankles to lay him out, stunned, on the passage floor.

The telsword stared into Islif's eyes, and she stared right back into his, putting a slow smile on her face. It was not a nice smile.

"Uh-ah-urkh," the Purple Dragon strangled, as she shook him gently. When she loosened her grip a trifle, he gasped quickly, "A-Anglond's Great Hall! W-where the revel—"

"*Thank* you," Islif said, dropping him to the floor. "And Vangey—pardon, Royal Magician Vangerdahast—would he be in that hall?"

"Y-yes," the telsword managed to croak, rubbing his bruised throat and wincing as a shrewd mace-blow from Semoor sent another of his fellow guards reeling and then slumping to the floor.

When he grabbed for his dagger, the tall, horse-faced woman slapped it away, clouted him across the side of the head on the backhand of her blow, and snatched his tabard up and over his head, blinding him.

"Tabards—good thought!" Florin snapped. "Collect them all!"

The moment she'd settled the tabard she'd taken over her head, Islif flung the door wide and strode through into the terrific din beyond, the rest of the Knights right behind her. Jhessail looked like a small girl wearing her father's borrowed tabard, Pennae's was more than a little wrinkled, and the two priests had none to wear, but Florin and Islif looked as stern and loyal as any Purple Dragon ever had. Florin waved the priests to the rear as the Knights strode after Islif.

So Semoor ended up being the last Knight in line. He swept a low bow to the groaning telsword as he stepped across the threshold.

The stricken Dragon took one last look at him and fainted.

* * * * *

The heat and din of the press in the heart of the crowded hall were on the verge of overwhelming Ildaergra Steelcastle. Looking not at all her customary bright, sharp, social-climbing self, she winced and looked around worriedly. "The envoy—is she coming at all, do you think?"

From beside her, Ramurra Hornmantle smiled dismissively. "Don't *fret* so, Ildaergra. Envoys always turn up late. It's the only way they have to show kings and queens that they do possess *some* power, albeit puny. Just relax, enjoy the sweets and smallbites—you see, if she'd been early, we wouldn't have been served these, now would we? And *look* at those heaped platters. We can gorge, my dear!—and this chance to get a good look at Anglond's Great Hall, and enjoy the evening. After all, you weren't going to hurry off anywhere, were you?"

Ildaergra sipped her latest flagon of firewine, smiled ruefully, and replied, "Hardly."

"Well, then," Ramurra said. "Just enjoy the company and the converse—look, there's the Royal Magician himself, not six paces from us!"

"Surrounded by a dozen-some barely begowned ladies all so feeble-brained as to be smitten with nasty old rogues of mages, I see," Ildaergra sniffed.

"I can get you through them to meet Vangerdahast himself, if you'd like."

"Oh, *would* you?"

* * * * *

"Our grand entrance," Semoor commented, "and we emerge behind a pillar. How fitting."

"Still the tongue, holywits," Jhessail said. "There are four tiers of balconies above us; they have to hold them up with something."

They stood in shadows beneath the balcony, amid many servants deftly gliding here and there with decanters and platters of smallbites in their hands. A few gave the bloody, disheveled Knights sharp looks or frowns, but the Purple Dragon tabards and holy symbols seemed to reassure them. One hurrying maid plucked a polishing-towel from her hip and tossed it to them. Pennae deftly caught it with a smile of thanks.

"Crusted silverfin cheese," Doust moaned from behind her, getting a whiff from some smallbites passing nearby. "In the name of Tymora, lass, feed a starving priest!"

The serving maid he'd called to turned with a grin. "There *are* no starving priests, saer, but by all means eat your fill."

Doust swept the platter out of her hands, agreeing, "No starving priests any more!"

Before the maid could protest, Pennae had scooped an armful of the greasy, flaky-crusted smallbites off the platter and thrust them at her fellow Knights. Doust gave her a hurt look and turned away to shield what was left with his shoulder, but his protest was lost amid the rumbles of the Knights' stomachs. They emptied Pennae's hands in a single breath, Semoor bending forward to lick her fingers until she snatched them away and slapped him with them.

That made the serving maid grin, shrug, and depart for another platter.

"There!" Florin said suddenly, pointing out into the brightly lit center of the hall, over the heads of courtiers, nobles, and commoners in their brightly hued best, all standing talking with drinks in their hands.

Standing quite near, in the midst of a throng of daringly gowned ladies hanging on his every growled word, was Vangerdahast.

The Knights hurried toward him. At the sight of them, Purple Dragons clad in full shining armor, with halberds in their hands, stepped away from pillars they'd been stationed at, and trotted to intercept the intruders.

"Stand aside," Florin murmured as the first guard moved to bar his way. The halberd came down to menace him, but the ranger slowed not a whit.

One of the ladies clustered around Vangerdahast saw the flash of the halberd descending as she glanced idly in that direction—and screamed.

As heads turned and guests started to stare and murmur, the Royal Magician of the Realm looked up, saw the Knights, and glared.

A guard thrust a halberd in Islif's way. She ducked under its head, grasped its shaft, and heaved, hurling the man aside. Finding herself in possession of the polearm, she flicked its other end between the ankles of the next hurrying guard—and then lost the halberd as he crashed forward onto it, nose-first, and went on to find the floor, hard.

A halberd jabbed at Pennae from another direction. She dived under its thrust and rolled swiftly across the floor to crash under its wielder's ankles, toppling him—into Florin's arms.

The ranger plucked the guard off his feet and hurled him bodily into the two guards right behind him, sending them all crashing down in a welter of bouncing halberds.

Lady revelers shrieked and tried to flee—and a reeling, off-balance guard stepped on the trailing gown of one buxom lady merchant and bared her to dethma and elegantly jeweled clout as her low-backed, lower-fronted gown tore from top to bottom. There were cries of both glee and rage at that—and Vangerdahast swept grandly out of his ring of admirers and spread his hands, rings catching fire on all of his fingers, to blast the Knights.

Florin desperately swept Pennae up off her feet, boosted her upright to his shoulder, and threw her forward and high into the air—as the Royal Magician's spell-blast slammed into the Knights, hurling them back. Pennae, aloft, escaped that roaring magic, but it flattened guards, servants, and guests alike, sweeping them all, bone-shakingly, past pillars to the back wall, to end up with the Knights in a chaos of bruised, interlocked, writhing folk.

Guests screamed, and their cries brought every head in the hall around and an astonished silence to the scene.

Ramurra Hornmantle and Ildaergra Steelcastle hastily drained their flagons, not taking their eyes off what was unfolding for an instant.

They saw Pennae land, drop into a crouch, and without pause spring up again like an acrobat, to deftly avoid the emerald beams of Vangerdahast's next magic—which struck plumes of smoke from the polished floor.

Pennae came crashing down into the Royal Magician's arms, bearing him to the floor and entwining herself around him to hiss into his startled face, "There's a conspiracy to kill you, Wizard! Don't look into or go near any crystal balls! Any moment now, word will come that both princesses are endangered—that's the signal!"

As Vangey blinked at her, Lord Maniol Crownsilver cried despairingly from halfway down the hall, "Lord Vangerdahast! Royal Magician! A rescue! A rescue! Ghoruld Applethorn told me to tell you I've—he's—captured the princesses! Gloating, that's it! Then he vanished right in front of my eyes, and I don't know where he's gone!"

"Oh, *tluin,*" Vangerdahast groaned, and took hold of Pennae's wrist in a grip of iron. "Go nowhere, little thief. *You* are going to explain all of this to me."

"Gladly, my lord," Pennae breathed in lavish imitation of an ardent, smitten lady.

The stout, bearded mage underneath her gave her a glare and growled, "Adventurers! Now get off my bladder and let me *up.*"

* * * * *

Wizard of War Beldos Margaster was, as usual, in his chambers. When events as large as this revel were unfolding, his scrying involved more than a dozen hovering-in-air crystal balls, and he preferred quiet solitude and room to work ordered as he saw fit, to use them in.

Wherefore he looked up, blinking, as the War Wizards Tathanter Doarmond and Malvert Lulleer bustled into his chambers at the head of a dozen Purple Dragons, who bore the bodies of Lady Laspeera and an ornrion of the Dragons on great decorative shields obviously torn down off the Palace walls.

"I've purge-poisoned the Lady Laspeera, and she's waking," Tathanter explained excitedly, without even a greeting, "but that's my one such spell. Can you see to this ornrion? We found them in the Long Passage. Its Palace-end guards were served the same way; all but two who came to us, warning of adventurers who must be in the Palace right now!"

Beldos Margaster frowned. "How so, when they'd have to wade through scores of other Dragons, on guard all over the cellars?"

"That's just what they've done," one of the Purple Dragons growled.

Margaster crooked a disbelieving eyebrow, then got a good look at the face of the ornrion on the shield, and hurried to a cabinet to pluck forth a vial.

"For this," he said, waving at both of the stricken, "potions are more reliable than the purge spell. That's why I've no such spell ready to cast."

He forced open the ornrion's mouth, emptied the vial into it, and held those slack lips together with his hand.

Almost instantly, Ornrion Taltar Dahauntul's still face creased, he started to cough, and then his eyes flew open.

They met Margaster's gaze a moment later, as the mage hastily took his fingers away, and Dauntless growled, "Gaster! Wanted to tell you, next I saw you: we left the Dragonfire swords behind us, in Halfhap! They're real after all! Flying and glowing, right enough. They're holding up most of the inn right now!"

Margaster looked interested, but said, "They'll have to wait until after you tell me what befell you and the Lady Laspeera. Here, that is, in the Long Passage, not in Halfhap."

Dauntless blinked. "Oh, *gods!* The Knights of Myth Drannor! They came out of Halfhap with us, but the moment the Lady Laspeera told them the Royal Magician was hunting them, they went mad! The thief slapped us both with a sleep-venom ring!"

Margaster glanced over at Laspeera; her eyelids were fluttering. Turning hastily to Tathanter and Malvert, he ordered, "Take this ornrion to the Battlebanners Room and keep him there until I come for him. Don't leave him and don't let him go anywhere. I'll see to the Lady L—"

"Oh, no, you won't, Gaster," Laspeera snapped, looking up at him. "You'll stay right here and relay all that's befalling, as the rest of us search the Palace for these Knights! I'll be having them in chains by nightfall!"

She heaved herself up from her shield, reeled, and caught hold of Dauntless for support.

"Leave him with me," she snapped at Tathanter and Malvert. Then her face changed, and she asked them rather wearily, "Wasn't there a revel here, this night?"

"Yes, Lady," Malvert replied hastily. "The reception for the envoy from Silverymoon."

Laspeera rolled her eyes and wobbled to her feet, leaning on Dauntless. "*That's* where they'll be. If I know my starving, thieving adventurers, they'll not be able to resist all the food and jewels! Lead me there!"

She strode out, visibly gaining strength with every step, and everyone went with her except Beldos Margaster.

Alone again, the old war wizard smiled faintly. Then he shrugged, opened another cabinet, took a pile of dark cloth from it, and shook out the uppermost cloth; it was a hood. Working quickly, he hooded each crystal ball and put it into the cabinet. When they were all closed away, the cabinet firmly latched, he went to the other end of the room and worked a spell.

When the horizontal whirlpool occurred in midair, Margaster bent over to peer into it, and kept his intent gaze upon it as it started to spin, and his scrying began again.

" 'Strordinary!" Lord Ildabray Indesm commented enthusiastically. "Hurled herself right at old Vangey, she did! Took him to the ground and rode him like a . . . like a . . ."

He suddenly became aware of his wife's cold-eyed scrutiny, and harrumphed into red-faced silence.

"*I* think," Lord Bellarogar Rowanmantle said loudly, "That the realm needs bold adventurers of that sort, to shake our Royal Magician right out of his confidence every tenday or so. Not to mention the entertainment his comeuppance affords us all."

Others standing near rolled their eyes. Lord Rowanmantle thought a lot of things, and all of them loudly.

"Now, now," Lord Horntar Dauntinghorn said soothingly. "We must remember that aside from bruised dignity and a few wine-stained gowns for which the Crown will no doubt compensate handsomely, no one was harmed. Our Dragons are back at their posts, halberds in hand once more, with no trace of blood on the floor. Moreover, all the ruffians went off in the company of Lord Vangerdahast, who claims ever that his haste and highhandedness befalls only for the good of the realm. And they *were* hurrying, all of them, so perhaps—"

"The day that sword-swinging adventurers are dedicated to the good of the realm," Lady Indesm said darkly, "is the day the madwits rise to rule and Cormyr as we know it shall be swept away. I pray to the gods that I not live to see that day!"

"Really," Ramurra Hornmantle murmured disgustedly to her friend Ildaergra, in the silence that followed that dramatic declaration. "If I could do it and escape death for it, I'd borrow a Dragon's dagger and answer her prayer for the gods forthwith! Whyever should *she* share in Cormyr's brighter future?"

• ✦ ✶ ✦ •

King Azoun IV of Cormyr, Dragon of Dragons, Conqueror Triumphant of Arabel and of Marsember, Lord of the Stormhorns and Thunder Peaks, and dozens of other titles he preferred to forget, looked down at the crown on the black velvet cushion with decided distaste. "Must I? Won't a simple circlet do? Or nothing at all? 'Tisn't as if the people don't know me!"

"You can if you *want* to insult the envoy, dear," Queen Filfaeril said reprovingly, taking up the crown to settle it expertly on his head, "but she *does* represent Silverymoon. And she is very beautiful."

She glided around him, adjusting the crown ever-so-slightly ere stepping back to survey him critically, from crown-spires to booted toe. "And goodness me, but I know full well that lasses swoon for a man in a crown."

Her impassively regal face marred only by a swift wink, she went to her knees in a smooth shifting of skirts, to plant a kiss on the flaring gold filigree of the ornate royal codpiece.

" 'Swooning' isn't exactly what I'd call it," he chuckled, lifting her to her feet and towing her by her chin to his lips.

Their kiss was long and ardent, and they moved against each other and murmured wordless need before Filfaeril pulled gently back to whisper, "Later. *After* you've tasted what Silverymoon has to offer."

"Fee," Azoun said reproachfully, "I'd not betray—"

"Hush," the Dragon Queen said softly, putting a finger across his lips. "I *know* you, Az. And you won't be betraying me—*if* Sune and Sharess smile upon you, and the lady does too—because you have my full and loving agreement in this."

She leaned in close again, to kiss one of his ears, and whispered into it, "Make Cormyr proud."

Azoun blinked at her, then grinned, and finally shook his head in admiration and said huskily, "Gods, I love you, lass. Don't ever change."

His queen faced away from him, deftly hiked her ornate ankle-length gown up to her waist to show him she was bare beneath, stuck out her tongue at him ere she let it fall again, and said, "Now we're *more* than fashionably late! Come! Anglond's Great Hall is a fair hike from here, and I can't roll along quickly in *this!*"

Chapter 29

Treason to Slay

For who stands forth bold, the realm to save
And face the bloody traitors' day?
We who loved the land, our lives we gave
Now rise from graves, treason to slay.

Tethmurra "Lady Bard" Starmar
from the ballad
The Dead, They March This Day
published in the Year of the Spur

"Ghoruld," Vangerdahast growled, letting Lord Crownsilver's head slip from between his hands. The noble's eyes rolled up in his head as he slid bonelessly to the floor, forgotten. "I might have known. Knights, come with me. It seems I can't trust a single war wizard just now. We've treason to slay this night!"

Treason, the whisper began around him, leaping from one excited Cormyrean to another, a murmur that spread outward, racing across the hall as swiftly as a shot from the bow of an expert archer.

Vangerdahast strode to an apparently solid painting on a wall—and stepped right through it as if was but empty air, the Knights of Myth Drannor hard on his heels.

Guests, guards, and servants alike gawked in startled silence. Then everyone spoke at once, rumor rising in a great wave of excited chatter.

In a deep stone chamber stood a ring of black stone plinths, each topped with a dark, lifeless crystal ball. Those squared fingers of stone stood waist-high, each in its own chalked circle on the stone floor, and each circle was linked by a chalk line to an empty central circle. One circle held no plinth, only a crystal ball on the floor—and that crystal was glowing, shapes and colors moving and flickering in its depths.

Ghoruld Applethorn stood over that sphere, watching and listening to what was unfolding in its depths. He saw Crownsilver slip to the floor, and the great secret growled aloud by Vangerdahast.

Applethorn chuckled then, and in his satisfied mirth spoke words to the crystal that he knew the Royal Magician could not hear.

"Crownsilver was about as competent as I expected, Vangey—and so are you. It doesn't matter *why* you come striding for me. Just so long as you come."

+ + ✦ + +

There came a pattern of tapping on a certain door deep in the gloom of one back corner of Anglond's Great Hall. The servant who'd been expecting this hailing eased the door open, making a swift gesture in mimicry of three fingers plucking harp strings.

That gesture was matched with a smile, and the servant opened the door wide. Resplendent in dark finery, Dalonder Ree slipped through. "Sorry I'm late," he hissed. "The hrasted *countryside's* changing! My favorite stream to follow through the King's Forest is gone! Clean *gone!*"

The servant gave the Harper ranger an incredulous look, but murmured, "No harm done. The king hasn't rolled in, yet, so you've missed nothing! The envoy's just entering now, yonder, and I doubt overmuch harm will come to her. See her maid, following at her hip? Well, in truth, her maid's deep in spell-sleep back in her guest chambers. That's Dove, wearing her shape."

"*Dove*? Well, I am unnecessary, then!"

"Oh, I'd not say that. They always need a lot of help mopping up all the blood, after."

+ + ✦ + +

"The princesses are safely with Beldos Margaster," Vangerdahast growled to the Knights, as they hastened into an empty room together. "So it's the king and queen we most have to worry about."

Ushering them in, he closed the door firmly and pointed at it. "Guard that," he ordered Islif, who wordlessly hefted her sword and took up a stance facing it.

Vangey nodded and pointed Doust at a taller-than-a-man painting on another wall, and Semoor at a wardrobe on a third. "Those are doors, too. Guard them. If any war wizard—or *anyone* else, even the king himself—tries to come in, shout out and try to stop them."

Returning the center of the room, he beckoned Florin, Pennae, and Jhessail to stand with him, and spread his hands on high, as if to dramatically commence spellcasting.

"Right," he barked. "No scrying crystals. Let's go hunting war wizard traitors. Applethorn, where are you?"

"Ah, so prudence at last takes hold of our Royal Magician," Ghoruld Applethorn purred, "despite the overconfidence that dooms him. Just who will protect *you,* Vangey? Your own oh-so-puissant spells? A handful of backcountry blunder-neck adventurers?"

Shaking his head, Applethorn unhurriedly worked a spell that turned him into the likeness of a plinth like all the others—a plinth with a hand that carefully lifted the glowing crystal atop itself and did something that made that sphere go dark like the rest.

Around that resting crystal, fingertips sank into the top of the plinth, as Applethorn's voice spoke mockingly from it. "So—behold—I hide me. Can you find me? In time? Before what Margaster unleashes finds *you?"*

"Careless, Ghoruld, careless," Margaster murmured, turning away from his scrying whorl. "Don't announce me and what I'm doing to all listening Cormyr! You're becoming expendable."

Kneeling on the stone floor, he flipped back a corner of the carpet to reveal a row of nine words chalked on the flagstones. Touching each in turn, he said it aloud with firm, grave precision.

Then he rubbed them all away.

In a dark, dusty secret passage elsewhere in the Royal Palace of Cormyr, each of Margaster's words sounded out of the empty air—one at a time, in turn—above a row of nine skulls resting on little stands along a shelf.

Each skull wore an old warrior's helm and each was connected by a trail of dried blood—a deliberately drawn line of blood—down from its stand to the shelf, and from the shelf all the way down the wall, and a little way across the floor to an unscabbarded sword lying on the flagstones.

As each word was spoken, the skull linked to it rocked, glowed briefly, then rose into the dusty air and melted away, leaving an empty helm floating in the air.

Dust swirled and coalesced, until it would have been clear to anyone watching—if there had been anyone alive to watch in that dark and deserted passage—that shadowy, wraithlike shoulders connected each empty helm to arms that seemed but more shadows, yet were able to lift, hold, and wield a sword.

Nine solid, real swords were plucked up from the floor, to be hefted and swung in eerie silence. The shadows trailed away raggedly below each set of shoulders; none of the nine shadow-things had a torso or legs. They were little more than ragged wraiths.

Nine helms turned this way and that, as if the emptinesses within them were looking at each other, and conferring.

Then, with one accord, nine bladewraiths flew down the passage.

✦ ✦ ✦

Amid the inevitable fanfare, the King and Queen of Cormyr entered Anglond's Great Hall arm in arm, giving the guests and courtiers serene smiles and nods.

Not letting his broad smile slip in the slightest, Azoun muttered to Filfaeril, "This has all the makings of a disaster."

"Now, Az," she murmured back fondly, "like most things, it's only a disaster if you *act* like it's a disaster." She patted his hand. "So don't. Seduce someone instead."

Azoun growled faintly, to let her know her teasing had been heard, and they proceeded smoothly on, pretending not to hear the whispers of "treason" that were loudly racing around the hall and raging along the balconies.

Filfaeril smiled up at the folk there, as she always did, then turned to look back over her shoulder at the balconies behind, to make sure no one felt ignored. She nudged their linked arms to signal her royal husband to do the same. Cheers rang out, from here and there across the hall, and were taken up by servants and Purple Dragons until the hall was a-roar.

Up on the balconies, merchants and their wives crowded the rails. Impassive, full-armored Purple Dragons stood among them, at intervals. Each held a cocked crossbow, pointed straight up at the ceiling, and was vigilantly surveying the crowd below.

Amid the hubbub, the royal couple glided across the miraculously clearing floor of the hall—that "miracle" caused by war wizard suggestion magics—to meet the envoy of Silverymoon.

She responded, moving forward at the same pace, as her tall, elegantly beautiful aides and maids fell away from around her—and Cormyreans all over Anglond's Great Hall gasped at the revealed beauty of the Lady Aerilee Hastorna Summerwood.

She was as tall as Azoun, and strikingly beautiful. Slender in dusk blue shimmerweave, as fluidly graceful as a wave riding across fair seas, she was a half-elf with dark, arched eyebrows, pale high cheekbones, a lush and kindly smiling mouth, and eyes like two great, deep sapphires. She was barefoot, and the shifting clingings of her ankle-length gown left little doubt to any eye that she was bare beneath it.

She greeted the King of Cormyr with a herald's respectful bow and fair words, but turned without pause to embrace Queen Filfaeril and give her a deep kiss, almost as if they were lovers. A long, tender kiss that left Azoun blinking in pleased surprise, and the hall buzzing with murmured comment.

"Oh, *joy,*" Dove and Dalonder Ree sighed in unison, from about sixty feet apart. "It begins."

"This," Dalonder added, as he watched the Lady Summerwood extend a long arm almost as an afterthought to gather the king into a three-way embrace, "is going to be an interesting evening."

* * * * *

Vangerdahast murmured something, and a tiny coffer appeared in midair in front of him.

He reached for it, opened it, and told Jhessail, "Touch only the unicorn-headed ring. Take it out, but *don't* put it on, or allow even the smallest part of any of your fingers to pass into its circle. Just hold it up in front of me."

She nodded and did so. A swift flick of Vangey's hand made the coffer go away again, and he carefully worked a spell on the ring.

A red glow rose from it, and began to pulse. Jhessail's face tightened in pain and she started to tremble. "Keep hold of it!" the Royal Magician snapped.

The lady Knight nodded grimly, as a scene slowly built in the air between them, of a deserted stone room lit by a single scrying crystal that was pulsing and glowing with the same red hue as the ring she was holding. In the depths of that crystal, the Knights could see a tiny image of themselves standing with Vangerdahast, in the room they were now in.

The crystal sat on a plinth of dark stone, one of a ring of identical plinths; the others all had dark, inactive crystal balls atop them. Every plinth was circled in chalk, and those circles were linked by raylike lines to a central, empty circle.

Peering hard at the plinths, Vangerdahast snapped, "See you the plinth under the glowing crystal, Florin? Look at the chalk drawn around it, at the slight variations in circle and line from what's been drawn around the other plinths. If the crystal went dark, could you tell that one plinth from the others?"

"I . . . yes," Florin said firmly. "Yes, I could."

"Good. That plinth is in truth a war wizard, a traitor to the realm. Go and slay him with steel, striking as fast as you can and keeping low, for he can with a word cause all those crystals to burst and spray deadly shards everywhere. Go out through the wardrobe, turn left, and run like a storm wind; my voice will guide you thereafter."

Without another word Florin raced across the room, drawn sword in hand, plunged through the wardrobe, and turned left.

✦ ✦ ✦ ✦ ✦

"Faster!" Laspeera snapped, as yet another guardpost of Purple Dragons moved to bar their way, uncertain frowns on their faces.

Tathanter Doarmund thrust his warshield spell forward like a battering ram, but on its flanks Dauntless in his tatters and most of the dozen other Purple Dragons were already plunging ahead. The ornrion bellowed, "Make way! Aside! *Get out of the tluining way!*"

When one palace guard stopped uncertainly, halberd raised, Dauntless smashed it aside with his fists and slammed the soldier into the passage wall. When the guard snarled a curse and reached for a dagger, a Purple Dragon rushing along behind Dauntless punched him hard in the throat, leaving him to reel and fall in the wake of the hurrying throng.

Tathanter, Malvert Lulleer, Laspeera, and the Dragons had already pounded along too many Palace corridors, striking aside servants and guards who hadn't gotten out of the way fast enough—but there were the doors to Anglond's Great Hall at last!

The door-guards took one look at them and flung the doors wide; Laspeera's band burst into the Great Hall, panting for breath but running hard.

As shrieking fine-gowned merchants' wives went sprawling, Dauntless and his dozen Dragons spread out, each racing through the thronged guests, sword out and looking for trouble.

Trouble, as in the Knights of Myth Drannor.

Pages, scribes, and courtiers from Silverymoon shouted in alarm and ran to surround and protect their lady. The envoy's maid raced to Lady Summerwood's side, eyes blazing with sudden silver flames.

A voice erupted then from the breastplate of every Purple Dragon in the hall: "Laspeera am I, of the Wizards of War of Cormyr. Loyal

Dragons and citizens, strike not at me, or those running with me! We serve the realm!"

"No sign of them!" one of those running Dragons bellowed from the far end of the hall, gasping for breath.

"None here!" another called. Other shouts followed, all announcing an utter lack of Knights of Myth Drannor from one end of the hall to the other.

Laspeera frowned, worked a swift spell—and Dauntless and his dozen, from wherever they were all across Anglond's Great Hall, were lofted into the air, rising upright to soar up onto the balconies. They promptly commenced to rage along those levels, peering and running.

The hall was in an uproar, but it died down when Dauntless thrust his way to the rail of the lowest balcony to wave at Laspeera and then spread his hands in a helpless "They're not here!" signal.

Grimly Laspeera turned to her king and queen, to tender her apologies—and stopped, her mouth hanging open in astonishment, as King Azoun gave her a broad, genuine smile ere turning to the Lady Summerwood and saying grandly, "Aerilee, at many of our revels we celebrate the vigilance of our war wizards and Purple Dragons with a mock chase, such this one you have just witnessed, to both entertain the citizenry and to remind them that the finest folk in all our realm watch over them constantly and vigorously! May I present Laspeera Naerinth, one of our foremost and most capable war wizards?"

Still dumbfounded, Laspeera found herself swept into the warm embrace of Silverymoon's envoy, whose enthusiastic kiss at first made her stiffen, then shrug, and then engage in as an equal partner in a warring of tongues.

"I'll bet you give great backrubs," she murmured, when at last their lips parted.

Airilee grinned impishly. "Oh, I do. Do you rub feet?"

Laspeera grinned back, and shrugged. "I'm willing to try."

• ✦ ✦ ✦ •

Up on the balcony, watching all the kissing, Dauntless slammed a fist down on the rail and growled, "Hrast! That could be *me,* down there!"

The nearest balcony guard looked him up and down, and shook his head. "Nay. You've not the legs for it."

Nearby Purple Dragons started to snicker, as Dauntless gave the guard a choice glare.

* * * * *

Semoor Wolftooth squeaked in surprise as the wardrobe doors in front of him crashed open in a great splintering of wood. Two dark, helmed shadow-things had just burst through them.

Barely half a breath later, five more shadow-things shredded the tall painting on the east wall to ribbons by arrowing through it, sword points first.

At the same time, the door the Knights had come in by crashed open under the onslaught of two more of Margaster's bladewraiths—who were met by Islif's snarling fury. Her swift-swung blade shattered a helm almost instantly, causing that bladewraith to fall into drifting dust, its sword clattering to the floor.

The other bladewraith raced past her shoulder, heading for the Royal Magician of Cormyr.

Vangerdahast spat out a word that boomed and rolled in all ears—and shattered three wraith-blades in midair, felling the shadow-thing racing for him and two that had burst in through the painting.

Jhessail shrieked and ducked away from a wraith that chased her, blade foremost. Pennae sprang into the air to catch hold of the candle-wheel lamp hanging from the ceiling. A wraith-blade laid open her back as she did, causing her to shout in pain.

Doust was proud of his grand technique when casting shields of faith, but threw it aside to stammer out the magic faster than he'd ever done. Jhessail had only just begun to shimmer in its protection when he shouted at her, "Right, *do* something to these!"

A moment later, a wraith-blade plunged through his guts, and he doubled up around it as it burst wetly out of his back, vomiting his blood all over Jhessail as he plunged face-first to the floor, kicking and writhing.

Semoor's sanctuary magic formed just in time, bladewraiths circling over him like flying angry eels but not striking. Overhead, Pennae kicked a wraith-blade away, swung hard on the lamp, and used its momentum to hurl herself feet-first down and across the room. She landed smoothly, bouncing to pluck up the fallen sword of the shadow-thing Islif had destroyed at the door.

Her pursuing bladewraith plunged down at her from behind, and would have spitted her as surely as it had served Doust, if its sword hadn't been slashed viciously aside by Islif, on her way to backhand another bladewraith away from Jhessail.

The mage of the Knights sat on the floor, her face a-drip with Doust's blood, frantically casting a spell. Across the room, Vangerdahast was chanting something too.

On hands and knees, Semoor scuttled across the room, trying to reach Doust. He saw the shimmering around Jhessail flicker violently as a shadow-thing hacked at it—twice, thrice, and then the magic winked out.

The wraith-blade thrust down again—and Semoor flung up his hands to ward it away from Jhessail's unprotected head. It sliced through his magic and then him, almost severing one of his hands.

The Anointed of Lathander stared in horror at the ruin dangling from his wrist, and started to scream.

Which was when Jhessail's battlestrike finally took effect, its bright leaping bolt sending the bladewraith wavering aside that had been circling to finish Semoor.

An instant later, Vangerdahast's chanting ended with the calm words "undeath to death"—and all five remaining wraiths collapsed in a clattering of falling swords and whirlwinds of corpse-dust.

"Islif," the Royal Magician snapped, without pause, "pry off *that* side of the doorframe. In a space behind you'll find a coffer of healing potions. Use what you need. Now, disturb me not!"

Pulling himself stiffly upright, he closed his eyes and hurled his will across the Palace, praying to Azuth that he'd be in time.

✦ ✦ ✦ ✦ ✦

"I'm in time! Turn right!" Vangerdahast's voice murmured abruptly, sounding as if the Royal Magician were standing where he could speak right into Florin's ear.

The ranger almost jumped, but obediently hurled himself around the turn, still racing along in darkness relieved only by the tiny glows that marked spyhole-swivel coverings.

"Slow down so you won't miss this turn—*right* turn," Vangey said, and Florin obeyed.

"Keep going past the first opening, turn left here, up the steps . . . along . . . down the steps, and turn right on the first landing . . . aye . . . now, see the glowing line? That's the edge of a panel—slide it hard away from you and go through, turning left immediately and moving fast and low!"

Panting, the ranger-Knight did just as he was bid, seeing the plinths as he plunged out and around them. There was the false one, as he ran on, past it. Vangey said not a word . . . ah, of course; the wizard could hear him, too!

Twisting back around the next plinth, Florin struck out backhand with the very tip of his blade at the false plinth—and felt his blade slice cloth, and flesh beneath.

There was a hoarse shriek, and the ranger flung himself at the floor and then bounced up off it, slamming into the unseen wizard before the man could say or do anything. If he could ruin any spellcasting—

They hit the floor together, Florin punching and kneeing, then stabbing and—being stabbed, that unseen dagger like icy flame punching into him, again and again.

"Down, Florin!" Vangerdahast roared. "Cover yourself!"

Trembling, sobbing in pain, Florin stabbed back at his foe, then clawed hold of unseen and blood-sticky cloth and hurled himself sideways, hitting the floor bruisingly hard but dragging the unseen, writhing man over on top of him. As he closed his eyes, a singing shriek heralded the shattering of all the crystals.

"Keep rolling!" Vangerdahast bellowed, right in Florin's ear. "Away, to the wall, and then make for the door! Let go of the carrion!"

The ranger obeyed, scrambling faster than he'd ever moved in his life before, and through a red haze of pain was dimly aware of the shards racing across the room with eerie slowness, drifting—drifting—

"Don't *watch* them, you backwoods thickneck idiot! *Get out of there!*"

Vangerdahast sounded angrier than Florin had ever heard him be before, so the ranger did as he was told.

* * * * *

The aftermath of Ghoruld Applethorn's last spell tore into him like a lightning storm, stabbing into his head and leaving his mind afire.

Vangerdahast went to his knees, gasping and clutching feebly at his skull—and was startled as firm hands pushed him upright and forced a potion vial to his lips.

Islif gave him a wry smile as he choked and coughed it down. Then she kissed him. "Thanks for saving our lives," she said. "And the realm. Again."

"Wench, have done!" Vangerdahast replied testily, trying to wave her away. "I've a spell to work!"

Islif rocked back on her heels to give him room, and the Royal Magician hastily worked an intricate magic that brought a blue haze down on the room.

When it lifted, long breaths later, he and the Knights were all lying or kneeling just as they had been—but in the center of Anglond's Great Hall, with a blood-spattered, wild-eyed Florin in front of them and something bloody, butchered, and in robes lying sprawled beside him.

A collective gasp of horror rose across Anglond's Great Hall. In the moment of awed silence that followed, the voice of the envoy of Silverymoon asked merrily, "And what does *this* celebrate?"

Epilogue

Above his scrying whorl, Beldos Margaster nodded grimly. So it was all going to end happily ever after. Except for war wizard traitors.

He might have only a few breaths more of life left to him, if he didn't speedily "get hence."

The portal to Halfhap—well, why not? Those Dragonfire swords . . .

Up on the balcony, Dauntless peered down at Florin, frowning, and then bellowed suddenly, "Hey! *Hoy!* My sword! Give my sword back, you confounded thief!"

Florin looked up and waved cheerfully. Dauntless exploded into a sputtering, wordless roar of fury and started to claw his way angrily along the rail toward a stair down.

Two hard-faced Purple Dragons closed hands on the furious ragtag warrior, one of them snapping, "That's enough, saer! Abate thy temper, saer!"

"What?" Dauntless roared at them. "*Take* your hands off me! I'm an ornrion of the Dragons, and—"

"Right, saer, and I'm the Princess Alusair!"

"Wrong, soldier! *I'm* the Princess Alusair," said a crisp voice from behind the struggling Dragons.

Everyone turned in astonishment. The Princess Alusair was

standing a few strides behind Dauntless and the soldiers grappling with him.

As they stared, she tore off her fine gown, to their gasps of amazement—literally ripping the fine silks and shimmerweave apart—to reveal, beneath, a leather bodice, mens' breeches, and high boots.

"Ornrion," the young princess snapped, "if I give you the finest blade you've ever owned—something with a spell or two on it, out of the royal armory—will you gift the one Florin Falconhand has to him, and forget all thoughts of arresting him?"

Dauntless blinked. "I . . . uh, yes, of course."

"Good," she said with a smile, and offered him her arm as if he was a grand noble rather than a dusty, sweaty soldier in tattered garb.

The Purple Dragons silently let go of him, and the ragtag ornrion came forward a little dazedly to take the proffered royal arm.

Its owner gave him a regal smile and said sweetly, "Now you may escort me down to meet Cormyr's latest hero. He saved my life back in Arabel, and I never got the chance to properly thank him."

Dauntless paled. "I—uh, your Highness, would that be wise? I'm no expert in matters of Court, but—"

"No, Ornrion, you're not. Nor am I wise. I am sick unto *death* of doing what's right and proper, and I'm going to stop. Here and now. So get me down there, without delay—and you've my full permission to draw your sword and carve up anyone who tries to stand in our way!"

Ornrion Taltar Dahauntul gulped. "Y-yes, your Royal Highness. At once." He drew his sword, saluted her, made sure her arm was settled in his just so, and started for the stairs.

* * * * *

Everyone was crowding around, the gabbling of excited questions rising to a nigh-deafening din. The only clear space was a little more than the reach of a long arm around Lady Summerwood and her maids, and when Jhessail caught the eye of one maid and saw a flash of silver in the wink sent in her direction, she knew why. She smiled happily at the disguised Lady in Green through a rapidly closing gap in the sea of silks, pearls, cloth-of-gold, glittering gems, shimmerweave, and jostling shoulders and elbows.

When she turned to tell Florin, an instant later, he was lost in the heart of a forest of crowding-forward Cormyreans.

"A battle, hoy?" Lord Cormrlryn shouted enthusiastically in the heart of that tangle, his monacle steaming over. "Did you butcher the traitors, lad? Hey?"

"Well, yes, one of them," Florin said mumbled politely, weaving his way to his feet. Aged and hairy noble hands were pounding him on the back, slapping at his shoulders, and waving in victorious fists in the air. Well, at least they weren't all trying to sword him . . .

He had Vangerdahast to thank for that. The wizard's bellow of, "Behold! The realm hath been *saved!"* had rolled from end to end of Anglond's Great Hall—magic, of course.

"Lord Bellarogar Rowanmantle," a noble as tall as Florin boomed loudly, enfolding the ranger's shoulder in a crushing grip. "A pleasure to make your acquaintance—"

"Dauntinghorn! Horntar Dauntinghorn! *Lord* Horntar Dauntinghorn!" another noble bellowed, bouncing his fist off Florin's chest as if it was a castle door he needed hard-of-hearing servants to come and open.

"Well met, hero! Any friend of Cormyr is a friend of mine!" another noble called, from behind Dauntinghorn's substantial shoulders. "I'm Lord Ildabray Indesm! I—*oogh!*—and this is my wife, the Lady Indesm!"

Florin tried not to grin at the evident sharpness of Lady Indesm's elbows, and became aware, beyond his own ring of admirers, of Lord Elvarr Spurbright struggling through the crowd like a caravel slicing stormy seas to reach the edge of the little open area around the Lady Summerwood.

Her maids turned to form a serenely smiling, unbreachable wall against him. "Aerilee!" Spurbright called over it, almost desperately, and the Lady Summerwood swept forward from between two maids with a brightening smile on her face and the delighted words, *"Elvarr!* Alustriel speaks of you often—and so do I!"

As the two embraced, kissing ardently before everyone in the hall, Florin saw Torsard standing behind his father, staring at the Lady Summerwood with helpless, brains-over-boots, smitten-quick love clear and deep on his face.

He had to turn his head away from that raw, swallowing longing—and found himself facing a tall, thin aging noble who nodded politely and said, "Well done, Sir Falconhand. Lord Rustryn Staglance offers his thanks and praise. If you're ever—"

"Are you *wed,* Sir Falconhand?" a sharp-tongued woman asked, thrusting herself up between Staglance and Florin like a fish leaping out of the sea. She had snapping black eyes and a long flow of hair adorned with a fine net of gold chains. Florin blinked not only at the gold and sparkling gems that were all over her, but at the upthrust bosom that those strings of begemmed chains were designed to lure his eyes down into.

"I am Ramurra Hornmantle," the woman said, leaning forward as if trying to climb his chest, "*wealthy* lady of taste and breeding, and I would be *honored*—"

"Ildaergra Steelcastle!" snapped another woman, tugging at Florin's arm. "I'm wealthier!"

"I believe," Semoor said sardonically, from somewhere close behind the ranger-Knight, "that Lathander is giving us all a little taste of our most rosy reward! As such, it would be almost blasphemous not to partake—"

Ildaergra Steelcastle reached out and hauled on the large whiskers of Lord Cormelryn in an attempt to elevate herself up and over Ramurra Hornmantle; the old noble roared in pain, his monacle springing forth on its fine gold chain to plunge straight down her bosom—just as Ramurra leaped straight up into the air, snarling, to fling Ildaergra over backward. The last Florin saw of her was the monacle, left behind in midair above the site of her landing.

"Saer!" another man called loudly from nigh Florin's left shoulder, "I am Arbitryce Heldanorn, Master Trader In Spices, Scents, and Wonders, and I was hoping to spend a few moments of your time in discussion of some schemes mutually benef—"

Beyond the spice-trader, Florin caught sight of Pennae wrapped around several finely dressed nobles, her hands at work almost as skillfully as theirs were groping clumsily. A look of disgust was passing over her face as deftly filched purse after ring was falling *through* her fingers—and she was turning her head to give Vangerdahast a glare.

The Royal Magician of Cormyr shouldered past Florin chuckling and murmuring in Pennae's direction, "Merely a side effect of my ironguard, little she-snake. Keeping a dagger or two from harming you is worth more than an ill-gotten bauble or two, hmm?"

"*There* she is!" another voice snapped. "Make way! Make way, all of you! I am Ornrion Delk Synond of the Purple Dragons, and this woman is a dangerous thief and would-be murderer, who has resisted arrest, assaulted Purple Dragons lawfully engaged in the prosecution of their sworn duty—"

"Oh, *belt* up, loudjaws!" a tall, red-faced woman snapped, as Telsword Grathus rudely thrust her aside, and Ornrion Synond stepped on her foot in his grand stride forward.

"And who are *you?*" Synond roared at her. "An accomplice?"

There was a dull ringing sound before she could reply, and the ornrion toppled face-first onto the telsword's heels.

"I am Goodwoman Kaylea Delruharmond," the woman told the unconscious Dragon rather uncertainly, her anger giving way to apprehension.

Behind the unconscious ornrion loomed the man who'd felled him: a crimson-faced, formidably tall and fat man in sauce-smeared robes, a dented skillet in his hand. "Always wanted to do that," he announced with satisfaction, grinning at Pennae and the rest of the Knights, beyond. "Master of the Kitchens Braerast Sklaenton, me. Heard you liked my smallbites!"

Telsword Grathus stumbled around to face the cook, sword grating out. That sword went straight up in the air as he suddenly fell over backward, deftly tripped by the same man who caught the sword out of the air, turned, and handed it to Pennae. "You might need this," he murmured, he said, as he stepped firmly on the telsword's throat. "Dalonder Ree, Harper. If ever you need me . . ."

Goodwife Deleflower Heldanorn would never have dreamed of backing into the Royal Magician of Cormyr and turning to grope at him and coo, "Oh, are *you* a Knight of Myth Drannor too?" if she'd caught proper sight of him in the press of bodies. She'd not have dared to say a word to him, or come within six strides of the man. However, Vangerdahast was rather shorter than she thought him to be, she did not get a good look at him, and she *did* grope.

For Vangerdahast, who liked to be the one to choose who groped him, or for that matter dared to speak to him, it was the proverbial flagon too many.

Anglond's Great Hall suddenly erupted in roiling red flames. Flames that burned not, but roared mightily, in a ring that soared toward the lofty ceiling and spread wings to take the shapes of young and snapping-jawed dragons.

There were gasps of awe and screams, and a sudden urgent movement to depart the crowd around Vangerdahast and the adventurers.

Cormyreans fled in all directions, leaving the Knights standing suddenly alone with a few unconscious, trampled fallen, the king and queen a few steps one way, and the envoy's maids a few steps the other.

Between those of Cormyr and those of Silverymoon stood Lady Summerwood and Lord Spurbright, locked in an oblivious embrace. With Torsard Spurbright standing uncertainly behind his father, poking his oblivious sire in the suddenly deepening silence.

"Pa? Dad? Lord Dad?" he quavered, his voice trailing away.

A ring of fascinated, scared faces now surrounded the cleared center of the hall.

"*Enough!*" Vangerdahast roared. "Let us have some civility. There's no need to push and shout and jostle!"

He turned to look all around, and then began to prowl, striding slowly with his hands clasped behind his back. "I mislike marauding rumor, and it does much damage in its wild flowerings besides. So, know you all: these adventurers, here before you, whom some of you already know as the Knights of Myth Drannor, personally chartered by the king—"

He bowed low to Azoun, who nodded.

"—and personal champions of the queen—"

The wizard bowed even lower to Filfaeril, who nodded and smiled.

"—have just, at great risk to their own lives, foiled a dastardly plot against the Crown *and* the person of the Lady Envoy of Silverymoon—"

He bowed in the direction of the Lady Summerwood, who was busily running her hands up under Lord Spurbright's best new silken tunic, her lips still locked on his, and paying the wider world not the slightest heed at all.

"—and that traitors among the nobility of Cormyr, subverted by evil wizards of Zhentil Keep, were involved!"

There was a gasp of horror and anger that was almost a roar, that then broke into an excited hubbub.

Vangerdahast cut through it with one word that brought utter silence down again in an instant, probably with the aid of his magic: *"However."*

He let the silence deepen, and added, "This is what we who serve the Crown of Cormyr *do*. This peril is now ended, and we have a most distinguished guest at our Court, and our attention should now be upon celebrating her embassy to us, our joy at her presence among us, and her every need."

He paused to stroll around Lord Spurbright and Lady Summerwood, as they murmured to each other, lips still locked together and eyes closed.

"As," the Royal Magician then added dryly, "our most dedicated agent Lord Elvarr Spurbright is so ably attending to."

Vangerdahast stepped back with a smile, and raised his arms to encourage the roar of mirth that followed. It rocked the hall, ringing deafeningly around the high vaulted ceiling and balconies—and when it began to diminish, a long breath later, he roared, "So let us have *revelry!*"

And the noise *really* began.

In the depths of that din, Pennae ducked back in among the Knights, grinned, and arched one eyebrow in the direction of the Royal Magician. "Did he actually *say* that? 'A dastardly plot'?"

"Dastardly," Semoor assured her solemnly. "Those are the worst kind."

Penna astonished him then by throwing her arms around him and kissing him.

* * * * *

Beldos Margaster drew in a breath of deep relief as he reached the portal to the ruined inn in Halfhap. Not only was it unguarded, but—if he was right—he'd reached it unseen. Now, if only this coffer of magical necessities, coins, and gems wasn't so hrasted *heavy*.

He strode forward, the moment of falling endlessly through chill blue mists followed, and then he was . . .

Standing under the open sky with the hovels and battered old shops of Halfhap all around him—amid the sagging ruins of what had been the Oldcoats Inn. Tumbled beams, splintered furniture, sagging upper floors all twisted and fire-blackened, and—

Wood creaked nearby. Margaster turned toward the sound and found himself staring into the hard faces of two grim, wounded Zhentilar warriors. Judging by the sacks of pans, kitchen knives, and the like they were carrying, they'd been camping out in the ruins trying to plunder anything of value. They both bore notched, well-used swords in their other hands.

Giving him stony looks, they hefted those blades and lurched toward him, spreading apart so as to come at him from two directions.

Margaster gave them a sneer and a swiftly hurled slaying spell—and got it right back in his face, as rings on their hands winked in unison.

Gods, the *pain!*

Staggering in agony, Beldos Margaster turned and fled, scrambling as swiftly as he could across the slippery chaos of the tumbled and fallen inn.

Chuckling grimly, the Zhents pursued him, moving more carefully. They knew there was nowhere for one old man whose spells couldn't touch them to run, to escape them.

Margaster, however, knew exactly where another portal stood. Whether there was still an inn standing around it or not, just ahead—here!—was one of the portals to Lord Yellander's hunting lodge. He plunged through it gratefully, greeting the blue mists once more for the brief moment that always seemed surprisingly long, and then stepped out into the hunting lodge. It'd be deserted, of course. He spared it not a glance, but whirled around and cast a spell that would close the portal forever, and hand him safety from brutish warriors.

It was a powerful magic, and a long one. Beldos Margaster had just triumphantly pronounced its last word when he heard crossbows crack in ragged unison behind him, and the hum of a volley of converging bolts rising angrily in his ears.

Here ends Book 2 of the tales of the Knights of Myth Drannor.
Their adventures are continued in The Sword Never Sleeps.

Ed Greenwood
presents

WATERDEEP

Time passes and so do men, but Waterdeep remains the same—
dangerous, full of intrigue, and in desperate need of heroes.

BLACKSTAFF TOWER
Steven E. Schend

In the wake of the Blackstaff's death, schemes and peril abound
over who will be the next to command Blackstaff Tower.
September 2008

MISTSHORE
Jaleigh Johnson

One woman must learn to stop running away—from the Watch,
from her powers, and from her past.
December 2008

Explore the richly textured city of Waterdeep with
master storyteller Ed Greenwood as your guide in an
action-packed series of adventures that will leave fans
of the FORGOTTEN REALMS® world breathless.

A Reader's Guide to

R.A. Salvatore's The Legend of Drizzt™

The Legend

When TSR published *The Crystal Shard* in 1988, a drow ranger first drew his enchanted scimitars, and a legend was born.

The Legacy

Twenty years and twenty books later, readers have brought his story to the world.

Drizzt

Celebrate twenty years of the greatest fantasy hero of a generation.

This fully illustrated, full color, encyclopedic book celebrates the whole world of The Legend of Drizzt, from the dark elf's steadfast companions, to his most dangerous enemies, from the gods and monsters of a world rich in magic, to the exotic lands he's visited.

Mixing classic renditions of characters, locales, and monsters from the last twenty years with cutting edge new art by award-winning illustrators including Todd Lockwood, this is a must-have book every Drizzt fan.

LISA SMEDMAN

The New York Times best-selling author of *Extinction* follows up on the War of the Spider Queen with a new trilogy that brings the Chosen of Lolth out of the Demonweb Pits and on a bloody rampage across Faerûn.

THE LADY PENITENT

BOOK I

SACRIFICE OF THE WIDOW

Halisstra Melarn has been a priestess of Lolth, a repentant follower of Eilistraee, and a would-be killer of gods, but now she's been transformed into the monstrous Lady Penitent, and those she once called friends will feel the sting of her venom.

BOOK II

STORM OF THE DEAD

As the followers of Eilistraee fall one by one to Halisstra's wrath, Lolth turns her attention to the other gods.

BOOK III

ASCENDANCY OF THE LAST

The dark elves of Faerûn must finally choose between a goddess that offers redemption and peace, or a goddess that demands sacrifice and blood. We know what a human would choose, but what about a drow?

June 2008

RICHARD A. KNAAK

THE OGRE TITANS

The Grand Lord Golgren has been savagely crushing all opposition to his control of the harsh ogre lands of Kern and Blöde, first sweeping away rival chieftains, then rebuilding the capital in his image. For this he has had to deal with the ogre titans, dark, sorcerous giants who have contempt for his leadership.

VOLUME ONE
THE BLACK TALON

Among the ogres, where every ritual demands blood and every ally can become a deadly foe, Golgren seeks whatever advantage he can obtain, even if it means a possible alliance with the Knights of Solamnia, a questionable pact with a mysterious wizard, and trusting an elven slave who might wish him dead.

VOLUME TWO
THE FIRE ROSE

Attacked by enemies on all sides, Golgren must abandon his throne to undertake the quest for the Fire Rose before Safrag, master of the Ogre Titans can locate it and claim supremacy over all ogres—and perhaps all of Krynn.

December 2008

VOLUME THREE
THE GARGOYLE KING

Forced from the throne he has so long coveted, Golgren makes a final stand for control of the ogre lands against the Titans . . . against an enemy as ancient and powerful as a god.

December 2009

JEAN RABE

THE STONETELLERS

"Jean Rabe is adept at weaving a web of deceit and lies, mixed with adventure, magic, and mystery."
—sffworld.com on *Betrayal*

Jean Rabe returns to the DRAGONLANCE® world with a tale of slavery, rebellion, and the struggle for freedom.

VOLUME ONE
THE REBELLION

After decades of service, nature has dealt the goblins a stroke of luck. Earthquakes strike the Dark Knights' camp and mines, crippling the Knights and giving the goblins their best chance to escape. But their freedom will not be easy to win.

VOLUME TWO
DEATH MARCH

The reluctant general, Direfang, leads the goblin nation on a death march to the forests of Qualinesti, there to create a homeland in defiance of the forces that seek to destroy them.

August 2008

VOLUME THREE
GOBLIN NATION

A goblin nation rises in the old forest, building fortresses and fighting to hold onto their new homeland, while the sorcerers among them search for powerful magic cradled far beneath the trees.

August 2009

Land of intrigue.
Towering cities where murder is business.
Dark forests where hunters are hunted.
Ground where the dead never rest.

To find the truth takes a special breed of hero.

THE INQUISITIVES

BOUND BY IRON
Edward Bolme

Torn by oaths to king and country, one man must unravel a tapestry of murder and slavery.

NIGHT OF THE LONG SHADOWS
Paul Crilley

During the longest nights of the year, worshipers of the dark rise from the depths of the City of Towers to murder . . . and worse.

LEGACY OF WOLVES
Marsheila Rockwell

In the streets of Aruldusk, a series of grisly murders has rocked the small city. The gruesome nature of the murders spawns rumors of a lycanthrope in a land where the shapeshifters were thought to have been hunted to extinction.

THE DARKWOOD MASK
Jeff LaSala

A beautiful Inquisitive teams up with a wanted vigilante to take down a crimelord who hides behind a mask of deceit, savage cunning, and sorcery.

In the shadow of the Last War, the heroes aren't all shining knights.

PARKER DeWOLF

The Lanternlight Files

Ulther Whitsun is a fixer. When you've got a problem, if you can't find someone to take care of it, he's your man—as long as you can pay the price. If you can't, or you won't . . . gods have mercy on your soul.

Book 1

The Left Hand of Death

Ulther finds himself in possession of a strange relic. His enemies want it, he wants its owner, and the City Watch wants him locked away for good. When a job turns this dangerous, winning or losing are no longer an option. It may be all one man can do just to stay alive.

Book 2

When Night Falls

Ulther teams up with a young and ambitious chronicler to stop a revolution. But treachery may kill him, and salvation comes from unexpected places.

July 2008

Book 3

Death Comes Easy

Gangs in lower Sharn are at each other's throats. And they don't care who gets killed in the battle. But now Ulther had been hired to put an end to the violence. And he doesn't care who he steps on to do his job.

December 2008